I0595383

Andrew K. H. Boyd

The Autumn Holidays of a Country Parson

Volume 1

Andrew K. H. Boyd

The Autumn Holidays of a Country Parson
Volume 1

ISBN/EAN: 9783337291778

Printed in Europe, USA, Canada, Australia, Japan

Cover: Foto ©Andreas Hilbeck / pixelio.de

More available books at **www.hansebooks.com**

THE

AUTUMN HOLIDAYS

OF A

COUNTRY PARSON.

BOSTON:

FIELDS, OSGOOD, & CO.,

SUCCESSORS TO TICKNOR AND FIELDS.

1869.

CONTENTS.

CHAPTER IX.

CHAPTER X.

CHAPTER XI.

CHAPTER XII.

CHAPTER XIII.

CHAPTER XIV.

CHAPTER XV.

CHAPTER XVI.

CHAPTER XVII.

———

CHAPTER I.

BY THE SEASIDE.

E have been here a little more than a week, all of us together. For if you be a man of more than five-and-thirty years, and if you have a wife and children, you have doubtless found out that the true way to enjoy your autumn holidays, and to be the better for them, is not to go away by yourself to distant regions where you may climb snowy Alps and traverse glaciers, in the selfish enjoyment of new scenes and faces. These things must be left to younger men, who have not yet formed their home-ties, and who know neither the happiness nor the anxieties of human beings, who spread a large surface on any part of which fortune may hit hard and deep. Let us find a quiet place where parents and children may enjoy the time of rest in company; where you will be free from the apprehensions of evil which (unless you be a very selfish person) you will not escape when the little things are a thousand miles away. And, to this end, one may well do without the sight of lakes, water-falls, streets, and churches, which it was pleasant once on a time to see. Upon this day, last year, I ascended the marvellous spire of Strasburg Cathedral. It was the brightest of all bright days. You went up and up, by little stairs winding through a lace-work of stone, which it makes one somewhat nervous to think of even now, till you emerged on a platform whence you looked down dizzily on the market-place hundreds of feet below; upon the town, all whose buildings looked so clean and well-defined in the smokeless air; upon the fertile level plain, stretching away towards Baden; and the ugly poplars, marking the course of the Rhine. It was all, to an untravelled man and an enthusiastic lover of Gothic architecture, interesting beyond expression: yet I would much rather be here.

For this is Saturday morning, and my parish is far away. There is no sermon to be thought of for to-morrow; and no multitude of sick folk to see; no pressure of manifold parochial cares. This is a very ugly cottage by a beautiful shore; and, through a simple pecuniary negotiation, the cottage is ours for the months of August and September. Looking up from this table, and looking out of the window, the first object you would see is a shaggy little fuchsia, covered with red flowers, waving about in a warm western wind. Beyond, there is a small expanse of green grass, in which I see, with entire composure, a good many weeds which would disquiet me much if the grass were my own. The little lawn is bounded by a wall of rough stone, half concealed by shrubs. And on the farther side, the top of the wall cutting sharp against it, weltering and toiling now in shadow, but a minute ago bright in sunshine, with the unnumbered dimple of little waves, spreads the sea. Now it has brightened again; and

three gleaming sails break the deep blue. Opposite, a
few miles off, there are grand Highland hills. Sometimes they look purple; sometimes, light blue; sometimes the sunshine shows a yellow patch of cornfield.
Never, for more than an hour or two, do those hills and
this sea look the same. They are always changing;
and the changes are extreme. You could no more tell
a stranger what this place is like, by describing it ever
so accurately as it is at this moment, than you could
worthily represent the most changeful human face by a
single photograph. In the sunset you may often see
what will make you understand the imagery of the Revelation, — a sea of glass mingled with fire; then the
mountains are of a deep purple hue, such as you would
think exaggerated if you saw it in a picture. Hardly
have the crimson and golden lights faded from the
smooth water, when a great moon, nearly full, rises
above the trees on this side, and casts a long golden
path, flickering and heaving; the stillness is such that
you fear to break it by a footfall. Then there have
been times, even within this week, when drenching
showers darkened the water and hid the opposite hills;
or when white-crested waves made the sea into a wild,
ridgy plain, and broke on the shingle hard by in foam
and thunder.

This is not a fashionable watering-place; you go back
to a quiet and simple life, coming here. No band of
music plays upon the black wooden pier, where the rare
steamboat calls daily. There is no such thing as a gay
promenade, frequented by brightly dressed people desirous to see and to be seen. There is no reading-
room, no billiard-room, no circulating library, no hotel,

no people who let out boats, no drinking-fountain. There is a post-office; but it is a mile distant. You would find here no more than a line of detached houses, a few extremely pretty, and more of them extremely ugly, reaching for somewhat more than a mile along the sea-shore. The houses, each with its shrubbery and lawn, greater or less, stand on a strip of level ground between the sea and a rocky wall of cliff, which follows the line of the beach at no great distance; doubtless an ancient sea margin. But now it serves as a beautiful background to the pretty houses, and it almost redeems the ugly ones; it is covered richly with trees, which through ages have rooted themselves in the crevices of the rock; and where the perpendicular wall forbids that vegetation, it is clothed with ivy so luxuriant, that you would hardly think those hearty leaves ever knew the blighting salt spray. By the sea-shore there runs a highway; the waves break within a few yards on a beach of rough shingly gravel. It is to be confessed, that this charming place lacks the level sand which the ebbing tide leaves for a firm, cool walking space at some time of every day. But your walks are not confined to the path to right and left along the sea-shore. You will discover pleasant ways, that lead to the country above the wooded and ivied cliff; and there you will find ripening harvest fields, and paths that wind through fragrant woods of birch, oak, and pine, and here and there the mountain-ash, with its glowing scarlet berries. But it is not what one understands by *a country side:* the whole landscape is gradually, but constantly, sloping upwards, till it passes into dark heathery hills, solitary as Tadmor in the wilderness. There the sportsman goes in search of grouse and deer; and thence you have views of the level blue water far below you, that are worth going many miles to see.

There are places along this seaside where your only walk is beside the sea. The hills rise almost from the water, an expanse of shadeless heather. But we are happier with our shady woodland walks. When the glare and heat are oppressive along the shore in the vacant afternoon, let us turn away from the road that skirts the beach, up this thickly wooded glen, through which a stream brawls from rock to rock, hardly seen for the leaves. You will not walk for a few yards under the pleasant shadow, till you find yourself so environed with ivy-grown trees, honeysuckle and wild flowers, that you might fancy the sea many miles off. And the oppressive light and heat and dust are gone. Let us go on, following the windings of the path and the water, till we reach a spot where a clear little brook, tumbling over rocks from far above us, crosses the road under a rude arch, to join the larger stream; and now let us sit down on a great stone, where the little brook, close by our feet, makes a leap into the dark entrance of the bridge. Here let us rest and be thankful. Many people find this a feverish world: let us rejoice in a nook so green and quiet. Ferns of many kinds cover the damp rocks: there is a thick canopy of green leaves overhead, through which you may see blinks of the brightest blue sky; and through which you may see an intense flickering of light, where the sun is struggling to pierce the dense shade. The air is fragrant and cool and moist: all around there is a thicket of evergreens and underwood, over which the tall trunks arise whose spreading branches make our grateful shadow.

We have all, young and old, wearied for this time; and here it is at last. The cheerful anticipation of it was something to help one through laborious summer days. For if you are to be in the country no more than two months in the year, the months beyond question should be August and September. Let us keep our cake as long as we can; let us make our holiday season late. June and July are delightful months amid rural scenes; but it would be dismal to go back to the hot town at the end of July, and think one had settled down for the winter. But, at the beginning of October, a little space of long dark evenings, and the growing crispness of the morning air, help to make one feel ready to take with good heart to the laboring oar again.

Yet, though this holiday time be so enjoyed by anticipation, I think that when the day comes on which you preach to your own congregation for the last time before leaving, you feel it rather a trial; and you turn your back upon your church with some regret and some misgiving. A clergyman's work is not like any other; you have not quite the school-boy's feeling when working days are over and holidays begin. For your work is not merely your duty, it is your happiness too; and though some folk may not understand it, you feel it something of a privation to think on a Sunday in your play-time that the bells are ringing, and the people assembling in the familiar place, and you not there. Happily, there are regions in this world where the clergyman's last Sunday at church, is likewise the last Sunday at church of a great part of the congregation. *It* is gathered, as usual, one day; and the next, scattered far and wide, by the seaside and among the hills.

And in this uncertain world, where when many hundreds of human beings are in one place to-day, no one can say who may be missing when they meet after some weeks' separation, I think that you, my friend, will preach with special kindness and heartiness on your last Sunday at home; and that you will be heard with special attention and sympathy. There will be a very perfect stillness as you pronounce the blessing for what may be the last time. And you will well remember the words and the music of the parting hymn. Taking your final look round your vestry, and round your emptied church, as you come away, you will feel the sorrow and anxiety which come of the vain delusion common to man, that the place where you worked and labored your best will not go on quite as well in your absence. Ah, my friend, some day you and I must leave our several churches for ever; and though we shall be kindly remembered and missed there for a while, they will come by and by to do without us. And very fit and right too. We are not such self-conceited fools as to wish it were otherwise. Yet it is cheering, each Tuesday morning through the holidays, when the letter comes by post, in which a kind friend, whom duty ties to his town work at this season, tells how all went well in the services of the Sunday before.

Then, following that parting day, comes one of confusion and worry and fatigue, — the day on which the family accomplishes the journey to the distant resting-place. Would that the age might come when human beings shall be able to do without baggage! Yet even baggage serves good moral ends. You are very thankful indeed, when, in the quiet evening, the cottage, or the more ambitious dwelling, is reached at last; and the manifold packing-cases, being counted up, are found to be all right. During the day, several times, you had quite resigned yourself to the conviction that half of them would never be found more.

There are simple statements which may be repeated many times, while yet no wise man will pull you up by declaring that he has heard the like before; for such simple statements are the irrepressible outflow of the present happy mood and feeling. You could not help uttering such, to any one to whom you might be talking out your heart. Suffer me now to declare, that there is no more precious blessing than rest. "The end of work is to enjoy rest." "The end and the reward of toil is rest." Yes, it is delightful to rest for a while from even the most congenial and beloved work. And rest is not merely delightful; it is needful. The time comes when the task drags heavily; when it is got through heartlessly, and by a painful effort often re-newed. Most busy men, busied with work that wears the brain and nervous system, have some little time of rest in their daily round, — some precious hour of quiet. There is generally the short breathing space between dinner and tea. But, as months pass, the nerves grow so irritable that many sounds and circumstances worry you; then is the hour when the organ-grinder painfully thrills you through. At this stage, busy men find the relief of a little pause, — a day or two away from work, no matter where. Arnold said, that the most restful days of the year were those spent in the long journeys by coach between Rugby and Fox How. A very eminent

and over-driven man lately told me, that when he is being wrought into a fever, he finds rest by going to London by the express train, and returning the next day.
The distance is four hundred miles going, and the like
returning,—eleven hours either way. But it is enjoyable to lean back in the carriage ; to read and to muse,
—sure that no one will speak to him on the business
of his profession. I have heard of a great man who
found the like relief in going to bed for two days or so.
There was physical repose ; and even the unreasonable
caller and tormentor, who would utterly disregard the
assurance that the Doctor was weary and could see no
one, was beaten by the assurance that the Doctor was in
bed. For the average human being, on being told that
the Doctor could see no one, would instantly say, " O,
but I know he will see ME !" But not even these re-
treats will stay the gathering weariness which grows on
body and mind as the seasons pass. And if you have
been at work from the beginning of October to the end
of July,—ten months with little relaxation,—then you
have fairly earned the autumn holiday-time. And your
rest will be not merely the reward of past work, but the
preparation for future. You are laying up the strength,
spirit, and patience needful for the winter months, if
you are to see that time. And you must act on the calculation that you are to see it. On dark Sunday afternoons in January, when gas is lit throughout the church,
and snow lies in the wintry streets, you may preach
your sermon with the greater heart and vigor for the
hours you sit now on a stone by the seaside, looking at
the waves, and for the bracing breezes that supply the
ozone the city lacks. So the diligent clergyman is as

1 *

much in the way of duty while enjoying his autumn
rest as while fulfilling the work of the remainder of the
year.

That you may thoroughly enjoy the autumn holidays,
it is essential that you should feel that they have been
fairly earned by long and hard work. You cannot feel
the delight of rest, unless by contrast with toil, hurry,
and weariness. All this quiet and beauty, to you and
me grateful as water to the thirsty, would be to people
who habitually live an idle life no better than something insufferably dull and stupid. Let us hope that
we have faithfully gone through the previous discipline,
that will make us relish simple quiet and peace. Some
people think it shows humility to say things against
themselves which they know are not true. They meek-
ly confess sins of which they are aware they are not
guilty; saying what they suppose must be true, instead
of what they feel to be true. Let us never do the like.
Few things are more fatal to a true and honest spirit.
For myself, I will say, without reserve, that in these
last ten months I have worked to the very best of my
ability and strength to fulfil my duty. And, if not very
much after all, I have done what I could. I can say
the like for certain dear friends in my own profession.
They never wilfully neglect any work; they never see
any thing that ought to be done, without trying to do it.
Unprofitable servants, doubtless, in the sight of One
above us; but, at least, we can look our fellow-men in
the face.

I suppose, my readers, we have all a picture in our
minds of the ideal autumn holidays. They never have
come; they are never to be. Yet we can think of

broad harvest fields, golden in sunshine; of magnificent trees, the growth of centuries; of green glades, with the startled deer; of the gray Gothic dwelling, large and hospitable; of a mode of life in which sickness, anxiety, vague fears, and pinching efforts to save shillings, are quite unknown. Yes, it is to be admitted that this ugly little cottage and its surroundings, physical and moral, are no more than a makeshift. But then, my friend, what more is all our life, and all our lot? We must make them do; we have great reason to be thankful for things as they are: but all this is not what we used to think of, when we were little children or hopeful youths. Let us train ourselves to look at lights rather than darks. There is such a thing as an eye for lights, and such a thing as an eye for darks. You know, when you look at a grand Gothic window,—the eastern window of a noble church; and when you look at a much smaller Gothic window, you may look either at the dark tracery of stone, or at the lights of gorgeous storied glass. Now, in a physical sense, it is well to look at each in turn. You may behold a really excellent window by this,—that the darks are beautiful in form, if you fix your attention on them only; and the lights are likewise beautiful in form, if you consider them by themselves. An inferior architect will give you the tracery beautiful, but the lights shapeless; or the lights pretty, but the tracery ugly. But, though it is well physically to have an eye for both darks and lights, it is best, usually, to look mainly at lights, as you contemplate the grand Gothic window of your lot and of circumstances. For many people look at the darks to the exclusion of the lights. They dwell on the worries of their condition, to the forgetfulness of its blessings and advantages. They contemplate the smoky chimney of their dining-room, to the forgetfulness of a hundred good things. They try to get other people to do the like. My friend Smith told me, that, once on a time, he had Mr. Jones to preach in his church. Smith's church holds fifteen hundred people, and it is perfectly filled by its congregation; of this circumstance Smith is pardonably proud. When Mr. Jones preached, the church was quite crowded, save that three seats (not pews, seats for a single person each) were vacant in a front gallery. But so keen was Mr. Jones's eye for darks, to the oblivion of lights, that after service he merely said to Smith, that he had remarked three seats empty in the gallery. Not one thought or word had he for the fourteen hundred and ninety-seven seats that were filled. Smith was a little mortified. But by and by he remembered, that the peculiar disposition of Mr. Jones was one that would inflict condign punishment upon itself. Then he was sorry, rather than angry. Yes, my friend, let us be glad, if we have an eye for the lights of life, rather than for its darks!

It is curious, how very soon the burden drops from one's back, when you come for your holidays to some place far away from your home and your duty. The relief is in direct proportion to the distance in miles. A hundred miles will suffice; a thousand are better. Very lightly does the care of your parish rest on you, when the parish is a thousand miles distant! Even a tenth part of that amount makes one feel as a horse must, when its harness is removed, and its shoes taken off, and it is turned out to grass. As you put on a tweed suit, and adopt a wide-awake hat, you forget the responsibilities and labors of past months ; you cease to be the same man. The careful lines are smoothed out of your face ; the hair pauses in growing gray. It is necessary, indeed, to the true sense of rest, that you should have the feeling of a good long horizon of time before you. A few days in the country, with the feeling that you are just going back to work, will not do ; the feverish pulse will keep by you. It is quite a different thing, when you know you have several weeks in prospect. Then you expatiate ; then you truly rest. Those good men who remain within a few miles of their parish, and who go back for each Sunday's duty, do not enjoy the feeling of the holiday-time at all. And feeling is the reality. It is not what a thing is in itself, but how it presents itself to you. You know how different a thing a railway-station, thirty miles from home, looks to you when you are to stop at it, and when you are to go on three hundred miles further.

It is pleasant, and at first a little perplexing, instead of setting to work after breakfast, to go forth and wander about the shore, or sit on a rock as long as you please, with the sense that you are neglecting nothing that needs to be done. You feel, as regards time, as a poor man who has suddenly inherited a large fortune must feel towards money. Strange, to have so much to spare of the thing of which before one had so little ! And how misty and unreal the scenes and the life that are distant and past grow to be ! I cannot at this minute, sitting on a warm stone by the sea in the morning sunshine, feel that at the entrance to a certain square stands in this same sunshine, with a little shrubbery before it, a certain church, Ionic as to its front elevation, which the writer well knows. It is always there when I go back; but I do not know what becomes of it in the mean while.

There is nothing more certain than this, that it will not answer to go to your resting-place to spend your holiday-time, without having thought of what you are to do while there. If the truth were told, it would be the confession of many men, that the enjoyment of their holidays was all in the anticipation and the retrospect; and that the holidays themselves were a very disappointing and tiresome time, very listless and weary. All this comes of their vaguely believing that, to enjoy the season of rest, all you have to do is to go to some quiet, retired place, and then some occupation will suggest itself, some mode of getting the due enjoyment out of the long-expected time. A clergyman might just as wisely ascend his pulpit, without having thought of what he is to say from it of his text and his sermon, and count upon these turning up at the moment they are needed. Before going to the seaside, you should carefully consider what you are to do there, and map out some little plan of life; not adhering to it, of course, should some pleasant deviation suggest itself. And every one must devise such a plan for himself, according to his own liking. Only let it be remembered, that it will not do to be absolutely vacant. Time will hang heavy; and then enjoyment is at an end. Different men have devised different modes of light occupation for their holiday-time; and that which suited one man might be most unsuitable for another. Mr. Jay, the eminent Non-conformist of Bath, tells us that it helped him to thoroughly enjoy his vacation, to write one little sermon in the morning of each day, and another in the evening. The sermons were certainly very brief; you might read each in five minutes; yet not every preacher would have regarded it as recreation to produce them. There are very many to whom sermon-writing does not come so easily; to whom a sermon is the thought of a week, not the diversion of an hour. Let it be said, that Mr. Jay's little sermons now fill four volumes, under the title of *Morning and Evening Exercises;* they provide a little pious reading for the mornings and evenings of a year. The writer is so very warm a Churchman, that he seldom looks at the volumes without regretting that the good man was not one; the more so, as it is plain that no conscientious scruple kept him out of his national church. Yet, let it be said, that if you read the little discourses daily, for a year, you will leave off with a very kindly and pleasant impression of their author. It is not that any one discourse is in any way specially brilliant, but that all are so evenly good; and they treat, in the most admirable spirit, not the matters on which good Christians differ, but those on which they all agree.

For men to whom the writing of sermons is not relaxation, but rather work, yet whose likings are quiet and scholarly, certain rules may be suggested. In addition to the physical employment of mountain excursions, yachting, riding, shooting, and the like, let abundance of reading be provided. Let the *Times* daily tell how the great world goes; let plenty of other newspapers come besides. Thus post-time will be a fresh sensation, even if very few letters appear, and these of very small interest. And, besides as many pleasant new books as you can get, let there be some large work, of many volumes, read perhaps long ago, yet worth reading again, and which could not be read satisfactorily amid the pressure of working days and months. And weeks before you come to the seaside, consider what this book shall be. Mine, this year, is Lockhart's *Life of Sir Walter Scott*, — an admirable history of a great and good man. If you have read it as a boy, read it once more as a man; and you will find how well you remember it. It is a sad history, certainly; and you will find many things to be thought of with deep regret: yet you will rise from it with a hearty admiration and affection for the greatest Scotchman. And often, as you go on, you will come on passages that will make you pause and muse, with the finger in the half-closed book.

But the writer's special occupation during these holidays is to revise and consider the essays which make up this volume. He has very little time now for writing such; and the little time is growing less. The spare hours of two years have gone to the production of this little book. It will always be pleasant to look back on time so pleasantly spent. And these chapters have already met so kind a reception, as they appeared in that dear old magazine in which the writer saw his earliest article in print and his latest, and in another magazine which professes to publish good words, though some people have declared it to be a bad and dangerous periodical, that the indulgent reader may easily understand how this volume has been added to the list of certain which have gone before. Let me wish for this book, that it may fall into as kind hands as the rest, and into as many.

It is a great thing to have some occupation, in a time and place like this, which implies no exertion. It is pleasant for a very small author to sit down on a rustic seat, under a shady tree, or on a rock by the sea, with the murmuring water lapping at one's feet; and there peacefully to read over one's essay. A distinguished American author has put on record the feelings with which he read his own first book. He says frankly, "I never read a more interesting volume!" Under the shadow of that illustrious precedent, it may be confessed, that though, when busy with serious work, you have something else to do than to read your own compositions, yet, in a season of leisure, it is light and pleasant employment for an author to do so. Somebody, once on a time, sent me a lengthened and friendly criticism of these essays, in which it was yet mentioned, as a ground of complaint, that no mental exertion was needful to follow them. That is precisely what their author wished; and he will be too glad to think that it is so. He has pioneered the road, through the jungle and up the pass: he trusts it is smooth and easy. Yet let it be said, that what is easy to read is, for the most part, difficult to write.

Let me be allowed a closing word. Why does the writer call himself a *country parson?* Years have passed since he left that beautiful green valley, with the river, the trees, and the hills, and went to a great city. But country parson is the name that suits him, and the name by which many kind friends know him. So he calls himself by it, just as his friend Smith calls himself Smith. It is not that that individual is a smith in fact; but that Smith is the name by which people have agreed to call and know him. The ancestor who first bore the name was in fact a smith; and the name of Smith continued to be handed down, after the fact of smith ceased. So let it be with the author's cherished designation.

And there is more. Though he now does the duty of a parish in a great city, it is the city in which, above all others, country and town are mingled in the most charming way. In the parish which he serves, you may even find beautiful shady walks, and expanses of grass and flowers, where you might think yourself far from town smoke and bustle; and indeed you are: for in that most beautiful of cities, there is no smoke and little bustle. May it be always so.

CHAPTER II.

CONCERNING UNPRUNED TREES.

O N this writing-table, here in a great city, there lie two large pruning-knives, unused for five years. They look inconsistent enough with the usual belongings of the work-room of the incumbent of a town parish, who, on week-days, walks about chiefly upon paving-stones, and on Sundays preaches to city folks. But Britons know that there are institutions which the wise man would preserve, though their day and their use have passed away; so is it with these knives, — buckhorn as to their handles, and black with rust as to their blades. The writer will never cast them away; will never lock them up in a drawer rarely visited, degrading them from the prominent and easily reached spot where they lay in years that are gone. Never again, in all likelihood, will those knives be used by the hand that was wont to use them; yet they serve their owner well when they bring back the pleasant picture of days when he was a country parson, and pruned many shrubs and trees; walking about leisurely in the enjoyment of snipping off, as a schoolmaster of my youth was accustomed to walk

down the rows of boys, busy in writing, here and there coming down with a heavy lash on some unlucky back, merely for his own recreation, and with no moral aim. Yes, there is a tranquil delight in pruning ; to a simple and unfevered mind, it is a very fascinating pursuit. And it is a good sign of a man, if he finds pleasure in it. Alas, we outgrow the days in which it makes us happy to prune trees !

The reader, who is given to pruning, knows how very much some trees need it. You know how horribly awkward and ugly an old bay becomes, after it has been untended for years. It has great branches which stick out most ungracefully. And it is likely enough that the whole tree is so inextricably grown into that un-gainly form, that it is best to saw it off about three or four feet from the ground, and to let it begin to grow anew. Thus, starting afresh, you may be able to make it a pretty and graceful object, though of much dimin-ished size. There are trees whose nature is such that they can do with little or no pruning. They don't need to be watched ; they cost no trouble. Such is a Portu-gal laurel ; such is a weeping birch ; such is a beech ; such is an oak. But not such is an Irish yew ; not such is an apple-tree, nor any kind of fruit-tree. And in the days when you were the possessor of trees, and were sometimes a good deal worried by the charge of them, I know you often thought what a blessing it is that there are some that need no pruning; some that, once put in their place, you may let alone. For there were some that needed ceaseless tending ; they grew horrible, un-less you were always watching them, and cutting off this and that little shoot that was growing in a wrong direction. It was an awful thing, standing beside some tree that had given you a great amount of trouble, to think what it would come to if it were just left to itself.

Most human beings are very like the latter order of trees; they need a great deal of pruning. Little odd habits, the rudiments of worse habits, need every now and then to be cut off and corrected. We should all grow very singular, ridiculous, and unamiable creatures, but for the pruning we have got from hands kind and unkind, from our earliest days; but for the pruning we are getting from such hands yet. Perhaps you have known a man who had lived for forty years alone. And you know what odd shoots he had sent out; what strange traits and habits he had acquired; what singular little ways he had got into. There had been no one at home to prune him; and the little shoots of eccentricity, of vanity, of vain self-estimation, that might have easily been cut off when they were green and soft, have now grown into rigidity. Woody fibre has been developed; and if you were to try to cut off the oddity now, it would be like trying to lop off a tough oak branch a foot thick with a penknife. You cannot do it; if you were to succeed in doing it, you would thereby change the whole man. Equally grown into rigid awkwardness with the man who has lived a very solitary life, the man is likely to be, who, for many years, has been the pope of a little circle of admiring disciples, no one of whom would ever contradict him, no one of whom would ever venture to say he judged or did wrong. In such a case, not merely are the angularities, the odd, ungainly shoots, not cut off; they are actually fostered. And a really good man grows into a bundle of awkwardnesses and oddities, and stiffens hopelessly into these. And these greatly lessen his influence and usefulness with people who do not know his real excellences. You cannot read the life of Mr. Simeon, of Cambridge, without lamenting that there was not some kind yet firm hand always near him, to prune off the wretched little shoots of self-conceit.and silliness which obscured, in great measure, the sterling qualities of the man. You may remember reading how, on an occasion on which some good ladies had collected pieces of needle-work to be sold for a missionary purpose, he came to behold them. He skipped into the room, held up his hands in a theatrical ecstasy of admiration, and went through various ungainly gambols, and uttered various wretched jokes, by way of compliment to the good ladies. I don't tell you the story at length; it is too humiliating. Now do you think the good man would ever have done this, had he lived among people who durst question his infallibility and impeccability? What a blessing it would have been for him had there been some one on such terms with him that he could say, " Now, Simeon, dear fellow, don't make a fool of yourself ! "

It is at once apparent, that when some really kind and judicious friend, or even some judicious person who is not a kind friend, says to you, as you are saying something, " Smith, you're talking nonsense; shut up, and don't make a fool of yourself," this fact is highly analogous to the fact of a keen pruning-knife snipping off a shoot that is growing in a wrong direction. And you may have seen a good man, accustomed to dwell among those who never dared to differ from him, look as if the world were suddenly coming to an end, when some courageous person said to his face what many persons had frequently said behind his back; to wit, that he was talking nonsense. You may find a house here and there in which the gray mare is the more energetic, if not the better horse; where the husband has been constrained by years of outrageous ill-temper to give the wife her own way; and where, accordingly, the mistress of the house has lived for thirty years without once being told she did wrong. The tree, that is, had never been pruned in all that time; and you may imagine what an ugly and disagreeable tree it had grown. For people who get their own way have nothing to repress their evil and ridiculous tendencies, except their own sense of propriety; and I have little faith in the practical guidance of that sense, unless it be reinforced and directed by the moral and æsthetic sense of other people. A tree, when pruned, suffers in silence; no doubt, it cannot like being pruned; it would like to have its own way. But the pruning of a human being, accustomed to his or her own way, is often accompanied by much moral kicking and howling. Such a person, in those years without pruning, has very likely got confirmed in many ridiculous and disagreeable habits; has learned to sit with his feet upon the mantle-piece; has come to use ungrammatical and ugly forms of speech; has grown into rubbing his nose, or twirling his thumbs, or making pills of paper while conversing with others. Indeed there is no reckoning the ugly growths into which unpruned human nature will develop itself; and self-conceited and haughty and petted folk deliberately deprive themselves of that salutary tending and pruning

which is needful to keep them in decent shape. There
was once a man, who was much given to advocating the
admission of fresh air; an excellent end. But, of course,
in advocating it, the word *ventilation* had frequently
to be used; and that man made himself ridiculous in the
eyes of all educated people by invariably pronouncing
the word as *ventulation*. For a long time, a youthful
relative of that man suffered in silence the terrible annoyance of listening to the word thus rendered; and
there are few more irritating things among the minor
vexations of life than to be compelled habitually to
listen to some vulgar and illiterate error in speech.
Perhaps you have felt a burning desire to prune a person, who talked of some trouble being *tremenduous ;* or
who said, he would rather go to Jericho *as* hear Dr.
Log preach; or who declared, the day to be *that* hot
that he was nearly killed. Oh, the thought of such ex-
pressions makes one's nerves tingle, and one's hand
steal towards the pruning-knife. But after long en-
durance, the youthful relative of the man who talked
about *ventulation* could stand it no longer, and ventured humbly to suggest that *ventilation* was the preferable way of setting forth the word. Ah, the tree did
not take the pruning peaceably! Wasn't there an explosion of vanity and spite and stupidity? Was not
the youthful individual scorched with furious sarcasm,
for pretending to know better than his seniors, and for
venturing to think that his betters could go wrong!
From that day forward, he resolved that however hideous the shoots of ignorance and conceit his seniors put
forth, *he* would not venture to correct them. For there
is nothing that so infuriates an uneducated and self-

sufficient man of more than middle age, as the faintest and best-disguised attempt to prune him. "Are you sure that your *data* is correct?" said a vulgar rich man to an educated poor man. "*Data* ARE correct, I think you mean," said the poor man (rather hastily), before going on to answer the question. The rich man's face reddened like an infuriated turkey-cock; and had there been a cudgel in his hand, he would have beaten the pruner upon the head. Yes; it is thankless work to wield the moral pruning-knife.

Probably among the class of old bachelors you may find the most signal instances of the evil consequence of going through life with nobody to prune one. I could easily record such manifestations of silliness and absurdity in the case of such men as would be incredible. Of course I am not going to do so. An old bachelor of some standing, living in a solitary house, with servants who dare not prune him, and with acquaintances who will not take the trouble to prune him, must necessarily, unless he be a very wise and good man, grow into a most amorphous shape. I beg the reader to mark the exception I make: for I presume he will agree with me when I say, that in the class of old bachelors and old maids may be found some of the noblest specimens of the human race. A judicious wife is always snipping off from her husband's moral nature little twigs that are growing in wrong directions. She keeps him in shape, by continual pruning. If you say anything silly, she will affectionately tell you so. If you declare that you will do some absurd thing, she will find means of preventing your doing it. And by far the chief part of all the common sense there is in this world belongs unquestionably to women. The wisest thing a man commonly does are those which his wife counsels him to do. It is not always so. You may have known a man do, at the instigation of his wife, things so malicious, petty, and stupid, that it is inconceivable any man should ever do them at all. But such cases are exceptional.

My friend Jones, when a boy of fourteen, went to visit a relative, a rich old bachelor. That relative was substantially a very kind person; that is, he gave Jones lots of money, and the like. But Jones, an observant lad, speedily took his relative's measure. The first evening Jones was with him, the old bachelor said, in a very cordial way, "Now, Tom, my boy, it is my duty to tell you something. You have been trained up to believe that your father" (a clergyman) "is an able and dignified person. It is right that you should know that he is a very poor stick."

Jones listened, without remark, but with rather a scared face. It was a trial to the young fellow. It was a shock to his belief in things in general, to hear his father thus spoken of. And Jones, who is now a man, tells me that though he said nothing, he inwardly groaned, looking at his wealthy relative. "You're a horrid old fool." And in all the years that have passed since then, Jones assures me he has not in the least modified that early opinion.

Now, don't you feel that no married man would have so behaved? Even if he were such an ass as to begin to say such a thing to a little boy, don't you feel his wife (if present) would have taken care that the sentence was never finished?

The same person began to tell Jones about the opera; and all of a sudden, to the lad's consternation, he burst out into some awful roars. Jones was terrified. He thought his relative had gone mad, or was suddenly seized by some unusual and terrible disease. But the old gentleman said, with great self-complacency, "That's just to give you some idea what the human voice is capable of!" Jones secretly thought that it gave him some idea what a fool an old gentleman might make of himself.

I have heard of an extremely commonplace man, who lived an utterly solitary life in London. He had gained considerable wealth : but he had nothing else to stand on ; and he was not rich enough to stand on that alone. The worthy man has been in his grave for many years. Having heard that Mr. Brown had stated that he did not know him, he exclaimed : "He does not know ME ! Well, there is no act of Parliament to make people know about me. All I can say is, that if he does not know about me, he is an ill-informed man !" This was not a joke. It was said in bitter earnest. For when a young fellow who was present showed a tendency to smile at this outburst of self-conceit nursed in solitude, the young fellow was furiously ordered out of the room.

Doubtless you have remarked, with satisfaction, how the little oddities of men who marry rather late in life are pruned away speedily after their marriage. You have found a man who used to be shabbily and carelessly dressed, with a huge shirt-collar frayed at the edges, and a glaring yellow silk pocket handkerchief, broken of these things, and become a pattern of neatness. You have seen a man whose hair and whiskers were ridiculously cut speedily become like other human beings. You have seen a clergyman, who wore a long beard, in a little while appear without one. You have seen a man, who used to sing ridiculous, sentimental songs, leave them off. You have seen a man who took snuff copiously, and who generally had his breast covered with snuff, abandon the vile habit. A wife *is* the grand wielder of the moral pruning-knife. If Johnson's wife had lived, there would have been no hoarding up of bits of orange peel, no touching all the posts in walking along the street, no eating and drinking with a disgusting voracity. If Oliver Goldsmith had been married, he would never have worn that memorable and ridiculous coat. Whenever you find a man whom you know little about, oddly dressed, or talking absurdly, or exhibiting any eccentricity of manner, you may be tolerably sure that he is not a married man. For the little corners are rounded off, the little shoots are pruned away, in married men. Wives generally have much more sense than their husbands, especially when the husbands are clever men. The wife's advices are like the ballast that keeps the ship steady. They are like the wholesome though painful shears, snipping off little growths of self-conceit and folly.

So you may see, that it is not good for man to be alone. For he will put out various shoots at his own sour will, which will grow into monstrously ugly and absurd branches, unless they are pruned away while they are young. But it is quite as bad, perhaps it is worse, to live among people with whom you are an oracle. There are many good Protestants who, by a long continuance of such a life, have come to believe their own infallibility much more strongly than the pope believes his. An only brother amid a large family of sisters is in a perilous position. There is a risk of his coming to think himself the greatest, wisest, and best of men ; the most graceful dancer, the most melodious singer, the sweetest poet, the most unerring shot; also the best-dressed man, and the possessor of the most beautiful hands, feet, eyes, and whiskers. And as the outer world is sure not to accept this estimate, the only brother is apt to be soured by the sharp contrast between the adulation at home and the snubbing abroad. A popular clergyman, with a congregation somewhat lacking in intelligence, is exposed to a prejudicial moral atmosphere. It is a dreadful sight to see some clergymen surrounded by the members of their flock. You see them, with dilated nostrils, inhaling the incense directly and indirectly offered. It irritates one to hear such a person spoken of (as I have heard in my youth) as " the dear man," " the precious man," or even, in some cases, " the sweet man." It is a great deal too much for average human nature to live among people who agree with all one says, and think it very fine. We all need " the animated No " ; a forest tree will not grow up healthily and strong unless you let the rude blasts wrestle with it and root it firmer. It is insufferable when any mortal lives in a moral hot-house. And if there be anything for which a clergyman ought to be thankful, it is if his congregation, though duly esteeming him for his office and for his work, have so much good sense as to refrain from spoiling him by deferring unduly to all his crotchets. Let there be as few worsted slippers as possible sent him ; no bouquets laid on his study table by youthful hands before he comes down stairs in the morning;

no young women preserving under a glass shade the glove they wore in shaking hands with him, that it may be profaned by no inferior touch. Let the phrase *dear man* be utterly excluded. A manly person does not want to be made a pet of. And if there be any occasion on which a man of sense, bishop or not, ought to be filled with shame and confusion, it is when man or woman kneels down and asks his blessing. Pray, how much is the blessing worth? What good will it do anybody? Most educated men have a very decided estimate of its value, which would be expressed in figures by a round O.

One great good of a great public school is the way in which the moral pruning-knife is wielded there. I do not mean by the masters, but by the republic of boys. Many a lad of rank and fortune, in whom the evil shoots of arrogance, self-conceit, contempt for his fellow creatures, and a notion that he himself is the mightiest of mortals, have been fostered at home by the adulation of servants, and cottagers, and tenantry, has these evil shoots effectually shred away. You have heard, of course, how the Duke of Middlesex and Southwark came to his title as a baby, and grew up under the care of obsequious tutors and governors till he had attained the age to go to school. The first evening he was there, he was standing at a corner of the playground, with a supercilious air, surveying the sports that were proceeding. A boy about his own size perceived him, and running up, said, with some curiosity, "Who are you?" "The Duke of Middlesex and Southwark," was the reply. "Oh," said the other boy, with awakened interest, "there's one kick for the

Duke of Middlesex and another for the Duke of South-wark "; and having thus delivered himself, he ran away. O, what a sharp pair of shears in that moment pruned off certain shoots which had been growing in that little peer's nature ever since the dawn of intelligence! The awful yet salutary truth was impressed, by a single les-son, that there were places in this world where nobody cared for the Duke of Middlesex and Southwark. And perhaps that painful pruning was the beginning of the discipline which made that duke, as long as he lived, the most unpretending, admirable, and truly noble of men.

There are few people in public life who in this age are not promptly pruned, where needful, by ever-ready shears. If the shoots of bumptiousness appear in a chief justice, they are instantly cut short by the tongue of some resolute barrister. If a prime minister, or even a loftier personage, evinces a disposition to neglect his or her duty, that disposition is speedily pruned by the *Times;* speaking in the name of the general sense of what is fit. And indeed the newspapers and reviews are the universal shears. If any outgrowth of folly, error, or conceit appear in a political man, or in a writer of even moderate standing, some clever article comes down upon it, and shows it up if it cannot snip it off. And if a wise man desires that he may keep, intellectually and æsthetically, in becoming shape, he will attentively consider whatever may be said or written about him by people who dislike him. For, as a general rule, people who don't like you come down sharply upon your real faults; they tell you things which it is very fit that you should know, and which nobody is likely to tell you but them. I have heard of one or two distinguished authors who made it a rule never to read anything that was written about themselves. Probably they erred in this. They missed many hints for which they might have been the better. And mannerisms and eccentricities developed into rigid boughs, which might have been readily removed as growing twigs.

A vain self-confidence is very likely to grow up in a man who is never subjected to the moral pruning-knife. The greatest men (in their own judgment) that you have ever known have probably been the magnates of some little village, far from neighbors. Probably the bully is never developed more offensively than in some village dealer, who has accumulated a good deal of money, and who has got a number of the surrounding cottages mortgaged to him. Such is the man who is likely to insult the conservative candidate, when he comes to make a speech before an election. Such is the man to lead the opposition to any good work proposed by the parish clergyman. Such is the man to become a church-rate martyr, or an especially offensive manager of Salem chapel. Such is the kind of man who, if he has children growing up, will refuse to let them express their opinion on any subject. A parent can fall into no greater mistake than to take the ground that he will never argue with his children, nor hear what they may have to suggest in opposition to any plan he may have proposed. For children very speedily take the measure of their parents; and have a perfectly clear idea how far their ability, judgment, and education justify their assuming the rank of infallible oracles. And it is infinitely better to let a lad of eighteen speak out his mind, than to have him like a boiler ready to burst with repressed views and feelings, and with the bitter sense of a petty and contemptible tyranny. Something has already been said of women who acquire the chief power in their own houses; whose husbands are cowed into ciphers; and whose infallibility is to be recognized throughout the establishment, under pain of some ferocious explosion. At last, some son grows up, and resists the established despotism. Infallibility and impeccability are conceded no longer. And the thick branches, consolidated by many years' growth, are lopped off painfully, which should have gone when they were slender shoots. Rely upon it, the man or woman who refuses to be peaceably and kindly pruned, will some day have to bear being rudely lopped.

There is one shoot which human nature keeps putting forth again, however frequently it is pruned away. It is self-conceit. *That* would grow into a terrible unwieldy branch, if it were not so often shred away by circumstances; that is, ·by God's providence. Everybody needs to be frequently taken down; which means, to have his self-conceit pruned away. And what everybody needs, most people (in this case) get. Most people are very frequently taken down.

I mean, even modest and sensible people. This wretched little shoot keeps growing again, however hard we try to keep it down. There is a tendency in each of us to be growing up into a higher opinion of ourself; and then, all of a sudden, that higher estimate is cut down to the very earth. You are like a sheep suddenly shorn: a thick fleece of self-complacency had

developed itself; something comes and all at once
shears it off, and leaves you shivering in the frosty air.
You are like a lawn, where the grass had grown some
inches in length, till some dewy morning it is mown
just as close as may be. You had gradually and insensibly come to think rather well of yourself and your
doings. You had grown to think your position in life
a rather respectable or even eminent one, and to fancy
that those around estimated you rather highly. But all
of a sudden, some slight, some mortification, some disappointment comes ; something is said or done that shows
you how far you have been deceiving yourself. Some
considerable place in your profession becomes vacant,
and nobody thinks of naming you for it. You are in
company with two or three men who think themselves
specially charged with finding a suitable person for the
vacant office : they name a score of possible people to
fill it, but not you. They never have thought of you :
or possibly they refrain from naming you, with the de-
sign of mortifying you. And so you are pruned close.
For the moment, it is painful. · You are ready to sink
down, disheartened and beaten. You have no energy
to do anything. You sit down blankly by the fire, and
acknowledge yourself a failure in life. It is not so
much that you are beaten, as that you are set in a lower
place than you hoped. Yet it is all good for us, doubtless. Few men can say they are too humble with it all.
And as even after all our mowings, prunings, and
shearings, we are sometimes so conceited and self-satisfied as we are, what should we have been had those
things not befallen us? The elf-locks of wool would
have been feet in length. The grass would have been

six feet high, like that of the prairies. And the shoot of vanity would have grown and consolidated into a branch, that would have given a lopsided aspect to the whole tree.

Happily, there is no chance of these things occurring. We seldom grow for more than a few days, without being pruned, mown, and shorn afresh. And all this will continue to the end. It is not pleasant; but we need it all. And we are all profiting by it. Possibly no one will read this page, who does not know that he thinks more humbly of himself now than he did ten years since; and ten years hence, if we live, we shall think of ourselves more humbly still.

Yes: we have all been severely pruned, in many ways. Perhaps our sprays and blossoms have been shred away by a knife so unsparing, that we are cut very much into the form of a pollarded tree. Perhaps we have been pruned too much, and the spring and the nonsense taken out of us only too effectually. Certain awkward knots are left in the wood, where some cherished hope was snipped off by the fatal shears, or some youthful affection (in the case of sentimental people) came to nothing; and it was like cutting a tree over, not far above the roots, when a man was made to feel that his entire aim in life was no better than a dismal failure. But it was all for the best; and defeat, bravely borne, is the noblest of victories. What an overbearing, insolent person you would have been, if you had always got your own way, if your boyish fancies had come true! What an odd stick you would have become, had you been one of the Unpruned Trees!

CHAPTER III.

CONCERNING UGLY DUCKS: BEING SOME THOUGHTS ON MISPLACED MEN.

SOME men's geese, it has occasionally been said, are all swans. Dr. Newman declares that this was so with the great Archbishop Whately of Dublin. Read this page, intelligent person; and you shall be informed about an Ugly Duck, and what it proved in truth to be.

Rather, you shall be reminded of what you doubtless know already. The story is not mine: it was originally devised by somebody much wiser and possibly somewhat better. I propose to do no more than tell afresh and briefly what has been told at much greater length before. No doubt it has touched and comforted many to read it. For there may be much wisdom and great consolation in a fairy tale.

Amid a family of little ducks, there was one very big, ugly, and awkward. He looked so odd and uncouth, that those who beheld him generally felt that he wanted a thrashing. And in truth, he frequently got one. He was bitten, pushed about, and laughed at by all the ducks, and even by the hens, of the house to which he belonged. Thus the poor creature was quite cast down under the depressing sense of his ugliness; and the members of his own family used him worst of all. He ran away from home, and lived for a while in a cottage with a cat and an old woman. Here, likewise, he failed to be appreciated. For chancing to tell them how he liked to dive under the water and feel it closing over his head, they laughed at him, and said he was a fool. All he could say in reply was, "You can't understand me!" "Not understand you, indeed," they replied in wrath, and thrashed him.

But he gradually grew older and stronger. One day he saw at a distance certain beautiful birds, snow-white, with magnificent wings. Impelled by something within him, he could not but fly towards them, though expecting to be repulsed and perhaps killed for his presumption. But suddenly looking into the lake below him, he beheld not the old ugly reflection, but something large, white, graceful. The beautiful birds hailed him as a companion. The stupid people had thought him an ugly duck, because he was too good for them. They could not understand him, nor see the great promise of that uncouth aspect. The ugly duck proved to be a Swan!

He was not proud, that wise bird; but he was very happy. Now, everybody said he was the most beautiful of all beautiful birds; and he remembered how, once upon a time, everybody had laughed at him and thrashed him. Yes: he was appreciated at his true value at last!

Possibly, my friendly reader, you have known various Ugly Ducks, — men who were held in little esteem, because they were too good for the people among whom they lived,—men who were held in little esteem, because it needed more wit than those around them possessed to discern the makings of great and good things under their first unpromising aspect. When John Foster, many years ago, preaching to little pragmatic communities of uneducated, stupid, and self-conceited sectaries, was declared by old women and young whipper-snappers, to be A PERFECT FOOL, he was an Ugly Duck of the first kind. When Keats published his earliest poetry, and when Mr. Gifford bitterly showed up all its extravagance and mawkishness, and positively refused to discern under all that the faculties which would be matured and tamed into those of a true poet, Keats was an Ugly Duck of the second kind. John Foster was esteemed an Ugly Duck at the time when he actually was a Swan, because the people who estimated him were such blockheads that they did not know a swan when they saw one. Keats was esteemed an Ugly Duck, because he really was an awkward, shambling, odd animal ; and his critic had not patience, or had not insight, to discern something about him that promised he would yet grow into that which a mere Duck could never be. For the creature which is by nature a Swan, and which will some day be known for such by all, may in truth be, at an early stage in its development, an uglier, more offensive, more impudent and forward, more awkward and more insufferable animal, than the creature which is by nature a Duck, and which will never be taken for anything more.

Yes, many men, with the gift of genius in them, and many more, with no gift of genius but with a little more industry and ability than their fellows, are regarded as little better than fools by the people among whom they live; more especially if they live in remote places in the country, or in little country towns. Some day, the Swans acknowledge the Ugly Duck for their kinsman: and *then* all the quacking tribe around him recognize him as a Swan. Possibly, indeed, even then, some of the neighboring ducks who knew him all his life, and accordingly held him cheap till the world fixed his mark, will still insist that he is no more than an extremely Ugly Duck, whom people (mainly out of spite against the ducks who were his early acquaintances) persist in absurdly calling a Swan. I have beheld a Duck absolutely foam at the mouth, when I said something implying that another bird (whose name you would know if I mentioned it) was a Swan. For the Duck, at college, had been a contemporary of the Swan: he had even played at marbles with the Swan, in boyhood; and so, though the Swan was quite fixed as being a Swan, the Duck never could bear to recognize him as such. On the contrary, he held him as an overrated, impudent, purse-proud, conceited, disagreeable, and hideously Ugly Duck. I remember, too, a very venomous and malicious old Duck, who never had done anything but quack (in an envious and uncharitable way too) through all the years which made him very old and exceedingly tough, giving an account of the extravagances and bombastic flights of a young Swan. The Duck vilely exaggerated the sayings of that youthful Swan. He put into the Swan's mouth words which the Swan had never uttered, and ascribed to the Swan sentiments (of a heretical character) which he very well knew the Swan abhorred. But even

upon the Duck's own showing, there was the promise
of something fine about the injudicious and warm-
hearted young Swan; and a little candor and a little
honesty might have acknowledged this. And it appeared to me a poor sight to behold the ancient Duck,
with all his feathers turned the wrong way with spite,
standing beside a dirty puddle, and stretching his neck,
and gobbling and quacking out his impotent malice, as
the beautiful Swan sailed gracefully overhead, perfectly
unaware of the malignity he was exciting in the muscle
which served the Duck for a heart.

It makes me ferocious, I confess it, to hear a Duck, or
a company of Ducks, abusing and vilifying a Swan;
and a good many Ducks have a tendency so to do. If
you ask one of very many Ducks, " What kind of a bird
is A ?" (A being a Swan), the answer will be, " Oh, a
very Ugly Duck !" If the present writer had the faintest pretension to be esteemed a Swan, he would not say
this. But he knows very well indeed that he can pretend to no more than to plod humbly and laboriously
along upon the earth, while other creatures sail through
the empyrean. He has seen, with wonder, several ill-
natured attacks upon himself in print, the *gravamen* of
the charge against him being that he does not and cannot write like A, B, and C, who are great geniuses.
Pray, Mr. Snarling, did he ever pretend to write like
A, B, and C? No; he pretends to nothing more than
to produce a homely material (with something real
about it) that may suit homely folk. And so long as a
great number of people are content to read what he is
able to write, you may rely upon it he will go on writing. As for you, Mr. Snarling, of course *you* can write

like A, B, and C. And in that case, your obvious course
is to proceed to do so. And when you do so, you may
be sure of this; that the present writer will never twist
nor misrepresent your words, nor tell lies to your prejudice.

It is a curious and interesting spectacle to witness
two Ducks discussing the merits of a Swan. I have
known a Duck attack a Swan in print. The Swan was
an author. The Duck attacked the Swan on the ground
that his style wanted elegance. And I assure you the
attack, for want of elegance of style, was made in language not decently grammatical. You may have heard
a Duck attack a Swan in conversation. The Swan was
a pretty girl. The charge was that the Swan's taste in
dress was bad. You looked at the Duck, and were
aware that the Duck's taste was execrable. Would
that we could "see ourselves as others see us!" Then
you would no longer see such sights as this, which we
may have witnessed in our youth. Two Ducks viciously
abusing a Swan, flying by; and pointing out that the
Swan had lost an eye, also a foot; and with wearisome
iteration dwelling on those enormities. And when you
looked carefully at the spiteful creatures, wagging their
heads together, hissing and quacking, you were aware
that (strange to say) each of them had but one foot and
one eye, and that, in short, in every respect in which
the Swan was bad, the Ducks were about fifty times
worse. Thus you may have known a very small and
shabby Duck, who scoffed at a noble Swan, because (as
he said) the Swan had no logic. Yet whenever that
Duck himself attempted to argue any question, he had
but one course, which was scandalously to misrepresent

and distort something said by the man maintaining the
other opinion, and then to try to raise against that man
a howl of heresy. Not indeed that that man, or any
one of his friends, cared a brass farthing for what the
shabby little Duck thought or said of him. Yet the
Duck showed all the will to be a viper, though nature
had constrained him to abide a Duck. And this was
the Duck's peculiar logic.

At this point the reader may pause, and ponder what
has been said. If exhausted by the mental effort of
attention, he may take a glass of wine. And then he
is requested to observe, that the writer considers himself to have made but one step in advance since he
finished the legend of the Ugly Duck, with which the
present work commenced. That step in advance was
to the principle:

THAT SOME MEN ARE HELD IN LITTLE ESTIMA-
TION BECAUSE THEY ARE TOO GOOD FOR THE PEOPLE
AMONG WHOM THEY LIVE. These are my MISPLACED
MEN.

Of course, not all misplaced men are what I understand by Ugly Ducks. For there are men who are
misplaced by being put in places a great deal too good
for them. You may have known individuals who could
not open their mouths but you heard the unmistakable
quack-quack, who yet gave themselves all the airs of
Swans. And probably a good many people honestly
took them for Swans, and other people, prudent, safe,
and somewhat sneaky people, pretended that they took
them for Swans, while in fact they did not. And when
perspicacious persons privately whispered to one another, "That fellow Stuckup is only a duck," it was be-

cause in fact he was no more. Yet Stuckup did not think himself so. I have not seen many remarkable human beings, but I have studied a few with attention; and I can say, with sincerity, that the peculiar animal known as the *Beggar on Horseback* is by far the greatest and most important human being I have ever known. Probably, my reader, you still hold your breath with awe, as you remember your first admission to the presence of a person whom you saw to be on horseback, but did not know to be a beggar who had attained that eminence. You afterwards learned the fact; and then you wondered you did not see it sooner. For now the beggar's dignity appeared to you to bear the like relation to that of the true man in such a place, that the strut of a king, with a tinsel crown, in a booth at a fair, bears to the quiet, assured air of Queen Victoria, walking into the House of Lords to open Parliament.

It is an unspeakable blessing for a man, that he should be put down among people who can understand him. For no matter whether a man is thought a fool by his neighbors because he is too good for them, or because he is realy a fool, the depressing effect upon his own mind is the same; unless indeed he have the confidence which we might suppose would have gone with the head and heart of Shakespeare, if Shakespeare appreciated himself justly. Very likely he did not. John Foster, great man as he was, could not have liked to see the little meeting-houses at which he held forth gradually getting empty, as the people of the congregation went off to some fluent blockhead with powerful lungs and a vacuous head. For many a day Archbishop Whately of Dublin was a misplaced man; feared and suspected just because that clear head and noble heart were so high above the sympathy or even the comprehension of many of those over whom he was set. A bitter little sectary would have been at first an infinitely more popular prelate; and the writer cannot refrain from saying with what delight, but a few months before that great man died, he saw, by the enthusiastic reception which the archbishop met, rising to make a short speech at a public meeting in Dublin of three thousand people, that justice was done him at last. He had found the place which was his due. They knew the noble Swan they had got, and knew that the honor he derived from the archiepiscopal throne was as a sand-grain when compared with the honor which he reflected on it. Yet he found the time hard to bear, when he was undervalued because he was too good; when men vilified him because they could not understand him. "I have tried to look as if I did not feel it," he said; "but it has shortened my life." Whereas our friend Carper, who for ten years past has held an eminent place for which he is about as fit as a cow, and which he has made ridiculous through his incompetence, — the wrong man in the wrong place, if such a thing ever was, — is entirely pleased with himself, and will never have his life shortened by any consideration of his outrageous incapacity. There were years of Arnold's life at Rugby during which he was an unappreciated man, just because he rose so high above the ordinary standard. If the sun were something new, and if you showed it for the first time to a company of blear-eyed men, they would doubtless say it was a most disagreeable object. And if there were no people of thoughtful hearts and of refined culture in the world, the author of *In*

Memoriam would no doubt pass among mankind for a fool. There are people who, through a large part of their life, are above the high-water-mark of popular appreciation. Wordsworth was so. He needed " an audience fit "; and it for many a day was " few." The popular taste had to be educated into caring for him. It was as if you had commanded a band of children to drink bitter ale and to like it. Even Jeffrey could write, " This will never do!" And you miss people as completely by shooting over their heads as by hitting the ground a dozen yards on this side of them. A donkey, in all honesty, prefers thistles to pine-apple. Yet the poor pine-apple is ready to feel aggrieved.

This misjudging of people, because they rise above the sphere of your judgment, begins early and lasts late. I have known a clever boy, under the authority of a tyrannical and uncultivated governor, who was savagely bullied and ignominiously ordered out of the room, because he declared that he admired the *Hartleap Well.* His governor declared that he was a fool, a false pretender, a villain. His governor sketched his future career by declaring that he would be hanged in this world, and sent to perdition in the next. All this was because he possessed faculties which his uncultivated tyrant did not possess. It was as if a stone-deaf man should torture a lover of music because he ventured to maintain that there is such a thing as sound. It was as if a man whose musical taste was educated up to the point of admiring the *Ratcatcher's Daughter* should vilipend and suspend by hemp a human being who should declare there was something beyond *that* in

Beethoven and Mendelssohn. And I believe that very often thoughtful little children are subjected to the great trial of being brought up in a house where they are utterly misunderstood by guardians and even by parents quite unequal to understanding them; and this has a very souring effect on the little heart. There are boys and girls, living under their fathers' roof, who in their deepest thoughts are as thoroughly alone as if they dwelt at Tadmor in the Wilderness. There are children who would sooner go and tell their donkey what was most in their mind than they would tell it to their father or their mother. In some cases, the lack of power to understand or appreciate becomes still more marked as childhood advances to maturity. You may have known a man recognized by the world as a very wise man for expressing to the world the self-same views and opinions whose expression had caused him to be adjudged a fool at home. "Do you know, Charlotte has written a book; and it's better than likely": was all the father of its author had to say about *Jane Eyre.* What a picture of a searing, blighting home atmosphere! You cannot read the story without thinking of evergreens crisping up under a withering east wind of three weeks' duration. And I could point to a country in Africa where men, who would be recognized as great men elsewhere, are thought very little of, because there is hardly anybody who can appreciate them and their attainments. I have known there an accomplished scholar, who in the neighboring kingdom of Biafra would be made a *clefrag* (corresponding to our bishop), who, living where he does, when spoken of at all, is usually spoken of contemptuously as A DOMINIE ; corresponding to our schoolmaster or college tutor, but the undignified way of stating the fact. Such a man is a great Greek scholar; but if he dwell among Africans, who know nothing earthly about Greek, and who care even less for it, what does it profit him? Alas, for that misplaced man! Thought an Ugly Duck because he lives at Heliopolis; while four hundred miles off, in the great University of Biafra, he would be hailed as a noble Swan by kindred Swans!

Almost the only order of educated men who have it not in their power to live among educated folk are the clergy. Almost all other cultivated men may choose. for their daily companions people like themselves. But in the Church, you have doubtless known innumerable instances in which men of very high culture were set down in remote rural districts, where there was not a soul with whom they had a thought in common within a dozen miles. It is all right, of course, in that broader sense in which everything is so; and doubtless the cure of souls, however rude and ignorant, is a work worthy of the best human heart and head that God ever made. Still it is sad to see a razor somewhat in-efficiently cutting a block, for which a great axe with a notched edge is the right thing. It is sad to see a cultivated, sensitive man in the kind of parish where I have several times seen such. You may be able to think of one, an elegant scholar, a profound theologian, a man of most refined taste, taken unhappily from the common-room of a college, and set down in a cold upland district, where there were no trees and where the wind almost invariably blew from the east; among people with high cheek-bones and dried-up complexions, of radical politics and dissenting tendencies, dense in ignorance and stupidity, and impregnable in self-confidence and self-conceit, and just as capable of appreciating their clergyman's graceful genius as an equal number of codfish would be. And what was a yet more melancholy sight than even the sight of the first inconsistency between the man and his place was the sight of the way in which the man, year by year, degenerated till he grew just the man for the place, and only a middling man for it. Yes, it was miserable to see how the Swan gradually degenerated into an Ugly Duck; how his views got morbid, and his temper ungenial; how his accomplishments rusted, and his conversational powers died through utter lack of exercise; till after a good many years you beheld him a soured, wrong-headed, cantankerous, petty, disappointed man. For luck was against him; and he had no prospect but that of remaining in the bleak upland parish, swept by the east wind, as long as he might live. And after a little while, he ceased entirely to go back to the university where he would have found fit associates; and he grew so disagreeable that his old friends did not care to visit him, and listen to his moaning. Now, you cannot long keep much above what you are rated at. At least, you must have an iron constitution of mind if you do. I daresay sometimes in old days an honorable and good man was constrained by circumstances to become a publican; I mean, of course, a Jewish publican. He meant to be honest and kind, even in that unpopular sphere of life. But when all men shied him; when his old friends cut him; when he was made to feel, daily, that in the common estimation publicans and sinners ranked together; I have no doubt earthly but he would sink to the average of his class. Or, as the sweetest wine becomes the sourest vinegar, he might not impossibly prove a sinner above all the other publicans of the district.

But not merely do ignorant and vulgar persons fail to appreciate at his true value a cultivated man: more than this, the fact of his cultivation may positively go to make vulgar and ignorant persons dislike and underrate him. My friend Brown is a clergyman of the Scotch Church, and a man who has seen a little of the world. Like most educated Scotchmen now-a-days, he speaks the English language, if not with an English accent, at least with an accent which is not disagreeably Scotch. He does not call a boat a bott; nor a horse, a hoarrse; nor philosophy, philozzophy; nor a road, a rodd. He does not pronounce the word *is* as if it were spelt eez, nor talk of a lad of speerit. Still less does he talk of salvahtion, justificahtion, sanctificahtion, and the like. He does not begin his church service by giving out either a *sawm* or a *samm;* in which two disgusting forms I have sometimes known the word *psalm* disguised. Brown told me that once on a time he preached in the church of a remote country parish, where parson and people were equally uncivilized. And after service the minister confided to him that he did not think the congregation could have liked his sermon. " Ye see," said the minister, " thawt's no the style o' langidge they're used wi'!" My friend replied, not without asperity, that he trusted it was not. But I could see, when he told me the story, that he did not quite like to be an Ugly Duck; that it irked him to think that, in fact, some vulgar boor with a different style o' langidge would have been much more acceptable to the people of Muffburgh. I am very happy to believe that such parishes as Muffburgh are becoming few; and that a scholar and a gentleman will rarely indeed find that he had better, for immediate popularity, have been a clod-hopper and an ignoramus. You have heard, no doubt, how a dissenting preacher in England demolished the parish clergyman in a discourse against worldly learn-ing. The clergyman, newly come, was an eminent scholar. "Do ye think Powle knew Greek?" said his opponent, perspiring all over. And the people saw how useless, and indeed prejudicial, was the knowledge of that heathen tongue.

And this reminds me that it will certainly make a man an Ugly Duck to be, in knowledge or learning, in advance of the people among whom he lives. A very wise man, if he lives among people who are all fools, may find it expedient, like Brutus, to pass for a fool too. And if he knows two things or three which they don't know, he had better keep his information to himself. Even the possession of a single exclusive piece of knowl-edge may be a dangerous thing. Long ago, in an an-cient university near the source of the Nile, the profes-sors of divinity regarded not the quantity of Greek or Latin words. The length of the vowels they decided in each case according to the idea of the moment. And their pronunciation of Scripture proper names, if it went upon any principle at all, went on a wrong one. A youthful student, named McLamroch, was reading an essay in the class of one of these respectable but ante-diluvian professors; and coming to the word *Thessa-*

lonica, he pronounced it, as all mortals do, with the accent on the last syllable but one, and giving the vowel as long. " Say Thessaloanica," said the venerable professor, with emphasis. " I think, *doctissime professor*," (for all professors in that university were *most learned by courtesy*,) " that Thessalonica is the right way," replied poor McLamroch. " I tell you it is wrong," shrilly shouted the good professor : " say Thessaloanica ! and let me tell you, Mr. McLamroch, you are most aboaminably affectit ! " So poor McLamroch was put down. He was an Ugly Duck. And he found by sad experience, that it is not safe to know more than your professor. And I verily believe, that the solitary thing that McLamroch knew, and his professor did not know, was the way to pronounce Thessalonica. I have heard, indeed, of a theological professor of that ancient day, who bitterly lamented the introduction of new fashions of pronouncing scriptural proper names. However, he said, he could stand all the rest ; but there were two renderings he would never give up but with life. These were Kapper-nawm, by which he meant Capernaum ; and Levvy-awthan, by which he meant Leviathan. And if you, my learned friend, had been a student under that good man, and had pronounced these words as scholars and all others do, you would have found yourself no better than an Ugly Duck, and a fearfully misplaced man.

A torrent of *wut*, sarcasm at new lights, and indignation at people who were not content to pronounce words (wrong) like their fathers before them, would have made you sink through the floor.

To be in advance of your fellow-mortals in taste, too,

is as dangerous as to be in advance of them in the pronunciation of Thessalonica. When Mr. Jones built his
beautiful Gothic house in a district where all other
houses belonged to no architectural school at all, all his
neighbors laughed at him. A genial friend, in a letter
in a newspaper, spoke of his peculiar taste, and called
him the *preposterous Jones.* And it was a current joke
in the neighborhood, when you met a friend, to say,
" Have you seen Jones's house ? " You then held up
both hands, or exclaimed, " Well, I never ! " Then
your friend burst into a loud roar of laughter. In a
severer mood, you would say, " That fellow ! Can't he
build like his fathers before him ? Indeed he never
had a grandfather. I remember how he was brought up
by his aunt, that kept a cat's-meat shop in Muffburgh,"
and the like. All this evil came upon Jones, because he
was a little in advance of his neighbors in taste. For
in ten years, hardly a house round but had some steep
gables, several bay-windows, and a little stained glass.
Their owners esteemed them Gothic ; and in one sense,
undoubtedly, some of them were Gothic enough. In
Scotland now people build handsome churches, and pay
all due respect to ecclesiastical propriety. But it is not
very long since a parish clergyman proposed to the authorities that a proper font should be provided for bap-
tisms, because the only vessel heretofore used for that
purpose was a crockery basin, used for washing hands ;
and one of the authorities exclaimed indignantly, " We
are not going to have any gewgaws in our church " : by
gewgaws meaning a decorous font. What could be done
with such a man ? Violently to knock his head against
a wall would have been wrong ; for no man should be

visited with temporal penalties on account of his honest opinions. Yet any less decided treatment would have been of no avail.

We ought all to be very thankful, if we are in our right place; if we are set among people whom we suit, and who suit us; and among whom we need neither to practise a dishonest concealment of our views, nor to stand in the painful position of Ugly Ducks and Mis placed Men. Yes, a man may well be glad, if he is the square man in the square hole. For he might have been a round man in a square hole; and then he would have been unhappy in the hole, and the hole would have hated him. I know a place where a man who should say that he thought Catholic Emancipation common justice and common sense would be hooted down even yet; would be told he was a villain, blinded by Satan. There is a locality, where morality indeed is very low, but where a valued friend of mine was held up to reprobation as a dangerous and insidious man, because he declared in print that he did not think it sinful to take a quiet walk on Sunday. In that locality, one birth in every three is illegitimate; but it was pleasant and easy, by abuse of the rector of a London parish, and by abuse of others like him, to compound for the neglect of the duty of trying to break Hodge and Bill, Kate and Sally, of their evil ways. I know a place where you may find an intelligent man, out of a lunatic asylum too, who will tell you that to have an organ in church is to set up images and go back to Judaism. I have lately heard it seriously maintained that to make a decorous pause for a minute after service in church is over, and pray for God's blessing on the worship in which you have joined, is "contrary to reason and to Scripture!" I know places where any one of the plainest canons of taste, being expressed by a man, would be taken as stamping him a fool. Now what would you do, my friend, if you found yourself set down among people with whom you were utterly out of sympathy; whose first principles appeared to you the prejudices of pragmatic blockheads, and to whom your first principles appeared those of a silly and Ugly Duck? One would say, "If you don't want to dwarf and distort your whole moral nature, get out of that situation." But then some poor fellows cannot. And then they must either take rank as Misplaced Men, or go through life hypocritically pretending to share views which they despise. The latter alternative is inadmissible in any circumstances. Be honest, whatever you do. Take your place boldly as an Ugly Duck, if God has appointed that to be your portion in this life. Doubtless, it will be a great trial. But you and I, friendly reader, set by Providence among people who understand us and whom we understand; among whom we may talk out our honest heart, and (let us hope) do so; in talking to whom we don't need to be on our guard, and every now and then to pull up, thinking to ourselves, "Now this sneaking fellow is lying on the catch for my saying something he may go and repeat to my prejudice behind my back"; how thankful we should be! I declare, looking back on days that have been, in this very country, I cannot understand how manly, enlightened, and honest men lived then at all! You must either have been a savage bigot, or a wretched sneak, or a martyr. The alternative is an awful one; but let us trust, my friend, that if you and I had lived then, we should, by God's grace, have been equal to it. Yes, I humbly trust that if we had lived then, we should either have been burned, hanged, or shot. For the days have been in which *that* must have been the portion of an honest man, who thought for himself, and who would be dragooned by neither pope, prelate, nor presbyter.

But now, having written myself into a heat of indignation, I think it inexpedient to write more. For it appears to me that to write or to read an essay like this ought always to be a relief and recreation. And those grave matters, which stir the heart too deeply, and tingle painfully through the nervous system, are best treated at other times, in other ways. Many men find it advisable to keep to themselves the subjects on which they feel most keenly. As for me, I dare not allow myself to think of certain evils of whose existence I know. Sometimes they drive one to some quiet spot, where you can walk up and down a little path with grass and evergreens on either hand, and try to forget the sin and misery you cannot mend: looking at the dappled shades of color on the grass; taking hold of a little spray of holly, and poring upon its leaves; stopping beside a great fir-tree, and diligently perusing the wrinkles of its bark.

So we shut up. So we cave in. O the beauty of these simple phrases, so purely classic!

CHAPTER IV.

OF THE SUDDEN SWEETENING OF CERTAIN GRAPES.

ANY years since, on a sunshiny autumn day, a gentleman named Mr. Charles James Fox, a lawyer of eminence, was walking with his friend Mr. Mantrap through a vineyard near Melipotamus. A vineyard in that region of the earth is not the shabby field of what look like stunted gooseberry bushes which you may see on the Rhine. For trellised on high, from tree to tree, there hung the ripe clusters, rich and red. One cluster, of especial size and beauty, attracted the attention of Mr. Fox. He had in his hand a walking-stick (made of oak, varnished to a yellow hue), with a hook at its superior end. With this implement he sought to reach that cluster of grapes, with the view of appropriating it to his personal consumption, possibly upon the spot. But after repeated attempts, he found he could not in any way attain it. Upon this, Mr. Fox, a man of ready wit intellectually, but morally no more than an average human being, turned off the little disappointment by saying to his friend, " O, bother: I believe the grapes are as sour as the disposition of Mr. Snarling." The friends prosecuted their walk; but after they had proceeded a few miles, it occurred to Mr. Mantrap that Mr. Fox had depreciated the grapes because he could not reach them. Mr. Mantrap mentioned the occurrence to various acquaintances, and gradually it came to be that, in the circle of Mr. Fox's friends, SOUR GRAPES grew a proverbial phrase, signifying anything a human being would like to get, and, failing to get, cried down.

These facts, now given to the public in an accurate fashion, were lately made the subject of a short narrative in a little volume of moral stories published by an individual whose name I do not mention. But by one of those misapprehensions which naturally occur when a story is conveyed by oral tradition, that gentleman (of whom I desire to speak with the utmost respect) represented that the person who acted in the way briefly described was not Mr. C. J. Fox, the eminent lawyer, but the well-known inferior animal which is termed a fox. A moment's thought may show how impossible it is to receive such a representation. For it is extremely doubtful whether a fox would care to eat grapes, even if he could get a cluster of the very finest; while the notion that such an animal could express his ideas in articulate language is one which could not possibly be received, unless by illiterate persons, residing at a great distance from a university town.

Should the reader have had any difficulty in grasping the full meaning of what has been said, it is requested that he should pause at this point, and read the preceding paragraphs a second or even a third time before proceeding further.

3 *

Sometimes, in this world, people dishonestly say that the grapes they have failed to reach are sour, though knowing quite well that the grapes are sweet. In this case, these people desire to conceal their own disappointment; and (if possible) to make the value of the grapes less to such as may ultimately get them. Sometimes, in this world, when people have done their best to reach the grapes and failed, they come to honestly believe that the grapes *are* sour. They do, in good faith, cease to care for them, and resign their mind quite cheerfully to doing without them. But there is no reckoning up the odd ways in which the machinery of thought and feeling within human beings works; and it is the purpose of the present dissertation to notice two of these.

One is, that when you get the grapes, and specially if you get them too easily, the grapes are apt, if not exactly to grow sour, yet in great measure to lose their flavor. When you fairly get a thing, you do not care for it so much. Many people have lately been interested and touched by a truthful representation in the pages of a very graceful, natural, and pure writer of fiction, whose pages (I have learned with some surprise) various worthy people think it wrong to read. That graceful and excellent writer shows us how a certain young man sought the love of a certain young woman, and how when that young man (not a noble or worthy man indeed) found the love of that poor girl given him so fully and unreservedly, he came not to care for it, and to think he might have done better. Lead him out and chastise him, my friend; and having done so, look into your own heart, and see whether there be anything like him. If you be a wise person, you may find reason severely to flagellate yourself. For it is the ungrateful and unworthy way of average human nature, to undervalue the blessings God gives us, if they come too cheaply and easily. Even Bruce, at the source of the Nile, thought to himself, "Is this all?" and Gibbon, looking out upon the Lake of Geneva, after writing the last lines of the *Decline and Fall*, tells us how he thought and felt in like manner.

This, however, is not my special subject. My subject is also connected with grapes; but it is a different phenomenon to which I solicit the reader's rapt and delighted attention. It is, how suddenly certain grapes grow sweet, when you find you can get them. You had no estimate at all of these grapes before, or you even thought them sour. But suddenly you find the hook at the end of your walking-stick can reach them, suddenly you find you can get them, and now you judge of them quite differently.

Many young women have thought, quite honestly, — and perhaps have said, in the injudicious way in which inexperienced people talk, — that they would not marry such and such a man upon any account. But some fine afternoon, the man in question asked them; and to the astonishment of their friends (some of whom would have been glad to do the like themselves), the young ladies gladly accepted the human being, held in such unfavorable estimation before. It just made all the difference, to find that the thing could be got. They began, all at once, to have quite a different estimate of the man; to think of him and of his qualifications in quite a different way. The grapes suddenly grew sweet; and instead of being contumeliously cast into the ditch, they were eaten with considerable satisfaction.

Even so have young clergymen, fresh from the university, thought that they would not on any account take such a small living or such a shabby church; and in a little while been very thankful to get one not so good. And I do not mean at present, in the case of either the young women or the young preachers, that they learn humbler ideas of themselves as time goes on, and come to lowlier expectations. *That*, of course, is true; but my present assertion is, that in truth when the thing is put within their reach, they come to think more highly of it; they come to see all its advantages and merits, they are not merely resigned to take it, — they are glad to get it. Many a man is now in a place in life, and very content and thankful to be there, which he would have repudiated the notion of his accepting very shortly before he accepted it with thankfulness.

The truth is, that if you look carefully, and look for some length of time, into the character of almost anything that is not positively bad, you will see a great deal of good about it. Friends in my own calling, do you not remember how, in your student days, you used to look at the shabby churches of our native land, where shabby churches are (alas!) the rule, and decorous ones the exception, and how you wondered then how their incumbents could stand them? You thought how much it would add to the difficulty of conducting public worship worthily to be obliged to do it under the cross-influence of a dirty, dilapidated barn, with a mass of rickety pews, where every arrangement would jar distressingly upon the whole nervous system of every man with a vestige of taste. You remember how your heart sunk as you looked at the vile wagon-roofed meeting-house in a dirty village street, with no churchyard at all round it ; or with the mangy, weedy, miserable-looking pound which even twenty years since was in many places thought good enough for the solemn sleep of the redeemed body, still united to the Saviour. And you remember how earnestly you hoped that you might be favored so highly as to attain a parish where the church was a building at least decent, and if possible fairly ecclesiastical. And yet it is extremely likely you got a remarkably shabby church for your first one; and it is in the highest degree probable that in a little you got quite interested in it, and thought it really very good. Of course, when my friend Mr. Snarling reads this, he will exclaim, What, is not the clergyman's work so weighty that it ought not to matter to him in the least what the mere outward building is like ? Is not the spiritual church the great thing? may not God be worshipped in the humblest place as heartily as in the noblest? And I reply to that candid person, who never misrepresented any one, and who never said a good word of any one, — Yes, my acquaintance, I remember all that. But still I hold that little vexatious external circumstances have a great effect in producing a feeling of irritation the reverse of devotional ; and I believe that we poor creatures, with our wandering thoughts and our cold hearts, are much more likely to worship in spirit, if we are kept free from such unfriendly influences, and if our worship be surrounded by all the outward decency and solemnity which are attainable. Give us a decorous building, I don't ask for a grand one; give us quietude and order in all its arrangements ; give us church music that soothes and cheers, and brings us fresh heart; give us an assemblage of seemingly devout worshippers. And these things being present, I do not hesitate to say that the average worshipper will be far more likely to offer true spiritual worship than in places to which I could easily point, where the discreditable building and the slovenly service are an offence and a mortification to every one with any sense of what is fit.

This, however, is by the bye. I could say much more on the subject. But I remember, thankfully, that it is a subject on which all educated persons now think alike, everywhere. It did not use to be so, once.

But not merely as regards churches, but as regards most other things, my principle holds true, that if you look carefully and for some time into the qualifications of almost anything not positively bad, you will discern a great deal of good about it. Take a very ordinary-looking bunch of grapes; take even a bunch of grapes which appears sour at a cursory glance: look at it carefully for a good while, with the sense that it is your own; and it will sweeten before your eyes. You pass a seedy little country house, looking like a fourth-rate farm-house: you think, and possibly say (if the man who lives in it be a friend of your own), that it is a wretched hole. The man who lives in it has very likely persuaded himself that it is a very handsome and attractive place. "What kind of manse have you got?" said my friend Smith to a certain worthy clergyman. "Oh, it is a beautiful place," was the prompt reply. It was in fact a dismal, weather-stained, whitewashed erection, without an architectural feature, with hardly a tree or an evergreen near it, standing on a bleak hillside. Smith heard the reply with great pleasure ; feeling thankful that by God's kind appointment a sensible man's own grapes seem sweet to him, which appear sour to everybody else, and to nobody sourer than to himself, before they became his own. The only wonder Smith felt was, that the good minister's reply had not been stronger. He was prepared to hear the good man say, " Oh, it is the most beautiful place in Scotland!" For people in general cannot express their appreciation of things, without introducing comparisons, and indeed superlatives. If a man's window commands a fine view, he is not content to say that it does command a fine view: no, it commands " the finest view in Britain." If a human being has an attack of illness, about a hundredth part as bad as hundreds of people endure every day, that human being will probably be quite indignant, unless you recognize it as a fact, that nobody ever suffered so much before. Take an undistinguished volume from your shelves, read it carefully in your leisure hours for several evenings, and that undistinguished volume will become (in your estimation) an important one. My friend Smith, when he went to his country parish, was obliged for several months to have his books in large packing-boxes, his study not being ready to receive them. He lived in a lonely rural spot, for many wintry weeks, all alone. It was a charming scene around, indeed ; warm with green ivy and yews and hollies through the brief daylight, but dreary and solitary through the long dark evenings to a man accustomed to gas-lit streets. Soon after settling there, Smith chanced to draw forth from a box a certain volume, which had remained for months in his bookcase unnoted: one among many more, all very like. And on every Sunday evening of that solitary time, Smith read in that volume. He read with pleasure and profit. Ever since then, he has thought the book a valuable and excellent one. It is distinguished among his books as the Bishop of Anywhere is among five hundred other clergymen; not that he is a whit wiser or better, but that he has been accidentally made more conspicuous. When Smith turns over its leaves now, the moaning of January winds through the pine wood comes back, and the brawl of a brook, winter-flooded. In brief, that cluster of grapes suddenly sweetened, because its merits were fairly weighed. If a thing be good at all, look at it and examine it, and it will seem better.

Now, a thing you have no chance of getting, you never seriously weigh the merits of. When you receive a half offer of a place in life, it is quite fair for you to say, " Offer it fairly and I shall think of it." You cannot take the trouble of estimating it now. It is a laborious and anxious thing to make up your mind in such a case. You must consider and count up and weigh possibly a great number of circumstances. You do not choose to undergo that fatigue, perhaps for no result. And if you be in perplexity what to do, the balance may be turned just by the fact that the thing is attainable. Hence the truth of that true proverb, that *Faint heart never won fair lady.* If you are fond of Miss Smith, and wish to marry her, don't speculate at home whether or not she will have you. Go and ask her. Your asking may be the very thing that will decide her to have you. And you, patron or electors of some little country parish which is vacant, don't say, " We need never offer it to such and such an eminent preacher; he would never think of it!" Go and try him. Perhaps he may. Perhaps you may catch him just at a time when he is feeling weary and exhausted; when he is growing old; when your offer may recall with fresh beauty the green fields and trees amid which he once was young; when he is sighing for a little rest. I could point out instances, more than one or two, in England and in Scotland, in which a bold offering of a bunch of grapes to a distinguished human being induced him to accept the grapes; though you would have fancied beforehand that they would have been no temptation to him. I have known a man who (in a moral sense) refused a pine-apple, afterwards accept a turnip, and like it. We have all heard of a good man who might have lived in a palace, holding a position of great rank and gain, and of very easy duty, who put that golden cluster of grapes aside, and by his own free choice went to a place of hard work and little fame or profit, to remain there one of the happiest as well as one of the noblest and most useful of humankind! And the only way in which I can account for various marriages is by supposing that the grapes suddenly grew irresistibly sweet, just when it appeared that they could be had. You may have known a fair young girl quite willingly and happily marry a good old creature, whom you would have said *a priori* she was quite sure to refuse. But when the old creature made offer of his faded self (and his unfaded possessions), the whole thing offered acquired a sudden value and beauty. He might be an odd stick; but then his estate had most beautiful timber. Intellectually and morally he might be inferior or even deficient; but then his three per cents formed a positive quantity of enormous amount. The whole thing offered had to be regarded as one bunch of grapes. And if some of the grapes were sour and shrivelled, a greater number of them were plump and juicy.

Nobody who reads this page really knows whether he would like to be lord chancellor or to live in a house like Windsor Castle. The writer has not the faintest idea whether he would like to be· Archbishop of Canterbury. We never even ourselves to such things as these. We don't seriously consider whether the grapes are sweet or sour, which there is not the faintest possibility of our ever reaching. When Mr. Disraeli (as he himself said in Parliament) " would have been very thankful for some small place," he had never lifted his eyes to the leadership of a certain great political party. Of that lofty cluster he had no estimate *then;* but the modest little bunch of twelve hundred a-year seemed attainable, and so seemed sweet. But he was a great man when he said " I am very glad now I did not get it !" He was destined to something bigger and loftier. And when that greater position at last loomed in view, and became possible, became likely, — we can well believe that the great orator began to estimate it; and that it became an object of honorable ambition when it was very near, and was all but grasped. When the prize is within reach, it becomes precious. When the Atlantic cable was being laid, you can think how precious it would seem when the vessels which were laying it had got within a mile or two of land. Yes, success, just within our grasp, grows inestimably valuable. The cluster of grapes, long striven after, and now at length just got hold of, — how sweet it seems !

My friend Mr. Brown had often remarked to me, " If ever there was a hideous erection on the face of the earth, it is that St. Sophia's Church; and I don't know a man less to be envied than the incumbent of so laborious and troublesome a parish." Brown and I were sitting on the wall of his beautiful churchyard in the country one fine summer day, when he made this remark, adding, " How much happier a life we have here in this pure air and among these sweet fields " (and indeed the fragrance of the clover was very delightful that day), " and with our kindly, well-behaved country people !" I need hardly mention, that Mr. Brown shortly afterwards succeeded to the vacant charge of St. Sophia's, a huge church in a great city. He was offered it in a kind way ; saw its claims and advantages in a new light ; accepted it, and is very happy in it. And recently he recalled to my memory his former estimate of it, and said how mistaken it was. He even added, that, although the architecture of St. Sophia's was not the purest Gothic (it is in fact not Gothic at all), still there is a simple grandeur about it, which produces a great effect upon the mind when you grow accustomed to it. " I used to laugh," he said, " at poor old Dr. Log when he declared it was the finest church in Britain but, do you know, some of its proportions are really unrivalled. Here, for instance, look at that arch " ; — and then he went on at considerable length. The truth was, that the grapes had suddenly sweetened. The position never thought of, or thought of only as quite unattainable, was a very different thing now.

I do not for a moment suppose any insincerity on the part of my friend. He quite sincerely esteemed the grapes as sour, when they hung beyond his reach. He quite sincerely esteemed them as sweet, when he came to know them better. But, as a general rule, whenever any man or woman undervalues and despises something which average human nature prizes and enjoys, we may say that if the grapes are fairly put within reach, they would suddenly and greatly sweeten. I speak of average human nature. There are exceptional cases. There is a great and good man who did not choose to be a bishop, who did not choose to be an archbishop. The test is, that he was offered these places and refused them. But there are a great many men, who could quite honestly say that they don't want to be bishops or archbishops. But then they have not been tried; and there are some that I should not like to try. I believe the lawn would brighten into effulgence, when it was offered. The opportunity of usefulness would appear so great, that it could not in conscience be refused. The grapes, being within reach, would grow so sweet, that those good men would forget their old professions, and (in the words of Lord Castlereagh) turn their backs upon themselves.

Perhaps you have known a refined young lady of thirty-nine years, who looked with disdain at her younger female friends when they got married. She wondered at their weakness in getting spoony about any man, and despised their flutter of interest in the immediate prospect of the wedding-day and all its little arrangements. The whole thing — trousseau, cards, favors, cake — was contemptible. Perhaps you have known such a mature young lady get married herself at last, and evince a pride and an exhilaration in the prospect such as are rarely seen. It was delightful to witness the maidenly airs of the individual to whom the bunch of grapes had finally become attainable; the enthusiastic affection she testified towards the romantic hero (weighing sixteen stone) to whom she had given her young affections; the anguish of perplexity as to the material and fashion of the wedding-dress; in short, the sudden sweetening of the grapes which had previously been so remarkably sour. There is nothing here to laugh at: it is a beneficent providential arrangement. In all walks of life you may have remarked the same. You may have known a hard-featured and well-principled servant, who, having no admirer, gave herself out as a man-hater, and believed herself to be one. But some one turning up who (let us hope) admired and appreciated her real excellence, that admirable young woman grew quite tremendous: first, in her pride and exultation that she had a beau; and secondly, in her admiration and fondness for him. Yes; turn out human nature with a pitch fork; and it will come back again.

Perhaps you have known a wealthy old gentleman, living quietly somewhere in the city (let the word be understood in its cockney sense), and going into no society whatever, who frequently professed to despise the vanities to which other folk attach importance. He utterly contemned such things as a fine house, a fashionable neighborhood, titled acquaintances, and the like; and he did it all quite sincerely. But nature had her way at last. That wealthy gentleman bought a house in an aristocratic West End square. His elation at finding himself there was pleasing, yet a little irritating. He could not refrain from telling everyone that he lived there. Occasionally he would cut short a conversation with a city acquaintance, by stating that he "must be home to dinner at half past seven in Berkeley Square." He speedily informed himself of the precise social standing of every inhabitant of that handsome quadrangle; and would even produce the " Court Guide," and tell an occasional visitor about the rank and connections of each name in the square. The delight with which he beheld a peer at his dinner-table may be conceived but not described. The grapes, in fact, had in all sincerity been esteemed as sour till he got possession of them. Then, all of a sudden, they became inconceivably sweet. So you may have beheld a plain, respectable man, who had made a considerable fortune in the oil trade, buy a property in the country and settle there. "I want nothing to do with your stuck-up gentry," said that respectable man. "I shall keep by my old friends Smith, Brown, and Robinson, who were apprentices with old McOily along with me, forty years ago." But when the carriage of the neighboring baronet drove up to the worthy man's door to call, it and its inmates were received with enthusiasm. There was, after all, a refinement of manner and feeling about gentle blood, not possessed by Smith and the others; and after a little intercourse with the family of the baronet, and with other similar families, poor Smith, Brown, and Robinson got so chilly a reception at the country house, and were so infuriated by the frequent mention and the high laudation of the landed families about (whom Smith and his friends did not know at all), that these old acquaintances quite dropped off; and the good old oil-merchant was left to the enjoyment of the grapes, formerly so sour and now so sweet. It is all in human nature. You may have known a cultivated man, with a small income, living in a city of very rich and not remarkably cultivated men. You may have heard him speak with much contempt of mere vulgar wealth, and of certain neighbors who possessed it. And you felt how easily that cultivated man might be led to change his tune. I have witnessed a parallel case. Once upon a time, the writer was walking along a certain country road, a walk of nine miles. He overtook a little boy walking along manfully by himself, — a little fellow of seven years old. The two wayfarers proceeded together for several miles, conversing of various subjects. It appeared, in the course of conversation, that the little boy, whose parents are very poor, never had any pocket-money. I don't believe he ever had a penny to spend in all his life. He stated that he did not care for money, nor for the good things (in a child's sense of that phrase) which might be bought with it. And parting from the little man, I could not but tip him a shilling. Every human being who will ever read this page would of course have done the same. It was his very first shilling. He tried to receive it with philosophic composure, as if he did not care a bit about it. But he tried with little success. It was easy to see how different a thing a shilling had suddenly grown. The grapes had all at once sweetened.

But it is the same way everywhere. An author without popular estimation thinks he can do quite well without it: he does not care for it. "The world knows nothing of its greatest men"; nor, let us add, of its best. Yet popular favor proves very pleasant, when it comes at last. So a barrister without briefs does not want them or value them, till they come. So with the schoolboy who does not care for prizes; so with the student at college whose prize essays fail, through the incompetence of the judges. So (I fear) with the very intellectual preacher who would rather have his church empty than full, and who (at present) thinks that only the stupid and blinded are likely to attend a church where all the seats are occupied. I have known clever young fellows, more than two or three, who at a very early age had outgrown all ambition; men who had in them the makings of great things, but by free choice took to a quiet and unnoted life; men whose university standing had been unrivalled, but who instead of aiming at like eminence afterwards, took to gardening, to evergreens and grass and trees; to contented walks through winter fields; to preaching to fifty rustic laborers; to reading black-letter books in chambers at the Temple, instead of trying for the Great Seal; quite happy, and quite sincere in thinking and saying they did not care for more eminent places. But at length, perhaps, success and eminence come, and they are very glad and pleased. Their views of these things are quite changed. They see that they can be more useful than they are. They feel that there was a good deal of indolent self-indulgence in the life they had been leading; that there is more in this life than to practise a refined Epicureanism, — at least while strength and spirits suffice for more. The day may come, when these shall be worn out, and then the old thing will again be pleasant.

Let us hear the sum of the whole matter. If there

be anything in this world which is in its nature agreeable to average humanity, yet which you think sour, the likelihood is, that, if you got it, it would grow sweet. You cannot finally turn out nature. Though you may mow it down very tightly, it will grow again, as grass does in the like contingency. And if there be in you evil and unworthy tendencies, which by God's grace you have resolved to extirpate, you must keep a constant eye upon them. You must knock them on the head not once for all, but daily and hourly.

There are things, perhaps, which you know you would like so much, yet which are so unattainable, that you will not allow yourself to think of them. *That* way lies your safety. If you allowed yourself to dwell upon them, and upon their pleasures and advantages, you would grow discontented with what you have. So, though you cannot help sometimes casting a hasty glance at the cluster of grapes, hanging high, which you would like, but which you will never have, yet don't look long at it. Don't sit down and contemplate it for a good while from various points of view, and think how much you would like it. *That* will only make you unhappy. And if you have known this world long, then you know this about it, that the thing you would like best is just the last you are ever likely to get. But of this I shall say no more. I said something like it once before, and got a shower of long letters controverting it.

If a young fellow fails in his profession, and then say he did not want to succeed, let us believe him. He is entitled to this. We do him, in most cases, no more than justice. The grapes have indeed grown sour, and it is a kind appointment of Providence that it is so.

4

But if success should come yet, you will find them sweeten again surprisingly.

In writing upon this subject, I have been led to think of many things, and to think of many old acquaintances. Not very cheerfully did the writer trace out the first page, still less so the last. How sadly short has many a one, of whom we expected great things, fallen of those expectations! Is there one of the clever boys and thoughtful lads that has done as much as we looked for? Not one.

The great thing, of course, that resigns one to this, and to anything else, is the firm belief that God orders all. "IT HAD PLEASED GOD to form poor Ned, A thing of idiot mind," wrote Southey. There the matter is settled. We have not a word more to say. "I was dumb; I opened not my mouth: BECAUSE THOU DIDST IT!"

We have all smiled at the fable of Æsop, of which the writer has given you the accurate version, and smiled at many manifestations we have seen in life showing its truth, and showing us how human nature, age after age, abides the self-same thing. I believe it is one of the most beneficent arrangements of God's providential government, that the grapes we cannot reach grow sour. But for *that*, this would be a world of turned heads and broken hearts. Who has got the purple clusters he in his childhood thought to get? Yet who (if a sensible mortal) cares? You were to have been a laurelled hero, — you are in fact a half-pay captain, glad to be made adjutant of a militia regiment. You were to have been Lord Chancellor of Great Britain, — you are, in fact, parish minister of Drumsleekie, with a smoky manse, and heritors who oppose the augmentation of your living. You were to have lived in a grand castle, possibly built of alternate blocks of gold and silver, — you live, in fact, in a plain house in a street, and find it hard enough to pay the Christmas bills. And you were to have been buried, at last, in Westminster Abbey, — while in fact you won't. But the beauty has faded off the things never to be attained, and the humble grapes you could reach have sweetened; and you are content. Yet there are grapes which, if submitted to your close inspection, would seem so sweet that in comparison with them those you have would seem very insipid; so you may be glad you will never see those grapes too near nor too long.

CHAPTER V.

CONCERNING THE ESTIMATE OF HUMAN BEINGS.

THE other day, talking with my friend Smith, I incidentally said something which implied that a certain individual, who may be denoted as Mr. X, was a distinguished and influential man. "Nonsense!" was Smith's prompt reply. "I saw Mr. X," continued Smith, "at a public meeting yesterday. He is a gorilla,—a yahoo. He is a dirty and ugly party. I heard him make a speech. He has a horribly vulgar accent, and an awkward, cubbish manner. In short, he is not a gentleman, nor the least like one!"

And having said this, my friend Smith thought he had finally disposed of X.

But I replied, "I grant all that. All you have said about X is true. But still I say he is a distinguished and influential man, a very able man,— almost a great man."

Smith was not convinced. He departed. I fear I have gone down in his estimation. I have not seen him since. Perhaps he does not want to see me. I don't care.

But my friend Smith's observations have made me think a good deal of a tendency which is in human nature. It is very natural, if we find a man grossly deficient in something about which we are able to judge, — and perhaps in the thing about which we are able best to judge, — to conclude that he must be all bad. In the judgment of many, it is quite enough to condemn a man, to show that he is a low fellow, with an extremely vulgar accent. We forget how much good may go with these evil things ; good more than enough to outweigh all these and more. There is great difficulty in bringing men heartily to admit the great principle which may be expressed in the familiar words, — For Better, for Worse. There · is great difficulty in bringing men really to see that excellent qualities may coexist with grave faults; and that a man, with very glaring defects, may have so many great and good qualities, as serve to make him a good and eminent man, upon the balance of the whole account. Though you can show that A owes a hundred thousand pounds, this does not certainly show that A is a poor man. Possibly A may possess five hundred thousand pounds, and so the balance may be greatly in his favor.

We all need to be reminded of this. It is very plain, but it is just very plain things that most of us practically forget. There are many folk who instantly, on discovering that A owes the hundred thousand pounds, proceed to declare him a bankrupt without further inquiry. Possibly the debt A owes is constantly and strongly pressed on your attention, while it costs some investigation to be assured of the large capital he possesses. There is one debt in particular which, if we find owed by any man, it

is hard to prevent ourselves declaring him a bankrupt
without more investigation.   Great vulgarity will commonly stamp a man in the estimation of refined people,
whatever his merits may be.   *That* is a thing not to be
got over.   If a man be deficient by *that* hundred thousand pounds, all the gold of Ophir will (in the judgment
of many) leave him poor.   Once in my youth, I beheld
an eminent preacher of a certain small Christian sect.
I knew he was an eloquent orator, and that he was
greatly and justly esteemed by the members of his own
little communion.   I never heard him speak, and never
beheld him save on that one occasion.   But, sitting near
him at a certain public meeting, I judged, from obvious
indications, that he never had brushed his nails in his
life.   I remember well how disgusted I was, and how
hastily I rushed to the conclusion that there was no good
about him at all.   Those territorial and immemorial
nails hid from my youthful eyes all his excellent qualities.   Of course, this was because I was very foolish and
inexperienced.   Men with worse defects may be great
and good upon the whole.   Or, to return to my analogy,
no matter how great a man's debts may be, you must
not conclude he is poor till you ascertain what his assets
are.   These may be so great as to leave him a rich man,
though he owes a hundred thousand pounds.

The principle which I desire to enforce is briefly this,
— that men must be taken *for better, for worse.*   There
may be great drawbacks about a thing, and yet the thing
may be good.   Many people think, in a confused sort of
way, that if you can mention several serious objections
to taking a certain course, this shows you should not take
that course.   Not at all.   Look to the other side of the

account. Possibly there are twice as many and twice as weighty objections to your not taking that course. There are things about your friend Smith that you don't like. They worry you. They point to a conclusion which might be expressed in the following proposition : —

SMITH IS BAD.

But if you desire to arrive at a just and sound estimate of Smith, your course will be to think of other things about Smith, which speak in a different strain. There are things about Smith you cannot help liking and respecting him for. And these point to a conclusion which a man of a comprehensive mind and of considerable knowledge of the language might express as follows : —

SMITH IS GOOD.

And having before you the things which may be said *pro* and *con*, it will be your duty first to count them, and then to weigh them. Counting alone will not suffice. For there may be six things which tell against Smith, and only three iu his favor; and yet the three may be justly entitled to be held as outweighing the six. For instance, the six things counting against Smith may be these : —

1. He has a red nose.

2. He carries an extremely baggy cotton umbrella.

3. He wears a shocking bad hat.

4. When you make any statement whatever in his hearing, he immediately begins to prove, by argument, that your statement cannot possibly be true.

5. He says *tremenduous* when he means *tremendous;* and talks of a *prizenter* when he means a *precentor.*

6. He is constantly saying, "How very curious!" also, "Goodness gracious!"

Whereas the three things making in Smith's favor may be these : —

1. He has the kindest of hearts.
2. He has the clearest of heads.
3. He is truth and honor impersonate.

Now, if the account stand thus, the balance is unquestionably in Smith's favor. And it is so with everything else as well as with Smith. When you change to a new and better house, it is not all gain. It is gain on the whole; but there may be some respects in which the old house was better than the new. And when you are getting on in life, it is not all going forward. In some respects it may be going back. It is an advance, on the whole, when the attorney-general becomes chancellor; yet there were pleasant things about the other way too, which the chancellor misses. It is, to most men, a gain on the whole to leave a beautiful rectory for a bishop's palace; yet the change has its disadvantages too, and some pleasant things are lost. When Bishop Poore, who founded Salisbury Cathedral in the thirteenth century, left his magnificent church amid its sweet English scenery, to be bishop of the bleak northern diocese of Durham, he must have felt he was sacrificing a great deal. Yet to be Bishop of Durham in those days was to be a Prince of the Church, with a Prince's revenue; and so Bishop Poore was, on the whole, content to go. I daresay in the thirteen years he lived at Durham before he died, he often wondered whether he had not done wrong.

You will find men who are good classical scholars

ready to think it extinguishes a man wholly to show that he is grossly ignorant of Latin and Greek. It is to be granted, no doubt, that as a classical training is an essential part of a liberal education, the lack of it is a symptomatic thing, like a man dropping his h's. He must be a vulgar man who talks about his Ouse and his Hoaks. And even so, to write about *rem quomodo rem,* as an eminent divine has done, raises awful suspicions. So it is with *macte estote puer.* Still, we may build too much on such things. By a careful study of English models, a man may come to have a certain measure of classical taste and sensibility, though he could not construe a chance page of Æschylus or Thucydides, or even an ode of Horace. Yet you will never prevent many scholars from sometimes throwing in such a man's face his lack of Latin and Greek, as though that utterly wiped him out. I cannot but confess, indeed, that there is no single fact which goes more fatally to the question, whether a man can claim to be a really educated person, than the manifest want of scholarship ; all I say is, that too much may be made of even this. You know that a false quantity in a Latin quotation in a speech in Parliament can never be quite got over. It stamps the unfortunate individual who makes it. He may have many excellent qualities, many things of much more substantial worth than the power of writing alcaics ever so fluently, yet the suspicion of the want of the education of a gentleman will brand him. Yet Paley was a great man, though, when he went to Cambridge to take his degree of Doctor of Divinity, in the *Concio ad Clerum* he preached on that occasion, he pronounced *profŭgus, profŭgus.* A shower of epigrams followed

Many a man, incomparably inferior to Paley on the whole, felt his superiority to Paley in the one matter of scholarship. Here was a joint in the great man's armor, at which it was easy to stick in a pin. Lockhart, too, was a very fair scholar, though you read at Abbotsford, above the great dog's grave, certain lines which he wrote :—

> " Maidæ marmoreâ dormis sub imagine, Maida,
> Ad januam Domini. Sit tibi terra levis ! "

You will find it difficult, if you possess a fair acquaintance with the literature of your own country, to suppress some little feelings of contempt for a man whose place in life should be warrant that he is an educated man, yet who is blankly ignorant of the worthy books in even his own language. Yet you may find highly respectable folk in that condition of ignorance ;— medical men in large practice; country attorneys, growing yearly in wealth as their clients are growing poorer; clergymen, very diligent as parish priests, and not unversed in theology, if versed in little else. I have heard of a highly respectable divine, of no small standing as a preacher, who never had heard of the *Spectator* (I mean, of course, Steele and Addison's *Spectator*), at a period very near the close of his life. And certain of his neighbors, who willingly laughed at that good man's ignorance, were but one degree ahead of him in literary information. They knew the *Spectator*, but they had never heard of Mr. Ruskin nor of Lord Macaulay. Still, they could do the work which it was their business to do, very reputably. And *that* is the great thing after all.

The truth is, that the tendency in a good scholar to despise a man devoid of scholarship, and the tendency in a well-read man to despise one who has read little or nothing besides the newspapers, is just a more dignified development of that impulse which is in all human beings to think A or B very ignorant, if A or B be unacquainted with things which the human beings first named know well. I have heard a gardener say, with no small contempt, of a certain eminent scholar, " Ah, *he* knows nothing; *he* does not know the difference between an arbutus and a juniper." Possibly you have heard a sailor say of some indefinite person, " *He* knows nothing; *he* does not know the foretop from the binnacle." I have heard an architect say of a certain man, to whom he had shown a certain noble church, " Why, the fellow did not know the chancel from the transept." And although the architect, being an educated man, did not add that the fellow knew nothing, *that* was certainly vaguely suggested by what he said. A musician tells you, as something which finally disposes of a fellow-creature, that he does not know the difference between a fugue and a madrigal. I remember somewhat despising a distinguished classical professor, who read out a passage of Milton to be turned into heroic Latin verse. One line was, —

" Fled and pursued transverse the resonant fugue ";

which the eminent man made an Alexandrine, by pronouncing fugue in two syllables, as FEWGEW. In fact, if you find a man decidedly below you in any one thing, if it were only in the knowledge how to pronounce fugue, you feel a strong impulse to despise him on the

whole, and to judge that he stands below you altogether.

Probably the most common error in the estimate of
human beings, is one already named; it is, to think
meanly of a man if you find him plainly not a gentleman. And I have present to my mind now a case
which we have all probably witnessed; namely, a set of
empty-headed puppies, of distinguished aspect and lan-
guid address, imperfectly able to spell the English language, and incapable of anything but the emptiest badi-
nage in the respect of conversation, yet expressing their
supreme contempt for a truly good man, who may have
shown himself ignorant of the usages of society. You
remember how Brummell mentioned it as a fact quite
sufficient to extinguish a man, that he was "a person
who would send his plate twice for soup." The judgment entertained by Brummell, or by any one like
Brummell, is really not worth a moment's consideration.
I think of the difficulty which good and sensible people
feel, in believing the existence of sterling merit along
with offensive ignorance and vulgarity. Yet a man
whom no one could mistake for a gentleman may have
great ability, great eloquence in his own way, great
influence with the people, great weight even with cultivated folk. I am not going to indicate localities or mention names, though I very easily could. No doubt, it is
irritating to meet a member of the House of Commons,
and to find him a vulgar vaporer. Yet, with all that,
he may be a very fit man to be in Parliament; and he
may have considerable authority there, when he sticks
to matters he can understand. And if refined and scholarly folk think to set such a one aside, by mentioning

that he cannot read Thucydides, they will find themselves mistaken.

It is to many a very bitter pill to swallow, a very disagreeable thing to make up one's mind to, yet a thing to which the logic of facts compels every wise man to make up his mind, that in these days men whose features, manners, accent, entire ways of thinking and speaking, testify to their extreme vulgarity, have yet great influence with large masses of mankind. And it is quite vain for cultivated folk to think to ignore such. Men grossly ignorant of history, of literature, of the classics, men who never brushed their nails, men who don't know when to wear a dress-coat and when a frock, may gain great popularity and standing with a great part of the population of Great Britain. Their vulgarity may form a high recommendation to the people with whom they are popular. It would be easy to point out places where anything like refinement or cultivation would be a positive hindrance to a man. Let not blocks be cut with razors. Let not coals be carried in gilded chariots. Rougher means will be more serviceable; and if people of great cultivation say, "A set of vulgar fellows, not worth thinking of"; and refuse to see the work such men are doing, and to counteract it where its effects are evil; those cultivated people will some day regret it. I occasionally see a periodical publication, containing the portraits of men who are esteemed eminent by a certain class of human beings. Most of those men are extremely ugly, and all of them extremely vulgar-looking. The natural impulse is to throw the coarse effigies aside, and to judge that such persons can do but little, either for good or ill. But if you inquire, you will find they are doing a great work, and wielding a great influence with a very large section of the population; the work and influence being, in my judgment, of the most mischievous and perilous character.

Then a truth very much to be remembered is, that the fact of a man's doing something conspicuously and extremely ill is no proof whatsoever that he is a stupid man. To many people it appears as if it were such a proof, simply because their ideas are so ill-defined. If a clergyman ride on horseback very badly, he had much better not do so in the presence of his humbler parishioners. The esteem in which they hold his sermons will be sensibly diminished· by the recollection of having seen him roll ignominiously out of the saddle, and into the ditch. Still, in severe logic, it must be apparent that if the sermons be good in themselves, the bad horsemanship touches them not at all. It comes merely to this, — that if you take a man off his proper ground, he may make a very poor appearance; while on his proper ground, he would make a very good one. A swan is extremely graceful in the water; the same animal is extremely awkward on land. I have thought of a swan clumsily waddling along on legs that cannot support its weight, when I have witnessed a great scholar trying to make a speech on a platform, and speaking miserably ill. The great scholar had left his own element, where he was graceful and at ease; he had come to another, which did not by any means suit him. And while he floundered and stammered through his wretched little speech, I have beheld fluent empty-pates grinning with joy at the badness of his appearance. They had got the great scholar to race with them; they in their own element, and he out of his. They had got him into a duel, giving them the choice of weapons; and having beat him (as logicians say), *secundum quid*, they plainly thought they had beat him *simpliciter*. You may have been amused at the artifices by which men, not good at anything but very fluent speaking, try to induce people, infinitely superior to them in every respect save that one, to make fools of themselves by miserable attempts at that one thing they could not do. The fluent speakers thought, in fact, to tempt the swan out of the water. The swan, if wise, will decline to come out of the water.

I have beheld a famous anatomist carving a goose. He did it very ill. And the faith of the assembled company in his knowledge of anatomy was manifestly shaken. You may have seen a great and solemn philosopher seeking to make himself agreeable to a knot of pretty young girls in a drawing-room. The great philosopher failed in his anxious endeavors, while a brainless cornet succeeded to perfection. Yet though the cornet eclipsed the philosopher in this one respect, it would be unjust to say that, on the whole, the cornet was the philosopher's superior. I have beheld a pious and amiable man playing at croquet. He played frightfully ill. He made himself an object of universal derision; and he brought all his good qualities into grave suspicion, in the estimation of the gay young people with whom he played. Yes, let me recur to my great principle,—no clergyman should ever hazard his general usefulness by doing anything whatsoever signally ill in the presence of his parishioners. If he have not a good horse, and do not ride well, let him not ride at all.

And if, living in Scotland, he be a curler; or, living in England, join in the sports of his people; though it be not desirable that he should display pre-eminent skill or agility, he ought to be a good player, — above the average.

It is an interesting thing to see how habitually, in this world, excellence in one respect is balanced by inferiority in another; how needful it is, if you desire to form a fair judgment, to take men for better, for worse. I have oftentimes beheld the ecclesiastics of a certain renowned country assembled in their great council to legislate on church affairs. And, sitting mute on back benches, never dreaming of opening their lips, — pictures of helplessness and sheepishness, — I have beheld the best preachers of that renowned country: I am not going to mention their names. Meanwhile, sitting in prominent places, speaking frequently and lengthily, speaking in one or two cases with great pith and eloquence, I have beheld other preachers, whose power of emptying the pews of whatever church they might serve had been established beyond question by repeated trials. Yet, by tacit consent, these dreary orators were admitted as the church's legislators; and, in many cases, not unjustly. There is a grander church, in a larger country, in which the like balance of faculties may be perceived to exist. The greater clergymen of that church are entitled *bishops*. Now, by the public at large, the bishops are regarded in the broad light of the chief men of the church; that is, the greatest and most distinguished men. Next, the thing as regards which the general public can best judge of a clergyman is his preaching. The general public, therefore, regard

the best preachers as the most eminent clergymen. But
the qualities which go to make a good bishop are quite
different from those which go to make a great preacher.
Prudence, administrative tact, kindliness, wide sympa-
thies, are desirable in a bishop. None of these things
can be brought to the simple test of the goodness of a
man's sermon. Indeed, the fiery qualities which go to
make a great preacher do positively unfit a man for
being a bishop. From all this comes an unhappy an-
tagonism between the general way of thinking as to
who should be bishops, and the way in which the people
who select bishops think. And the general public is
often scandalized by hearing that this man and the
other, whom they never heard of, or whom they know
to be a very dull preacher, is made a bishop; while this
or that man, who charms and edifies them by his admirable sermons, is passed over. For the tendency is in-
veterate with ill-cultivated folk, to think that if a man
be very good at anything he must be very good at everything. 'And with uneducated folk, the disposition is almost ineradicable, to conclude that if you are very ignorant on some subject they know, you know nothing; and
that if you do very ill something as to which they can
judge, you can do nothing at all well. Pitt said of
Lord Nelson, that the great admiral was the greatest
fool he ever knew, when on shore. A less wise man
than Pitt, judging Nelson a very great fool on shore,
would have hurried to the conclusion that Nelson was a
fool everywhere and altogether. And Nelson himself
showed his wisdom, when informed of what Pitt had
said. "Quite true," said Nelson; "but I should soon
prove Pitt a fool if I had him on board a ship." It

may, indeed, be esteemed as certain that Pitt's strong common-sense would not have failed him, even at sea; but when he was rolling about in deadly sea-sickness, and testifying twenty times in an hour his ignorance of nautical affairs, it may be esteemed as equally certain that the sailors would have regarded him as a fool.

I have heard vulgar, self-sufficient people in a country parish relate with great delight instances of absence of mind and of lack of ordinary sense, on the part of a good old clergyman of great theological learning, who was for many years the incumbent of that parish. A thoughtful person would be interested in remarking instances in which an able and learned man proved himself little better than a baby. But it was not for the psychological interest that those people related their wretched little bits of ill-set gossip. It was for the purpose of conveying, by innuendo, that there was no good about that simple old man at all; that he was, in fact, a fool *simpliciter*. But if you, learned reader, had taken that old man on his own ground, you would have discovered that he was anything but a fool. "What's the use of all your learning," his vulgar and ignorant wife was wont to say to him, "if you don't know how to ride on horseback, and how turnips should be sown after wheat?"

You may remember an interesting instance, in the *Life of George Stephenson*, of two great men supplementing each the other's defects. George Stephenson was arguing a scientific point with a fluent talker who knew very little about the matter; but though Stephenson's knowledge of the subject was great, and his opinions sound, he was thoroughly reduced to silence. He

had no command of language or argument. He had a
good case, but he did not know how to conduct it. But
all this happened at a country-house where Sir William
Follett was likewise staying. Follett saw that Stephenson was right, and he was impatient of the triumph of
the fluent talker. Follett, of course, had magnificent
powers of argument, but he had no knowledge whatever
of the matter under discussion. But, privately getting
hold of Stephenson, Follett got Stephenson to coach
him up in the facts of the case. Next day, the great
advocate led the conversation once more to the disputed
question; and now Stephenson's knowledge and Follett's
logic combined smashed the fluent talker of yesterday
to atoms.

Themistocles, every one knows, could not fiddle, but
he could make a little city a big one. Yet the people
who distinctly saw he could not fiddle were many, while
those who discerned his competence in the other direction were few. So, it is not unlikely that many people despised him for his bad fiddling, failing to remark
that it was not his vocation to fiddle. Goldsmith wrote
The Vicar of Wakefield and *The Good-natured Man*;
yet he felt indignant at the admiration bestowed by a
company of his acquaintances upon the agility of a monkey; and, starting up in anger and impatience, exclaimed, "I could do all that myself." I have heard
of a very great logician and divine, who was dissatisfied
that a trained gymnast should excel him in feats of
strength, and who insisted on doing the gymnast's feats
himself; and, strange to say, he actually did them.
Wise men would not have thought the less of him
though he had failed; but it is certain that many aver-

age people thought the more of him because he succeeded.

There are single acts which may justly be held as
symptomatic of a man's whole nature; for, though done
in a short time, they are the manifestation of ways of
thinking and feeling which have lasted through a long
time. To have written two or three malignant anonymous letters may be regarded as branding a man finally.
To have only once tried to stab a man in the back may
justly raise some suspicion of a man's candor and honesty ever after. You know, my reader, that if A poi-
sons only one fellow creature, the laws of our country
esteem that single deed as so symptomatic of A's whole
character, that they found upon it the general conclusion
that A is not a safe member of society; and so, with all
but universal approval, they hang A. Still the doing
of one or two very malicious and dishonorable actions
may not indicate that a man is wholly dishonorable and
malicious. These may be no more than an outburst of
the bad which is in every man, cleared off thus, as
electricity is taken out of the atmosphere by a good
thunder-storm. I am not sure what I ought, in fairness,
to think of a certain individual, describing himself as a
clergyman of the Church of England, who has formed
an unfavorable opinion of the compositions of the present writer, and who, every now and then, sends me an
anonymous letter. It is, indeed, a curious question,
how a human being can deliberately sit down and spend
a good deal of time in writing eight rather close pages
of anonymous matter of an unfriendly, not to say abusive character, and then send it off to a man who is a

total stranger. What are we to think of this individual? Are we to think favorably of him as a clergyman and as a gentleman? He has sent me a good many letters; and I shall give you some extracts from the last. For the sake of argument, let it be said that my name is Jones. I am a clergyman of the Established Church in a certain county. But my correspondent plainly thinks it a strong point to call me a Dissenter, which he does several times in each of his letters. Of course, he knows that I am not a Dissenter; but this mode of address seems to please him. I give you the passages from his last letter *verbatim*, only substituting Jones for another name, of no interest to anybody:—

Rev. Jones (Dissenting Preacher):—

I have read your *Sermons* from *curiosity*. They exhibit your invincible conceit, like all your other works. Your notion as to the resurrection of the *old body* is utterly *exploded*, except amongst such divines as Dr. Cumming (who is *not* eminent, as you assert), and similar riff-raff.

There is now-a-days no Sabbath. The Scotch, who talk of a "Sabbath," are fools and ignorant fanatics. I am glad to see that *you*, Jones, were well castigated by a London paper for lending your name to a hateful crusade of certain fanatics in Edinburgh (including the odious Guthrie), against opening the *parks* to the people on Sunday. I intend to visit Edinburgh or Glasgow some *Sunday*, and to walk about, *as a clergyman*, between the services, with some little ostentation, in order to show my contempt of the local custom. Let any

low Scotch Presbyterian lay hands on me at his peril!
Ah, Jones, you evidently dare not say your soul is your
own in Scotland!

Neither Caird nor Cumming are men of first-rate
ability. Cumming is a mere dunce, not even *literate.*
How *can* you talk of understanding the works of Mr.
Maurice? Of course not: you are too low-minded and
narrow-souled! But do not dare to disparage such exalted merit. Say you are a fool, and blind, and we may
excuse you.

You are clearly unable to appreciate excellence of
any kind. Your assertion, that the doctrines of *the*
Church, *our* Church, are *Calvinistic,* is a *false* one.
Calvinism is now confined to illiterate tinkers, Dissenters, Puritans, and low Scotch Presbyterians.

Your constant use of the phrase, " My friends," in
your sermons, is bad and affected. We are not your
"friends"; and you care nothing for your hearers, except to gain their applause!

I remain, Sir Jones, with no *very great* respect,

Your obedient servant,

P. A.

P. S.—Poor A. K. H. B. Why not A. S. S.!

Now, my reader, how shall we estimate the man that
wrote this? Can he be a gentleman? Can he be a
clergyman? I have received from him a good many
letters of the same kind, which I have destroyed, or I
might have culled from them still more remarkable
flowers of rhetoric. In a recent letter he drew a very
unfavorable comparison between the present writer and
the author of *Friends in Council.* In that unfavorable

comparison I heartily concur; but it may be satisfactory to Mr. P. A. to know that immediately after receiving his letter I was conversing with the author of *Friends in Council*, and that I read his letter to my revered friend. And I do not think Mr. P. A. would have been gratified if he had heard the opinion which the author of *Friends in Council* expressed of P. A. upon the strength of that one letter. Let us do P. A. justice. For a long time he sent his anonymous letters unpaid, and each of them cost me twopence. For some time past he has paid his postages. Now this is an improvement. The next step in advance which remains for P. A. is to cease wholly from writing anonymous letters.

Now to conclude:—

There is great difficulty in estimating human beings; that is, in *placing* them (in the racing sense) in your own mind. And the difficulty comes of this, that you have to take a conjunct view of a man's deservings and ill-deservings; the man's merit is the resultant of all his qualities, good and bad. In a race the comparison is brought to the single point of speed,—or, more accurately speaking, to the test, which horse shall, on a given day, pass the winning-post first. Every one understands the issue; and the prize goes on just the one consideration. Great confusion and difficulty would arise if other issues were brought in; as for instance, if a man were permitted to say to the owner of the winner, "You have passed the post first, but then my horse has the longest tail, and, upon the strength of that fact, I claim the cup." Yet, in placing human beings (mentally) for the race of life, the case is just so. You are making up your mind, "Is this man eminent or obscure? is he deserving or not? is he good or bad?" But there is no one issue to which you can rightly bring his merits. He may exhibit extraordinary skill and ability in doing some one thing; but a host of little disturbing circumstances may come to perplex your judgment. Mr. Green was a good scholar and a clever fellow; yet I have heard Mr. Brown say, " Green! ah, he's a beast! Do you know, he told me he always studies without shoes and stockings!" And then there is a difficulty in saying what importance ought to be attached to those disturbing causes, as well as whether they exist or not. One man thinks a long tail a great beauty, another attaches no consequence to a long tail. One man concludes that Mr. Green is a beast because he studies without shoes or stockings; another holds *that* as an indifferent circumstance, not affecting his estimate of Green. I fear we can come to no more satisfactory conclusion than this,— that of Green, and of each human being, there are likely to be just as many different estimates as there are people who will take the trouble of forming an estimate of them at all.

You will remark, I have been speaking of estimates, honestly formed and honestly expressed. No doubt we often hear and often read estimates of men, which estimates have been plainly disturbed by other forces. No wise man will attach much weight to the estimate of a successful man, which is expressed by a not very magnanimous man whom he has beaten. If A sends an article to a magazine, and has it rejected, he is not a competent judge of the merit of the articles which appear in that number in which he wished his to be. You would not ask for a fair estimate of Miss Y's singing from a young lady who tries to sing as well and fails. You would not expect a very reliable estimate of a young barrister, getting into great practice, from poor Mr. Briefless, mortified at his own ill-success. You would not look for a very flattering estimate of Mr. Melvill or Bishop Wilberforce from a preacher who esteems himself as a great man, but who somehow gets only empty pews and bare walls to hear him preach. Sometimes, in such estimates, there are real envy and malice, as shown by intentional misrepresentation and mere abuse. More frequently, we willingly believe, there is no intention to estimate unfairly; the bias against the man is strong, but it is not designed. A writer cut off from the staff of a periodical, though really an honest man, has been known to attack another writer retained on that staff. Let me say that, in such a case a very high-minded man would decline to express publicly any estimate, being aware that he could not help being somewhat biassed.

Let this be a rule:—

If we think highly of one who has beaten us, let us say out our estimate warmly and heartily.

If we think ill of one who has beaten us, let us keep our estimate to ourselves. It is probably unjust; and even if it be a just estimate, few men of experience will think it so.

5 *   G

CHAPTER VI.

REMEMBRANCE.

SHALL I, because I have seen the subject which has been simmering in my mind for several past days treated beautifully by another hand, resolve not to touch that subject, and to let my thoughts about it go? No, I will not.

It was a little disheartening, no doubt, when I looked yesterday at a certain magazine, to find what I had designed to say said far better by somebody else. But then Dean Alford said it in graceful and touching verse: I aimed no higher than at homely prose.

Sitting, my friend, by the evening fireside,—sitting in your easy chair, at rest, and looking at the warm light on the rosy face of your little boy or girl, sitting on the rug by you, — do you ever wonder what kind of remembrance these little ones will have of you, if God spares them to grow old? Look into the years to come: think of that smooth face, lined and roughened; that curly hair, gray; that expression, now so bright and happy, grown careworn and sad, and you long in your grave. Of course, your son will not have quite forgot you. He will sometimes think and speak of his father who is gone. What kind of remembrance will he have of you? Probably very dim and vague.

You know for yourself, that when you look at your little boy in the light of the fire, who is now a good deal bigger than in the days when he first was able to put a soft hand in yours and to walk by your side, you have but an indistinct remembrance of what he used to be then. Knowing how much you would come to value the remembrance of those days, you have done what you could to perpetuate it. As you turn over the leaves of your diary, you find recorded with care many of that little man's wonderful sayings; though, being well aware that these are infinitely more interesting to you than to other people, you have sufficient sense to keep them to yourself. There are those of your fellow-creatures to whom you would just as soon think of speaking about these things as you would think of speaking about them to a jackass. And you have aided your memory by yearly photographs, thankful that such invaluable memorials are now possible, and lamenting bitterly that they came so late. Yet, with all this help, and though the years are very few, your remembrance of the first summer that your little boy was able to run about on the grass in the green light of leaves, and to go with you to the stable-yard and look with admiration at the horse, and with alarm at the pig voraciously devouring its breakfast, is far less vivid and distinct than you would wish it to be. Taught by experience, you have striven with the effacing power of time; yet assuredly not with entire success. Yes, your little boy of three years old has faded somewhat from your memory; and you may discern in all this the way in which you will gradually fade from his. Never forgotten, if you have been the parent you ought to be, you will be remembered vaguely. And you think to yourself, in the restful evening, looking at the rosy face, Now, when he has grown old, how will he remember me? I shall have been gone for many a day and year; all my work, all my cares and troubles, will be over; all those little things will be past and forgot, which went to make up my life, and about which nobody quite knew but myself. The table at which I write, the inkstand, all my little arrangements, will be swept aside. That little man will have come a long, long way since he saw me last. How will he think of me? Will he sometimes recall my voice, and the stories I told, and the races I used to run? Will he sometimes say to a stranger, "That's his picture, not very like him"; will he sometimes think to himself, "There is the corner where he used to sit; I wonder where his chair is now?"

Cowper, writing at the age of fifty-eight, says of his mother: "She died when I had completed my sixth year, yet I remember her well. I remember too a multitude of maternal tendernesses which I received from her, and which have endeared her memory to me beyond expression." For fifty-two years the over-sensitive poet had come on his earthly pilgrimage since the little boy of six last saw his mother's face. Of course, at that age, he could understand very little of what is meant by death; and very little of that great truth, which Gray tells us he discovered for himself, and which very few people learn till they find it by experience, that in this world a human being never can have more than one mother. Yet we can think of the poor little man, finding daily that no one cared for him now as he used to be cared for, finding that the kindest face he could remember was now seen no more. And doubtless there was a vague, overwhelming sorrow at his heart, which lay there unexpressed for half a century, till his mother's picture sent him by a relative touched the fount of feeling, and inspired the words we all know :—

> "I heard the bell tolled on thy burial day;
> I saw the hearse that bore thee slow away;
> And, turning from my nursery window, drew
> A long, long sigh, and wept a last adieu!
>
> But was it such? — It was. Where thou art gone,
> Adieus and farewells are a sound unknown.
> May I but meet thee on that peaceful shore,
> The parting word shall pass my lips no more!"

Nobody likes the idea of being quite forgot. Yet sensible people have to make up their mind to it. And you do not care so much about being forgotten by those beyond your own family circle. But you shrink from the thought that your children may never sit down alone, and, in a kindly way, think for a little of you after you are dead. And all the little details and interests which now make up your habitude of life seem so real, that there is a certain difficulty in bringing it home to one that they are all to go completely out, leaving no trace behind. Of course they must. Our little ways, my friend, will pass from this earth; and you and I will be like the brave men who lived before Agamemnon. A clergyman who is doing his duty diligently does not like to think that when he goes he will be so soon forgotten in his old parish and his old church. Bigger folk, no doubt, have the same feeling. A certain great man has been entirely successful in carrying out his purpose; which was, he said, to leave something so written that men should not easily let it die. But that which is nearest us touches us most. We sympathize most readily with little men. Perhaps you preached yesterday in your own church to a large congregation of Christian people. Perhaps they were very silent and attentive. Perhaps the music was very beautiful, and its heartiness touched your heart. The service was soon over; it may have seemed long to some. Then the great tide of life that had filled the church ebbed away, and left it to its week-day loneliness. The like happens each Sunday. And many years hence, after you are dead, some old people will say, Mr. Smith was minister of this parish for so many years. That is all. And looking back for even five or ten years, a common Sunday's service is as undistinguished in remembrance as a green leaf on a great beech-tree now in June, or as a single flake in a thick fall of snow.

Probably you have seen a picture by Mr. Noel Paton, called *The Silver Cord Loosed*. It is one of the most beautiful and touching of the pictures of that great painter. I saw it the day before yesterday, not for the first or second time. People came into the place where it was exhibited, talking and laughing; but as they stood before that canvas, a hush fell on all. On a couch, there is a female figure lying dead. Death is unmistakably there, but only in its beauty; and beyond, through a great window, there is a glorious sunset sky.

"Thy sun shall no more go down, neither shall thy moon withdraw herself, for the Lord shall be thine ever-lasting light, and the days of thy mourning shall be ended." Seated by the bed, there is a mourner, with hidden face, in his first overwhelming grief. Looking at that picture in former days, I had thought how "at evening time there shall be light," but looking at it now, with the subject of this essay in my mind, I thought how that man, so crushed meanwhile, if the first grief do not kill him (and the greatest grief rarely kills the man of sound physical frame), would get over it, and after some years would find it hard to revive the feelings and thoughts of this day. People in actual modern life are not attired in the picturesque fashion of the mourner in Mr. Noel Paton's picture, but it is because many can from their own experience tell what a human being in like circumstances would be feeling that this detail of the picture is so touching. And the saddest thing about it is not the present grief, it is the fact that the grief will so certainly fade and go. And no human power can prevent it. "The low beginnings of content" will force themselves into conscious existence, even in the heart that is most unwilling to recognize them. You will chide yourself that you are able so soon to get over that which you once fancied would darken all your after days. And all your efforts will not bring back the first sorrow, nor recall the thoughts and the atmosphere of that time. When you were a little boy, and a little brother pinched your arm so that a red mark was left, you hastened down-stairs to make your complaint to the proper authority. On your way down, fast as you went, you perceived that the red mark was fading out, and becoming invisible. And did you not secretly give the place another pinch to keep up the color till the injury should be exhibited? Well, there are mourners who do just the like. I think I can see some traces of *that* in *In Memoriam*. In sorrow that the wound is healing, you are ready to tear it open afresh. And by observing anniversaries, by going to places surrounded by sad associations, some human beings strive to keep up their feelings to the sensitive point of former days. But it will not do. The surface, often spurred, gets indurated; sensation leaves it, and after a while, you might as well think to excite sensation in a piece of India rubber by pricking it with a pin, as think to waken any real feeling in the heart which has indeed met a terrible wound, but whose wound is cicatrized. All this is very sad to think of. Indeed, I confess to thinking it the very sorest point about the average human being. Great grief may leave us, but it should not leave us the men we were. There are people in whose faces I always look with wonder, thinking of what they have come through, and of how little trace it has left. I have gone into a certain room, where everything recalled vividly to me one who was dead. Furniture, books, pictures, piano, how plainly they brought back the face of one far away! But the regular inmates of the house had no such feeling; had it not, at least, in any painful degree. No doubt, they had felt it for a while, and outgrown it; whereas to me it came fresh. And after a time it went from me too.

You know how we linger on the words and looks of the dead after they are gone. It is our sorrowful protest against the power of Time, which we know is taking these things from us. We try to bring back the features and the tones; and we are angry with ourselves that we cannot do so more clearly. "Such a day," we think, "we saw them last: so they looked: and such words they said." We do *that* about people for whom we did not especially care while they lived: a certain consecration is breathed about them now. But how much more as to those who did not need this to endear them! You ought to know the lines of a true and beautiful poet about his little brother who died:—

> " And when at last he was borne afar
>   From the world's weary strife,
> How oft in thought did we again
>   Live o'er his little life!
>
> " His every look, his every word,
>   His very voice's tone,
> Came back to us like things whose worth
>   Is only prized when gone! "

I wish I could tell Mr. Hedderwick how many scores of times I repeated to myself that most touching poem in which these verses stand. But I know (for human nature is always the same) that, when the poet grew to middle age and more, those tones and looks that came so vividly back in the first days of bereavement would grow indistinct and faint. And now, when he sits by the fire at evening, or when he goes out for a solitary walk, and tries to recall his little brother's face, he will grieve to feel that it seems misty and far away.

> " I cannot see the features right,
>   When on the gloom I strive to paint
> The face I knew; the hues are faint,
>   And mix with hollow masks of night."

5 *

And you will remember how Mr. Hawthorne, with his sharp discernment of the subtle phenomena of the mind, speaking in the name of one who recalled the form and aspect of a beautiful woman not seen for years, says something like this: When I shut my eyes, I see her yet, but a little wanner than when I saw her in fact.

Yes; and as time goes on, a great deal wanner. I have remarked that even when the outlines remain in our remembrance, the colors fade away.

Thus true is it, that as for the long absent and the long dead, their remembrance fails. Their faces, and the tones of their voice, grow dim. And sometimes we have all thought what a great thing it would be to be able at will to bring all these back with the vividness of reality. What a great thing it would be if we could keep them on with us, clearly and vividly as we had them at the first! When your young sister died, oh how distinctly you could hear, for many days, some chance sentence as spoken by her gentle voice! When your little child was taken, how plainly you could feel, for a while, the fat little cheek laid against your own, as it was for the last time! But there is no precious possession we have which wears out so fast as the remembrance of those who are gone. There never was but one case where that was not so. Let us remember it as we are told of it in the never-failing Record: there are not many kindlier words, even there :—

"But the Comforter, which is the Holy Ghost, whom the Father will send in my name, He shall teach you all things, and bring all things to your remembrance, whatsoever I have said unto you."

So you see in *that* case the dear remembrance would never wear out but with life. The Blessed Spirit would bring back the words, the tones, the looks, of the Blessed Redeemer, as long as those lived who had heard and seen Him. He was to do other things, still more important; but you will probably feel what a wonderfully kindly and encouraging view it gives us of that Divine Person, to think of Him as doing all that. And while we have often to grieve that our best feelings and impulses die away so fast, think how the Apostles, everywhere, through all their after years, would have recalled to them when needful *all things* that the Saviour had said to them; and how He said those things; and how He looked as He said them. *They* had not to wait for seasons when the old time came over them; when through a rift in the cloud, as it were, they discerned for a minute the face they used to know; and heard the voice again, like distant bells borne in upon the breeze. No: the look was always on St. Peter, that brought him back from his miserable wander; and St. John could recall the words of that parting discourse so accurately, after fifty years.

The poet Motherwell begins a little poem with this verse: —

> " When I beneath the cold red earth am sleeping,
>> Life's fever o'er,
> Will there for me be any bright eye weeping
>> That I 'm no more?
> Will there be any heart sad memory keeping
>> Of heretofore? "

Now that is a pretty verse, but to my taste it seems tainted with sentimentalism. No man really in earnest could have written these lines. And I feel not the slightest respect for the desire to have " bright eyes weeping" for you, or to have some vague indefinite "heart" remembering you. Mr. Augustus Moddle, or any empty-headed lackadaisical lad, writing morbid verses in imitation of Byron, could do that kind of thing. The man whose desire of remembrance takes the shape of a wish to have some pretty girl crying for him (which is the thing aimed at in the mention of the "bright eye weeping") is on precisely the same level, in regard to taste and sense, with the silly, conceited block-head who struts about in some place of fashionable resort, and fancies all the young women are looking at him. Why should people with whom you have nothing to do weep for you after you are dead, any more than look at you or think of you while you are living? But it is a very different feeling, and an infinitely more respectable one, that dwells with the man who has out-grown silly sentimentalism, yet who looks at those whom he holds dearest; at those whose stay he is, and who make up his great interest in life; at those whom *he* will remember, and never forget, no matter where he may go in God's universe; and who thinks, Now, when the impassable river runs between,—when I am an old remembrance, unseen for many years,—and when they are surrounded by the interests of their after life, and daily see many faces but never mine; how will they think of me? Do not forget me, my little children whom I loved so much, when I shall go from you. I do not wish you (a wise, good man might say) to vex yourselves, little things; I do not wish you to be gloomy or sad; but sometimes think of your father and mother when they are far away. You may be sure that, wherever they are, they will not be forgetting you.

CHAPTER VII.

ON THE FOREST HILL: WITH SOME THOUGHTS TOUCHING DREAM-LIFE.

HY is it that that purple hill will not get out of my mind to-night? I am sure it is not that I cared for it so much when I could see it as often as I pleased. I suppose, my reader, that you know the painful vividness with which distant scenes and times will sometimes come back unbidden and unwished. No one can tell why. And now, at 11.25 P. M., when I have gone up to my room far away from home, and ought to go to bed, that hill will not go away. There is no use in trying. And nothing can be more certain than that if I went to bed now, I should toss about in a fever till 4 or 5 A. M. Well, as a smart gallop takes the nonsense out of an aged horse which has shown an unwonted friskness, there is something which will quiet this present writer's pulse, and it shall be tried. Come out, you writing-case; come forth, the foolscap, the ink-bottle, the little quill that has written many pages. And now you may come back again before the mind's eye, purple hill, not seen for years.

I shut my eyes, which if opened would behold many

things not needful to be noted, and then the scene arises. In actual fact, the writer is surrounded by the usual furniture of a bedroom in a great railway hotel in a certain ancient city; and occasional thundering sounds, and awful piercing screeches, speak of arriving and departing trains somewhat too near. I have walked round the city upon the wall; and reaching a certain spot I sat down in the summer twilight, and looked for a long time at the old cathedral, which is not gray with age; on the contrary, it is red, as though there lingered about its crumbling stones the sunsets of seven hundred summers. The day was, as we learn from Bishop Blomfield's *Life*, wherein to be the chief minister of that noble church was esteemed as a very poor preferment. And this estimation is justified by the statement that the annual revenue of the bishop was not so very many hundred pounds. But who shall calculate the money value of the privilege of living in this quaint old city, whose streets carry you back for centuries; and of worshipping, as often as you please, under that sublime roof; of breathing the moral atmosphere of the ancient place; and of looking from its walls upon those blue hills and over those rich plains? Surely one might here live a peaceful life of worship, thought, and study, amid Gothic walls and carved oak and church music. And if any ordinary man should declare that he could not be content with all this, just let me get him by the ears. Wouldn't I shake him!

But all this is a deviation. And if there is anything on which the writer prides himself, it is the severity of his logic. You will not find in his pages those desultory and wandering passages which attract the unthinking to the works of Archbishop Whately and Mr. John Stuart Mill. And from this brief excursion he returns to the severe order of thought which is natural to him.

I shut my eyes, as has been already remarked. The railway hotel, the thundering trains, and the yelling engines vanish, and the old scene arises. It is a bright autumn afternoon. The air is very still. The sun is very warm, and makes the swept cornfields golden. The trees are crimson and brown, and crisped leaves rustle beneath your foot. It is a long valley, with hills on either side, and a river flowing down it. A path winds by the river side, through the fields; and there, in front, is the purple hill. An Englishman would think it pretty high. It is more than twelve hundred feet in height. The upper part of it is covered with heather. It rises like a great pyramid, closing in the valley. There are two or three little farm-houses half-way up it. Above these it is solitary and still.

I wonder, this evening, being so far away, yet with painful distinctness seeing all that, whether I am there in fact as well as feeling? Would some country lad, returning late from market, discern a shadowy figure walking slowly along the path, and bawl out and run away, recognizing me?

If you believe various recent books, you will understand that when you think very intently of a place or person, it is not improbable that some misty eidolon of yourself is present to the person or at the place. I cannot say that I think this fact well authenticated.

I walk on, not in the summer night, but in the autumn afternoon. I want to climb the hill, as I have done so often in departed days. So I lay aside the pen, and bend down my head on my hands.

I have been there, if ever I was in my life. It is not every day one can sit in a very hard easy-chair, and take such a walk, nearly two hundred miles off.

Through the long grass, with a dry rustle under one's feet, by the river's side; up through a little wood of firs, till the highway is gained; over a one-arched bridge, that spans a little rocky gorge, where a stream, smaller than the river, tumbles over a shelf of rock, making a noisy waterfall, now white as country snow that has lain but a night; up a steep and rough road, with birches on either hand, and a brook flowing down on one side, that brawls in rainy weather, but only murmurs on the still autumn day; up and up till the hedges give place to walls of rude stones, built without mortar; and till rough slopes of heather spread away on either side; up and up till the path ceases, and you sit down on a great bowlder of granite in the lonely bosom of the hill: through all that I have been. A long way below this, but a longer way above the wooded valley, which you now see in its whole extent, you may discern the smoke rising from a farm-house, screened a little by a clump of rather scraggy pines. There is a sick man there, — an aged man whom I go to see frequently. I went to the farm-house door, a black and white dog barking furiously; there a pleasant, comely, young face welcomed me. I went in and found my old friend sitting by his warm fireside, which was, indeed, a great deal too warm for any one who had been striving up that stiff ascent. I saw his face and heard his voice, though he has been dead for years. I saw the sheep feeding on the hill around; I heard a cart passing noisily along a road far below; I saw the long gleam of the river, down in the valley, and the horizon of encircling hills: saw and heard all these things as really as though they had been present. Memory is certainly a most wonderful thing. It is very capricious. Sometimes it recalls things very faintly and dimly; sometimes, with a vividness that makes one start. Can it be so long ago! And it selects in a very arbitrary fashion what it will choose to remember. The faces and voices we would most desire to recall, it allows to fade away; and scenes and people we did not particularly care for, it now and then sets before us with this strange vividness of force and color. I did not cherish any special regard for the old farmer; and the walk up the hill was not a very great favorite. Yet to-night something took me by the collar and walked me up that path, and set me down beside the old man's chair.

I have come back. It has exorcised the hill, to write all this about it. I had an eerie feeling, like that which De Quincey tells he had for many nights about the Malay to whom he gave the great piece of opium. But now the hill is appeased. All these odd, inexplicable states of thought and feeling are transitory. And it is much better that they should be so. Hard work crowds them out: it is only in comparative leisure they come at all.

But we are not to suppose that only weak and fanciful persons know by experience these mental phenomena.

What may be called *Dream-life* (that is, spending some part of one's time in an imaginary world), is a thing in which some of the hardest-headed of human beings have had their share. And this little walk which the writer has had to-night in a place far away, and as upon a day that is left far behind, helps him to understand some of those singular things which are recorded of the extent to which many men have spent their time in castles in the air, and of the persistency with which they have dwelt there, to the forgetfulness of more tangible interests. If ever there was a man who was not a morbid day-dreamer, it was Sir James Mackintosh. Sir James Mackintosh was known to mankind in general as an acute metaphysician, a forcible political writer, a brilliant talker. The greatest place he ever held, to the common eye, was that of Recorder of Bombay. And he held that place just the shortest time he possibly could to earn his pension. How many men knew, looking at the homely Scotchman, what his true place in life was? Had he not told us himself, we should hardly have believed it. He was Emperor of Constantinople! And a laborious and anxious position he found it. He (mentally) promoted many of his friends to important offices of state; and his friends by their indiscretion and incompetence caused him an immense deal of trouble. Then the empire was always getting involved in the most vexatious complications, which seriously affected the emperor's sleep and general health. He always felt like a man playing a very intricate game of chess. No wonder he was sometimes very absent and distracted. You would say he might have escaped all this by resigning his crown; but he could not arrange satisfactorily to do that. A thoughtless person smiles at these things ; but to Mackintosh they were among the most serious things of his life. A man of bread-and-butter understanding would explain it by saying that Mackintosh was cracked ; but then we all know that he was not cracked. Yet in his disengaged hours, regularly as they came, was the thread of his history taken up where it had been dropped last time ; and he was the emperor, laden with an emperor's cares. It was not, as with the actor Elliston, received with great applause on the stage at Drury Lane, and fancying himself a king just long enough to bestow a blessing upon the audience, till he was pulled up by a burst of laughter. Nor was it like Alexander the Great, according to Dryden, who " assumed the god " for only a very limited period. Neither was the astute philosopher's notion of an emperor the childish one. He was not emperor, to sit on a throne and receive homage and make a grand appearance on grand occasions, but to go through intricate calculations and hard work, and to undergo great anxiety.

In short, Sir James Mackintosh, being a great man, indulged in dream-life on a great scale. But commonplace human beings do it in a way that suits themselves and their moderate aspirations. The poor consumptive girl, who, on a dark December evening, is propped up with pillows, and gets you to sit beside her while she tells you how much stronger and better she feels, how by spring she will be quite well again, and how delightful the long walks will be in the summer evenings, while you know she will never see the black-thorn in blossom, nor the green leaves on the tree : she is doing just what the great metaphysician used to do. And the little schoolboy, far away from home, a thoughtful, bullied little fellow, does it too, when he pictures out the next holiday-time, and his getting away from all this to be with those who care for him. Possibly more people than you would think make up for the dulness of their actual life in some such way. They take pleasure in fancying what they would like in their vacant hours. And unless you wish your mind to become very small and dry, you will have such hours. No matter how hard-worked you may be, they are attainable. You remember what Charles Lamb once wrote to a friend: "If you have but five consolatory minutes between the desk and the bed, make much of them, and live a century in them." Human beings, living even the most prosaic lives, have sometimes their enchanted palace, and live in it a great deal. Have you not sometimes, my reader, pictured out the life you would like, not in the least expecting it, or even really wishing it, any more than Mackintosh really looked to be made Emperor of Constantinople? And when you have set your heart on something happening, which is very likely not to happen, it is quite right to please yourself by picturing out the best: all the more that this is all the enjoyment of it you are likely to have. If we have all suffered a great deal of pain through the anticipation of evils which never came, we have all probably enjoyed a great deal of pleasure through the anticipation of pleasant things which were never to be. We have lived a good deal in castles which were never to be built, but in the air. When we tried for something we did not get, you remember well how we used, in vacant hours, to plan out all the mode of life, even to its minute details; enjoying it only the more keenly through the intrusion of the fear that only in this airy fashion should we ever lead that life which we should have enjoyed so much. Of course, it is not expedient to waste in dreaming over noble plans the precious hours which might have gone far to turn our dreams into serviceable realities. It is foolish for the lad at college to spend, in thinking how proud his parents would be, and how pleased all his friends, if he were to carry off all the honors that were to be had, the time which, if devoted to hard work, might have gained at least some of those soon-forgotten laurels. It may be said here, by way of parenthesis, that one of the very last visions in which ambitious youth need indulge is the vision of being recognized as great and distinguished in the place of your birth or your early days. A prophet has no honor in his own country. I have a friend, greatly revered, who expresses an opposite opinion. He maintains, in a charming volume, that if you rise to decent eminence in life, the people who knew you as a boy will be proud of you, and will help to push you on farther. " I see, with my mind's eye," says my friend, "a statue of Dunsford, erected in Tollerporcorum." Dunsford was a native of Tollerporcorum; and having recorded the conversation of his *Friends in Council*, would probably be thus distinguished. There are portions of this earth where the fact is just the contrary. Tollerporcorum is just the last place where certain Dunsfords I know are likely to have a statue. Dunsford's early acquaintances cannot bear the moderate success which has attended Dunsford in life; they regard *Friends in Council* as a very poor work; and a college acquaintance, who never forgave Dunsford the medals he won there, now and then abuses Dunsford in the Tollerporcorum newspaper. I lately visited a certain Tollerporcorum, — an ancient town in a fair tract of country. That Tollerporcorum had its Dunsford. Dunsford started from small beginnings, but gradually rose about as high as a human being well can in a certain portion of Scandinavia. But the fashionable and intellectual · thing in Tollerporcorum was to ignore Dunsford and his career altogether. Nobody cared about him or it. Dunsford sometimes went back to Tollerporcorum; and the Tollerporcorum people diligently shut their eyes to his existence. Every envious little wretch who had stuck in the mud thus avenged himself on Dunsford for having got on so far. In the latter years of his honored life, Dunsford hardly ever visited Tollerporcorum; and when the great man died, it was never proposed at Tollerporcorum to erect so much as a drinking-fountain to his memory.

Here ends the parenthesis. Take up the broken thread of thought. It is right and pleasant to gain at least the pleasure of anticipation out of happy things that are not to be. And when you see a sanguine person in a state of great enjoyment through such anticipation, you will not, unless you have in you the spirit of my old friend Mr. Snarling, try to throw a damp upon all this innocent happiness by pointing out, with great force of logic, how very little chance there is of the anticipation being realized. That is only the stronger reason for enjoying in this way that which you are not likely to enjoy in any other. There is hardly a more touching sight than the sight of a human being, old or young, happy in the anticipation of any pleasant thing which he will never reach. With what a rosy face and what bright eyes your little boy of five years old confides to you all he is to do when he is a man! Great are the grandeur and fame in which he is to live, many are to be his horses, and numerous his dogs; but a great feature in his plan always is, how happy he is to make his father and mother. Ah! little man, before those days come your father and mother will be far away.

And a reason why a wise man, desirous to economize the enjoyment there is in this life, and to make it go as far as possible, will often quietly luxuriate in the prospect of what he secretly knows is not likely to happen, is this certain fact, that in this world the thing you would like best is the thing you are least likely to get. *That* is a fact which, as we get on through life, we come to know extremely well. Yes, if you set your heart on a thing, whoever gets it, *you* won't. You may get something else, perhaps something better, but not *that*. If you have such an enthusiasm for Gothic architecture that you sometimes think no one could enjoy it so much, if you feel that it would sensibly flavor all your life to live in a Gothic house or to worship in a Gothic church, then, though everything else about them be all you could wish, rely on it, your church and house will be Palladian. And you will often meet men whose belongings are Gothic, who tell you they are very beautiful, very uncomfortable, that the church is destroying their lungs, and the house giving them perpetual cold in their heads, and who greatly envy you. Of course, all this is gratifying, to a certain degree. It serves to make you content.

I have known a man who lived in a house which was

extremely comfortable, and extremely ugly. No one
could ever say to what school of architecture, in particular, his residence was to be referred. And the
country round was very ugly and bare. But, like the
farmer in Virgil, in that exquisite passage in one of
the *Georgics, regum æquabat opes animo;* he could
picture out, at will, a charming English manor-house,
of hospitable-looking red brick with stone dressings;
oriel-windowed, steep-gabled, with great wreathed chim-
neys, with environing terraces, with magnificent horse-
chestnuts ever blazing in the glory of June. You
thought he was walking a bleak moorland road, dreary
and dismal; but in truth the warm breeze was
shaking the blossoms overhead, and making a chequered
dancing shade on soft green turf below. And there
yearly comes a certain season, when very many human
beings practise on themselves a delusion something like
his. I mean Christmas-time. Who ever spent the
ideal Christmas? I should like very greatly to behold
that person. I have never done so yet: never spent a
Christmas in all my life in the ideal way. You ought
to be living in a noble Gothic house, somewhere in the
midland counties of England. There ought to be a
large and gay party, spending the holidays there.
There ought to be an exquisite old church near. There
ought to be bracing frost, and cheerful snow. All hearts
should seem touched and warmed by the sacred associations of the season. There should be an oaken hall,
and a vast wood-fire; holly and mistletoe; and of course
roast beef and plum-pudding and strong ale for every
poor person near. You should be living, in short, at
Bracebridge Hall, exactly as it was when Washington

Irving described it, and with all the same people. It need not be said that in fact the Christmas time and its surroundings are quite different from all this. You sit down by yourself, and try to get up the feeling of the time by reading Washington Irving and Mr. Dickens's *Christmas Carol.* The *Illustrated London News* is a great help to ordinary imaginations at that season. On the actual Christmas-day, rainy, muddy, tooth-aching, ill-tempered, you turn over the pictures in that excellent journal ; and you find the ideal Christmas there. My friend Smith once told how he spent his first Christmas-day in his little country parsonage. Luckily there was snow. He provided that his servants, three in number, should have the means of a little enjoyment. He worked hard all the forenoon writing a sermon, whose subject was not the Nativity. And for an hour before dinner he walked alone, up and down a little gravelled walk with evergreens on each side, looking at the leaden sky and the solitary fields, and trying to feel as if he were at Bracebridge Hall. He tried with small success. Then, having dined in solitude on turkey and plum-pudding, he read the pleasant Christmas chapter in *Pickwick,* and tried to get up an enthusiasm about the enjoyment which, for the sake of argument, might be conceived as existing in many houses that night. Finally, he concluded that he was unsuccessfully trying to humbug himself, and ended by reading Butler's *Analogy* in a good deal of bitterness of heart.

Very early in our intelligent life, our personality begins to cut us off from those nearest us. Unless a parent have a much deeper insight and sympathy than

6

most parents have, he loses knowledge very early of the real inward life of his children. At first, it is like wading in shallow water; but it is not long till it shelves down into depths beyond your diving. The little thoughtful face you see every day; the little heart within you know just as much as you know the outer side of the moon. No doubt, if this be so, it is in a great measure your own fault. There are many parents to whom their children, young or old, would no more confide the things they really care for and think about than they would confide these to the first cabman at the next stand. But beyond this, the little things soon begin to have a world of their own, not known to any but themselves. You may have known young children who wearied for the hour when they might get to bed, and begin to think again; take up the history where they left it off last night. Of course, the history and the world were very different from the fact. Kings and queens, heroes and giants, elves and fairies, palaces and castles, these being oftentimes enchanted, were common there. Also clear views of the kind of life they would live when they grew up; a life in which coaches and six, suits of armor, and the like, were not unknown.

It is a mercy for some people, that circumstances keep them down. Their lot circumscribes their opportunity of making fools of themselves. My friend Smith, already named, is a clergyman. His church is a plain one. Such is his craze for Gothic architecture, that I tremble to think what would have become of him if he had chanced to attain a magnificent church dating from the eleventh century, — a church with stately ranks of shafts, echoing aisles, storied window, crusaders' statues, rich oak carving, and monumental brasses, standing amid grand old trees. I fear he would have spent great part of his time in admiring and enjoying the structure; in sitting on a gravestone outside and looking at it; in walking up and down inside it, and the like. It would have been a great feature in his life. It is much safer and better that he has been spared that temptation. The grand building, of course, has fallen to somebody who does not care for it at all. In a former age, there was a barrister who would have keenly enjoyed being made a judge. Probably no man ever made a judge would have delighted so much in the little accessories of that eminent position, — the curious garb, and the varied dignity wherewith the administrators of the law are surrounded. How tremendously set up he would have been, if he could once have sentenced a man to be hanged! The writer was present when the name of that person was suggested to an individual who could have made him what he wished to be. That individual was asked whether he might not do. That individual did not open his lips, but he shook his head slowly from side to side several times. For thus goes on this world.

Probably most human beings, now and then, have short glimpses of cheerfulness and light-heartedness, which make them think how much more and better might be made of this life. You have seen a charming scene, bathed in a glorious sunshine, and you have thought, Now, it might always be like this. Sometimes there comes a hopefulness of spirit, in which all difficulties and perplexities vanish; in which everything seems delightful, and all creatures good. This is the potential of happiness in man. Of course, it is seldom reached, and never for long. Most people are more familiar with the converse case, in which everything looks dark and amiss,— the season of perplexity, despondency, depression. Probably this comes many times more frequently than the other. Let me say, my reader, that we know the reason why.

The truth is, it is not needful to our enjoyment of many things that we should fancy any connexion between ourselves and them. You read a pleasant story, and like it, without fancying yourself its hero or heroine. Never in your life, perhaps, have you spent a week in a house like Bracebridge Hall; and you are never likely to do that. Yet you enjoy the sunshiny volume; and you thank its author for many hours of quiet, thoughtful enjoyment, for which you felt the better. And, indeed, much of what is pleasing and beautiful you enjoy most when you never think of it in relation to yourself. Take the most pleasing development of human comeliness, which is doubtless in the case of young women. Let it be admitted that there are few things more pleasing and interesting to the rightly-constituted mind than the sight of sweet girlish faces and graceful girlish forms, and the tones of the pleasant voices that generally go with them. But there is no doubt earthly, that in grave middle age, you have much more real pleasure in these things than in feverish youth. Let us suppose, my reader, that you are a man in years. Those who were young girls in your day are middle-aged women now: they are past. But you look with the kindest interest on the fair young faces of another generation. A young lad is eager to commend himself to

the notice and admiration of these agreeable human beings. He is filled with bitter enmity at other lads more
successful than himself in gaining their favor. His
whole state of mind in the circumstances leads him into
a host of absurdities: the contemplative mind sees him
in the light of an ass. Now, you are beyond and above
all these things. You look with pure pleasure and kindness at the fairest beings of God's creation; and you
look at the fair sight and enjoy it as you look at Ben
Lomond, or at the setting sun, without the faintest wish
to make it your own. It is the entire absence of personal interest that makes your interest so pleasant, and
so unmingled with any disagreeable feeling. I remember to have read, in a religious biography, a statement
made by a very clever and good man about a certain
beautiful girl, called away in early youth. "I found
myself," he said, "looking at her with an interest for
which I could not account." Was that unsophisticated
simplicity real? Not able to account for the interest
with which you look at a pleasant sight! I think it
might be accounted for. Though indeed when we go to
first principles, we get beyond the reach of logical ex-
planation. In strictness, you may not be able to say
why the tear comes to your eye when you look at a
number of little children, and think what is before them.
In strictness, you may not be able to say why it was that
so many people found themselves shedding tears, on a
day in Westminster Abbey, when they saw the Crown
placed on the head of a certain young girl who, in after
years, was destined to gain the love of most hearts in
Britain as the best of Queens. Yet a great many
thoughtful persons have recorded that they were affected

alike in beholding that sight.   So there must have been something in the sight to awaken the emotion.

These are the things of which the writer thought in the circumstances already set out.   Probably it has made you sleepy to read all this.   It had the contrary effect to write it; for when the writer at length wearily sought his couch, he could not sleep at all.

CHAPTER VIII.

A REMINISCENCE OF THE OLD TIME: BEING SOME THOUGHTS ON GOING AWAY.

I AM sure you know how, as we advance in life, hours come in which we feel an impulse to sit down for a little, and try to revive an old feeling, before it dies away; and many of our old feelings are dying away, and will ultimately die out altogether. It is partly through use, and partly because our system, physical and psychical, is growing less sensitive as we go on. We do not feel things now as we used to do. We are getting stronger, the robuster nerves of middle age do not receive the vivid impressions of earlier years, and there are faintly-flavored things which they cease to appreciate at all. We have come out from the green fields, and from the shady woodlands, and we are plodding along the beaten highway of life. It is the noon now, not perhaps without some tendency to decline towards evening; and we look back to the dawn and to the morning, when the air was cool and fresh, and when the sky was clear. And we have grown hardened to the rougher work of the present time. We have all got lines pretty deeply drawn upon our faces, and a good many gray hairs. And if

one could see a middle-aged soul, no doubt you would
see about it something analogous to being wrinkled and
gray. No doubt you would likewise discern something
analogous to the thickening and toughening of the skin
in the case of the middle-aged hand. Neither hand nor
heart feels so keenly.

There is no help for it, but still one cannot help regretting it, the way in which things lose their first fresh
relish by use. We ought to be getting more enjoyment
out of things than we do. A host of very small matters, which we pass without ever noticing, would afford
us real and sensible pleasure if we had not grown so
accustomed to them. Prince Lee Boo, as we used to
read, was moved to ecstatic wonder and delight by the
upright walls and the flat ceiling of an ordinary room.
They were new to him. There was a young Indian
chief, many years ago, who came from the Far West to
London, and was for a season a lion in fashionable
society. He was a manly, clever young fellow, but in
his English months he never got over his unsophisticated enjoyment of the furniture of English houses.
And thoughtless folk despised him, when they ought
rather to have envied him, as they witnessed his delight
in the contemplation of a dinner-table where he had
been accustomed to see a stretched bull's hide, and of
plates, knives and forks, carpets, mirrors, window-cur-
tains, and wash-hand stands. All these great luxuries,
and a thousand more, *he* appreciated at their true value;
while civilized men and women, through familiarity,
had arrived at contempt of them. Which was right,
the civilized folk or the savage man ? Is it the human
being who sees least in the things around him that

ought to be proud, or is not the man rather to be envied who discerns in simple matters qualities and excellences which others do not discern? If you had so worn out your eyes by constant use that you could no longer see, *that* would be nothing to plume yourself on ; you would have no right to think you had attained a position of superiority to the remainder of the human race, in whom the optic nerve still retained its sensitiveness. Yet there are people who are quite proud that their mind has had its nerves of sensation partially paralyzed, and who would like you to think that those nerves are entirely paralyzed. " I don't remark these things," they will say with an air of disdain, when you point out to them some of the little material advantages which we enjoy in this country now-a-days. They convey that they think you must be a weak-minded person because you do remark these things, because you still feel it a curious thing to leave London in the morning, and after ten hours and a half of unfatiguing travelling to reach Edinburgh in the evening; or because you still are con-scious of a simple-minded wonder when you send a mes-sage five hundred miles, and get your answer back in a quarter of an hour. If there be a mortal whom I de-spise, it is the man who is anxious to impress you with the fact that he does not care in the least for anything. The human being who is proud because he has reached the *nil admirari* stage is just a human being who is proud because a creeping paralysis has numbed his soul.

Yet without giving in to it, and without being proud of it, you are aware that the keen relish goes from that which you grow accustomed to. I have indeed heard it

said concerning certain individuals whose supercilious
and lofty air testified that some sudden rise in life had
turned their head, that they lived in a state of constant
surprise at finding themselves so respectable. But this
statement was not true in its full extent. For after
being for several years in a position for which nature
never intended him, even Dr. Bumptious (before his
elevation his name was Toady) must have grown to a
certain measure accustomed to it. Even other people
got accustomed to it. And though his incompetence for
his place remained just as glaring as ever, they ceased
to remark it, and came to accept it as something in the
nature of things. You know, we do not perplex ourselves by inquiring every morning why there are such
creatures as wasps, toads, and rattlesnakes. But if
these beings were of a sudden introduced into this world
for the first time, it would be different.

It is to be lamented that the very fresh and sensible
enjoyment which we derive from very little things, when
they are new to us, passes so completely away when
they grow familiar. I remark that my fellow-creatures,
who inhabit houses in this street, are very far from being
duly thankful for the great privilege we possess in having a post-office at the end of it. You write your letters in the forenoon after you have completed your more
serious work, and upon each envelope you stick the representation of a face which is very familiar to us all,
and very dear. If you are a wise man, you post your
letters for yourself; and accordingly the first thing you
do daily, when you go forth to your out-door business or
duty, is to proceed to that little opening which receives
the expression of so much care, so much kindness, so

much worry, so much joy and sorrow, and to drop the documents in. Not many of the human beings who post letters and who receive them have any habitual sense of the supreme luxury they enjoy in that familiar institution of the post-office. Into that little opening goes your letter; a penny secures its admission, and obtains for it very distinguished consideration; and in a little while the most ingenious mechanism that has been devised by the most ingenious minds is hard at work conveying your letter, at tremendous speed, by land or sea; till next morning, unerring as the eagle upon its eyrie, it swoops down upon the precise dwelling at which you aimed it. When I say it swoops down upon a dwelling in the country, I mean to express poetically the fact that it comes jogging along in a cart drawn by a little white pony, which stops for the purposes of conversation whenever it meets anybody in the wooded lane I have in my mind. But in saying that the inhabitants of this street are not duly thankful for the post-office at the corner, I did not mean merely that they fail to understand what a blessing to Britain the system of postal communication is. Everybody, on ordinary days, fails to understand *that*. I was thinking of something else. I was thinking of the luxury of having a receiving-house so near. When I lived in the country, the post-office was five miles distant; and if you missed the chance of sending away your letters in the morning by the cart drawn by the white pony, you must wait till next day, or you must send a special messenger to the old-fashioned town of red freestone dwellings, standing by a classic river's side. Let not that town be mentioned save in complimentary terms. Let me learn by the

misfortune of another. An eminent native of the district which surrounds it, known in the world of letters,
once upon a time published some remarks upon that
town, disguising its pretty name in another of somewhat
ludicrous sound. And when that eminent man shortly
afterwards strove to persuade the inhabitants to send
him to represent them in Parliament, the old offence
was raked up, and it did him harm. This, however, is
a digression. Let us return. When I came from the
country, to live in this city, I felt it a great privilege,
and something to be enjoyed freshly every time, to take
my letters to the post-office, two hundred yards off. It
was delightful. Not once in the day, but (if need were)
half a dozen times, could you write your letter, and in
three minutes have it in the post-office. There was
something very fresh and enjoyable in the reflection, as
you stood by the receiving-house window, Now here in
these minutes I am in the same position in which half
an hour's smart driving, or an hour and a quarter's
steady walking, would have placed one in departed
days! Wonderful! But now, after several years of
the enjoyment of this privilege, the fresh wonder has
worn away. The edge of enjoyment is dulled. And
though I try hard, in going to the post-office, to feel
what a blessing it is, I cannot feel it as I would wish.
Yes, the enjoyment of the post-office is gone in great
measure ; even as the unutterable greenness discerned
by the stranger goes from the summer trees among
which you have come to feel yourself at home ; even as
the sound of Niagara becomes inaudible to the waiters
at the Niagara Hotel ; even as the bishop who was
plucked at college gradually ceases to be astonished at

finding himself a bishop; even as Miss Smith, in a few weeks after she is married, no longer feels it strange to be called Mrs. Jones; even as the readers of what is with bitter irony called a *religious newspaper* lose their first bewilderment at finding a human animal writing an article filled with intentional misrepresentation, lying, and slandering, and ending the article by taking God to witness that in abusing the man he hates for his success and eminence, he is actuated by a simple regard to the Divine glory.

And thus it is, remembering how the old time and the old way fade out, that the writer has resolved to give a little space of comparative rest to reviving (as far as may be) something which used to have a strongly felt character of its own in years which are gone, and which are melting into blue distance fast. Let me seek to bring up again the atmosphere of Going Away, as it used to be, and to be felt. No doubt there is a certain fancifulness about moral atmospheres; not all men feel them alike; and there are robust natures which probably do not feel them at all. When a man comes to describe a house, a landscape, a mode of life, not as these are in literal fact, but as these impress himself, then we get into a realm of uncertainty and fancy. When a man ceases to say of a dwelling that it is built of red brick, that it has so many windows in front, that it is so many stories high, that it has evergreens of such kinds round it, and the like; and when the man goes on to describe the house by quite other characteristics, — saying that it is a sleepy-looking house, a dull house, a hospitable-looking house, an eerie strange-looking house, a house that makes you feel queer, — then you feel that though the man may convey to another man, who is in sympathy with himself, a very true impression of the fact as it presents itself to him, still there are many people to whom such descriptions are really quite unintelligible ; and that those who are most capable of understanding them are least likely to agree as to their truth. It is so with what I have called moral atmospheres ; the pervading characteristic of a time, a scene, a way of life, a human being. Nor can it be admitted that there is anything of morbid sensitiveness in being keenly aware of these. Most people know the vague sort of sense that you have of being in a remote pastoral country, or of being in a busy town. You feel a difference in the morning whenever you awake, and before you have fully gathered up your consciousness ; it pervades your very dreams. You remember periods of your life about which there was a kind of flavor ; strongly felt, but indescribable to others ; not to be expressed in any spoken words ; Mendelssohn or Beethoven might have come near expressing it in music ; and it comes back upon you in reading some passage in *In Memoriam* which has nothing to do with it, or in looking at the first yellow crocus in the cold March sunshine, or in walking along a, lane with blossoming hawthorn on either hand, or in smelling the blossoms of an apple-tree. And when you look back, you feel the atmosphere surround you again with its fragrance a good deal gone, and with its colors faded. It is a misty, ghost-like image of a past life and its surroundings that steals vaguely before your mental sight ; and possibly it cannot be more accurately or expressively described than by saying that the old time comes over you.

Doubtless external scenery has a great deal to do in the production of that general sense of a character pervading one's whole mode of life, which I mean by a moral atmosphere. It is especially so if you lead a lonely life, or if you have not many companions, and these not very energetic or striking. How well many men in orders remember the peculiar flavor of the time when they first began their parochial duty! Years afterwards, you go and walk up and down in the church where you preached your first sermons, and you try to awaken the feeling of that departed time. It comes back in a ghostly, unsubstantial way; sometimes it refuses to be wakened up at all. And the feeling, whatever it may be, is (to many men) very mainly flavored by the outward scene in which that time was spent. I can easily believe that there are persons on whose mood and character no appreciable impression is produced by external scenery: probably the reader knows one or two. They have usually high cheek-bones, smoke-dried complexions, and disagreeable voices; they think Mr. Tennyson a fool, and tell you that *they* cannot understand him, in a tone that conveys that in their judgment nobody can. I have known men who declared honestly that they did not think Westminster Abbey in the least a more solemn place than a red brick meeting-house with a flat ceiling, and with its inner walls chastely whitewashed, or papered with a paper representing yellow marble. My acquaintance with such individuals was slight, and by mutual consent it speedily ceased. Give us the man who frankly tells you how different a man he is in this place from what he is in that, how outward nature casts its light or its shadow upon all his thinking

and feeling. What would you be, my friend, if you lived
for months by a misty Shetland sea, or amid a wild Irish
bogland, or in a wooden châlet at Meyringen, or on a flat
French plain, with white ribbons of highway stretching
across it, bordered with weary poplars; or under the
shadow of castle-crowned crags upon the Rhine, or amid
the bustle of a great commercial town, or in the classic
air of an ancient university city, with a feast of Gothic
everywhere for the eyes, and with courts of velvety turf
that has been velvety turf for ages? But here I get
into the region of the fanciful; and though holding very
strongly a certain theory about these things, I am not
going to set it out here. Yet I cannot but believe that,
when you read men's written thoughts, you may readily,
if you be of a sensitive nature, *feel* the surroundings
amid which they were written. Turn over the volume
which was written in the country by a man keenly alive
to outward things and their influences, and you will be
aware of a breeziness about the pages,—a fresher air
seems to breathe from them, the atmosphere of that simple life and its little cares. Turn over the Best of all
books: read especially the accounts of patriarchal times
in Genesis: and (inspiration apart) you will feel the
presence of something indefinitely more than the bare
facts recorded. You will feel the fresh breeze come to
you over the ocean of intervening centuries: you will
know that a whole life and its interests surround you
again. And there seems to me no more marked difference between fictitious stories written by men of genius
and written by commonplace people than this, that the
commonplace people make you aware of just the inci-
dents they record, while the man of genius makes you

aware of a vast deal more, — of the entire atmosphere of the surrounding circumstances and concerns and life. You will understand what is meant when I remind you of the wonderful way in which the battle of Waterloo is made to surround and pervade a certain portion of the train of events recorded in that thoroughly true history, Mr. Thackeray's *Vanity Fair.*

Now all that is pleasant. I mean to the writer, not necessarily to the reader. The writer has to produce a multitude of pages, which to produce is of the nature of grave work; and in them he must hold right on, and discuss his subject under no small sense of responsibility. But such pages as this are his play; and he may without rebuke turn hither and thither, and pluck the wild flowers on either side of the path. O how hard work it is to write a sermon; and, when one is in the vein, how easy it is to write an essay! And, in saying that all this is pleasant, the thing present to the author's mind was the very devious course which his train of thought has followed since the first sentence of this dissertation was written. I have a great respect for certain men, who write in a logical and scholarly way. I admire and esteem such. When I read their productions at all, I do so after breakfast, when one's wits are fully awake. But in the evening, by the fireside, when the day's work and worry are over, and there remains the precious little breathing-space, I would rather not read them. Neither do I desire here to write like them.

Going Away is my subject. Going Away and its atmosphere, as it used to be, and as it is to many people now. Going Away from home. Not Going Away for ever; not Going Away for a long time; not Going

Away under painful circumstances. Ordinary and commonplace Going Away.

And let me tell you, intrepid travellers, who think nothing of flying away to London, to Paris, to Chamouni, to Constantinople, that Going Away for a week or two, and to a distance not exceeding a hundred miles, is a very serious thing to a quiet, stay-at-home person. A multitude of contingencies suggest themselves in its prospect; there is the vague fear of the great, terrible outside world. It is as when a little boat, that has been lying safe in some sheltered cove, puts out to sea, to face the full might of winds and waves; when a lonely human being, who for months has plodded his little round of work and care, looking at the same scenes, and conversing with the same people, musters courage to go away for a little while. There is a considerable inertia to overcome; some effort of resolution is needed. When you have lived an unvaried life for many weeks in a quiet country place, your wish is to sit still. Yet there are great advantages which belong to people who have seen little or nothing. They have so keen a sense of interest, and so lively an impression of the facts, in beholding something new. By and by they come to take it easily. You look out of the window of the railway carriage, and in. reply to something said by a fellow-traveller, you say, "Ah, that 's Berne, or that 's Lausanne," and you return to your *Times* or your *Saturday Review*. You look forth on the left hand, as the train rounds a curve, and say, "Strasburg spire; very fine. Four hundred and fifty feet high. It does not look nearly so much from this point." Now once it was very different. It was a vivid sensation to see for the first time some town in England, or some lake or hill in Scotland. My friend Smith told me that once, for more than six years, beginning when he was eight-and-twenty, he never had stirred ten miles from his home and his parish, save when he went in the autumn for a few weeks to the seaside; and then he went always to the same place, a journey of four hours or so. It would have done him much good — had he been able sometimes through those years which were very anxious and very trying ones — to have the benefit of a little change of scene. But he could not afford it; and in those days of depressed fortune, he had, literally, not a friend in this world, beyond the little circle of his own home. He had, indeed, some acquaintances; but they were able to understand him or sympathize with him about as much as a donkey could. But better days came, as (let us trust) they will come, through hard work and self-denial, to most men, by God's blessing; and Smith could venture on the great enterprise of a journey to London. Ah! an express train was a great thing to him; and a journey of three hundred miles an endless pilgrimage. And he told me himself (he is in his grave now, and no one who knew him will know him by what has been said of him) that it was an extraordinary feeling to look out of the carriage-window, and to think, Now Cambridge is only a few miles off, over these flats! And farther on, when the trains glided by the capital of the Fens, and the noble mass of Peterborough Cathedral loomed through the misty morning, it was a stranger object to him than St. Sophia or even the Mosque of Omar would be to you; and he thought how curious a thing it would be to live on that wide

plain, in that quiet little city, under the shadow of that
magnificent pile. Probably, my friend, you have been
long enough in many striking places to feel their first
interest and impression go, to feel their moral atmosphere become inappreciable. You feel all *that* keenly
at first; but gradually the place becomes just like anywhere else. After a while, the inner atmosphere over-
powers the outer; the world within the breast gives its
tone and color to the scene around you. I believe
firmly, that if you want to know a place vividly and
really (I mean a town of moderate extent), you ought to
stay in it just a day and no more. By remaining longer,
you may come to know all the churches and shops, and
the like; but you will lose the pervading atmosphere
and character of the whole. First impressions are always
the most vivid; and I firmly believe they are in the
vast majority of cases the most truthful. An observant
and sensitive man, spending just a day in a town with
twenty thousand inhabitants, knows what kind of place
that town is far better than an ordinarily observant
person who has lived in it for twenty years.

The truth is, that a little of a thing is usually far
more impressive than the whole of it, or than a great
deal of it. Don't you remember how, when you were
a child, lying in bed in the morning, you used to watch
the daylight through the shutters? And you remember how bright it looked, through the narrow line where
the shutters hardly met: it was like a glowing fire. At
length, the shutters were thrown back, and they let in
all the day; and it was nothing so bright. Even if the
morning was sunshiny, there was a sad falling off;
and perhaps the morning was dull and rainy. Even

so is the glimpse of Peterborough from the passing express train, infinitely finer than the view of Peterborough to the man who lives in it all the year round. Even so has the quiet life of a cathedral city a charm to the visitor for a day, who has come from a land where cathedrals are not, which fades away to such as spend all their days in the venerable place, and come to have associations not merely of glorious architecture and sublime music, but likewise of many petty ambitions, jealousies, diplomacies, and disappointments ; and, in short, of Mr. Slope and Mrs. Proudie. Yes, a little of a thing is sometimes infinitely better than the whole ; and it is the little which especially has power to convey that general estimate of a pervading characteristic which we understand by perceiving the moral atmosphere. And besides this, you may have a surfeit of even the things you like best. You heartily enjoy a little country Gothic church; you linger on every detail of it ; it is a pure delight. But a great cathedral is almost too much: it wearies you, it overwhelms you. You may get, through one summer day, as much enjoyment out of Sonning Church as out of York Minster. That perfection of an English parish church, with its perfect vicarage, by the beautiful Thames, is like a friend with whom you can cordially shake hands: the great minster is like a monarch to be approached on bended knee. Most people remember a case in which a thousandth part would have been far better than the whole: I mean, the Great Exhibition in that fine shed which the nation declined to buy. You would have enjoyed the sight of a little of what was gathered there ; but the whole was a fearful task to get through.

I never beheld more wearied, dazed, stupefied, disgusted, and miserable countenances, than among rich and poor under that roof. I wonder whether any mortal ever really enjoyed that glare and noise and hubbub, or felt his soul expanded under the influence of that huge educational institution. Too many magazines or books, too, coming together, convert into a toil what ought to be a pleasure. You look at the mass, and you cannot help thinking what a deal you have to get through. And that thought is in all cases fatal to enjoyment. Whenever it enters the heart of a little boy, contemplating his third plate of plum-pudding, the delight implied in plum-pudding has vanished. Whenever the hearer listens to the preacher describing what he is to do in the first and second place, and so on to the fifth or sixth, the enjoyment with which most sermons are heard is sensibly diminished. And even if you be very fond of books, there is a sense of desolation in being turned loose in a library of three hundred thousand volumes. That huge array is an incubus on your spirit. There is far more sensible pleasure when you go into a friend's snug little study, and diligently survey his thousand or twelve hundred books. And you know that if a man has a drawing-room a hundred feet long, he takes pains to convert that large room into a little one, by enclosing a warm space round the fire with great screens for his evening retreat. Yes, a little is generally much better than a great deal.

A thing which precedes Going Away is packing up. And this the wise man will do for himself, the more so if he cannot afford to have any one to do it for him. There is a great pleasure in doing things for yourself.

And here is one of the compensations of poverty. You open for yourself the parcel of new books you have bought, and with your own hand you cut the leaves. A great peer, of course, could not do this, I suppose. The volumes would be prepared for his reading, and laid before him with nothing to do but to read them. Now, it ought to be understood, that the reading of a book is by no means the only use you can put it to, or the only good you can get out of it. There is the enjoyment of stripping off the massive wrappings in which the volumes travelled from the bookseller's shop, through devious ways, to the country home. There is the enjoyment of cutting the leaves, which, if you have a large ivory paper knife, is a very sensible one. There is the enjoyment of laying the volumes after their leaves are cut upon your study table, and sitting down in an arm-chair by the fireside, and calmly and thoughtfully looking at them. There is the enjoyment of considering earnestly the place where they shall be put on your shelves, and then of placing them there, and of arranging the volumes which have been turned out to make room for them. All these pleasures you have, quite apart from the act of reading the books; and all these pleasures are denied to the rich and mighty man who is too great to be allowed to do things for himself. He has only the end : we have both the end and the means which lead up to it. And the greater part of human enjoyment is the enjoyment of means, not of ends. There is as much solid satisfaction in going out and looking at your horse in his warm stable as in riding or driving him. An eminent sportsman begins a book in which he gives an account of his exploits in hunting

in a foreign country, by fondly telling how happy he
was in petting up his old guns till they looked like new,
and in preparing and packing ammunition in the prospect of setting off on his expedition. You can see that
these tranquil and busy days of anticipation and preparation at home were at least as enjoyable as the more
exciting days of actual. sport which followed. Now,
however much a duke might like to do all this, I
suppose his nobility would oblige him to forego the
satisfaction.

If you have a wife and children (and for the purposes of this essay I suppose you to have both), the
multitude of trunks and packing-cases in which their
possessions are bestowed in the prospect of going away,
are sought out and packed apart from any exertion or
superintendence on your part. Your share consists in
writing addresses for them, and in counting up the
twenty-three things that are assembled in the lobby
before they are loaded on cart, cab, or carriage. I have
remarked it as a curious thing, that when a man with
his wife and two or three children and three or four
servants go to the seaside in autumn, the articles of luggage invariably amount to twenty-three. And it has
ever been to me a strange and perplexing thought, how
so many trunks and boxes are needed, and how, through
various changes by land and sea, they get safely to their
destination. There are few positions which awaken
more gratitude and satisfaction in the average human
being, than (having arrived at the seaside place) to see
the twenty-three things safe upon the little pier, after
the roaring steamer which brought them has departed,
and the little crowd has dispersed ; when, amid the still-

ness, suddenly become audible, you tell the keeper of the pier to send your baggage to the dwelling which is to be your temporary home. A position even more gratifying is as follows: when, returning to town, your holiday over, you succeed, by the aid of two liberally-tipped porters, in recovering all your effects from the luggage-van of the railway-train, amid an awful crowd and confusion on the platform, and accumulating them into a heap, for whose conveyance you would assuredly be called to pay extra but for the judicious largesse already alluded to; then in seeing them piled in and upon three cabs, in which you slowly wend your way to your door; and finally, in the lobby, whence they originally started, counting up your twenty-three things once more. Yes, there is much pleasure attendant on the possession and conveyance of luggage; a pleasure mingled with pain, indeed, like most of our pleasures; a pleasure dashed with anxiety and clouded with confusion, yet ultimately passing into a sense of delightful rest and relief, as you count up the twenty-three things and find them all right, which you had hardly dared to hope they would ever be.

So much having been said concerning the general luggage of the family, let us return to the thought of your own personal packing. You pack your own portmanteau, arranging things in that order which long usage has led you to esteem as the best. And if you be a clergyman, you always introduce into that receptacle your sermon-case with two or three sermons. You do this, if you be a wise man, though there should not appear the faintest chance of your having to preach anywhere, — having learned by experience how often and how unexpectedly such chances occur. And then, when your portmanteau is finally strapped up and ready to go, you look at it with a moralizing glance, and think how little a thing it looks to hold such a great deal. It is like a general principle, including a host of individual cases. It is like a bold assertion, which you accept without thinking of all it implies. And in a short time that compendium of things immediately needful will be one among a score like it in the luggage-van. Thus, the philosopher may reflect, is every man's own concern the most interesting to himself, because every man knows best what is involved in his own concern.

There are many associations about the battered old leathern object, and it is sad to remark that it is wearing out. It is to many people a sensible trial to throw aside anything they have had for a long time. And this thing especially, which has faithfully kept so many things you intrusted to it, and which has gone with you to so many places, seems to cast a silent appealing look at you when you think it is getting so shabby that you must throw it aside. Some day you and I, my friend, will be like an old portmanteau; and we shall be pushed out of the way to make room for something fresh. Probably it is worldly wisdom to treat trunks and men like that single-minded person, Mr. Uppish, who steadfastly cuts his old friends as he gradually gets into a superior social stratum. Doubtless he has his reward.

It is invariably on Monday morning that certain human beings Go Away, in the grave and formal manner which has been spoken of. I mean, with an entire family, and with the twenty-three trunks, many of them very large ones. Not unfrequently a perambulator is present, also a nursery crib. And going at that especial period of the week, there is a certain thing inevitably associated with Going Away. That thing is the periodical called the *Saturday Review*. It comes every Monday morning; and you cut the leaves after breakfast and glance over it, but you put off the reading of it till the evening. But on those travelling days this paper is associated with the forenoon. Breakfast is a hasty meal that day. The heavy baggage, if you dwell in the country, has gone away early in a cart, — the railway station is of course five miles off. And then, just a quarter of an hour after the period you had named to your man-servant, round comes the phaeton which can hold so much. It comes at the very moment you really desired to have it, — for knowing that your servant will always be exactly a quarter of an hour too late, you always order it just a quarter of an hour before the time you really want it. Phaeton of chocolate hue, picked out with red and white; horse of the sixteen hands and an inch, jet black of color, well-bred in blood, and gentle of nature, where are you both to-night? Through the purple moorlands, through the rich cornfields, along the shady lanes, up the High-street of the little town, we have gone together; but the day came at length when you had to go one way and I another; and we have each gone through a good deal of hard work doubtless since then. Pleasant it is, driving home from the town in the winter afternoon, and reaching your door when it has grown pretty dark; pleasant is the flood of mellow light that issues forth when your door is opened; pleasant is it to witness the unloading of the vast amount and

variety of things which, in various receptacles, that far
from ponderous equipage could convey; pleasant to
witness the pile that accumulates on the topmost step
before your door; pleasant to behold the bundle of books
and magazines from the reading-club; pleasanter to see
the less frequent parcel of those which you can call your
own; pleasant to see the manifold brown-paper parcels
enter the house, which seems to be such a devouring
monster, craving ceaseless fresh supply. All this while
the night is falling fast, and the great trees look down,
ghost-like, upon the little bustle underneath them. Then.
phaeton and horse depart; and in a little you go round
to the stable-yard, and find your faithful steed, now dry
and warm, in his snug stall, eagerly eating, yet bearing
in a kindly way a few pats on the neck and a few pulls
of the ears. And your faithful man-servant is quite
sure to have some wonderful intelligence to convey to
you, picked up in town that afternoon. In the country,
you have not merely the enjoyment of rich summer
scenery, of warm sunsets, and green leaves shining gold-
en; there is a peculiar pleasure known to the thorough
country man in the most wintry aspects of nature. The
bleak trees and sky outside, the moan of the rising wind
presaging a wild night, and the brawl of the swollen
brook that runs hard by, all make one value the warmth
and light and comfort within doors about forty times as
much as you could value these simple blessings in a
great city, where they seem quite natural, and matters
of course. Of course, a great man would not care for
these things, and would despise the small human being
that does care for them. Let the great man take his
own way, and let the small human being be allowed to
follow his in peace.

This, however, is a deviation to an evening on which you come home; whereas our proper subject is a morning on which you go away from home. The phaeton has come to the door; many little things go in; finally the passengers take their seats, and the thick rugs are tucked in over their knees; then you take the reins (for you drive yourself), and you wind away outward till you enter the highway. The roads are 'smooth and firm, and for all the heavy load behind him, the black horse trots briskly away. Have I not beheld a human being, his wife, two children, a man-servant, and a woman-servant, steadily skimming along at a respectable nine miles an hour, with but one living creature for all the means of locomotion? And the living creature was shining and plump, and unmistakably happy. The five miles are overcome, and you enter the court-yard of your little railway station. There in a heap, cunningly placed on the platform where the luggage-van may be expected to rest when the train stops, is your luggage. The cart has been faithful: there are the twenty-three things. You have driven the last mile or two under a certain fear lest you might be too late; and that fear will quicken an unsophisticated country pulse. But you have ten minutes to spare. There are no people but your own party to divide the attention of the solitary porter. At length, a mile off, along the river bank, you discern the sinuous train: in a little the tremendously energetic locomotive passes by you, and the train is at rest. You happily find a compartment which is empty, and there you swiftly bestow your living charge; and having done this you hasten to witness the safe embarkation of the twenty-three trunks and packages.

All this must be done rapidly, and of course you take much more trouble than a more experienced traveller would. And when at length you hurriedly climb into your place, you sink down in your seat, and feel a delicious sense of quiet. The morning has been one of worry, after all. But now you are all right for the next four hours. And that is a long look forward. You keenly appreciate this blink of entire rest. Your unaccustomed nerves have been stretched by that fear of being late; then there was the hurry of getting the children into their carriage, and seeing after the twenty-three things; and now comes a reaction. For a few miles it is enough just to sit still, and look at the faces beside you and opposite you, and especially to watch the wonder imprinted on the two round little faces looking out of the window. First, looking out on either side there is a deep gorge; great trees; rocks .on one side, and on the other side a river. By and by the golden gleam of ripe cornfields in the sunshine on either hand lightens up all faces. And now, forth from its bag comes the *Saturday Review;* and you read it luxuriously, with frequent pauses and lookings out between. Do the keen, sharp, brilliant men who write those trenchant paragraphs ever think of the calm enjoyment they are providing for simple minds? Although you do not care in the least about the subject discussed, there is a keen pleasure in remarking the skill and pith and felicity with which the writer discusses it. You feel a certain satisfaction in thinking that every Monday since that periodical started on its career, you have read it. It is a sort of intellectual thing to do. You reflect with pleasure on the statement made on oath by a witness in a famous trial. He described a certain person as "a sensible and intelligent man who took in the *Times*." What proof, then, of scholarly likings, and of power to appreciate what not everybody can appreciate, should be esteemed as furnished by the fact that a man pays for and reads the *Saturday Review*?

Now here, my reader, we have reached the very article of GOING AWAY. Many are the thoughts through which we approached it: here it is at last. Behold the human being, about the first day of August, seated in a corner of a railway carriage, whose cushions are luxurious, and whose general effect is of blue cloth within, and varnished teak without. Opposite the human being sits his wife. Pervading the carriage you may behold two children. And carefully tending them, and seeking vainly to keep them quiet, you may (in very many cases, for such excellent persons are happily not uncommon) discern a certain nurse, who is as a member of that little family circle; more than a trusted and valued servant, even a faithful friend. That is how human beings Go Away. That is the kind of picture which rises in the writer's mind, and in the mind of very many people in a like station in this life, when looking back over not many years.

There is a certain cumbrous enjoyment in all Going Away, bearing with you all these *impedimenta;* even when you are going merely for a Christmas week or the like. But the great Going Away is at the beginning of your autumn holidays. And thinking of this, I feel the prospect change from country to town: I think how the human being, wearied out by many months of hard work amid city bustle and pressure, leaves these behind; how the little children shut up their school-books, and their tired instructors are off for their turn of much-needed recreation; how the churches are emptied, and the streets deserted; how the congregation, assembled in one place on the last Sunday of July, is before the next one scattered far and wide, like the fragments of a bursting bombshell. But it is not now, in this mid-term of work, that one can recall the feelings of commencing holiday-time. Meanwhile, you are out of sympathy with it; and every good thing is beautiful in its time.

Was it worth while thus to revive things so long past? It has been pleasant for the writer; and a hundred things not recorded here have been awakened in the retrospect. And when these pages meet the right people's eye, they may serve to recall simple modes of being and doing which are melting fast away. For the experience of ordinary mortals is remarkably uniform; and most of the people you know are in many respects extremely like yourself. Now let us cease and sit down and think. There is indeed a temptation to go on. One would rather not stop in the middle of a page; I mean a manuscript page; and it is almost too much for human nature to know that we may add a few sentences more, and they will not be cut off. And there are positions too much for human nature. A sense of power and authority, as a general rule, is more than the average man can bear. Not long since I beheld, in the superhuman dignity of a policeman, something which deeply impressed this on my mind. The kitchen chimney of this dwelling caught fire. It is contrary to municipal law to let your kitchen chimney catch fire, and very properly so ; so there was a fine to be paid. On a certain day I was told there was a policeman in the kitchen, who desired an interview. I proceeded thither and found him there. No language can convey an idea of the stern and unyielding severity of that eminent man's demeanor. He seemed to think I would probably plead with him to let Justice turn from her rigid course ; and he sought by his whole bearing to convey that any such pleading would be futile ; and that, whatever might be said, the half-crown must be paid, to be applied to public purposes. When I entered his presence, he sternly asked me what was my name. Of course he knew my name just as well as I did myself; but there was something in the requirement fitted to make me feel my humble position before him. And having received the information, he made a note of it in a little book ; and, conveying that serious consequences would follow, he departed. A similar manifestation may be found in the case of magistrates in small authority. I have heard of such an individual who dispensed justice from a seedy little bench, with an awful state. He sat upon that bench all alone ; and no matter of the smallest importance ever came before him. Yet when expressing his opinion, he never failed to state that THE COURT thought so and so. A vague impression of dignity thus was made to surround the workings of the individual mind. It once befell, that certain youthful students, in a certain university, had a strife with the police ; and being captured by the strong arm of the law, were conveyed before such a magistrate. Sitting upon the judgment seat, he sternly upbraided the youths for their

7 *

discreditible behaviour; adding, that it gave him special sorrow to witness such lawless violence in the case of individuals who were receiving a university eddication. He did not know, that unhappy magistrate, that there stood at his bar one whose audacious heart quailed not in his presence. "Stop," exclaimed that unutterably irreverent youth, interrupting the stern magistrate; "let me entreat you to pronounce the word properly; it is not EDDICATION, it is EDUCATION." And the magistrate's dignity suddenly collapsed, like a blown-up bladder when you insert a penknife. This incident is recorded to have happened at Timbuctoo, in the last century. I have no doubt the story is not true. Hardly any stories are true. Yet I have often heard it related. And like the legend of *The Ass and the Archbishop*, which is utterly without foundation, you feel that it ought to be true.

CHAPTER IX.

CONCERNING OLD ENEMIES.

IT may be assumed as certain, that most readers of this page have on some occasion climbed a high hill. It may be esteemed as probable, that when half-way up, they felt out of breath and tired. It is extremely likely that, having come to some inviting spot, they sat down and rested for a little, before passing on to the summit. Now, my reader, if you have done all that, I feel assured that you must have remarked as a fact that, though when you sit down you cease to make progress, you do not go back. You do not lose the ground already gained. But if you ever think at all, even though it should be as little as possible, you must have discerned the vexatious truth that in respect of another and more important kind of progress, unless you keep going on, you begin to go back. You struggle, in a moral sense, up the steep slope; and you sit down at the top, thinking to yourself, "Now *that* is overcome." But after resting for a while you look round; and lo! insensibly you have been sliding down, and you are back again at the foot of the eminence you climbed with so much pain and toil.

There are certain enemies with which every worthy human being has to fight, as regards which you will feel, as. you go on, that this principle holds especially true; the principle that if you do not keep going forward, you will begin to lose ground and go backward. It is not enough to knock these enemies on the head for once. In your inexperienced days you will do this; and then, seeing that they look quite dead, you will fancy they will never trouble you any more. But you will find out, to your painful cost, that those enemies of yours and mine must be knocked at the head repeatedly. One knocking, though the severest, will not suffice. They keep always reviving, and struggling to their feet again; a little weak at first through the battering you gave them, but in a very short time as vigorous and mischievous as ever. The Frenchman, imperfectly acquainted with the force of English words, and eager that extremest vengeance should be wreaked on certain human foes, cried aloud, " KILL THEM VERY OFTEN "! And *that*, my friend, as regards the worst enemies we have got, is precisely what you and I must do.

If we are possessed of common sense to even a limited amount, we must know quite well who are our worst enemies. Not Miss Limejuice, who tells lies to make you appear a conceited, silly, and ignorant person. Nor Mr. Snarling, who diligently strives to prevent your reaching something you would like, because (as he says) the disappointment will do you good. Not the human curs that gnarr at your heels when you attain some conspicuous success or distinction ; which probably you worked hard for, and waited long for. Not these. " A man's foes," by special eminence and distinction, are even nearer him than "they of his own house:" a man's worst enemies are they of his own heart and soul. The enemies that do you most harm, and probably that cause you most suffering, are tendencies and feelings in yourself. If all within the citadel were right, if the troop of thoughts and affections *there* were orderly and well-disposed and well-guided, we should be very independent of the enemies outside. Outside temptation can never make a man do wrong till something inside takes it by the hand, and fraternizes with it, and sides with it. The bad impulse within must walk up arm in arm with the bad impulse from without, and introduce it to the will, before the bad impulse from without, however powerful it may be, can make man or woman go astray from right. All this, however, may be taken for granted. What I wish to impress on the reader is this: that in fighting with these worst enemies, it is not enough for once to cut them down; smash them, bray them in a mortar. If you were fighting with a Chinese invader, and if you were to send a rifle-bullet through his head, or in any other way to extinguish his life, you would feel that he was done with. You would have no more trouble from *that* quarter. But once shoot or slash the ugly beast which is called Envy, or Self-Conceit, or Unworthy Ambition, or Hasty Speaking, or general Foolishness, and you need not plume yourself that you will not be troubled any more with him. Let us call the beast by the general name of BESETTING SIN; and let us recognize the fact, that though you never willingly give it a moment's quarter, though you smash in its head (in a moral sense) with a big stone, though you kick it (in a moral sense) till it seems to be lying quite

lifeless, in a little·while it will be up again as strong
as ever. And the only way to keep it down is to knock
it on the skull afresh every time it begins to lift up its
ugly face. Or, to go back to my first figure : you have
climbed, by a hard effort, up to a certain moral elevation.
You have reached a position, climbing up the great
ascent that leads towards God, at which you feel resigned to God's will, and kindly disposed to all your
fellow-creatures, even to such as have done you a bad
turn already, and will not fail to do the like again.
You also feel as if your heart were not set, as it once
used to be, upon worldly aims and ends ; but as if you
were really day by day working towards something
quite different and a great deal higher. You feel humble, patient, charitable. You sit down there, on that
moral elevation, satisfied with yourself, and thinking to
yourself, Now, I am a humble, contented, kindly,
Christian human being; and I am so for life. And let
it be said thankfully, if you keep always on the alert,
always watching against any retrogression, always with
a stone ready to knock any old enemy on the head,
always looking and· seeking for a strength beyond your
own, — you may remain all *that* for life. But if you
grow lazy and careless, in a very little while you will
have glided a long way down the hill again. You will
be back at your old evil ways. You will be eager to
get on, and as set on this world as if this world were
all, you will find yourself hitting hard the man who
has hit you, envying and detracting from the man
who has surpassed you, and all the other bad things.
Or if you do not retrograde so far as *that*, if you pull
yourself up before the old bad impulse within you comes

to actual bad deeds, still you will know that the old bad impulse within you is stirring, and that, by God's help, you must give it another stab.

Now this is disheartening. When, by making a great effort, very painful and very long, you have put such a bad impulse down, it is very natural to think that it will never vex you any more. The dragon has been trampled under the horse's feet, its head has been cut off; surely you are done with it. You have ruled your spirit into being right and good; into being magnanimous, kindly, humble. And then you fancied you might go ahead to something more advanced; you had got over the *Pons Asinorum* in the earnest moral work of life. You have extirpated the wolves from your England, and now you may go on to destroy the moles. The wolves are all lying dead, each stabbed to the heart. You honestly believe that you had got beyond them, and that whatever new enemies may assail you, the old ones, at least, are done with finally. But the wolves get up again. The old enemies revive.

I have sometimes wondered whether those men who have done much to help you and me in the putting down of our worst enemies, have truly and finally slain those enemies as far as concerns themselves. Is the man, in reading whose pages I feel I am subjected to a healthful influence, that puts down the unworthy parts of my nature, and that makes me feel more kindly, magnanimous, hopeful, and earnest than when left to myself, — is that man, I wonder, always as good himself as for the time he makes me? Or can it be true that the man who seems not merely to have knocked on the head the lower impulses of his own nature, but to have done good to you and me, my friend, by helping to kill those impulses within us, has still to be fighting away with beasts, like St. Paul at Ephesus; still to be lamenting, on many days, that the ugly faces of suspicion, jealousy, disposition to retaliate when assailed, and the like, keep wakening up and flying at him again? I fear it is so. I doubt whether the human being lives in whom evil, however long and patiently trodden down, does not sometimes erect its crest, and hiss, and need to be trodden down again. Vain thoughts and fancies, long extinguished, will waken up; unworthy tendencies will give a push now and then. And especially I believe it is a great delusion to fancy that a man who writes in a healthy and kindly strain *is* what he counsels. If he be an honest and earnest man I believe that he is striving after that which he counsels, and that he is aiming at the spirit and temper which he sets out. I think I can generally make out what are a moral or religious writer's besetting sins, by remarking what are the virtues he chiefly magnifies. He is struggling after those virtues, struggling to break away from the corresponding errors and failings. If you find a man who in all he writes is scrupulously fair and temperate, it is probable that he is a very excitable and prejudiced person, but that he knows it, and honestly strives against it. An author who always expresses himself with remarkable calmness is probably by nature a ferocious and savage man. But you may see in the way in which he restricts himself in the matter of adjectives, and in which he excludes the superlative degree, that he is making a determined effort to put down his besetting sin. And probably he fancies, quite honestly, that he has finally knocked that enemy on the head. The truth no doubt is, that it is because the enemy is still alive, and occasionally barking and biting, that it is kept so well in check. There is just enough of the old beast surviving to compel attention to it: the attention which consists in keeping a foot always on its head, and in occasionally giving it a vehement whack. The most eminent good qualities in human beings are generally formed by diligent putting down of the corresponding evil qualities. It was a stutterer who became the greatest ancient orator. It was a man who still bore on his satyr face the indications of his old satyr nature who became the best of heathens. And as with Socrates and Demosthenes, it has been with many more. If a man writes always very judiciously; rely upon it he has a strong tendency to foolishness; but he is keeping it tight in check. If a man writes always very kindly and charitably, depend upon it he is fighting to the death a tendency to bitterness and uncharitableness.

A faithful and earnest preacher, resolved to say no more than he has known and felt, and remembering the wise words of Dean Alford, "What thou hast not by suffering bought, presume thou not to teach," would necessarily show to a sharp observer a great deal of himself and his inner being, even though rigidly avoiding the slightest suspicion of egotism in his preaching; and it need hardly be said that egotism is not to be tolerated in the pulpit.

After you have in an essay or a sermon described and condemned some evil tendency that is in human nature, you are ready to think that you have finally overcome it. And after you have described and commended some good disposition, you are ready to think that you have attained it, and that you will not lose it again. And for the time, if you be an honest man, you *have* smashed the foe, you *have* gained the vantage ground. But, woe's me, the good disposition dies away, and the foe gradually revives and struggles to his legs again. Let us not fancy that because we have been (as we fancied) once right, we shall never go wrong. We must be always watchful. The enemy that seemed most thoroughly beaten may (apart from God's grace) beat us yet. The publican, when he went up to the temple to pray, expressed himself in a fashion handed down to all ages with the *imprimatur* upon it. Yet, for all his speaking so fairly, the day might come when, having grown a reformed character and gained general approbation, he would stand in a conspicuous place, and thank God that he was not as other men. Let us trust *that* day never came. Yet, if the publican had said to himself, as he went down to his house, Now I have attained an excellent pitch of morality; I am all right; I am a model for future generations, — that day would be very likely to come.

It is a humiliating and discouraging sight to behold a man plainly succumbing to an enemy which you fancied he had long got over. You may have seen an individual of more than middle age making a fool of himself by carrying on absurd flirtations with young girls, who were babies in long-clothes when he first was spoony. You would have said, looking at such a man's outward aspect, and knowing something of his history, that years had brought this compensation for what they had taken away, that he would not make a conspicuous ass of himself any more. But the old enemy is too much for him; and O how long that man's ears would appear, if the inner ass could be represented outwardly! You may have seen such a one, after passing through a discipline which you would have expected to sober him, evincing a frantic exhilaration in the prospect of his third marriage. And you may have witnessed a person evincing a high degree of a folly he had unsparingly scourged in others. I have beheld, in old folk, manifestations of absurdity all very well in the very young, which suggested to me the vision of a stiff, spavined, lame, broken-down old hack, fit only for the knacker, trying to jauntily scamper about in a field with a set of spirited, fresh young colts. And looking at the spectacle, I have reflected on the true statement of the Venerable Bede, that there are no fools like old fools.

But here it may be said, that we are not to suppose that a thing is wrong, unless it can bear to be looked back on in cold blood. Many a word is spoken, and many a deed done, and fitly too, in the warmth of the moment, which will not bear the daylight of a time when the excitement is over. Mr. Caudle was indignant when his wife reminded him of his sayings before marriage. They sounded foolish now in Caudle's ears. This did not suffice to show that those sayings were not very fit at the time; nor does it prove that the tendency to say many things under strong feeling is an enemy to be put down. You have said, with a trembling voice, and with the tear in your eye, things which are no discredit to you, though you might not be disposed to say the like just after coming out of your bath in the morning. You needed to be warmed up to a certain pitch; and then the spark was struck off. And only a very malicious or a very stupid person would remind you of these things when you are not in a correspondent vein.

And now that we have had this general talk about these old enemies, let us go on to look at some of them individually. It may do us good to poke up a few of the beasts, and to make them arise and walk about in their full ugliness, and then to smite them on the head as with a hammer. Let this be a new slaying of the slain, who never can be slain too often.

Perhaps you may not agree with me when I say that one of these beasts is Ambition. I mean unscrupulous self-seeking. You resolved, long ago, to give no harbor to that, and so to exclude the manifold evils that came of it. You determined that you would resolutely refuse to scheme, or push, or puff, or hide your honest opinions, or dodge in any way, for the purpose of getting on. You know how eager some people are to let their light shine before men, to the end that men may think what clever fellows those people are. You know how anxious some men are to set themselves right in newspapers and the like, and to stand fair (as they call it) with the public. You know how some men, when they do any good work, have recourse to means highly analogous to the course adopted by a class of persons long ago, who sounded a trumpet before them in the streets to call attention to their charitable deeds. I know individuals who constantly sound their own trumpet, and that a very brazen one, — sound it in conversation, in newspaper paragraphs, in advertisements, in speeches at public meetings. But you, an honest and modest person, were early disgusted by that kind of thing, and you determined that you would do your duty quietly and faithfully, spending all your strength upon your work, and not sparing a large per centage of it for the trumpet. You resolved that you would never admit the thought of setting yourself more favorably before your fellow-creatures. You learned to look your humble position in the face, and to discard the idea of getting any mortal to think you greater or better than you are. Yes, you hope that the petty self-seeking, which keeps some men ever on the strut and stretch, has been outgrown by you; yet if you would be safe from one of the most contemptible foes of all moral manhood, you must keep your club in your hand, and every now and then quiet the creature by giving it a heavy blow on the head. St. Paul tells us that he had "*learned* to be content." It cost him effort. It cost him time. It was not natural. He came down, we may be sure, with many a heavy stroke on the innate disposition to repine when things did not go in the way he wanted them. And that is what we must do.

As you look back now, it is likely enough that you recall a time when self-seeking seemed thoroughly dead in you. You were not very old, perhaps, yet you fancied that (by God's help) you had outgrown ambition. You did your work as well as you could, and in the evening you sat in your easy-chair by the fireside, looking not without interest at the feverish race of worldly competition, yet free from the least thought of running in it. As for thinking of your own eminence, or imagining that any one would take the trouble of talking about you, *that* never entered your mind. And as you beheld the eager pushing of other men, and their frantic endeavors

to keep themselves before the human race, you wondered
what worldly inducement would lead you to do the like.
But did you always keep in that happy condition? Did
you not, now and then, feel some little waking up of the
old thing, and become aware that you were being drawn
into the current? If so, let us hope that you resolutely
came out of it, and that you found quiet in the peaceful
backwater, apart from that horrible feverish stream.

There is another old enemy, a two-headed monster,
that is not done with when it has been killed once. It
is a near relative of the last: it is the ugly creature
Self-Conceit and Envy. I call it a two-headed monster,
rather than two monsters; it is a double manifestation
of one evil principle. Self-conceit is the principle as it
looks at yourself; Envy is the same thing as it looks at
other men. I fear it must be admitted that there is in
human nature a disposition to talk bitterly of people
who are more eminent and successful than yourself, and
though you expel it with a pitchfork, that old enemy
will come back again. This disposition exists in many
walks of life. A Lord Chancellor has left on record
his opinion, that nowhere is there so much envy and
jealousy as among the members of the English bar.
A great actor has declared that nowhere is there so
much as among actors and actresses. Several authors
have maintained that no human beings are so bitter at
seeing one of themselves get on a little, as literary folk.
And a popular preacher has been heard to say that
envy and detraction go their greatest length among
preachers. Let us hope that the last statement is erroneous. But I fear that these testimonies, coming

from quarters so various, lead to the conclusion that envy and detraction (which imply self-conceit) are too natural and common everywhere. You may have heard a number of men talking about one man in their own vocation who had got a good deal ahead of them, and who never had done them any harm, except thus getting ahead of them; and you may have been amazed at the awful animosity evinced towards the successful man. But success in others is a thing which some mortals cannot forgive. You may have known people savagely abuse a man because he set up a carriage, or because he moved to a finer house, or because he bought an estate in the country. You remember the outburst which followed when Macaulay dated a letter from Windsor Castle. Of course, the true cause of the outburst was that Macaulay should have been at Windsor Castle at all. Let us be thankful, my friend, that such an eminent distinction is not likely to happen either to you or me; we have each acquaintances who would never forgive us if it did. What a raking up of all the sore points in your history would follow, if the Queen were to ask you to dinner! And if you should ever succeed to a fortune, what unspeakable bitterness would be awakened in the hearts of Mr. Snarling and Miss Limejuice! If their malignant glances could lame your horses as you drive by them with that fine new pair, the horses would limp home with great difficulty; and if their eyes could set your grand house on fire, immediately on the new furniture going in, a heavy loss would fall either upon you or the insurance company.

But this will not do. As you read these lines, my friend, you picture yourself as the person who attains the eminence and succeeds to the fortune ; and you picture Miss Limejuice and Mr. Snarling as two of your neighbors. But what I desire is, that you should change the case ; imagine your friend Smith preferred before you, and consider whether there would not be something of the Snarling tendency in yourself. Of course, you would not suffer it to manifest itself; but it is there, and needs to be put down. And it needs to be put down more than once. You will now and then be vexed and mortified to find that, after fancying you had quite made up your mind to certain facts, you are far from really having done so. Well, you must just try again. You must look for help where it is always to be found. And in the long run you will succeed. It will be painful, after you fancied you had weeded out self-conceit and envy from your nature, to find yourself some day talking in a bitter and ill-set way about some man or some woman whose real offence is merely having been more prosperous than yourself. You thought you had got beyond that. But it is all for your good to be reminded that the old root of bitterness is there yet ; that you are never done with it ; that you must be always cutting it down. A gardener might as justly suppose that because he has mown down the grass of a lawn very closely to-day, the grass will never grow up and need mowing again, as we fancy that because we have unsparingly put down an evil tendency within us, we shall have no more trouble with it.

Did nature give you, my friend, or education develope in you, a power of saying or writing severe things, which might stick into people as the little darts stick into the bull at a Spanish bull-fight ? I believe that there are few persons who might not, if their heart would let them, acquire the faculty of producing disagreeable things, expressed with more or less of neatness and felicity. And in the case of the rare man here and there, who says his ill-set ·saying with epigrammatic point, like the touch of a rapier, the ill-setness may be excused, because the thing is so gracefully said. We would not wish that tigers should be exterminated; but it is to be desired that they should be very few. Let there be spared a specimen, here and there, of the graceful, agile, ferocious savage. But you, my reader, were no great hand at epigrams, though you were ready enough with your ill-set remark; and after some experience, you concluded that there is something better in this world than to say things, however cleverly, that are intended to give pain. And so you determined to cut that off, and to go upon the kindly tack; to say a good and cheering word whenever you had the opportunity; to be ready with a charitable interpretation of what people do; and never to utter or to write a word that could vex a fellow-creature, who (you may be sure) has quite enough to vex him without your adding anything. Perhaps you did all this, rather overdoing the thing. Ill-set people are apt to overdo the thing when they go in for kindliness and geniality. But some day, having met some little offence, the electricity that had been storing up during that season of repression, burst out in a flash of what may, by a strong figure, be called forked lightning; the old enemy had got the mastery again. And indeed a hasty temper, founding as it does mainly on irritability of the nervous system, is never quite got over. It may be much aggravated by yielding to it, and much abated by constant restraint; but unless the beast be perpetually seen to, it is sure to be bursting out now and then. Socrates, you remember, said that his temper was naturally hasty and bad, but that philosophy had cured him. I believe it needs something much more efficacious than any human philosophy to work such a cure. No doubt, you may diligently train yourself to see what is to be said in excuse of the offences given you by your fellow-creatures, and to look at the case as it appears from their point of view. This will help. But though ill-temper, left to its natural growth, will grow always worse, there is a point at which it has been found to mend. When the nervous system grows less sensitive through age, hastiness of temper sometimes goes. The old enemy is weakened; the beast has been (so to speak) hamstrung. You will be told that the thing which mainly impressed persons who saw the great Duke of Wellington in the last months of his life, was what a mild, gentle old man he was. Of course, every one knows that he was not always so. The days were, when his temper was hot and hasty enough.

And thus thinking of physical influence, let us remember that what is vulgarly called nervousness is an enemy which many men know to their cost is not to be got over. The firmest assurance that you have done a thing many times, and so should be able to do it once more, may not suffice to enable you to look forward to doing it without a vague tremor and apprehension. There are human beings, all whose work is done without any very great nervous strain; there are others in whose vocation there come many times that put their whole nature upon the stretch. And these times test a man. You know a horse may be quite lame, while yet it does not appear in walking. Trot the creature smartly, and the lameness becomes manifest. In like manner a man may be nervous, particular, crotchety, superstitious, while yet this may not appear till you trot him sharply. Put him at some work that must be done with the full stretch of his powers, and then you will see that he has got little odd ways of his own. I do not know what is the sensation of going into battle, and finding oneself under fire; but short of that, I think the greatest strain to which a human being is usually subjected is that of the preacher. A little while ago, I was talking with a distinguished clergyman, and being desirous of comparing his experience with that of his juniors, I asked him, —

1. Whether, in walking to church on Sunday to preach, he did not always walk on the same side of the street? Whether he would not feel uncomfortable, and as if something were going wrong, if he made any change?

2. Whether when waiting in the vestry, the minute or two before the beadle should come to precede him into church, he did not always stand on the same spot? Whether it would not put him out of gear, to vary from that?

My eminent friend answered all these questions in the affirmative. Of course there are a great many men to whom I should no more have thought of proposing such questions than I should think of proposing them to a rhinoceros. Such men, probably, have no little ways; and if they had, they would not admit that they had.

But my friend is so very able a man, and so very sincere a man, that he had no reason to be afraid of any one thinking him little, though he acknowledged to having his little fancies. And indeed, when you come to know people well, you will find that they have all ways that are quite analogous to Johnson's touching the tops of all the posts as he walked London streets. They would not exactly say, that they are afraid of anything happening to them if they deviated from the old track, but they think it just as well to keep on the safe side, by not deviating from it.

Possibly there was a period in your life in which you had no objection to get into controversies upon political or religious subjects with other men; which controversies gradually grew angry, and probably ended in mutual abuse, but assuredly not in conviction. But having remarked, in the case of other controversialists, what fools they invariably made of themselves; having remarked their ludicrous exaggeration of the importance of their dispute, and the malice and disingenuousness with which they carried on their debate (more especially if they were clergymen); having remarked, in brief, how very little a controversialist ever looks like a Christian, — you turned, in loathing, from the whole thing, and resolved that you would never get into a controversy, public or private, with any mortal upon any subject any more. Stick to that resolution, my friend; it is a good one. But you will occasionally be tempted to break it. Whenever the old enemy assails you, just think what a demagogue or agitator, political or religious, looks like in the eyes of all sensible and honest men!

Perhaps you had a tendency to be suspicious, and

you have broken yourself of it. Perhaps your temptation was to be easily worried by little cross-accidents, and to get needlessly excited. Perhaps your temptation was to laziness, to putting off duty till to-morrow, to untidiness, to moral cowardice. Whatever it was, my friend, never think yourself so cured of an evil habit, that you may cease to mow it down. If Demosthenes had left off attending to his speaking, he would have relapsed into his old evil ways. If St. Paul, after having learned to be content, had ceased to see to that, he would gradually have grown a grumbler.

I am going to close this little procession of old enemies which has passed before our eyes by naming a large and general one. It is Folly. My friend, if you have attained to any measure of common sense now, you know what a tremendous fool you were once. If you do not know that, then you are a fool still. Ah, reader, wise and good, you know all the weakness, the silliness, the absurd fancies and dreams, that have been yours. I presume that you are ready to give up a great part of your earlier life: you have not a word to say for it. All your desire is that it should in charity be forgotten. But surely you will not now make a fool of yourself any more. There shall be no more now of the hasty talking, the vaporing about your own importance, the idiotic sayings and doings you wish you could bury in Lethe; and which you may be very sure certain of your kind friends carefully remember and occasionally recall. But now and then the logic of facts will convince you that the old enemy is not quite annihilated yet, and you say something you regret the moment it is uttered; you do something which indicates that you have lost your head for the time.

Let it be said, in conclusion, as the upshot of the whole matter, that the wise man will never think he is safe till he has reached a certain place where no enemy can assail him more. I beg my friend Mr. Snarling to take notice, that I do not pretend to have pointed out in these pages the worst of those old enemies that get up again and run at us after they had been knocked on the head once, and more than once.

If this had been a sermon, I should have given you a very different catalogue, and one that would have awakened more serious thoughts. Not but that those which have been named are well worth thinking of. The day will never come, in this world, on which it will be safe for us to sit down in perfect security, and to say to ourselves, now we need keep no watch; we may (in a moral sense) draw the charge from our revolver because it will not be needed; we may fall asleep, and nothing will meddle with us the while. For all around us, my friend, are the old enemies of our souls and our salvation; some aiming at nothing more than to make us disagreeable and repulsive, petty and jealous; others aiming at nothing less than to make us unfit for the only home where we can know perfect rest and peace; some stealing upon us more stealthily, silently, fatally, than ever the Indian crept through the darkness of night upon the traveller nodding over his watch-fire; some coming down upon us, strong and sudden as the tiger's agile spring. Well, we know what to do: we must watch and pray. And the time will come at length when the pack of wolves shall be lashed off for ever; when the evil within us shall be killed outright, and beyond all reviving; and when the evil around us shall be gone.

CHAPTER X.

AT THE CASTLE: WITH SOME THOUGHTS ON MICHAEL SCOTT'S FAMILIAR SPIRIT.

NOT on a study-table in a back parlor in a great city shall these little blue pages be covered with written characters. Every word shall be written in the open air. The page shall be lighted by sunshine that comes through no glass, but which is tempered by coming through masses of green leaves. And this essay is not to be composed; not to be screwed out, to use the figure of Mr. Thackeray; not to be pumped out, to use the figure of *Festus*. It shall grow without an effort. When any thought occurs, the pencil shall note it down. No thought shall be. hurried in its coming.

You know how after a good many months of constant work, with the neck always at the collar, you grow wearied and easily worried. Little things become burdensome; and the best of work is felt as a task. You cannot reason yourself out of that; ten days' rest is the thing that will do it. Be thankful if then you can have such a season of quiet in as green and shady a nook of country as mortal eyes could wish to see; in a nook like this, amid green grass and green trees, and the wild flowers of the early summer. For this is little more than midway in the pleasant month of May.

It is a very warm, sunshiny morning. This is a little open glade of rich grass, lighted up with daisies and buttercups. The little glade is surrounded by large forest-trees ; under the trees there is a blaze of primroses and wild hyacinths. A soft west wind, laden with the fragrance of lilac and apple blossoms, wakes the gentlest of sounds (in a more expressive language than ours it would have been called *susurrus*) in the topmost branches, gently swaying to and fro. The swaying branches cast a flecked and dancing shadow on the grass below. Midway the little glade is beyond the shadow ; and there the grass, in the sunbeams, has a tinge of gold. A river runs by, with a ceaseless murmur over the warm stones. Look to the right hand, and there, over the trees, two hundred yards off, you may see a gray and red tower motionless above the waving branches ; and lower down, hardly surmounting the wood, a stretch of massive wall, with huge buttresses. Tower and wall crown a lofty knoll, which the river encircles, making it a peninsula. Wallflower grows in the crannies ; a little wild apple-tree, covered with white blossoms, crowns a detached fragment of a ruined gateway ; sweetbrier grows at the base of the ancient walls ; ivy and honeysuckle climb up them ; and where great fragments of fallen wall testify to the excellence of the mortar of the eleventh century, wild roses have rooted themselves in masses, which are now only green. That is THE CASTLE, all that can be seen of it from this point. There is more to be said of it hereafter. Hard by this spot, two little children are sitting on the grass, to whom some one is reading a story.

The wise man will never weary of looking at green grass and green trees. It is an unspeakable refreshment to the eye and the mind; and the daily pressure of occupation cannot touch one here. One wonders that human beings who always live amid such scenery do not look more like it. But some people are utterly unimpressionable by the influences of outward scenery. You may know men who have lived for many years where Nature has done her best with wood and rock and river; and even when you become well acquainted with them, you cannot discover the faintest trace in their talk or in their feeling of the mightily powerful touch (as it would be to many) which has been unceasingly laid upon them through all that time. Or you may have beheld a vacuous person at a picnic party, who, amid traces of God's handiwork that should make men hold their breath, does but pass from the occupation of fatuously flirting with a young woman like himself, to furiously abusing the servants for not sufficiently cooling the wine.

A great many of the highly respectable people, we all know, are entirely in the case of the hero of that exquisite poem of Wordsworth's, which Jeffrey never could bring himself to like: —

> " But Nature ne'er could find her way
>   Into the heart of Peter Bell.

> " In vain, through every changing year,
>   Did Nature lead him as before ;
>   A primrose by a river's brim
>   A yellow primrose was to him,
>   And it was nothing more."

A human being ought to be very thankful if his disposition be such that he heartily enjoys green grass and green trees; for there are clever men who do not. In a little while I shall tell you of an extraordinary and anomalous taste expressed on that subject by one of the cleverest men I know. If a man has a thousand a year, and his next neighbor five hundred, and if the man with five hundred makes his income go just as far as the larger one (and an approximation to doing so may be made by good management), it is plain that these two mortals are, in respect to income, on the same precise footing. The poorer man gets so much more enjoyment out of his yearly revenue as makes up for the fact that the richer man's revenue is twice as great.

There is a like compensation provided for the lack of material advantages in the case of many men, through their intense appreciation of the beauty of natural scenery, and of very simple things. A rich man may possess the acres, with their yearly rental; a poor man, such as a poet, a professor, a schoolmaster, a clergyman, or the like, may possess the landscape which these acres make up, to the utter exclusion of the landed proprietor. Perhaps, friendly reader, God has not given you the earthly possessions which it has pleased Him to give to some whom you know, but He may have given you abundant recompense by giving you the power of getting more enjoyment out of little things than many other men. You live in a little cottage, and your neighbor in a grand castle; you have a small collection of books, and your neighbor a great one of fine editions in sumptuous bindings and in carved oak cases; yet you may have so great delight in your snug house, and your familiar volumes, that in regard of actual enjoyment you may be the more enviable man. A green field with a large oak in the middle, a hedge of blossoming hawthorn, a thatched cottage under a great maple, twenty square yards of velvety turf, — how really happy such things can make some simple folk!

Of course it occurs to one that the same people who get more enjoyment out of little pleasures will get more suffering out of anything painful. Because your tongue is more sensitive than the palm of your hand, it is aware of the flavor of a pineapple which your palm would ignore, but it is also liable to know the taste of assafœtida, of which your palm would be unconscious. The supersensitive nervous system is finely strung to discern pain as well as pleasure. No one knows, but the over-particular person, what a pure misery it is to go into an untidy room, if it be your own. There are people who suffer as much in having a tooth filed as others in losing a limb. A Frenchman, some years since, committed suicide, leaving a written paper to say he had done so because life was rendered unendurable through his being so much bitten by fleas. This is not a thing to smile at. That poor man, before his reason was upset, had probably endured torments of which those around had not the faintest idea. I have heard a good man praised for the patience with which he bore daily for weeks the surgeon's dressing of a very severe wound. The good man was thought heroic. I knew him well enough to be sure that the fact was that his nature was dull and slow. He did not suffer as average men would have suffered under that infliction. There are human beings in touching whose moral nature you feel you are touching the impenetrable skin of the hippopotamus. There are human beings in touching whose moral nature you feel you are touching the bare tip of a nerve. Eager, anxious men are prone to envy imperturbable and slow-moving men. My friend Smith, who is of an eager nature, tells me he looks with a feeling a few degrees short of veneration on a massive-minded and immovable being, who in telling a story makes such long pauses at the end of each sentence that you fancy the story done. Then poor Smith breaks in hastily with something he wants to say, but the massive-minded man, not noticing him, continues his parable till he pauses again at the end of another sentence. And Smith is made to feel as though he were very young.

I have said that likings vary in regard to such matters as the enjoyment of this scene. O this green grass, rich, unutterably green, with the buttercups and daisies, with the yellow broom and the wild bees, and the environment of bright leafy trees that inclose you round; to think that there are people who do not care for you! It was but yesterday, in a street of a famous and beautiful city, I met my friend Mr. Keene. Keene is a warm-hearted, magnanimous, unselfish, brave, out-spoken human being, as fine a fellow as is numbered among the clergy of either side of the Tweed. Besides these things, he is an admirable debater; fluent, ready, eloquent, hearty, fully persuaded that he is right, and that his opponents are invariably wrong, and not without some measure of smartness and sharpness in expression. Keene approached me with a radiant face, the result partly of inherent good nature, and partly of a very hot summer day. He had come to the city to take part in the debates of the great ecclesiastical council of a northern country. I was coming to this place. He was entering the city, in fact, for many days of deliberation and debate; I was departing from it for certain days of rest and recreation. I could not refrain from displaying some measure of exultation at the contrast between our respective circumstances. "I shall be lying to-morrow," I said, "on green grass under green trees, while you will be existing" (the word used indeed was stewing) " in that crowded building, with its feverish atmosphere highly charged with carbonic-acid gas." To these words Keene replied, with simple earnestness : "I shall be quite happy there; I don't care a straw for green grass and green leaves!" Such was the sentiment of that eminent man. I pity him sincerely!

Here I paused, and thought for a little of the great ecclesiastical council and of lesser ecclesiastical councils, and the following reflection suggested itself : —

Our good principles are too often like Don Quixote's helmet. We arrive at them in leisure, in cool blood, with an unexcited brain, which is commonly called a clear head; then in actual life they too commonly fail at the first real trial. Don Quixote made up his helmet carefully with a visor of pasteboard. Then, to ascertain whether it was strong enough, he dealt it a blow with his sword; thereupon it went to pieces.

In like manner, in our better and more thoughtful hours, we resolve to be patient, forgiving, charitable, kind-spoken, unsuspicious, — in short Christian, for *that* includes all, — and the first time we are irritated we fail. We grow very angry at some small offence; we speak harshly, we act unfairly. I have heard a really good man preach. Afterwards I heard him speak in a lesser ecclesiastical council. He preached (so far as the sentiments expressed went) like an angel. He argued like just the reverse.

Ah, we make up our helmets with pasteboard. We resolve that henceforth we shall act on the most noble principles. And the helmets look very well so long as they are not put to the test. We fancy ourselves charitable, forgiving, Christian people, so long as we are not tried. A stroke with a sword, and the helmet goes to tatters. An attack on us, a reflection on us, a hint that we ever did wrong, and oh, the wretched outburst of wrath, bitterness, unfairness, malignity!

Of course, the best of men, as it has been said, are but men at the best. Let us be humble. Let there be no vain self-confidence ; and especially let us, entering on every scene that can possibly try us, (and when do we escape from such a scene?) earnestly ask the guidance of that Blessed Spirit of Whom is every good feeling and purpose in us, and without Whom our best resolutions will snap like reeds just when they are needed most to stand firm.

There is more to be said about the Castle. It is not a castle to which you go that you may enjoy the society of dukes and other nobles, such as form the daily associates of the working clergy. By the payment of a moderate weekly stipend, this castle may become yours. The castle is in ruins ; but a little corner amid the great masses of crumbling stones, which were placed here by strong hands dead for eight hundred years, has been patched up so as to make an unpretending little dwelling ; and there you may find the wainscotted rooms, the quaint panelled ceilings of mingled timber and plaster, the winding turret stairs, the many secret doors, of past centuries. The castle stands on a lofty promontory of no great extent, which a little river encircles on two sides, and which a deep ravine cuts off from the surrounding country on the other two sides. You approach the castle over an arch of seventy feet in height, which spans the ravine. In former days it was a drawbridge. The bridge runs out of the inner court of the castle; midway in its length it turns off at almost a right angle, till it joins the bank on the other side of the ravine. That little bridge makes a charming place to walk on, and it is a great deal longer than any quarter-deck. It is all grown over with masses of ancient ivy, the fragrance of a sweetbrier hedge in the castle court pervades it at present; you look down from it upon a deep glen, through which the little river flows. The tops of the tall trees are far beneath you ; there are various plane-trees with their thick leaves. Wherever you look, it is one mass of rich foliage. Trees fill up the ravine, trees clothe the steep bank on the other side of the river, trees have rooted themselves in wonderful spots in the old walls, trees clothe the ascent that leads from the castle to that little summit near, crowned with one of the loveliest creations of the Gothic architect's skill. *That* is the chancel of a large church, of which only the chancel was ever built; and if you would behold a little chapel of inexpressible perfection and beauty, if you would discern the traces of the faithful and loving toil of men who have been for hundreds of years in

their graves, if you would look upon ancient stones that
seem as if they had grown and blossomed like a tree,
then find out where that chapel is, and go and see it.

But you pass over the bridge; and under a ruined
gateway, where part of a broken arch hangs over the
passer-by, you enter the court. On the right hand,
ruined walls of vast thickness. The like on the left
hand, but midway there is the little portion that is habi-
table. Enter: pass into a pretty large wainscotted parlor; look out of the windows on the further side. You
are a hundred feet above the garden below, — for on that
side there is below you story after story of low-browed
chambers, arched in massive stone, and lower still, the
castle wall rises from the top of a precipice of perpendicular rock. On the further side from the river, the
chambers are hewn out of the living stone. What a
view from the window of that parlor first mentioned!
Beneath, the garden, bright now with blossoming apple-
trees, bounded by the river, and, beyond the river, a
bank of wood three hundred feet in height. A little
window in a corner looks down the course of the stream;
there is a deep dell of wood, one thick luxuriance of foliage, with here and there the gleam of the flowing water.

This is our place of rest. Add to all that has been
said an inexpressible sense of a pervading quiet.

Do you find, when you come to a place where you are
to have a brief holiday, a tendency to look back on the
work you have been doing, and to estimate what it has
come to after all? And have you found, even after
many months of grinding as hard as you could, that it
was mortifying to see how little was the permanent re-

sult? Such seems to be the effect of looking back on work. One thinks of a case parallel to the present feeling. There was Jacob, looking back on a long life, on a hundred and twenty years, and saying, sincerely, that his days had been few and evil. Now, in a blink of rest, my friend, look back on the results you have accomplished in those months of hard work. You thought them many and good at the time, now they seem to be no better than few and evil. It is humiliating to think how little permanent result is got by a working day. To bring things to book, to actually count and weigh them, always makes them look less. You may remember a calculation made by the elder Disraeli, as to the amount of matter a man could read in a lifetime. It is very much less than you would have thought, — perhaps one tenth of what an ordinary person would guess. Thackeray, in his days of matured and practised power, thought it a good day's work to write six of the little pages of *Esmond*. A distinguished and experienced author told me that he esteemed three pages of the *Quarterly Review* a good day's work. Some men judge a sermon, which can be given in little more than half an hour, a sufficient result of the almost constant thought of a week. Six little pages, as the sole abiding result of a day on which the sun rose and set, and the clock went the round of the four-and-twenty hours, — on which you took your bath, and your breakfast, and read your newspaper, and in short went through the round of employments which make your habitude of being. Six pages, — skimmed by the reader in five minutes! The truth is, that a great part of our energy goes just to bear the burden of the day, to do the work of the time, and we have only the little surplus of abiding possession. The way to keep ourselves from getting mortified and disheartened when we look back on the remaining result of all our work, is to remember that we are not here merely to work, — merely to produce that which shall be an abiding memorial of us. It is well if all we do and bear is forming our nature and character into something which we can willingly take with us when we go away from this life.

This morning after breakfast I was sitting on the parapet of the bridge already mentioned, looking down upon the tops of two plane-trees, and feeling a great deal the better for the sight. I believe it does good to an ordinary mortal to look down on the top of a large tree, and see the branches gently waving about. Little outward phenomena have a wonderful effect in soothing and refreshing the mind. Some men say the sight and sound of the sea calms and cheers them. You know how when a certain old prophet was beaten and despairing, the All-wise thought it would be good for him to behold certain sublime manifestations of the power of the Almighty. We cannot explain the rationale of the process, but these things do us good. A wise and good and most laborious man told me that when he feels overworked and desponding, he flies away to Chamouni and looks at Mont Blanc, and in a few days he is set right. It was not a fanciful man who said that there is scenery in this world that would soothe even remorse. And for an ordinary person, not a great genius and not a great ruffian, give us a lofty bridge whence you may look down upon a great plane-tree.

All this, however, is a deviation. Sitting on the bridge and enjoying the scene, this thought arose: Greatly as one enjoys and delights in this, what would the feeling be if one were authoritatively commanded to remain in this beautiful place, doing nothing, for a month? And one could not but confess that the feeling would not be pleasant. The things you enjoy most intensely you enjoy for but a short time, then you are satiated. When parched with thirst, what so delightful as the first draught of fair water? But if you were compelled to drink a fourth and fifth tumbler, the water would become positively nauseous. So is it with rest. You enjoy it keenly for a little while, but constrained idleness, being prolonged, would make you miserable. Ten days here are delightful; then back, with fresh appetite and vigor, to the dear work. But a month here, thus early in the year, would be a fearful infliction. You have not earned the autumn holidays as yet.

It is in human nature, that when you feel the pressure of anything painfully, you fancy that the opposite thing would set you right. When you are extremely busy and distracted by a host of things demanding thought, you think that pure idleness would be pleasant. So, in boyhood, on a burning summer day, you thought it would be delicious to feel cold. You went to bathe in the sea, and you found it a great deal too cold.

Charles Lamb, for a great part of his life, was kept very busy at uncongenial work. Oftentimes, through those irksome hours, he thought how pleasant it would be to be set free from that work forever. So he said that if he had a son, the son should be called NOTHING TO DO, and he should do nothing. Of course, Elia

spoke only half-seriously. We know what he meant.
But, in sober earnest, we can all see that NOTHING TO
DO would have been a miserable as well as a wicked
man. He would assuredly have grown a bad fellow;
and he would just as surely have been a wretched
being.

Every one knows the story of Michael Scott and his
Familiar Spirit. Of late I have begun to understand
the meaning of that story.

Michael Scott, it is recorded, had a Familiar Spirit
under his charge. We do not know how Michael Scott
first got possession of that Spirit. Probably he raised
it, and then could not get rid of it : like the man who
begged Dr. Log to propose a toast, and then Dr. Log
spoke for three quarters of an hour. Michael Scott
had to provide employment for that being, on pain of
being torn in pieces. Michael gave the Spirit very
difficult things to do. They were done with terrible
ease and rapidity. The three peaks of the Eildon Hills
were formed in a single night. A weir was built across
the Tweed in a like time. Michael Scott was in a terrible state. In these days, he would probably have
desired the Spirit to make and lay the Atlantic Tele-
graph Cable. But a happy thought struck him. He
bade his Familiar make a rope of sea-sand. Of course,
this provided unlimited occupation. The thing could
never be finished. And the wizard was all right.

These things are an allegory. Michael Scott's Familiar Spirit is your own mind, my friend. Your own
mind demands that you find it occupation ; and if you
do not, it will make you miserable. It is an awful

thing to have nothing to do. The mill within you demands grist to grind; and if you give it none, it still grinds on, as Luther said; but it is itself it grinds and wears away. My friend Smith, having overworked his eyes at college, was once forbid to read or write for eighteen months. It was a horrible penance at first. But he devised ways of giving the machine work; and during that period of enforced idleness, he acquired the power of connected thinking without writing down each successive thought. Few people have that power. One of the rarest of all acquirements is the faculty of profitable meditation. Most human beings, when they fancy they are meditating, are in fact doing nothing at all, and thinking of nothing.

You will remember what was once said by a lively French writer, — that we commonly think of idleness as one of the beatitudes of heaven; while we ought rather to think of it as one of the miseries of hell. It was an extreme way which that writer took of testifying to the tormenting power of Michael Scott's Familiar Spirit.

And one evil in this matter is, that it is just the men who lead the most active and useful lives, who are making Michael Scott's Spirit more insatiable. You give it abundance to do; and so when work is cut off from it, it becomes rampageous. You lose the power of sitting still and doing nothing. You find it inexpressibly irksome to travel by railway for even half an hour, with nothing to read. For the most handy way of pacifying the Spirit is to give it something to read. People tell you how disgusting it was when they had to wait for three quarters of an hour for the train at some little country railway station. Michael Scott's Spirit was worrying and tormenting them, being kept without employment for that time. You know to what shifts people will have recourse, rather than have the Familiar Spirit coming and tormenting them. To give grist to the mill, to provide the Familiar Spirit with something to do, on a railway journey of twelve hours, they will read all the advertisements in their newspaper : they will go back a second and a third time over all the news ; they will even diligently peruse the leading article of the *Little Pedlington Gazette*. They read the advertisements in *Bradshaw*. They try to make out, from that publication, how to reach, by many corresponding trains, some little cross-country place to which they never intend to go. Anything rather than be idle. Anything rather than lean back, quite devoid of occupation, and feel the Familiar Spirit worrying away within, as Prometheus felt the vulture at his liver. When I hear a young fellow say of some country place where he has been spending some time, that it is a horribly slow place, that it is the deadest place on earth, I am aware that he did not find occupation there for Michael Scott's Familiar Spirit.

One looks with interest at people in whose case that Spirit seems to have been lulled into torpidity, has been brought to what a practical philosopher called *a dor-mouse state*. I read last night in a book how somebody "leant his cheek on his hand and gazed abstractedly into the fire." One who has trained the Familiar Spirit to an insatiable appetite for work can hardly believe such a thing possible. You may remember a picture in a volume of the illustrated edition of the *Waverley Novels*, which represents a plump old abbot, sitting satisfied in a large chair, with the light of the fire on his face, doing nothing, thinking of nothing, and quite tranquil and content. One sometimes thinks, Would we could do the like! That fat, stupid old abbot had led so idle a life that the muscular power of the Familiar Spirit was abated, and its craving for work gone.

When you are wearied with long work, my reader, I wish you may have a place like this to which to come and rest. How good and pleasant it is for a little while! Your cares and burdens fall off from you. How insignificant many things look to one, sitting on this green grass, or looking over this bridge down into the green dell, that worried one in the midst of duty! If you were out in a hurricane at sea, and your boat got at last into a little sheltered cove, you would be glad and thankful. But only for a short time. In a little, you would be weary of staying there. We are so made that we cannot for any length of time remain quiescent and do nothing. And we cannot live on the past. The Familiar Spirit will not chew the cud, so to speak; you must give him fresh provender to grind. Perhaps there have been days in your life which were so busy with hard work, so alive with what to you were great interests, so happy with a bewildering bliss, that you fancied you would be able to look back on them and to live in them all your life, and they would be a possession for ever. Not so. It is the present on which we must live. You can no more satisfy Michael Scott's Spirit with the remembrance of former occupations and enjoyments than you can allay your present hunger with the remembrance of beef-steaks brought you by the plump head-waiter at "The Cock," half a dozen years ago. Each day must bring its work, or the Spirit will be at you and stick pins into you.

A power of falling asleep enables one to evade the Spirit. At night, going to bed, looking for a sleepless night, how many a man has said, Oh for forgetfulness! When you have escaped into *that* realm, the Spirit can trouble you no more. You know the wish which Hood puts on the lips of Eugene Aram, tortured by an unendurable recollection, that he could shut his mind and clasp it with a clasp, as he could close his book and clasp it. Few men are more to be envied than those who have this power. Napoleon had it. So had the Duke of Wellington. At any moment either of these men could escape into a region where they were entirely free from the pressure of those anxieties which weighed them down while awake. Once the Duke, with his aide-de-camp, came galloping up to a point of the British lines whence an attack was to be made. He was told the guns would not be ready to open for two hours. "Then," said he, "we had better have a sleep." He sat down in a trench, leant his back against its side, and was fast asleep in a minute. That great man could at any time escape from Michael Scott's Spirit; could get into a country where the Spirit could not follow him. For in dreamless sleep you escape from yourself.

I have been told that there is another means of lulling that insatiable being into a state in which it ceases to be troublesome and importunate. It is tobacco. Some men say that the smoking of that fragrant weed soothes them into a perfect calm, in which they are pleasurably conscious of existing, but have no wish to do anything. Let me confess, notwithstanding, that I esteem smoking

as one of the most offensive and selfish of the lesser
sins. When I see smoke pouring out of the window
of a railway carriage not specially allotted to smokers,
I go no farther for evidence that that carriage is occupied by selfish snobs.

Young children have Michael Scott's Familiar Spirit
to find employment for, just as much as their seniors.
Who does not yet remember the horrible feeling which
you expressed when a child by saying you had *nothing
to do?* I have just heard a little thing say to his mother, "Read me a story to make the time pass quick."
That was his way of saying, "to pacify the Familiar
Spirit." And we talk of *killing Time*, as though he
were an enemy to be reduced to helplessness. There is
an offensive phrase which sets all the idea more distinctly. There are silly fellows who ask you what
o'clock it is by saying, "*How goes the enemy?*" This
phrase indeed suggests thoughts too solemn and awful
for this page. Let me ask, in a word, if Time be such,
how about Eternity? But in every such case as those
named, the enemy is not Time. It is Michael Scott's
Familiar Spirit demanding occupation. How fast Time
goes, when the Spirit is pleasantly or laboriously employed! When people talk of killing Time, they mean
knocking that strange being on the head, so to speak;
stunning it for the hour. *That* may be done, but it is
soon up again, importunate as ever.

I suppose, my reader, that you can remember times
in which the face you loved best looked its sweetest;
and tones, pleasanter than all the rest, of the voice that
was always pleasantest to hear; thoughtful looks of the

little child you seek in vain in the man in whom you lost it; and smiles of the little child that died. Touched as with the light of eternity, these things stand forth amid the years of past time; they are as the mountain tops rising over the mists of oblivion; they are the possessions which will never pass your remembrance till you cease to remember at all. And you know that Nature too has her moments of special transfiguration; times when she looks so fair and sweet that you are compelled to think that *she* would do well enough (for all the thorns and thistles of the Fall), if you could but get quit of the ever-intruding blight of sin and sorrow. Such a season is this bright morning, with its sunshine that seems to us (in our ignorance) fair and joyous enough for that place where there is no night; with its leaves green and living (would they but last) as we can picture of the Tree of Life; with its cheerful quiet that is a little foretaste of the perfect rest which shall last forever. It is very nearly time to go back to work, but we shall cherish this remembrance of the place; and so it will be green and sunshiny through winter days.

CHAPTER XI.

CONCERNING THE RIGHT TACK: WITH SOME THOUGHTS ON THE WRONG TACK.

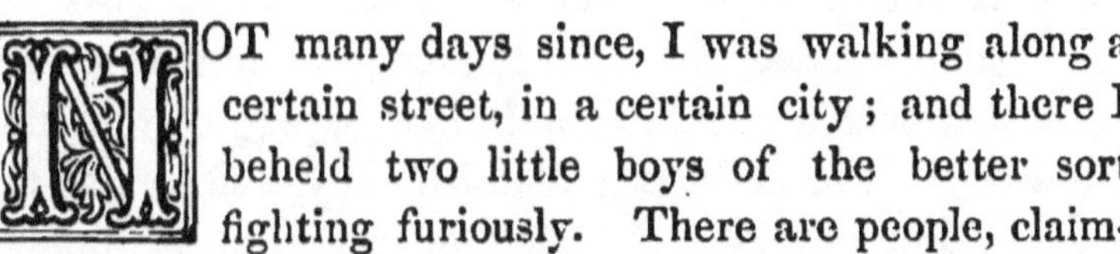

OT many days since, I was walking along a certain street, in a certain city; and there I beheld two little boys of the better sort fighting furiously. There are people, claiming to be what is vulgarly called Muscular Christians, who think that a certain amount of fighting among boys is to be very much encouraged, as a thing tending to make the little fellows manly and courageous. For myself, I believe that God's law is wise as well as right; and I do not believe that angry passion (which God's law condemns), or that vindictive efforts to do mischief to a fellow-creature (which God's law also condemns), are things which deserve to be in any way encouraged, or are things likely to develop in either man or boy the kind of character which wise and good people would wish to see. Accordingly I interposed in the fight, and sought to make peace between the little men; supporting my endeavors by some general statement to the effect that good boys ought not to be fighting in that way. They stopped at once: no doubt both had had enough of that kind of thing. For one had a bloody nose, and the other had a rudimentary black eye, which next morning would be manifest. But one of them defended himself against the charge of having done anything wrong, by saying, with the energy of one who was quite assured that he had the principles of eternal justice on his side, " I have a right to hit him, because he hit me first ! "

Of course, these were suggestive words. And I could not but think to myself, walking away from the little fellows after having composed their strife, Now *there* is the principle upon which this world goes on. There is not a deeper-rooted tendency in human nature than that which is exhibited in that saying of that fine little boy. For he *was* a fine little boy, and so was the other. The great principle on which most human beings go, in all the relations and all the doings of life, is just that which is compendiously expressed in the words, " I have a right to hit you, if you hit me first." You may trace the manifestations of that great principle in all possible walks of life, and among all sorts and conditions of men. One man or woman says something unkind of another: the other feels quite entitled to retaliate by saying something unkind of the first. And this tendency appears early. I once heard a little boy of four years old say, with some indignation of manner : " Miss Smith said I was a troublesome monkey : if she ever says *that* again, I'll say that she is an ugly old maid ! " One man says, in print, something depreciatory of another ; finds fault with something the other man has said, or written, or done. Then the other man retorts in kind : pays off the first man by publishing something depreciatory of *him*. A great many of the political essays which we read in the newspapers, and a great many of the reviews of books we meet, are manifestly dictated and inspired by the purpose to revenge some personal offence, to clear off scores by hitting the man who has hit you. A sharp, clever person reads the book written by an enemy, with the determination to pick holes in it ; not that the book is bad, or that he thinks it bad ; but its author has given him some offence, and *that* is to be retaliated. You remember, of course, that very clever and very bitter article on Mr. Croker's edition of Boswell's *Life of Johnson,* which is contained in Lord Macaulay's selection of essays from the *Edinburgh Review.* Was there any mortal who supposed that when Macaulay's own *History of England* appeared, Mr. Croker would review it otherwise than with a determination to find faults in it? Was there any mortal surprised to find that Mr. Croker, having been hit by Macaulay, endeavored to hit Macaulay again? And if Macaulay's *History* had been absolutely immaculate, had been a thousand times better than it is, do you suppose *that* would appreciably have affected the tone of Mr. Croker's review of it? I am far from saying that Mr. Croker deliberately made up his mind to do injustice to Lord Macaulay. It is likely enough he thought Macaulay richly deserved all the ill he said of him. A great law of mind governs even human beings who never came to a formal resolution of obeying it ; as a stream never pauses to consider whether, at a certain point, it shall run downhill or up. When Sir Bulwer Lytton, in his poem of *The New Timon,* alluded to Mr. Tennyson in disparaging terms as *Miss Alfred,* no one was surprised to read, in a few

days, that terribly trenchant copy of verses in which
Mr. Tennyson called Sir Bulwer a Bandbox, and showed
that the true Timon was quite a different man from the
Bandbox with his mane in curl-papers. For such is the
incongruous imagery which the reader will carry away
from that poem. And if you happen, my reader, to be
acquainted with three or four men who have opportunity
to carry on their quarrels in print, or by speeches in
deliberative assemblies, and if you refuse to take part
in the quarrels which divide them, and keep resolutely
on friendly terms with all, you will be struck by the
fact that the system of mutual hitting and retaliation,
carried on for a while, quite incapacitates these men for
doing each other anything like justice. Each will occasionally caution you against his adversary as a very
wicked and horrible person ; while you, knowing both,
are well aware that each is in the main an able and
good-hearted human being, not without some salient
faults, of course ; and that the image of each which is
present to the mind of the other is a frightful carica-
ture ; is about as like the being represented as the most
awful photograph ever taken by an ingenious youthful
amateur is like you, my good-looking friend. I have
named deliberative assemblies. Everybody knows in
how striking a fashion you will find the great principle
of retaliation exhibited in such ; and nowhere, I lament
to say, more decidedly than in presbyteries, synods, and
general assemblies, where you might naturally expect
better things. I have heard a revered friend say, that
only the imperative sense of duty would ever lead him
to such places ; and that the effect of their entire tone
upon his moral and spiritual nature was the very reverse

of healthful. One man, in a speech, says something sharp of another: of course, when the first man sits down, the second gets up, and says something unkind of his brother. And you will sometimes find men, with a calculating rancor, and with what Mr. Croker, speaking of Earl Russell, called "a spiteful slyness," wait their opportunity, that they may deal the return blow at the time and place where it will be most keenly felt. Now all this, which is bad in anybody, is more evidently bad in men who on the previous Sunday were, not improbably, preaching on the duty of forgiving injuries. All clergymen have frequent occasion to repeat certain words which run to the effect, "And forgive us our trespasses, as we forgive them that trespass against us." Yet you may find a clergyman here and there whose reputation is high as a very hard hitter, and as one who never suffers any breath of assault to pass without keenly retaliating. If you touch such a man, however distantly; if, in the midst of a general panegyric, you venture to hint that anything he has done is wrong, he will flare up, and you will have a savage reply. You know the consequence of touching *him*, just as you know the consequence of giving a kick to a ferocious bulldog. Now, is that a fine thing? Is it anything to boast of? I have heard a middle-aged man (not a clergyman) state in an ostentatious manner, that he never forgot an offence; that whoever touched him would some day (as schoolboys say) *catch it*. All this struck me as tremendously small. In the case of most people who talk in that way, it is not true. They are not nearly so bad as they would like you to think them. They don't cherish resentments in that vindictive way.

But if it were true, it would be nothing to be proud of. I have heard a man boast that he had never thanked anybody for anything all his life. I thought him very silly. He expected me to think him very great. I well remember how, in a certain senate, after two older members, each a wise and good man when you got him in his right mind, had spent some time in mutual recrimination, a younger member took occasion to point out that all this was very far from being right or pleasing. To which one of the good men replied, in a ferocious voice, and with a very red face, as if *that* answer settled the matter, "*But who began it?*" No doubt, the other *had* begun it; and that good man took refuge in the angry schoolboy's principle, "I have a right to hit him, because he hit me!"

I have been speaking, you see, of those little offences, and those little retaliations, which we have occasion to observe daily in the comparative trimness and restraint of modern life, and in a state of society where a certain Christian tone of feeling, and the strong hand of the law, limit the offences which can be commonly given, and the vengeance which can be commonly taken. My good friend A, who has been several times attacked in print by B, would probably kick B, if various social restraints did not prevent him. But, however open the way might be, I really don't believe that A would cut B's throat, or burn his house and children and other possessions. No; I don't think he would. Still, there is nothing I less like to do than to talk in a dogmatic and confident fashion. If Mr. C applies to the university of D for the honorary degree of Doctor of Music, and is refused that distinction, mainly (as C believes) through the opposition of Professor E, although C may retort upon E by a malicious article in a newspaper, containing several gross falsehoods, I really believe, and I may say I hope, and even surmise, that C, even if he had the chance, would not exactly poison E with strychnine. And I may say that I firmly believe, from the little I have seen of C's writings (by which alone I know him), that nothing would induce C to poison E, if C were entirely assured that if he poisoned E, he (C) would infallibly be detected and hanged. But we are cautious now, and, through various circumstances, our claws have been cut short. It was different long ago. Of course we all know how, in the old days, insult or injury was often wiped out in blood; how it was a step in advance even to establish the stern principle of " an eye for an eye and a tooth for a tooth, hand for hand, foot for foot, burning for burning, wound for wound, stripe for stripe." For *that* principle made sure that the retaliation should at least not exceed the first offence; while formerly, and even afterwards, where that principle was not recognized, very fanciful offences and very small injuries sometimes resulted in the quenching of many lives, in the carrying fire and sword over great tracts of country, and in the perpetuating of bloody feuds between whole tribes for age after age. You know that there have been countries and times in which revenge was organized into a scientific art; in which the terrible *vendetta*, proclaimed between families, was maintained through successive centuries, till one or the other was utterly extinguished, and a regularly kept record preserved the story how this and the other member of the proscribed race had been ruined, or imprisoned in a hopeless dungeon, or by false testimony brought within the grasp of cruel laws, or directly murdered outright by some one of the race to which was committed the task of vengeance. You know how the dying father has, with his latest breath, charged his son to devote himself to the destruction of the clan that lived beyond the hill or across the river, because of some old offence whose history was almost forgot; you know how the Campbell and the Macgregor, the Maxwell and the Johnstone, the Chattan and the Quhele — in Scotland — were hereditary. foes, and how, in many other instances, the very infant was born into his ancestors' quarrel. You have heard how a dying man, told by the minister of religion that now he must forgive every enemy as he himself hoped to be forgiven, has said to his surviving child, " Well, *I* must forgive such a one, but my curse be upon you if *you* do!" I am not going to give you an historical view, or anything like an historical view, of a miserable subject, but every reader knows well that there is not a blacker nor more deplorable page in the history of human kind than that which tells us how faithfully, how unsparingly, how bloodily, the great principle of returning evil for evil has been carried out by human beings; the great rule, not of doing to others as you would that they should do to you, but of doing to others as they have done to you, or perhaps as you think they would do to you if they had the chance; in short, the great fundamental principle of universal application, set out in the words of my little friend with the inchoate black eye, " I have a right to hit him, because he hit me first!"

Now, all this kind of thing is what I mean by THE WRONG TACK.

My friendly reader, there is another way of meeting injury and unkindness, and a better way. The natural thing, unquestionably, is to return evil for evil. The Christian thing, and the better way, is to "overcome evil with good." There was a certain Great Teacher, who was infinitely more than a Great Teacher, who taught all who should be His followers till the end of time, that the right thing would always be to meet unkindness with kindness; to forgive men their trespasses as we hope our Heavenly Father will forgive ours; to love our enemies, bless them that curse us, do good to them that hate us, and pray for them which despitefully use us and persecute us, — if such people be. And an eminent philosopher, whom some people would probably appreciate more highly if he had not been also an inspired apostle, spoke not unworthily of his Divine Master when he said, "Recompense to no man evil for evil; dearly beloved, avenge not yourselves. If thine enemy hunger, feed him; if he thirst, give him drink. Be not overcome of evil, but overcome evil with good."

Now, all this kind of thing is what I mean by THE RIGHT TACK.

There is no need at all to try formally to define what is intended by the Right Tack. Everyone knows all about it, and its meaning will become plainer as we go on. Of course, the general idea is, that we should try to meet unkindness with kindness; unfairness with fairness; a bad word with a good one. The general idea is this: Such a neighbor or acquaintance has spoken of you unhandsomely, has treated you unjustly. Well, you determine that *you* will not go and make yourself as bad as he is, and carry on the quarrel, and increase the bad feeling that already exists, by trying to retort in kind, — by saying a bad word about *him*, or by doing *him* an unfriendly turn. No, you. resolve to go upon another tack entirely. You will treat the person with scrupulous fairness. You try to think kindly of him, and to discover some excuse for his conduct towards you; and if an opportunity occurs of doing him a kind turn, you do it, frankly and heartily. Let me say, that if you try, in a fair spirit and in a kind spirit, to discover some excuse for the bad way in which that person has treated you, or spoken of you, you will seldom have much difficulty in doing so. You will easily think of some little provocation you gave him, very likely with. out in the least intending it; you will easily see that your neighbor was speaking or acting under some mis- conception or mistake; you will easily enough think of many little things in his condition — painful, mortify- ing, anxious things — which may well be taken as some excuse for worse words and doings than ever proceeded from him concerning you. Ah, my brother, most people in these days, if you did but know all their condition, all about their families and their circumstances, have so many causes of disquiet and anxiety and irritation to fever the weary heart and to shake the shaken nerves, that a wise and good man will never make them of- fenders for a hasty word, or even for an uncharitable suspicion or an unkind deed, very likely hardly said or done till it was bitterly repented. My friend Smith, who is one of the best of men, was one day startled, at- tending a meeting of a certain senatorial body, to hear Mr. Jones get up and make a speech in the nature of a most vicious attack upon Smith. Smith listened attentively to a few paragraphs, and then, turning to the man next to him, put the following question : " I say, Brown, is not that poor fellow's stomach often very much out of order ? " — " He suffers from it horribly," was the true reply. " Ah, that 's it, poor fellow," said Smith ; " I see what it is that is exacerbating his temper and making him talk in that way." And when Jones sat down, Smith got up with a kindly face, — I don't mean with a provokingly benevolent and ·forgiving look, — and in a simple, earnest way, justified the conduct which had been attacked in a manner which conveyed that he was really anxious that Jones should think well of him, — all this without the slightest complaint of Jones's bitterness, or the least reference to it. Smith had only done Jones justice in all this. He had done no more than allow for something which ought to be allowed for, and Jones was fairly beaten. After the meeting he went to Smith and asked his pardon, saying that he really had been feeling so ill that he did not know very well what he was saying. Smith shook hands with poor Jones in a way that warmed Jones's heart, and they were better friends than ever from that day forward. But in the lot of many a man there are worse things than little physical uneasinesses, for which a wise man will always allow in estimating an offence given. Yes, there are people with so much to embitter them, — poor fellows so sadly disappointed, — clever, sensitive men so terribly misplaced, so grievously tried, with their keenly sensitive nature so daily rasped, so horribly blistered by coarse, uncongenial natures and by unhappy circumstances, — that I am not afraid to say that a truly good man, if such a poor fellow pitched into him ever so bitterly, or did anything short

of hitting him over the head with a more than commonly thick stick, would do no more than beg the poor fellow's pardon.

But mind, too, my friend, that all this kindly way of
judging your fellow-creatures — all this returning of
good for evil — must be a real thing, and not a pretence. It must not be a hypocritical varnishing over of
a deep, angry, and bitter feeling within us. It must not
be something done with the purpose of putting our
neighbor still further and still more conspicuously in the
wrong. And far less must it consist in mere words with
no real meaning. Neither must it consist, as it sometimes in fact does, in saying of an offending neighbor,
"I bear him no malice; I forgive him heartily; I make
no evil return for his infamous conduct towards me";
when in truth, in the very words of forgiveness, you
have said of your offending neighbor just the very worst
you could say. You may remember certain lines which
appeared in a London newspaper several years since,
which purported to be a free translation into rhyme of a
speech made in the House of Peers by an eminent
bishop. In that speech the blameless prelate spoke of a
certain order of men whose tastes were very offensive to
him. He said they

> "... Were the vilest race
> That ever in earth or hell had place.
> He would not prejudge them: no, not he;
> For his soul o'erflowed with charity.
> Incarnate fiends, he would not condemn;
> No, God forbid he should slander them.
> Foul swine, their lordships must confess
> He used them with Christian gentleness.
> He hated all show of persecution, —
> But why were n't they sent to execution?"

I have no doubt whatever that these lines (which form part of a considerable poem) are an extreme exaggeration of what the bishop did actually say; yet I have just as little doubt that in his speech the bishop did exhibit something of that tone. For I have known human beings, not a few, who diligently endeavored to combine the forgiving of a man with the pitching into him just as hard as they conveniently could. Now, that will not do. You must make your choice. You cannot at the same time have the satisfaction of wreaking your vengeance upon one who has injured you, and likewise the magnanimous pleasure of thinking that you have Christianly forgiven him. Your returning of good for evil must be a real thing. It must be done heartily, and without reservation in your own mind, or it is nothing at all. Uriah Heep, in Mr. Dickens's beautiful story, forgave David Copperfield for striking him a blow. But Uriah Heep never did anything more vicious, more thoroughly malignant, than that hypocritical act. But it was vicious and malignant, just because it was hypocritical. In matters like this, sincerity is the touchstone.

I suppose most readers will agree with me when I say that I know no Christian duty which is so grievously neglected by people claiming to be extremely good. There is no mistake whatever as to what is the Christian way of meeting an unkindness or an unfriendly act; it is very desirable that professing Christians had more faith in its efficiency! It would be well if we could all heartily believe, and act upon the belief, that our Maker knows and advises the right and happy way of meeting a bad turn when it may be done to us, how-

ever naturally our own hearts may suggest a very different way! But I fear that our experience of life has
convinced most of us, that this duty of returning good
for evil is one that is very commonly and very thoroughly shelved. A great many people set it aside, as something all very good and proper, very fit for the Bible to
recommend, setting up (as the Bible of course ought to
do) a perfect ideal, but as something that *will not work*.
We have all a little of that feeling latent in us. And
here and there you may find a human being, perhaps a
person of an exceedingly loud and ostentatious religious
profession, who is so touchy, so ready to take offence,
and then so vindictive and unsparing in following up the
man that gave it, and in retaliating by word and deed,
— by abusive speeches and malicious writings and ill-set
demeanor generally, — that it is extremely plain that,
though that man might sympathetically shake his head
if he were told to "overcome evil with good," and accept *that* as a noble precept, still his real motto ought
rather to be that simple and compendious rule of life,
"I will hit you if you hit me!"

I am going to point out certain reasons which make
me call the rule of meeting evil with good *the Right
Tack*, and the rule of meeting evil with evil *the Wrong
Tack*. For one thing, the Right Tack is the effectual
way. What the second thing is I don't choose to tell
you till you arrive at it in the regular course of diligently reading these pages. Let there be no skipping.
So, for one thing at a time, the Right Tack is the effectual thing.

Of course, the natural impulse is to return a blow,
and to resent an injury or insult. *That* is the first thing

that we are ready to do. We do that almost instinctively, certainly with little previous reflection. And a
brute does *that* just as naturally as a man. It is nothing
to boast of that you stand on the same level as a vicious
horse, or a savage bulldog, or an angry hornet. But
then, *that* does not *overcome* the evil. No, it perpetu-
ates and increases it. It provokes a rejoinder in kind;
that provokes another, and thus the mischief grows, till
from a small offence at the beginning, vast and comprehensive sin and misery have arisen. But go on the
other tack, and you will soon see, from the little child
at play up to the worn man with his long experience of
this world, how the soft answer turns away wrath, and
the kind and good deed beats the evil. There is a beautiful little tract called *The Man that killed his Neighbors*,
which sets forth how a good man, coming to a cantankerous district, by pure force of persevering and hearty
kindness, fairly killed various unfriendly neighbors, who
met him with many unfriendly acts. He killed the
enemy; that is, he did not kill the individual man, but
the enemy was altogether annihilated, and the individual
man continued to exist as a fast friend. There is something left in average human nature even yet, which
makes it very hard indeed to go on doing ill to a man
who goes on showing kindness to you. You may get
that tract for twopence; go and pay your twopence, and
(after finishing this essay) read that tract. No doubt
there is so much that is mean and unworthy in some
hearts, and people so naturally judge others by themselves, that there may be found those who cannot understand this returning of good for evil, who will suspect
there is something wrong lurking under it, and who will

not believe that it is all sincere and hearty. And many an honest and forgiving heart has felt it as a trial to have its good intentions so misconceived. My friend Green once wrote an article in a magazine. In a certain brilliant weekly periodical there appeared a notice of that article, finding fault with it. And a week or two after, in another article in the magazine, Green, in a good-natured way, replied to the notice in the weekly periodical, and while defending himself in so far, admitted candidly that there was a good deal of truth in the strictures of the weekly periodical. Green did all that, just as bears and lions growl and fight, because it was "his nature too," it cost him no effort; and assuredly there was no hypocritical affectation in what he did. He felt no bitterness,. and so he showed none. He was amused by the clever attack upon him, and showed that he was amused. Some time after this, I read an ill-natured notice of Green in a newspaper, in which, among his other misdoings, there was reckoned up this rejoinder to the brilliant weekly periodical. He was likened to Uriah Heep, already mentioned; he was accused of hypocrisy, of arrogant humility, and the like. Of course it was manifest to all who knew Green, that his assailant knew as much about Green's character as he does about the unexplored tracts of Central Africa. But a mean-spirited man cannot even understand a generous one ; and the assailant could not find it in himself to believe that Green was a frank, honest man, writing out of the frankness of an unsuspecting heart. So, X and Y were once attacked in print by Z. X thereafter cut Z. Y remained on friendly terms with Z, as previously. Y pointed out to X that it is foolish to quarrel with a man for attacking you, even severely, upon properly critical grounds. Y further said that he would never quarrel with a man who attacked him even in the most unfair way; that he would treat the attacking party with kindness, and try to show him that his unfavorable estimate was a mistaken one. "Ah!" replied X, "you are scheming to get Z to puff you!" To meet evil with good, X plainly thought, is a thing that could not be done in good faith, and just because it is the right thing to do. There must be some underhand, unworthy motive; and the greatest obstacle that you are likely to find, in habitually meeting evil with good, will be the misconstruction of your conduct by some of the people that know you. No doubt Uriah Heep himself and all his relatives will be ready to represent that you are a humbug and a sneak. Well, it is a great pity; but you cannot help *that*. Go on still on *the Right Tack*, and by and by it will come to be understood that you go upon it in all honesty and truth, and with no sinister nor underhand purpose. And when this comes to be understood, then the evil in almost every case will be overcome, and that effectually. No human being, unless some quite exceptionally hardened reprobate, will long go on doing ill to another who only and habitually returns good for it.

This is not an essay for Sunday reading: it is meant to be quietly read over upon the evening of any day from Monday till Saturday inclusive. But that is no reason why I should not say to you, my friend, that you and I ought to bring the whole force of our Christian life and principle to bear upon this point. Let us determine that, by the help of God's Holy Spirit, without whom we can do nothing as we ought, we shall faithfully go upon the right tack through all the little ruffles and offences of daily life. If the sharp retort comes to your lips, remember that it touches the momentous question whether you are a Christian at all, or not, that you hold that sharp word back, and say a kind one. If Mr. A. or Miss B. (a poor old maid, soured a good deal by a tolerably bitter life) speak unkindly of you, or do you some little injustice, say a good word or do a good deed to either of them in return. Pray for God's grace to help you habitually to do all *that*. It will not be easy to do all *that* at the first; but it will always grow easier the longer you try it. It will grow easier, because the resolution to go on the right tack will gain strength by habit. And it will grow easier too, because when those around you know that you honestly take Christ's own way of returning an injury, not many will have the heart to injure you: very few will injure you twice. I have the firmest belief, that the true system of mental philosophy is that which is implied in the New Testament; and that there never was any one who knew so well the kind of thing that would suit the whole constitution of man, and the whole system of this universe, as He who made them both.

One case is worth many reasonings. Let me relate a true story. Not many years since there was in Mesopotamia a Christian merchant; of great wealth, and with the Right Spirit in him. A neighboring trader, who did not know much about the Christian merchant, published a calumnious pamphlet about him. The Christian merchant read it: it was very abusive and wicked and malicious. In point of style it was something like the little document which contains the articles about *Good Words* which appeared in a newspaper called *Christian Charity*. The Christian merchant, I repeat, read the pamphlet. All he said was, that the man who wrote it would be sorry for it some day. This was told the libellous trader, who replied that he would take care that the Christian merchant should never have the chance of hurting him. But men in trade cannot always decide who their creditors shall be; and in a few months the trader became a bankrupt, and the Christian merchant was his chief creditor. The poor man sought to make some arrangement that would let him work for his children again. But every one told him that this was impossible without the consent of Mr. Grant. *That* was the Christian merchant's honored name. "I need not go to *him*," the poor bankrupt said; "I can expect no favor from *him*."—"Try him," said somebody who knew the good man better. So the bankrupt went to Mr. Grant, and told his sad story of heavy losses, and of heartless work and sore anxiety and privation, and asked Mr. Grant's signature to a paper already signed by the others to whom he was indebted. "Give me the paper," said Mr. Grant, sitting down at his desk. It was given, and the good man, as he glanced over it, said, "You wrote a pamphlet about me once;" and, without waiting a reply, handed back the paper, having written something upon it. The poor bankrupt expected to find *libeller* or *slanderer*, or something like that written. But no: there it was, fair and plain, the signature that was needed to give him another chance in life. "I said you would be sorry for writing that pamphlet," the good man went on. "I did not mean it as a threat. I meant that some day you would know me better, and see that I did not deserve to be attacked in that way. And now," said the good man, "tell me all about your prospects; and especially tell me how your wife and children are faring." The poor trader told him, that to partly meet his debts he had given up everything he had in the world; and that for many days they had hardly had bread to eat. "That will never do," said the Christian merchant, putting in the poor man's hand money enough to support the pinched wife and children for many weeks. "This will last for a little, and you shall have more when it is gone; and I shall find some way to help you, and by God's blessing you will do beautifully yet. Don't lose heart: I 'll stand by you!" I suppose I need not tell you that the poor man's full heart fairly overflowed, and he went away crying like a child. Yes, the Right Tack is the effectual thing! To meet evil with good fairly beats the evil, and puts it down. The poor debtor was set on his feet again: the hungry little children were fed. And the trader never published an attack upon that good man again as long as he lived. And among the good man's multitude of friends, as he grew old among all the things that should accompany old age, there was not a truer or heartier one than the old enemy thus fairly beaten! Yes, my reader: let us go upon the Right Tack!

And now for the other reason I promised to give you why I call all this the Right Tack. It is not merely the most effectual thing; it is the happiest thing. You will feel jolly (to use a powerful and classical expression) when, in spite of strong temptation to take the other way, you resolutely go on the right tack. I suppose that when the poor trader already named went away with his full heart, feeling himself a different man from what he had been when he entered the merchant's room, and hastening home to tell his wife and children that he had found God's kind angel in the shape of a white-haired old gentleman in a snuff-colored suit, and wearing gaiters, — I suppose there would not be many happier men in this world than that truly Christian merchant prince. He was very much accustomed, indeed, to the peculiar feeling of a man who has returned good for evil; but this feeling is one which no familiarity can bring into contempt. But suppose Mr. Grant had gone on the other tack; said, "You libelled me once, it is my turn now; you shall smart for it." I don't think any of us would envy him his malignant satisfaction. And when he went home that night to his grand house, and enjoyed all the advantages which came of his great wealth, I don't think he would relish them more for thinking of the bare home where the poor debtor had gone, with his last hopes crushed, and for thinking of the little hungry children, — of little Tom sobbing himself to sleep without any supper, — of little Mary, somewhat older, saying with her thin, white face, that she did not want any. At least, if he *had* found happiness in all this, most human beings, with human hearts, would class him with devils, rather than with men. Give me Lucifer at once, with horns and hoofs, rather than the rancorous old villain in the snuff-colored suit!

It causes suffering to ordinary human beings to be

involved in strife. It is a dull, rankling pain. It has a cross-influence on all you do. And reading your Bible, and praying to God, it will often come across you with a sad sense of self-accusing. You will not be able to entirely acquit yourself of blame. You will feel that all this is not very consistent with your Christian profession, with your seasons at the communion-table, with your prayers for forgiveness as you hope to be forgiven, with the remembrance that in a little while you must lay down your weary head and die. The man who has dealt another a stinging blow in return for some injury, the man who has made an exceedingly clever and bitter retort, in speech or in writing, may feel a certain complacency, thinking how well he has done it, and what vexation he has probably caused to a fellow-sinner and fellow-sufferer. But he cannot be happy. He *cannot!* He cannot know the real glow of heart that you will feel, my reader, when God's blessed Spirit has helped you with all your heart to do something kind and good to an offending brother. Yes, it is the greatest luxury in which a human being can indulge himself, the luxury of going upon the Right Tack when you are strongly tempted to go upon the Wrong!

I must speak seriously. I cannot help it. All this is unutterably important, and I cannot leave you, my friend, with any show of lightness in speaking about it. All this is of the very essence of our religion; it goes to the great question, whether or not we are Christian people at all; it touches the very ground of our acceptance with God, and the pardon of our manifold sins. There are certain words never to be forgotten: "If ye forgive men their trespasses, your Heavenly Father will also forgive you. But if ye forgive not men their trespasses, neither will your Father forgive your trespasses." Yes, the taint of rankling malice in our hearts, when we go to God and ask for pardoning mercy, will turn our prayers into an imprecation for wrath. "Forgive us our debts, as we forgive our debtors"; forgive us our sins against Thee, just as much as we forgive other men their offences against us; that is, not at all! Think of the unforgiving man or woman who returns evil for evil going to God with *that* prayer! I cannot say how glad and thankful I should be if I thought that all this I have been writing would really influence some of those who may read this page to resolve, by God's grace, that when they are daily tempted to little resentments by little offences, — and it is only by these that most Christians in actual life are tried, — they will habitually go on the Right Tack ! But remember, my friend, that nothing you have read is more real and practical, — nothing bears more directly upon the interests of the life we are daily leading, with all its little worries, trials, and cares, — than what I say now, that it is only by the help and grace of the Holy Spirit of God that you can ever thoroughly and effectually do what I mean by going upon the Right Tack. A calm and kindly temperament is good ; a disposition to see what may be said in defence of such as offend you is good ; and doubtless these are helps, but something far more and higher is needed. There must be a loftier and more excellent inspiration than that of the calm head and the kind heart. You will never do anything rightly, never anything steadfastly, that goes against the grain of human nature, except by the grace of that Blessed One who makes us new creatures in Christ. There will be something that will not *ring sound* about all that meeting evil with good, which does not proceed from the new heart, and the right spirit sanctified of God.

Now, let there be no misunderstanding of all this, and no pushing it into an extreme opposed to common sense. All this that has been said has been said concerning the little offences of daily life. As regards these, I believe that what I have called the Right Tack is the effectual thing and the happy thing. But I am no advocate of the principle of non-resistance. I am no member of the Peace Society. I have no wish to see Britain disband her armies, and dismantle her navy, and lie as a helpless prey at the mercy of any tyrant or invader. No: I should wish our country's claws to be sharp and strong; *that* is the way to prevent the need for their use from arising. I should, with regret, but without conscientious scruple, shoot a burglar who intended to murder me. I heartily approve the blowing of a rebel sepoy away from a cannon. And though the punishment of death, as inflicted in this country, is a miserable necessity, still I believe it is a necessity, and a thing morally right, in almost every case in which it is inflicted. All that has been said about the returning of good for evil is to be read in the light of common sense. There are bad people whom you cannot tame or put down, except by the severe hand of Justice. And in taming them in the only possible way you are doing nothing inconsistent with the views set forth in these pages. It would take too much time to argue the matter fully out; and it is really needless. A wrongheaded man, a member of the Peace Society, has published a pamphlet in which he frankly tells us that if he and his wife and children were about to be murdered by a burglar, and if there was no possibility of preventing this murdering except by killing the burglar, then it would be the duty of a Christian to die as a martyr to his principles, and peaceably allow the burglar to murder him and his family. Really there is nothing to be said in reply to such a puzzle-head, except that I would just as soon believe that black is white as that *that* is a Christian duty. There are exceptional human beings who are really wild beasts, and who must be treated precisely as a savage wild beast should be treated. And even in the matter of injuries of a less decided character than the murdering of yourself, your wife, and children, it is as plain as need be that a wise and good man may very fitly defend himself against the aggression of a ruffian. When Mr. Macpherson threatened to thrash Dr. Johnson for expressing doubts as to the genuineness of Ossian, Dr. Johnson was quite right to provide a stick of great size and weight, and to carry it about with him for the purpose of self-defence. And while desirous to obey the spirit of the Saviour's command, there are few things of which I feel more certain, than that if a blackguard struck my good friend Dr. A on the right cheek, the blameless divine would not turn the other also. Nor need we make the least objection to the motto of a certain Northern country, which conveys that people had better be careful how they do that country any wrong, inasmuch as that country won't stand it. There is nothing amiss in the "*Nemo me impune lacesset.*" Don't meddle with us; we have not the least wish to meddle with you.

CHAPTER XII.

CONCERNING NEEDLESS FEARS.

AT the present moment I feel very uncomfortable ; not physically, but mentally and morally. And I do not know why. What I mean is, that a little ago some disagreeable thought was presented to my mind which put me quite out of sorts. And though I have forgot what the disagreeable thought was, its effect remains, and I still feel out of sorts. I am aware of a certain moral aching which I cannot refer to its cause. I suppose, my reader, you have often felt the like. You have been conscious of a certain gloom, depression, bewilderment, — not remembering what it was that started it. But after a little time it suddenly flashes on you, and you remember the whole thing.

I can imagine a man going to be hanged, waking up on the fatal morning with a dull aching sense of something wrong, he does not know what, till all at once the dreadful reality glares upon him. Some of us have had the experience, as little boys, when coming back to consciousness on the morning of the day we had to return to school, far away from home. In certain cases, returning to school is to a boy not many degrees less unendurable than being hanged is to a man. Of course there is no remorse in the case of the little schoolboy, and here is a discrepance between the cases suggested. But indeed it is vain to estimate the relative crushing powers of two great trials. Each at the time is just as much as one can bear.

But (to go back a little) just as a strong hand, seven hundred years since, set a large stone in its place in a cathedral wall, and the stone remains there to-day, though the hand that placed it is gone and forgot, in like manner some painful reflection jars the human mind and puts it out of joint, and it remains jarred and out of joint after the painful reflection has passed away. A cloud passes between us and the sun, and a sudden gloom and chill fall upon all things. But, strange to say, in the moral world, after the cloud that brought the gloom and chill has passed, the gloom and chill remain. And thus a human being may feel very uncomfortable, and know that he has good reason for being uncomfortable, yet not know what the reason is. If you receive ten letters before breakfast, you open them all and read them hastily. It is very likely that one of the ten contains some rather disagreeable communication. You forget, in a minute, as you skim the newspaper and take your breakfast, what that disagreeable communication was; yet still you take your breakfast with a certain weight upon your spirits, with a certain vague sense of something amiss.

What is it that is wrong this Saturday evening at 9.10 p. m.? Nothing is wrong physically. Too thankful would this writer be if he could but be assured that on all the Saturday evenings of his life he would be as happily placed as he is now. To-morrow he is to preach at his own church, and during the week all but gone he hath prepared two new discourses to be preached on that day. Indurated must be that man's conscience, or very lightly must that man take his work, who does not feel a certain glow of satisfaction on the Saturday evening of a week wherein he has prepared two new discourses. You remark, I don't say two new sermons. No sensible mortal can prepare, or would try to prepare, two new sermons in one week. But he may prepare one sermon and one lecture, which (being added one to the other) will be found to amount to two discourses. But any one who knows the long and hard work which goes to the production of a sermon which people may be expected to listen to, will feel, as he sews up his manuscript, the peculiar satisfaction which attends the contemplation of " something attempted, something done."

Yes, I remember now. Something I thought of this morning has come with me all the day, making me feel gloomy even while forgetting what it was. You know how a severe sting from a nettle leaves behind it a certain starting pain, hours after the first heat of the sting is gone. So it was here. And in this, too, is a point of difference between the material and moral world. In the material world, if a table stands on three legs, and you in succession saw off the three legs, the table goes down. But in the moral world (especially in the case of old women), if a belief or a feeling founds upon three reasons (or legs), though you in succession take away those reasons, the table often still stands as before.

The physical table cannot do without legs. The moral table often stands firmest when it has no legs whatever. The beliefs which men often hold most resolutely are those for which not merely they can give no reason, but for which no reason could be given by anybody.

I was thinking of the fears which eat the heart out of so many lives. And this was my reflection.

When I was a boy, there was exhibited in London what was called a Centrifugal Railway. Let me request you earnestly to attend to the subjoined diagram.

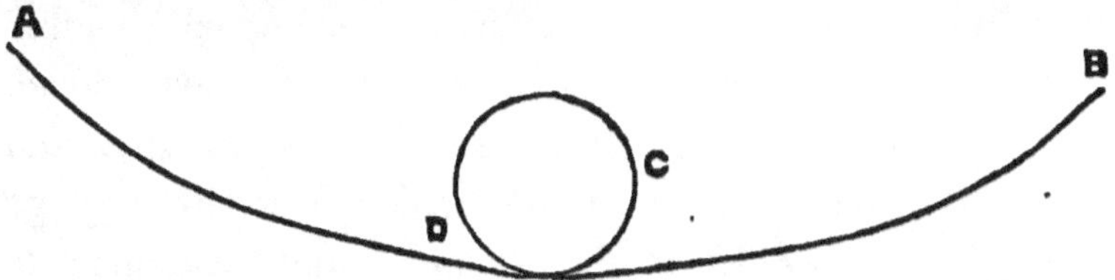

The line A D C B represents the Centrifugal Railway. You started from the point A in a little carriage. It acquired a very great velocity in running down the descent from A to D; a velocity so great that it ran right round the circle C, turning the passenger with his head downwards, and finally got safely to B. At the point B the passenger got out, and if he were a person of sense (which, under the circumstances, was by no means probable), he resolved never to travel by the Centrifugal Railway any more.

Now, you observe that in turning the circle C the passenger was in a very critical position. He had good reason to be thankful when the circle was fairly turned, and he had, with unbroken bones, reached B. And it struck me, that all our life here is like the circle C on the Centrifugal Railway. I shall be able to think differently in a day or two, more hopefully and cheerfully;

but it was borne in upon me that after all, my friends, we are doing no more in this life than getting round the circle C; and that there are so many risks in the way, that we may be very glad and thankful when it is done. He was a wise man in former days who said (let me translate his words into my peculiar idiom), "I call no man happy before he has got round the circle C." And desponding times will come to all, in which they will think of the innumerable sad possibilities which hang over them, and the sorrowful certainties which are daily drawing nearer, and the dangers of getting off the line altogether and going to destruction. I look ahead, many a one will sometimes be disposed to say, and there are many, many things which I know may go wrong. O, I would be thankful if I and those dear to me were safely round the circle C, and had got safely to the point B; even though some people shrink from that latter point as long as they possibly can.

Of course, this is a gloomy kind of view; but such views will sometimes push themselves upon one, and will not be put off. I hope it will go away shortly. It will go away all the sooner for my having made you partaker of it. I have in my mind an abstract eidolon, an image of the reader of this page, who is my confidential friend. To him I have told very many things which I have hardly ever told to any one else. And I want him to take his share of this vexatious view about the circle C, that so it may lie lighter on myself. All this life, of push, struggle, privation, trickery, getting on, failure; all this life, in which one man becomes chancellor, and another prime minister, and another a weary careworn drudge, and another a self-satisfied blockhead, and another a poor needlewoman laboring eighteen hours a day for a few pence ; all this life, of kings and priests and statesmen, of cripples and beggars, of joyful hearts and sorrowful hearts, of scheming and working, as if there were no other world, — is no more than our getting round the circle C. We are cast on that incline that begins from A, at our birth ; and our business is to get safely to B.

Every day that dawns upon many people is a little circle C. In the morning they are aware that various things may go wrong in it ; and of course they do not know what the day may bring forth. We are environed by many unknown dangers ; and any day we may say the hasty word, or do the foolish thing, which may involve us in great trouble. Even the most sagacious and prudent man may some day be taken off his guard. And the accidents which may befall us are quite innumerable. It is a wonder we have got on so far in life as we have, so little battered by the chances of the way. You know some one who went out from his own home on a frosty day, and in three minutes came back pale and fainting, having fallen and fractured his wrist. The pain was great ; and the seclusion from work was absolute for a while. What could we do if the like happened to us ? Some one else thought but one step of a stair remained for him to descend, while in fact there were two ; and the consequences of that misapprehension remained with him painfully to the end of his life. And thus, looking back on last year, one feels it was a most protracted and perilous circle C. It was made up of days, each of which might have brought we know not what with it. We have got

10 *   o

safely round that circle, indeed ; but at the beginning
we were not sure that we should. If we could have had
such an assurance it would have spared us many fears.
These fears are for the most part forgot when we look
back, and feel how needless they were. But they were
very real things at the time they were felt, and they
were a terrible drawback from the pleasures of anticipation and of actual fact. When you look back on a few
weeks or months of foreign travel, the whole thing has
a fixed and certain look, — the thing that has been is a
thing for ever. But what a shifting tract of shadows it
was when you were looking forward to it, and a tract
not without several alarming spectres vaguely stalking
about over it. Now we know that we got safely back,
but when we started we did not know that we should.
It was like leaving the point A, and flying round the
circle C ; whereas now we have reached the point B,
and we have forgot our emotions in actually flying round
the circle.

Two or three days ago, three friends of the writer sailed
from Southampton, on their way to Egypt and the Holy
Land. They are to be away three months. They are
experienced travellers, and have seen very many cities
and men, and doubtless they started with no feelings but
those of pleasurable anticipation. When I heard of
their going my first feeling was one of envy. How delightful to cast aside all this perpetual toil that overtasks
one's strength, and keeps one ever on the stretch, and
have three months for the mind to regain its elasticity,
much diminished by its being kept always bent! And
then, what strange, unfelt moods of thought and feeling
one would experience when surrounded by the scenes

and associations of those tracts of this world! You would accumulate store of new ideas and remembrances; and in the first sermons and essays you would write after returning, you would be (in a moral sense) curveting about like a young colt in a pasture, and not plodding like an old steady hack along the highway! But when I tried to put myself (in fancy) in the place of my friends; when I thought of the long, unknown way, and of the unsettled tribes of men; when I thought of Mr. Buckle at Damascus; when I thought of possible fevers and of most certain bugs; when I thought how when human beings go to the East for three months, they may chance never to come back at all, — then to a quiet, stay-at-home person, who has seen hardly anything, the circle C appeared invested with many grounds of alarm; and I was reconciled to the fact that I was not stepping on board the *Ellora* amid a great roar of escaping steam, nor going down to the choky little berth, and surveying my belongings there. Thus did I repress the rising envy in my breast. But when my friends come back again, portentous images with huge beards; when they have made the Nile, and Olivet, and Gethsemane, and the Dead Sea, a possession for as long as memory serves them; when they have got fairly and triumphantly round the circle C, and happily reached the point of safety B, — then, I fear, the envious feeling will recur.

O, if we could but get quit of our needless fears! Of those fears (that is) which take so much from the enjoyment of life, and which the result proves to have been quite groundless!

Some folk, with very robust nervous systems, probably know but little of these. But from large experience of my fellow-creatures, rich and poor, and from careful investigation of their features, I begin to conclude that such fears are very common things. Most middle-aged faces have an anxious look. You can see, even when they bear a cheerful expression, that they are capable in a moment of taking that painful aspect of anxiety and apprehension. I do not mean by fear the indulgence of physical cowardice; happily few of the race that inhabits Britain will, on emergency, prove deficient in physical pluck. But I mean that most middle-aged people, who have children, are somewhat cowed by the unknown Future; and that the too ready imagination can picture out a hundred things that may go wrong. *Anxius vixi*, wrote the man in the Middle Ages; and anxious we live yet, and probably always will live, in this world.

If you go out in the dark expecting to see a ghost, you will very likely take a white sheet hung on a hedge for one. And even so, people in their feverish state of apprehension sometimes are dreadfully frightened by things which in a calmer mood they would discern had nothing alarming about them. Every one is sharp enough to see this in the case of other people. You will find a man who will say to you, " What a goose Smith is to worry himself about that table-cloth on the holly, and declare it is an apparition, and that it has bad news for him"; and in a few minutes you will be aware that the man who says all this is furtively looking over his shoulder at a white donkey feeding under a thick hedge, and dreading that it is a polar bear about to devour him.

It is curious to think how often these needless fears,

which cause so much unnecessary anxiety and misery, are the result of pure miscalculation, and this miscalculation not made in a hurry, but deliberately. I have a friend who told me this:—When he was married, he had exactly £ 500 a year, and no means of adding to that income. So as he could not increase his income, his business was to keep down his expenditure below it. But neither he nor his wife knew much about household management; and (as he afterwards found) he was a good deal victimized by his servants. After doing all he could to economize, he found, at the end of the third month of his financial year, that he had spent exactly £ 125. Four times £ 125, he calculated, made £ 600 a year, which was just £ 100 more than he had got; so the debtor's prison appeared to loom in view, or some total change in his mode of life, which it seemed almost impossible for him to make, without very painful circumstances; and, for weeks, the thought almost drove him distracted. Day and night it never was absent. At length, one day, brooding over his prospects, he suddenly discovered that four times 125 make just 500, and not 600; so that all his fears were groundless. He was relieved, he told me; but somehow his heart had been so burdened and sunk by those anxious weeks, that though the cause of anxiety was removed, it was a long time before it seemed to recover its spring.

Now my friend had all his wits about him. There was nothing whatever of that causeless delusion which shades off into insanity. But somehow he thought that $125 \times 4 = 600$; and his conclusion was that ruin stared him in the face.

I have heard of a more touching case. A certain

man brought to a friend a sum of money, rather less than a hundred pounds, and asked the friend to keep it for him. He said it was all he had in the world, and that he did not know what he was to do when it was gone. He had been a quite rich man; but one of those swindling institutions whose directors ought to be hung, and are not, had involved him in great money responsibilities by its downfall. In a few days after leaving the money with his friend, the poor man committed suicide. Then his affairs were examined by competent persons; and it was found that after meeting all possible liabilities, he had been worth several hundreds a year. But the poor fellow had miscalculated; and here was the tragic consequence.

No doubt, he had been so terribly apprehensive, that he had been afraid to make a thorough examination as to how his affairs stood. Human beings often undergo much needless fear, because they are afraid to search out all the facts. For fear of finding the fact worse than they fear, they often fear what is much worse than the fact. They go on through life thinking they have seen a ghost, and miserable in the thought; whereas, if they had but screwed their courage to the point of examining, they would have found it was no more than a table-cloth drying upon a line between two poles. O, that we could all, forever, get rid of this moral cowardice! If you think there is something the matter with your heart, go to the doctor and let him examine. Probably there is nothing earthly wrong. And even if there be, it is better to know the worst than live on week after week in a vague, wretched fear. Let us do the like with our affairs. Let us do the like with our religious difficulties, with our theological perplexities. The very worst thing you can do is to lock the closet door when you think probably there is a skeleton within. Fling it wide open; search with a paraffin lamp into every corner. A hundred to one, there is no skeleton there at all. But from youth to age, we must be battling with the dastardly tendency to walk away from the white donkey in the shadow, which we ought to walk up to. I have seen a little child, who had cut her finger, entreat that it might just be tied up, without ever being looked at; she was afraid to look at it. But when it *was* looked at, and washed and sorted, she saw how little a thing it was for all the blood that came from it; and about nine-tenths of her fear fled away.

You have heard of Mr. Elwes, the wealthy miser, frightening a guest by walking into his bedroom during the night, and saying, " Sir, I have just been robbed of seven guineas and a half, which was all I had in the world!" Here, of course, we enter the domain of proper insanity. For the fears which a man of vast fortune has lest he may die in the workhouse belong essentially to the same class with those of the man who thinks he is glass, and that if he falls he will break; or who thinks he is butter, and if he goes near the fire he will melt. And though all needless fears are morbid things, which the healthy mind would shake off, yet there is a vast distance between the morbid apprehensions and the morbid depressions of the practically sane man, and the phenomena of the mind which is truly insane.

The truth seems to be, that some people must have a

certain amount of misery; and it will attach itself to any peg. If not to this, then to another; but the misery is *due*. And I defy you by any means to lift such people above the slough of their apprehensions. As you remove each cause of alarm, they will fix upon another. First, they fear that their means will not carry them from year's end to year's end. *That* fear proves groundless. Next they fear that though their present income is ample, somehow it will fall off. *That* fear proves groundless. Next, they are in dread as to the provision for their children; and here, doubtless, most men can find a cause of anxiety that will last them through all their life. But it is their nature to be always imagining something horrible. They live in dread that they may quarrel with some friend, or that some general crash will come some day, they don't know how. And if all other causes of apprehension were absolutely removed, they would make themselves wretched to a suitable degree by fearing lest an earthquake should swallow up Great Britain, or that Dr. Cumming's calculations as to the end of the world may prove true. In short, if a human being be of a nervous, anxious temperament, it is as certain that such a human being will find some peg to hang his fears upon, as it is that a man, who is the possessor of a hat, will find something, wherever he goes, to hang it or lay it upon.

All this seems to be especially true in the case of people who have been heavily tried in youth. Human beings may be subjected to a treatment in their early years that seems to take the hopeful spring out of them. Unless where there is very unusual stamina of mind and body, they never quite get over it. You may damage a man so that he will never quite get over it, — you may give the youthful mind a wrench whose evil effect will cling to it through all life. There are things in the moral world which are like an injury to the spine, — never recovered from; but that grows and strengthens with the man's growth and strength; and no good fortune, no happiness coming afterwards, can ever make amends. The evil has been done, and it cannot be undone.

You have beheld a horse, no more than six years of age, but which is dull and spiritless, and its forelegs somewhat bent and shaky. Why are these things so? It has easy work now, good feeding, kind usage. Yes, but it was driven when too young. It was set to hard work then, and the creature never has got over it and never will. It is too late for any kindness now to make up for the mischief done at three years old.

I am firmly persuaded it is so with many human beings. They had an unhappy home as little boys, the love of the beautiful in nature and art was starved out in them. They were committed to the care of a self-conceited person, utterly devoid of common sense. All mirth was forbidden as something sinful. Life was made hard and savorless. They grew up under a bitter sense of injustice and oppression, and with the conviction that they were hopelessly misunderstood. Or, later, the weight of care came down upon them very heavily. There are many people who, for most of the years between twenty and thirty, never know what a light heart is. And by such things as these the spring of the spirit is broken. A dogged steadfastness of purpose may remain, but the elasticity is gone. The writer has no knowledge of Mr. Thackeray's character and career except from the accounts of these which have been published since his death by some who knew him well. But it is strongly impressed on one in reading these, that, amid all the success and fame and love of his latter years, a certain tone of melancholy remained, testifying that former days of unappreciated toil, of care, and anxiety, had left a trace that never could go. It is only of a limited and exceptional order of troubles that the memorable words can be spoken with any shade of truth: *Forsan et hæc olim meminisse juvabit.* I do not believe that the memory of pure misery can ever be other than a miserable thing.

If this were a sermon, I should now go on to set forth, at full length, what I esteem to be the best and worthiest means of getting free from those needless fears of which we have been thinking. But in this essay, I pass these briefly by for the present; and proceed to suggest a lesser cure for needless anxiety, which is not without its wholesome effect on some minds.

I believe that when you are worrying yourself by imagining all kinds of evils as likely to befall you, it will do you a great deal of good to be allowed to see something of other people who are always expecting something awful to happen, and with a morbid ingenuity devising ways of making themselves miserable. You will discern how ridiculous such people look; how irritating they are; how, so far from exciting sympathy, they excite indignation. The Spartans were right to make their slaves drunk, and thus to cure their children of the least tendency to the vice of drunkenness, by letting them see how ugly it looks in another. I

request Mr. Snarling to take notice, that when I say the
Spartans were right in doing this, I don't mean to say
that they did an act which is in a moral sense to be
commended or justified. All I mean is, that they took
a very effectual means to compass the end they had in
view. You never feel the badness of your own faults
so keenly as when you see them carried a little further
in somebody else. And so a human being, naturally
very nervous and evil-foreboding, is corrected, when he
sees how absurd it looks in another. My friend Jones
told me, that, after several months of extremely hard
head-work, which had lowered his nervous system, he
found himself getting into a way of vaguely dreading
what might come next, and of receiving his letters in
the morning with many anticipations of evil. But happily a friend came to visit him, who carried all this
about a hundred degrees further, who had come through
all his life expecting at least an earthquake daily, if not
the end of the world. And Jones was set right. In
the words of Wordsworth, " He looked upon him, and
was calmed and cheered." Jones saw how like a fool
his friend seemed; and there came a healthy reaction;
and he opened his letter-box bravely every morning,
and was all right again. Yes, let us see the Helot
drunk, and it will teach us to keep sober. My friend
Gray told me that for some little space he felt a growing tendency to scrubbiness in money matters. But
having witnessed pinching and paring (without the least
need for them) carried to a transcendent degree by
some one else, the very name of economy was made to
stink in his nostrils; and he felt a mad desire to pitch
half-crowns about the streets wherever he went. In

this case the reaction went too far; but in a week or two Gray came back to the middle course, which is the safest and best.

But, after all, the right and true way of escaping from what Dr. Newman has so happily called "care's unthankful gloom," and of casting off needless fears, lies in a different direction altogether. It was wise advice of Sidney Smith, when he said that those who desire to go hopefully and cheerfully through their work in this life should "take short views"; not plan too far ahead; take the present blessing and be thankful for it. It was indeed the best of all possible advice; for it was but a repetition, in another form, of the counsel of the Kindest and Wisest, "Take, therefore, no thought for the morrow, for the morrow shall take thought for the things of itself: Sufficient unto the day is the evil thereof." There is no doubt whatever that the true origin of all these forebodings of evil is our lack of trust in God. We all bear a far greater burden of anxiety than we need bear, just because we *will* try to bear our burden for ourselves, instead of casting it on a stronger arm. We try to provide for our children and ourselves, forgetting the sure promise to all humble Christian people, that "the Lord will provide." And when we seek to cast off our load of care by the help of those comfortable words of Holy Scripture which invite us to trust everything to God, we try too much to reason ourselves into the assurance that we need not be so care-laden as we are. We forget that the only way in which it is possible for us to believe these words in our heart, and to take the comfort of them, is by heartily asking God that they may be carried home to us with the irresistible demonstration of the Holy Spirit. How the circle C would lose its fears, if we did but feel, by His gracious teaching, that it is the way which God designed for us, and that He will "keep us in all our ways!" Whenever I see man or woman, early old with anxiety, and with a face deeply lined with care, I think of certain words which deserve infinitely better than to be printed in letters of gold, and I wish that such a one, and that all I care for, were numbered among the people who have a right to take these words for their own:—

"Be careful for nothing; but in everything, by prayer and supplication, with thanksgiving, let your requests be made known unto God. And the peace of God, which passeth all understanding, shall keep your hearts and minds through Christ Jesus."

CHAPTER XIII.

BEATEN.

O you know this peculiar feeling? I speak to men in middle age.

To be bearing up as manfully as you can; putting a good face on things; trying to persuade yourself that you have done very fairly in life after all; and all of a sudden to feel that merciful self-deception fail you, and just to break down; to own how bitterly beaten and disappointed you are, and what a sad and wretched failure you have made of life?

There is no one in the world we all try so hard to cheat and delude as ourself. How we hoodwink that individual, and try to make him look at things through rose-colored spectacles! Like the poor little girl in Mr. Dickens's touching story, we *make believe very much*. But sometimes we are not able to make believe. The illusion goes. The bare, unvarnished truth forces itself upon us, and we see what miserable little wretches we are; how poor and petty are our ends in life, and what a dull weary round it all is. You remember the poor old half-pay officer, of whom Charles Lamb tells us. *He* was not to be disillusioned. He asked you to hand him the silver sugar-tongs in so confident a tone, that though your eyes testified that it was but a tea-spoon, and that of Britannia metal, a certain spell was cast over your mind. But rely on it, though that half-starved veteran kept up in this way before people, he would often break down when he was alone. It would suddenly rush upon him what a wretched old humbug he was.

Is it sometimes so with all of us? We are none of us half-satisfied with ourselves. We know we are poor creatures, though we try to persuade ourselves that we are tolerably good. At least, if we have any sense, this is so. Yet I greatly envied a man whom I passed in the street yesterday; a stranger, a middle-aged person. His nose was elevated in the air; he had a supercilious demeanor, expressive of superiority to his fellow-creatures, and contempt for them. Perhaps he was a prince, and so entitled to look down on ordinary folk. Perhaps he was a bagman. The few princes I have ever seen had nothing of his uplifted aspect. But what a fine thing it would be to be able always to delude yourself with the belief that you are a great and impor-tant person; to be always quite satisfied with yourself and your position. There are people who, while repeat-ing certain words in the litany, feel as if it was a mere form, signifying nothing, to call themselves *miserable sin-ners*. There are some who say these words sorrowfully from their very heart, feeling that they express God's truth. They know what weak, silly, sinful beings they are; they know what a poor thing they have made of life, with all their hard work, and all their planning and scheming. In fact, they feel beaten, disappointed, down. The high hopes with which they started are blighted; were blighted long ago. They think, with a bitter laugh, of their early dreams of eminence, of success, of happiness; and sometimes, after holding up for a while as well as they could, they feel they can do it no longer. Their heart fails them. They sit down and give up altogether. Great men and good men have done it. It is a comfort to many a poor fellow to think of Elijah, beaten and sick at heart, sitting down under a scrubby bush at evening far in the bare desert, and feeling there was no more left, and that he could bear no more. Thank God that the verse is in the Bible.

" But he himself went a day's journey into the wilderness, and came and sat down under a juniper-tree; and he requested for himself that he might die, and said, It is enough: now, O Lord, take away my life, for I am not better than my fathers."

I thought of Elijah in the wilderness the other night. I saw the great prophet again. For human nature is the same in a great prophet as in a poor little hungry boy.

At nine o'clock on Saturday evening, I heard pitiful, subdued sobs and crying outside. I know the kind of thing that means some one fairly beaten: not angry, not bitter; smashed. I opened the front door, and found a little boy, ten years old, sitting on the steps, crying. I asked him what was the matter. I see the thin, white, hungry, dirty little face. He would have slunk away, if he could: he plainly thought his case beyond all mending. But I brought him in, and set him on a chair in the lobby, and he told his story. He had a large bundle of sticks in a ragged sack,—firewood. At three o'clock that afternoon, he had come out to sell them. His mother was a poor washerwoman, in the most wretched part of the town: his father was killed a fortnight ago by falling from a scaffold. He had walked a long way through the streets: about three miles. He had tried all the afternoon to sell his sticks, but had sold only a halfpenny worth. He was lame, poor little man, from a sore leg, but managed to carry his heavy load. But at last, going down some poor area stair in the dark, he fell down a whole flight of steps, and hurt his sore leg so that he could not walk, and also got a great cut on the forehead. He had got just the half-penny for his poor mother: he had been going about with his burden for six hours, with nothing to eat. But he turned his face homewards, carrying his sticks, and struggled on about a quarter of a mile, and then he broke down. He could go no farther. In the dark cold night he sat down and cried. It was not the cry-ing of one who hoped to attract attention: it was the crying of flat despair.

The first thing I did (which did not take a moment) was to thank God that my door-steps had been his juni-per-tree. Then I remembered that the first thing God did when Elijah broke down was to give him something to eat. Yes, it is a great thing to keep up physical nature. And the little man had had no food since three o'clock till nine. So there came, brought by kind hands (not mine), several great slices of bread and butter (jam even was added), and a cup of warm tea. The spirit began to come a little into the child; and he thought he could manage to get home, if we would let him leave his sticks till Monday. We asked him what

he would have got for his sticks if he had sold them all :
ninepence. Under the circumstances, it appeared that
a profit of a hundred per cent was not exorbitant, so he
received eighteen pence, which he stowed away somewhere in his rags, and the sack went away, and returned with all the sticks emptied out. Finally, an old
gray coat of rough tweed came, and was put upon the
little boy, and carefully buttoned, forming a capital great
coat. And forasmuch as his trowsers were most unusu-
ally ragged, a pair of such appeared, and being wrapped
up were placed in the sack along with a good deal of
bread and butter. How the heart of the child had by
this time revived! He thought he could go home
nicely. And having very briefly asked the Father of
the fatherless to care for him, I beheld him limp away
in the dark. All this is supremely little to talk about.
But it was quite a different thing to see. To look at
the poor starved little face, and the dirty hand like a
claw ; to think of ten years old ; to think of one's own
children in their warm beds ; to think what all this would
have been to one's self as a little child. O, if I had a
four-leaved shamrock, what a turn-over there should be
in this world !

When the little man went away, I came back to my
work. I took up my pen, and tried to write, but I could
not. I thought I saw many human beings besides
Elijah in the case of that child. I tried to enter into
the feeling (it was only too easy) of that poor little
thing in his utter despair. It was sad enough to carry
about the heavy bundle hour after hour, and to sell only
the halfpenny worth. But it was dreadful, after tumbling down the stair, to find he was not able to walk ;

and still to be struggling to carry back his load to his bare home, which was two miles distant from this spot. And at last to sit down in misery on the step in the dark night, stunned. He would have been quite happy if he had got ninepence, God help him. When I was a boy, I remember how a certain person who embittered my life in those days was wont to say, as though it summed up all the virtues, that such a person was a man who looked at both sides of a shilling before spending it. It is such a sight as the little boy on the step that makes one do the like, that helps one to understand the power there is in a shilling. But many human beings, who can give a shilling rather than take it, are as really beaten as the little boy. They too have got their bags, filled with no matter what. Perhaps poetry, perhaps metaphysics, perhaps magazine articles, perhaps sermons. They thought they would find a market, and sell these at a great profit, but they found none. They have fallen down a stair, and broken their leg and bruised their head. And now, in a moral sense, they have sat down in the dark on a step, and, though not crying, are gazing about them blankly.

Perhaps you are one of them.

CHAPTER XIV.

GOSSIP.

HO invents the current lies? I suppose a multitude of people give each their little contribution, till the piece of malignant tattle is formed into shape.

There are many people, claiming to be very religious people, who are very willing to repeat a story to the prejudice of some one they know, though they have very little reason to think it true, and have strong suspicions that it is false. There is a lesser number of respectable people, who will positively invent and retail a story to the prejudice of some one they know, being well aware that it is false. In short, most people who repeat ill-natured stories may be arranged in these two classes:—

1. People who lie.

2. People who lie, and know they lie.

The intelligent reader is requested to look upon the words which follow, and then he will be informed about a malicious, vulgar, and horribly stupid piece of gossip:—

Mr. and Mrs. Green

always

Dress for Dinner.

My friend Mr. Green lately told me, that quite by accident he found that in the little country town where he lives, and of which indeed he is the vicar, it had come to be generally reported that in every bedroom in his house a framed and glazed placard was hung above the mantelpiece, bearing the above inscription. Miss Tarte and Mr. Fatuous had eagerly disseminated the rumor, though it was impossible to say who had originated it. Probably Miss Tarte had one day said to Mr. Fatuous that Mr. Green ought to have such a placard so exhibited, and that some day Mr. Green probably would come to have such a placard so exhibited. A few days afterwards Mr. Fatuous said to Miss Tarte that he supposed Mr. Green must have his placards up by this time. And next day, on the strength of that statement, Miss Tarte told a good many people that the placards were actually up. And the statement was willingly received and eagerly repeated by those persons in that town who are always delighted to have something to tell which shows that any one they know has done something silly or bad. At last a friend of Mr. Green's thought it right he should know what Mr. Fatuous and Miss Tarte were saying. And Mr. Green, who is a resolute person, took means to cut these individuals short. My friend has exactly one spare bedroom in his house, and no one who is not an idiot need be told that no such inscription was ever displayed or ever dreamt of in his establishment. Next Sunday Mr. Green preached a sermon from the text, *Thou shalt not bear false witness against thy neighbor.* And after pointing out that it was unnecessary that the commandment should forbid false witness to the advantage of one's neighbor, inasmuch as nobody was likely ever to bear *that,* he went on to point out, with great force of argument, that if man or woman habitually told lies to the prejudice of their neighbors, their Christian character might justly be held as an imperfect one, even though they should attend all the week-day services and missionary society meetings within several miles. Mr. Fatuous and Miss Tarte complained that this was very unsound doctrine. And Miss Tarte wrote a letter to the *Record,* in which she stated that the vicar habitually preached the doctrines of Bishop Colenso.

One is most unwilling to believe it, yet I am compelled by the logic of facts to think that malice towards all their fellow-creatures is an essential part of the constitution of many people. All the particles of matter, we know, exert on each other a mutual repulsion. Is it so with the atoms that make up human society? Many people dislike a man just because they know nothing about him. And when they come to know something about him, they are sure to dislike him even more. In a simple state of society, if you disliked a man you would knock him on the head. If an Irishman, you would shoot him from behind a hedge. The modern civilized means of wreaking your wrath on the man you dislike is different. You repeat tattle to his prejudice. You tell lies about him. This is the weapon of warfare in Christian countries. Two things there are the wise man will not trust, if said by various persons we all know: —

1. Anything to their own advantage.
2. Anything to their neighbor's prejudice.

It is a bad sign of human nature, that many men

should have so much to say to the prejudice of any one they know. But it is a much worse sign of human nature that many men should hear with delight, and speak with exaggeration, anything to the prejudice of people whom they know nothing about. The man you know may have given you offence. The man of whom you know nothing cannot possibly have done so; and if you hate him, and wish to do him harm, it can only be because you are prepared to hate the average specimen of your race. We all know those who, if they met a fellow-creature out in the lonely desert, would see in him not a friend but an enemy, and would prepare to shoot him or hamstring him unobserved. For the people I mean prefer to deal their blow unseen. There are those who, as boys at school, would never have a fair fight with a companion, but would secretly give him a malicious poke when unobserved. And such men, I have remarked, carry out the system when they have reached maturity. They will not boldly face the being they hate, but they secretly disseminate falsehoods to his disadvantage.

But it is sad to think that the hasty judgments men form of one another are almost invariably unfavorable ones. It is sad to think that people come to have such malignant feeling towards other people who are quite unknown to them. A short time ago, at a public meeting, Mr. Jones was proposed as a suitable person to be the town beadle. Jones did not want the beadleship, being already in possession of a preferable situation of the same character. When his name was proposed, an old individual rose to oppose him. That was all natural. But this individual was not content to oppose Jones's claims to the beadleship, he positively gnashed his teeth

in fury at Jones. He had no command of language,
and could but imperfectly express his hatred; but he
foamed at the mouth, the veins of his head swelled up,
and he trembled in every limb with eager wrath, as he
declared that he would never consent to Jones being
beadle; that if Jones was appointed beadle he himself
(his name was Mr. Curre) would forthwith quit the town,
and never again enter it. Curre had never exchanged
a word with Jones in all his life; yet he hated Jones, and
the mention of Jones's name thus infuriated him, even
as a scarlet rag a bull. Poor Curre was not a bad-
hearted fellow after all, and at a subsequent period
Jones made his acquaintance. Now, one great principle
Jones holds by is this, that if any man hate you, it must
be in some measure your own fault; you must in some
way have given offence to the man. So Jones, who is a
very genial and straightforward person, asked Curre to
tell him honestly why he had so keenly opposed his appointment to the beadleship, adding that he feared he
had given Curre offence in some way or other, though
he had never intended it; and Curre, after some hesi-
tation and with a good deal of shame, replied, " Well,
the fact is, I could not bear to see you riding such a fine
horse, and Mr. Sneakyman told me you paid a hundred
and twenty pounds for it."—" My friend Curre," was the
reply, " I gave just forty for that horse, and how could
you believe anything said by Sneakyman?" Curre assured Jones that the reason why he had disliked him was
just that he knew so little of him, and that when he
came to know him his dislike immediately passed into a
real warm and penitent regard. And when Curre died
soon after, he left Jones ten thousand pounds. Curre

had no relations, so it was all right; and Jones had nine-teen children, so it was all right for him too.

Reader, take a large sheet of paper, — foolscap paper. Take a pen. Sit down at a table where there is ink. Write out a list of all the persons you dislike, adding a brief statement of the reason or reasons why you dis-like each of them.

Having written accordingly, ask yourself this ques-tion: Am I doing well to be angry with these persons? Have they given me offence to justify this dislike?

And now listen to this prophecy. You will be obliged to confess that they have not. You will feel ashamed of your dislike for them. You will resolve to cease dis-liking them.

Believe one who has tried. Here on this table is a large foolscap page. Three names did I write down of people I disliked; then I wrote down the cause why I disliked the first, and it looked, being written down, so despicably small, that I felt heartily ashamed. And now, you large page, go into the fire; and with you these dislikes shall perish. At this moment I don't dislike any human being, and if anybody dislikes me I hope he will cease doing so. If ever I gave him offence, I am sorry for it.

Yet I cannot quite agree with Jones in thinking that, in every case where dislike is felt, it is at least in part the fault of the disliked person. In many cases it is: not in all. A retired oilman of large wealth bought a tract of land, and went to reside on it. He found that his parish clergyman drove a handsome carriage, and had a couple of men-servants. The old oilman was in-furiated. The clergyman's wife erected a conservatory:

11*.

the oilman had an epileptic fit. Now all this was entirely the oilman's own fault. A retired officer went to live in a certain rural district. He dined at six o'clock. Several people round, who dined at five, took mortal offence. O for the abolition of white slavery! When will human beings be suffered to do as they please?

I have remarked, too, that most stupid people hate all clever people. I have witnessed a very weak and silly man repeat, with a fatuous and feeble malignity, like a dog without teeth trying to bite, some story to the prejudice of an eminent man in the same profession. And even worse: you may find such a man repeat a story not at all to the disadvantage of the eminent man, under the manifest impression that it *is* to his disadvantage. I have rarely heard Mr. Snarling say anything with more manifest malignity, than when he said that my friend Smith had bought a fire-proof safe in which to keep his sermons. Well, was there any harm in that? " Bedwell said he would take nothing under the chancellorship," said Mr. Dunup. Perhaps Bedwell should not have said so; but the fact proved to be that he got the chancellorship.

Clergymen of little piety or ability, and with empty churches, dislike those clergymen whose churches are very full. You may discern this unworthy feeling exhibited in a hundred pitiful, spiteful little ways. I have remarked, too, that the emptier a man's church grows, the higher becomes his doctrine. And flagrant practical neglect of duty is in some cases compensated by violent orthodoxy, the orthodoxy being shown mainly by accusing other people of heterodoxy.

Unworthy people hate those who do a thing better

than themselves. An inefficient rector empties his church. He gets a popular curate who fills it. The parishioners present the curate with a piece of plate. Forthwith the rector dismisses the curate. Or perhaps the rector dare not venture on that. He waits till the curate gets a parish of his own; and then he diligently excludes him from the pulpit whence his sermons were so attractive. His old friends shall never see or hear him again, if the rector can prevent it. And further, the rector and his wife disseminate wretched little bits of scandal as to the extravagant sayings and doings of the curate, all exaggerated and mostly invented.

The heroic way of taking gossip is that in which the old Earl Marischals took it, when it was a more serious thing than now. Above the door of each of their castles, there were written on the stone these words:—

THEY HAIF SAYD:

QHAT SAYD THEY?

LAT THEM SAY!

CHAPTER XV.

ARCHBISHOP WHATELY ON BACON.*

THIS is in every way a remarkable book. We have before us in this volume the most generally popular work of the greatest and meanest man of his time, with a Commentary of Annotations by the man who, of all living authors, approaches in many of his intellectual characteristics nearest to Bacon himself. We find in the writings of Archbishop Whately the same independence of thought which distinguishes the writings of Bacon; the same profusion of illustration by happy analogies which is characteristic of Bacon's later works; the same clearness, point, and precision of style. We do not wonder that the accomplished prelate, accustomed (as he tells us in his Preface) to write down from time to time the observations which suggested themselves to him in reading Bacon's *Essays*, should have found them grow beneath his hand into a volume; and we cannot but regard it as a boon conferred upon all educated men, that this volume has been given to the world. Nor must we omit to remark, in this age of readers for mere entertainment,

* Bacon's Essays: with Annotations by Richard Whately, D. D., Archbishop of Dublin.

that although the volume be a large one, written by an archbishop, and consisting of comments upon the thoughts of a great philosopher, the book is invested with such an attractive interest, that it cannot fail to prove a readable and entertaining one, even to minds unaccustomed to high-class thought and incapable of severe thinking. The somewhat severe terseness of the *Essays* is relieved by the lighter and more popular tone of the Annotations. Archbishop Whately's mind is of that nature that it takes up each of a vast range of subjects with equal ease, and apparently with equal gusto; grappling with a great difficulty or unravelling a great perplexity with no more appearance of effort than when lightly touching a social folly, such as might have invited the notice of the author of *The Book of Snobs*, or when playfully blowing to the winds an error not worth serious refutation. Hardly ever in the range of literature have we observed the workings of an intellect in which nervous strength is so combined with delicate tact. We are reminded of Mr. Nasmyth's steam-hammer, which can smash a mass of steel in shivers, or by successive taps drive a nail through a half-inch plank.

We are thankful that in noticing this book, we are concerned rather with the annotator than with the essayist; for not without much pain can we look back on Lord Bacon's history. There is something jarring in the mingled feelings of admiration and disgust with which we think of Bacon's greatness and meanness; his intellectual grasp, his keen insight, his wit, his imagination (sober in its wildest flights), his serene temper, his brilliant conversation, his courtly manners, his freedom from arrogance and pretence; and then, on the

other side, his cold heart and mean spirit, his low and
unworthy ambition, his despicable selfishness, his flagrant dishonesty, his crawling servility, his perfidy as a
friend, his sneakiness as a patriot, his corruption as a
judge.   As to his intellectual greatness there can be no
question ; though there can be no error more complete
than to regard him as the inventor or discoverer of the
Inductive Philosophy.   He did not invent it; he did
not skilfully apply it.   His philosophy differed from
that which preceded it less in method than in aim ; and
it is glory enough to have mainly contributed to turn
the thoughts and the efforts of thoughtful and energetic
men away from the profitless philosophy of the schools
to the practical good of mankind.   In the *commodis hu-
manis inservire* we have the end and the spirit of the
Baconian philosophy.

The *Essays* constitute Bacon's most popular work, if
not his greatest.   They illustrate in thought and style
what was said of him by Ben Jonson, that " No man
ever spoke more neatly, more pressly, more weightily,
nor suffered less emptiness, less idleness, in what he
uttered."   Their subjects are well known.   We have in
them the thoughts of Bacon on a considerable range of
matters, briefly expressed, most of them not occupying
more than a page or two.   They may have been written,
many of them, at a short sitting, though they manifestly
give us the results of mature and protracted thought.
And here and there occur those pregnant, suggestive
sentences which Archbishop Whately has taken as texts
for his own observations.   The Archbishop reminds us
in his preface, by way of guarding himself from the imputation of presumption in adding to what Bacon has

said on many subjects, that the word "essay," which
has now come to signify a full and careful treatise on a
subject, was in Bacon's day more correctly understood
as meaning a slight sketch to be filled up and followed
out; a something *to set the reader a-thinking;* and the
Annotations, which form by a great deal the larger
part of the book, contain the reflections and remarks
which have been suggested to the Archbishop in his
reading of the *Essays.*

The Annotations are of all degrees, from a sentence
or two of inference or illustration to a pretty full discourse on some topic more or less directly suggested by
Bacon. The writer frequently presses opinions which
he has elsewhere maintained, and gives many extracts
from his own published works. We also find several
quotations from other authors, selected (we need not
say) with great judgment; and showing us incidentally
how wide is the Archbishop's reading, and how completely he keeps up with whatever is valuable in even
the lighter literature of the day. In that portion of
this volume which is properly Dr. Whately's own, we
have the acute observations of a writer who knows both
books and men; of a keen observer; a thinker almost
always sound amid extraordinary independence and
originality; a master of a style so beautifully lucid alike
in thought and expression, that we hardly feel, as we
follow in the track, how difficult it would be to tread
that path without the direction of a guide so able and so
sympathetic.

The characteristics of Archbishop Whately are very
marked; and his negative characteristics not less so
than his positive. No thoughtful man can become

acquainted with his writings, without being struck quite as much by what this distinguished prelate *is not*, as by what he *is*. Indeed, what the Archbishop of Dublin is not, is perhaps the thing which at first impresses us most deeply. We discover in his works the productions of a mind which can apply itself to the most diverse subjects, and give forth the soundest and shrewdest sense on all, expressed in the most felicitous forms. We cannot but remark his vast information; and his ripe wisdom, moral, social, and political. But, after all, the thing that strikes us most is, how thoroughly different Archbishop Whately is from most people's idea of an archbishop. We associate with so elevated a dignitary a certain ponderousness of mind; we assume that his intellect must be a machine which by its weight and power is rather unfitted for light work; and we are taken by surprise when we find a prelate so dignified combining with the graver strength of understanding a liveliness, pith, and point, a versatility, wit, and playfulness, which, without taking an atom from that respect which is due to his high position, yet put us at our ease in his presence, and fit him for the attractive discussion of almost every topic which can interest the scholar and the gentleman. The general idea of an archbishop is of something eminently respectable, perhaps rather dull and prosy; never startling us in any way by thought or style; looking at all the world through his own medium, and from his own elevated point of view; and above all, an intensely *safe man*. The very reverse of all this is Archbishop Whately. Never, indeed, does he say anything inconsistent with his dignified position; but his works show him to us (and we know him by his works alone) as the independent thinker, often thinking very differently from the majority of men, — the thorough man of the world, in the true sense of that phrase, — perfectly versant in the ways of living men, from the tricks of the petty tradesman up to the diplomacies of cabinets and the social ethics of exclusive circles, — at home in the literature of the hour no less than in the weightier letters of philosophy, theology, and politics, — the master of eloquent logic, from the heavy artillery which demolishes a stronghold of error or scepticism, to the light touch that unravels a paradox or puts a troublesome simpleton in his right place, — the master of wit, from the half-playful breath which shows up a little social folly, to the scathing sarcasm which turns the laugh against the scoffer, and which shows the would-be wise as the most arrant of fools.

As for Archbishop Whately's positive characteristics, we believe that most of his intelligent readers will agree with us when we place foremost among these his acuteness and independence of thought. The latter of these qualities he possesses almost in excess. We believe that to the Archbishop of Dublin the fact that any opinion is very generally entertained, so far from being a recommendation, is rather a reason for regarding it with suspicion. It is amusing how regularly we find it occurring in the prefaces to his works, that one reason for the publication of each is his belief that erroneous views are commonly entertained as to the subject of it. And when we consider how most men receive their opinions upon all subjects ready-made, we cannot appreciate too highly one who, in the emphatic sense of the phrase,

Q

thinks for himself. It is right to add that there is hardly an instance in which so much originality of thought can be found in conjunction with so much justice and sobriety of thought. In Archbishop Whately's writings we have independence without the least trace of wrong-headedness. His views, especially in his *Lectures on a Future State*, on *Good and Evil Angels*, and on the *Characters of the Apostles*, are often startling at the first glance, because very different from those to which we have grown accustomed; but he generally succeeds in convincing us that his opinion is the sound and natural one; and where he fails to carry our conviction along with him, he leaves us persuaded of his good faith, and sensible that much may be said on his part.

Another striking characteristic of Archbishop Whately is, his extraordinary power of illustrating moral truths and principles by analogies to external nature. Not even Abraham Tucker possessed this power in so eminent a degree; and the Archbishop's illustrations are always free from that grossness and vulgarity which often deform those of Tucker, who (as he himself tells us) did not scruple to take a figure from the kitchen or the stable, if it could make his meaning plainer. We cannot call to mind any English author who employs imagery in such a profuse degree, yet without the faintest suspicion of that nerveless and aimless accumulation of figures and comparisons which constitutes what is vulgarly termed *floweriness* of style. We have no fine things put in for mere fine-writing's sake. Dr. Whately's illustrations are not only invariably apt and striking; they really *illustrate* his point, they *throw light upon it,* and make it plainer than it was before. They are hardly ever long drawn out; consisting very frequently in a happy analogy suggested in one clause of a sentence, — the writer being anxious to make that step in his reasoning clear, yet too much bent upon the ultimate conclusion he is aiming at to linger upon that step longer than is necessary to make it so.

To these literary qualifications we add, that Archbishop Whately's information, though evidently reaching over a vast field, is yet minutely accurate in the smallest details; and, without the least tinge of pedantry, the fine scholarship of the writer often shines through his work. It is almost superfluous to allude to the invariable clearness, point, and felicity of the Archbishop's English style, which often warms into eloquence of the highest class, — effective and telling, without one grain of claptrap.

We should give an imperfect view of the characteristics of the Archbishop of Dublin, if we did not mention, as a marked one, his intense honesty of purpose, his evident desire to arrive at exact truth, and his carefulness to state opinions and arguments with perfect fairness. Nor should his fearless out-spokenness be forgotten. He does not hesitate to call an opponent's argument nonsense when he has proved it to be so. "Often very silly, and not seldom very mischievous," * is his description of the speculations of writers of the Emerson school. Our readers are perhaps acquainted with the Archbishop's remarks upon some of the German writers of the present day : —

"The attention their views have attracted, considering their extreme absurdity, is something quite wonderful. But

* Preface, p. v.

there are many persons who are disposed to place *confidence* in any one, in proportion, not to his *sound judgment*, but to his *ingenuity* and *learning;* qualifications which are sometimes found in men (such as those writers) who are utterly deficient in common-sense and reasoning powers, and knowledge of human nature, and who consequently fall into such gross absurdities as would be, in any matter unconnected with religion, regarded as unworthy of serious attention." *

It is impossible to read the Annotations without feeling what an acute observer of men is Archbishop Whately. How carefully, in his passage through life, has his quick eye gathered up the characteristics of those persons with whom he has been brought in contact, — their pretensions, foibles, tricks, and errors ; and how well he turns his recollections to account, when an example or illustration is needed! We likewise find many indications that he has been keenly alive, not more to the ways of men than to the little phenomena of nature. We refer our readers particularly to a passage on the degrees of cold which are experienced in the course of a single night (p. 305) ; and we wonder how many persons, even of those who generally live in the country, are aware of the following fact : —

" Any one who is accustomed to go out before daylight will often, in the winter, find the roads full of liquid mud half an hour before dawn, and by sunrise as hard as a rock. Then those who have been in bed will often observe that ' it was a hard frost last night,' when in truth there had been no frost at all till daybreak." — p. 305.

And the final feature we remark in Archbishop Whately's character is one which must afford the highest satis-

* Lectures on the Characters of Our Lord's Apostles, p. 166.

faction to all who have, in their own experience, found earnest personal religion existing most markedly in conjunction with great weakness, ignorance, and prejudice; and to all who have ever mingled in the society of able and cultivated men, who thought that contemptuously to put religion aside was the indication of mental vigor and enlightenment. It is most satisfactory to find the writings of one of the strongest-minded men of his time all pervaded and inspirited by a religious principle and feeling, earnest, unaffected, really practical and influential, — as perfectly free from weakness as from self-assertion and self-conceit.

We believe that from this volume of Annotations we could construct a tolerably complete scheme of Archbishop Whately's views on politics, morals, social ethics, and the general conduct of life. We have some indication of his peculiar tastes and bent from observing which among Bacon's *Essays* he passes by without remark. He has little to say concerning "Masques and Triumphs." We should judge that his nature has little about it of that "soft side" which leads to take delight in the recurrence of periodical festal occasions, with their kindly remembrances: we should judge that a solitary Christmas would be much less of a trial to him than it would be to us; although the instances of Dickens and Jerrold prove that the warmest feeling about such seasons and associations is quite consistent with even extreme opinions on the side of progress. Then the Archbishop passes the Essays on " Building " and " Gardens " without a word; although these subjects would have set many men off into a rhapsody of delighted details and fancies. We judge that Dr.

Whately has not a very keen relish for external nature *for its own sake ;* his chief interest in it appears to be in the tracing of analogies between the material and moral worlds. The fact that Bacon's ideas both on Building and Gardening are now quite out of date would be only the stronger reason to many men for launching out upon the subject; and how deeply could some sympathize with Bacon in his ideal picture of a princely palace, — one of those delightful palaces in the air about whose site there are permitted no drawbacks or shortcomings on the part of Nature, — round which ancestral woods grow at a moment's notice, and within whose view noble rivers, fed by no springs, can flow up-hill, — and in whose architecture expense and time need never be thought of. But not many men are likely ever to live in palaces ; not many more, perhaps, would care to picture out such a life for themselves ; and we prefer to Bacon's palace, the delightful description in Mr. Loudon's *Encyclopædia of Architecture,* of what he calls the *Beau Ideal English Villa.*

We have long regarded the Archbishop of Dublin as, in several respects, almost the foremost man of this day. It says little for the age's intelligence, that while Dr. Cumming's paltry claptraps sell by scores of thousands of copies, Archbishop Whately commands an audience, fit indeed, but comparatively few ; for his writings possess a very high degree of that most indispensable, though not highest, of all qualities, *interest.* He is never heavy nor tiresome. Very dull people may understand, though they may not appreciate him. But we are persuaded that his archbishopric lessens the number of his readers. Readers for mere amusement are afraid to begin what has been written by so great a man.

We need hardly say that it is wholly impossible within the limits of a short article to give any just idea, either of the variety of topics which the Archbishop has discussed, or of the manner in which he has discussed them. Bacon himself described his *Essays* as " handling those things wherein both men's lives and persons are most conversant "; and Archbishop Whately's Annotations, ranging over the same wide field, can be described, as to their scope, in no more definite terms. But the same necessary want of unity which makes the book so hard to speak of as a whole renders it the easier to consider in its separate parts. It consists of precious detached pieces, each of which loses nothing by being individually regarded. But before glancing at some of the topics which the Archbishop has treated, we wish to give our readers a few specimens of those admirable illustrations of moral truths by physical analogies which form so striking a feature of his writings : —

" There are two kinds of orators, the distinction between whom might be thus illustrated. When the moon shines brightly we are apt to say, ' How beautiful is this *moonlight!* ' but in the daytime, ' How beautiful are the trees, the fields, the mountains !' — and, in short, all the *objects* that are illuminated; we never speak of the sun that makes them so. Just in the same way, the really greatest orator shines like the sun, making you think much of the *things* he is speaking of; the second-best shines like the moon, making you think much of *him* and his *eloquence*." — (p. 327, Annotation on Essay " Of Discourse.")

" In most subjects, the utmost knowledge that any man can attain to, is but ' a little learning ' in comparison of what he remains ignorant of. The view resembles that of an American forest, in which the more trees a man cuts down, the greater is the expanse of wood he sees around him." — (p. 446, Annotation on Essay " Of Studies.")

In an annotation on the Essay "Of Negotiating," Archbishop Whately mentions, as a caution to be observed, that in combating, whether as a speaker or a writer, deep-rooted prejudices, and maintaining unpopular truths, the point to be aimed at should be, to adduce what is sufficient, and *not much more* than is sufficient, to prove your conclusion. You affront men's self-esteem, and awaken their distrust, by proving the *extreme absurdity* of thinking differently from yourself; and —

" in this way the very clearness and force of the demonstration will, with some minds, have an opposite tendency to the one desired. Laborers who are employed in *driving wedges* into a block of wood are careful to use blows of no greater force than is just sufficient. If they strike too hard, the elasticity of the wood will *throw out the wedge.*" — (p. 432.)

On the Essay "Of Praise," Archbishop Whately remarks, with admirable truth, that it is needless to insist, as many do, upon the propriety of not being wholly indifferent to the opinions formed of us; as that tendency of our nature stands more in need of *keeping under* than of encouraging or vindicating: —

" It must be treated like the grass on a lawn which you wish to keep in good order: you neither attempt nor wish to *destroy* the grass; but you mow it down from time to time, as close as you possibly can, well trusting that there will be quite enough left, and that it will be sure to grow again." — (p. 491.)

On the Essay "Of Youth and Age," we have many excellent remarks upon the fact to which the experience of most men bears testimony, that great precocity of understanding is rarely followed by superior intellect in after-life; and more especially that there is nothing less promising than, in early youth, "a certain full-formed, settled, and, as it may be called, *adult* character : " —

" A lad who has, to a degree that excites wonder and admiration, the character and demeanor of an intelligent man of mature years, will probably be *that*, and nothing more, all his life, and will cease accordingly to be anything remarkable, because it was the precocity alone that ever made him so. It is remarked by greyhound-fanciers that a well-formed, compact-shaped puppy never makes a fleet dog. They see more promise in the loose-jointed, awkward, clumsy ones. And even so, there is a kind of crudity and unsettledness in the minds of those young persons who turn out ultimately the most eminent." — (p. 405.)

How admirably true! We heartily wish that many injudicious parents would lay this to heart. Who is there who does not remember, how, at school and college, some cautious, slow-speaking, never-committing-himself lad, whose seeming precocity of judgment was mainly the result of stolidity of understanding and slowness of circulation, was evermore thrust as a grand exemplar before the view of those whose quicker intellect and warmer heart often got them into scrapes from which *he* kept clear, but promised what *he* could never attain, till the very name of prudence, discretion, reserve, became hateful and disgusting! And how regularly that pattern boy or lad has proved in after-life the dullard and booby which his young companions, in their more natural frank-heartedness, instinctively knew and felt he was even then!

12

On the Essay "Of Friendship" the Archbishop observes : —

"It may be worth noticing as a curious circumstance, when persons past forty before they were at all acquainted form together a very close intimacy of friendship. For grafts of *old* wood to *take*, there must be a wonderful congeniality between the trees." — (p. 276.)

On Bacon's remark, that "a man that is young in years may be old in hours, if he have lost no time," the Archbishop says, —

"And this may be, not only from his having had better opportunities, but also from his understanding better how to learn by experience. Several different men, who have all had equal, or even the very same experience, — that is, have been witnesses or agents in the same transactions, — will often be found to resemble so many different men looking at the same book. One, perhaps, though he distinctly sees black marks on white paper, has never learned his letters; another can read, but is a stranger to the *language* in which the book is written ; another has an *acquaintance* with the language, but understands it imperfectly; another is familiar with the *language*, but is a stranger to the subject of the book, and wants power or previous instruction to enable him fully to take in the author's drift; while another again perfectly comprehends the whole." — (p. 400.)

In an annotation on the Essay "Of Dispatch," we find some thoughts on the advantage of knowing when to act with promptitude and when with deliberation, and of being able suitably to meet either case. Then the Archbishop goes on as follows : —

"If you cannot find a counseller who *combines* these two kinds of qualification (which is a thing not to be calculated

on), you should seek for some of each sort, — one to devise and
mature measures that will admit of delay; and another to
make prompt guesses, and suggest sudden expedients. A
bow, such as is approved of by our modern toxophilites, must
be *backed* — that is, made of *two* slips of wood glued together:
one a very *elastic*, but somewhat *brittle* wood; the other much
less elastic, but very *tough*. The one gives the requisite
spring, the other keeps it from breaking. If you have two
such counsellers as are here spoken of, you are provided with
a *backed* bow." — (p. 250.)

Describing the two opposite sorts of men who equally
precipitate a country into anarchy, the one sort by obstinately resisting all innovations, and the other by reck-
lessly hurrying into violent changes without reason, the
Archbishop says : —

" The two kinds of absurdity here adverted to may be
compared respectively to the acts of two kinds of irrational
animals, a moth and a horse. The moth rushes into a flame,
and is burned; and the horse obstinately stands still in a stable that is on fire, and is burned likewise. One may often
meet with persons of opposite dispositions, though equally
unwise, who are accordingly prone respectively to these opposite errors; the one partaking more of the character of the
moth, and the other of the horse." — (p. 244.)

Mr. Macaulay tells us, and experience confirms his
statement, that it is not easy to make a simile go on all-
fours, and incomparably more difficult to attain strict
accuracy when an analogy is drawn out to any length.
But Archbishop Whately overcomes this difficulty.
There is no hitch whatever in the following comparison,
though it runs to very minute and exact details : —

" The effect produced by any writing or speech of an argumentative character, on any subject on which diversity of opinion prevails, may be compared — supposing the argument to be of any weight — to the effects of a fire-engine on a conflagration. That portion of the water which falls on solid stone walls is poured out where it is not needed. That, again, which falls on blazing beams and rafters, is cast off in volumes of hissing steam, and will seldom avail to quench the fire. But that which is poured on woodwork that is just beginning to kindle, may stop the burning; and that which wets the rafters not yet ignited, but in danger, may save them from catching fire. Even so, those who already concur with the writer as to some point, will feel gratified with, and perhaps bestow high commendation on, an able defence of the opinions they already hold; and those, again, who have fully made up their minds on the opposite side, are more likely to be displeased than to be convinced. But both of these parties are left nearly in the same mind as before. Those, however, who are in a hesitating and doubtful state, may very likely be decided by forcible arguments; and those who have not hitherto considered the subject may be induced to adopt opinions which they find supported by the strongest reasons. But the readiest and warmest approbation a writer meets with will usually be from those whom he has *not* convinced, because they were convinced already. And the effect the most important and the most difficult to be produced he will usually, when he does produce it, hear the least of." — (p. 432.)

We do not know where to find a comparison more correct or more beautiful than that with which the highly-gifted prelate concludes his remarks on those writers who inculcate morality, with an exclusion of all reference to religious principle. He gives us to understand that the resolute manner in which Miss Edgeworth, in her works, ignored Christianity, was the result of an entire disbelief in its doctrines. But even this sad fact leaves her open to the charge of having falsified poetical truth; inasmuch as it cannot be denied that Christianity, true or false, does exist, and does exercise a material influence on the feelings and conduct of some of the believers in it. And to represent all sorts of people as involved in all sorts of circumstances, while yet none ever makes the least reference to a religious motive, is artistically unnatural. The graver objection still remains, that the moral excellences described in non-religious fictions as existing, cannot exist, cannot be realized, except by resorting to principles which, in those fictions, are unnoticed. And the young reader should therefore be reminded —

" that all these ' things that are lovely and of good report,' which have been placed before him, are the genuine fruits of the Holy Land, though the spies who have brought them bring also an evil report of that land, and would persuade us to remain wandering in the wilderness." — (p. 468.)

In pointing out the unfairness to a new colony of making it the receptacle of the blackguards and scape-graces of the old country, by the system of penal transportation, the Archbishop happily illustrates the way in which people of not very logical minds are brought to associate things which are not merely unconnected, but inconsistent : —

" In other subjects, as well as in this, I have observed that two distinct objects may, by being dexterously presented again and again in quick succession, to the mind of a cursory reader, be so associated together *in his thoughts* as to be conceived capable, when in fact they are not, of being *actually* combined in practice. The fallacious belief thus induced bears a striking resemblance to the optical illusion effected by that ingenious and philosophical toy called the 'thaumatrope'; in which two objects painted on opposite sides of a card — for instance, a man and a horse, a bird and a cage — are, by a quick rotatory motion, made so to impress the eye in combination, as to form one picture, of the man on the horse's back, — the bird in the cage, &c. As soon as the card is allowed to remain at rest, the figures, of course, appear as they really are, separate and on opposite sides. A mental illusion closely analogous to this is produced, when, by a rapid and repeated transition from one subject to another alternately, the mind is deluded into an idea of the actual combination of things that are really incompatible. The chief part of the defence which various writers have advanced in favor of the system of penal colonies consists, in truth, of a sort of intellectual thaumatrope. The prosperity of the colony, and the repression of crime, are, by a sort of rapid whirl, presented to the mind as combined in one picture. A very moderate degree of calm and fixed attention soon shows that the two objects are painted on *opposite sides* of the card." — (p. 334.)

On the risk run by superstitious persons of falling into grave error : —

" Minds strongly predisposed to superstition may be compared to heavy bodies just balanced on the verge of a precipice. The slightest touch will send them over; and then the greatest exertion that can be made may be insufficient to arrest their fall." — (p. 155.)

Illustration is sometimes the most cogent of argument. A volume of reasoning against ultra-conservatism would not equal, for general impression, the following plain statement of the case : —

" Is there not, then, some reason for the ridicule which

Bacon speaks of, as attaching to those 'who too much reverence old times?' To say that no changes shall take place is to talk idly. We might as well pretend to control the motions of the earth. To resolve that none shall take place *except* what are undesigned and accidental, is to resolve that though a clock may gain or lose indefinitely, at least we will take care that it shall never be regulated. 'If time' (to use Bacon's warning words) 'alters things to the worse, and wisdom and counsel shall not alter them to the better, what shall be the end?'" — (pp. 236, 237.)

We shall throw together, without remark, some further examples of Archbishop Whately's power of illustrating the moral by the physical. So marked a feature in his intellectual portraiture deserves, we think, extended notice. But it is only by studying the Annotations for themselves, that our readers can form any just idea of the affluence and exuberance of happy imagery with which they sparkle all over:—

"To these small wares, enumerated by Bacon, might be added a very hackneyed trick, which yet is wonderfully successful, — to affect a delicacy about mentioning particulars, and hint at what you *could* bring forward, only you do not wish to give offence. 'We could give many cases to prove that such and such a medical system is all a delusion, and a piece of quackery; but we abstain, through tenderness for individuals, from bringing names before the public.' 'I have observed many things — which, however, I will not particularize — which convince me that Mr. Such-a-one is unfit for his office; and others have made the same remark; but I do not like to bring them forward,' &c., &c.

"Thus an unarmed man keeps the unthinking in awe, by assuring them that he has a pair of loaded pistols in his pocket, though he is loth to produce them." — (p. 210.)

" A man who plainly perceives that, as Bacon observes, there are some cases which call for promptitude,. and others which require delay, and who has also sagacity enough to perceive *which* is which, will often be mortified at perceiving that he has come too late for some things, and too soon for others; that he is like a skilful engineer, who perceives how he could, fifty years earlier, have effectually preserved an important harbor which is now irrecoverably silted up, and how he could, fifty years hence, though not at present, reclaim from the sea thousands of acres of fertile land at the delta of some river." — (p. 203.)

" As in contemplating an ebbing tide, we are sometimes in doubt, on a short inspection, whether the sea is really receding, because, from time to time, a wave will dash farther up the shore than those which have preceded it, but, if we continue our observation long enough, we see plainly that the boundary of the land is on the whole advancing; so here, by extending our. view over many countries and through several ages, we may distinctly perceive the tendencies which would have escaped a more confined research." — (p. 300.)

" An ancient Greek colony was like what gardeners call a *layer;* a portion of the parent tree, with stem, twigs, and leaves imbedded in fresh soil till it had taken root, and then severed. A modern colony is like handfuls of twigs and leaves pulled off at random, and thrown into the earth to take their chance." — (p. 341.)

" ' *There be that can pack the cards, and yet cannot play well.*'

" Those whom Bacon here so well describes are men of a clear and quick sight, but short-sighted. They are ingenious in particulars, but cannot take a comprehensive view of a whole. Such a man may make a good captain, but a bad general. He may be clever at surprising a picket, but would fail in the management of a great army and the conduct of a campaign. He is like a chess-player who takes several pawns, but is checkmated." — (p. 215.)

"The truth is, that in all the *serious* and important affairs of life men are attached to what they have been used to ; in matters of *ornament* they covet novelty ; in all systems and institutions, — in all the ordinary business of life, — in all fundamentals, — they cling to what is the established course ; in matters of detail, — in what lies, as it were, on the surface, — they seek variety. Man may, in reference to this point, be compared to a tree whose stem and main branches stand year after year, but whose leaves and flowers are fresh every season." — (p. 228.)

"In no point is the record of past times more instructive to those capable of learning from other experience than their own, than in what relates to the history of *reactions*.

"It has been often remarked by geographers that a river flowing through a level country of soft alluvial soil never keeps a straight course, but winds regularly to and fro, in the form of the letter S many times repeated. And a geographer, on looking at the course of any stream as marked on a map, can at once tell whether it flows along a plain (like the river *Meander*, which has given its name to such windings), or through a rocky and hilly country. It is found, indeed, that if a straight channel be cut for any stream in a plain consisting of tolerably soft soil, it never will long continue straight, unless artificially kept so, but becomes crooked, and increases its windings more and more every year. The cause is, that any little wearing away of the bank in the softest part of the soil, on one side, occasions a *set* of the stream against this hollow, which increases it, and at the same time drives the water aslant against the opposite bank a little lower down. This wears away that bank also ; and thus the stream is again driven against a part of the first bank, still lower ; and so on, till by the wearing away of the banks at these points on each side, and the deposit of mud (gradually becoming dry land) in the comparatively still water between them, the course of the stream becomes sinuous, and its windings increase more and more.

12 *

R

"And even thus, in human affairs, we find alternate movements, in nearly opposite directions, taking place from time to time, and generally bearing some proportion to each other in respect of the violence of each; even as the highest flood-tide is succeeded by the lowest ebb." — (p. 175.)

Very beautifully, in the following paragraph, does the Archbishop illustrate the law that whatever is to last long, must grow slowly : —

" We hear of volcanic islands thrown up in a few days to a formidable size, and in a few weeks or months sinking down again or washed away; while other islands, which are the summits of banks covered with weed and drift-sand, continue slowly increasing year after year, century after century. The man that is in a hurry to see the full effect of his own tillage should cultivate annuals, not forest-trees. The clear-headed lover of truth is content to wait for the result of his. If he is wrong in the doctrines he maintains, or the measures he proposes, at least it is not for the sake of immediate popularity. If he is right, it will be found out in time, though perhaps not in *his* time. The preparers of the *mummies* were (Herodotus says) driven *out of the house* by the family who had engaged their services, with execrations and stones; but their work remains sound after three thousand years." — (p. 503.)

Although these extracts have been given mainly to exemplify Archbishop Whately's mode of enforcing and illustrating his views, they may have served likewise to give our readers some notion of the variety of topics treated in this volume, and of the Archbishop's opinions upon some of these. We hardly know how to attempt a description of the *matter* of the work as distinguished from its *manner*. There are scores of paragraphs among the Annotations which might each supply material for extended review; and we had marked many interesting passages with the intention of discussing at some length the views contained in them. But, even after weeding out of our list the topics which appeared of minor interest (the process was that of *thinning* rather than of weeding), so many remain, that we can do no more than glance at two or three.

In the second edition of the work just published, we find no material differences when compared with the first. Archbishop Whately's opinions have been too well considered to admit of change within a few months' space. But the minute reader will find here and there many little additions, which afford pleasant proof that the author is still thinking upon the subjects treated; and which promise that, rich as this volume already is in wisdom and eloquence, it may yet be further enriched by the further observation and reflection of its writer. In the former edition the Essay " On Faction " was followed by no remarks; in the present edition it is followed by several annotations, — some of them suggested, we may believe, by recent occurrences in America. The following passage, of special interest at the present time, points out forcibly the advantage of having in a state *aliquid impercussum*, — a central rallying-point detached from all party, and to which all parties may profess attachment : —

" Bacon's remark, that a prince ought not to make it his policy to ' govern *according to respect to factions*,' suggests a strong ground of preference of *hereditary* to elective sovereignty. For when a chief — whether called king, emperor, president, or by whatever name — is *elected* (whether for life, or for a term of years), he can hardly avoid being the head of a party. He who is elected will be likely to feel aversion towards those who have voted against him; who may be, perhaps, nearly half of his subjects. And they again will be likely to regard him as an *enemy*, instead of feeling loyalty to him as their prince.

. "And those again who have voted *for* him, will consider him as being under an *obligation* to them, and expect him to show to them more favor than to the rest of his subjects; so that he will be rather the head of a party than the king of a people.

"Then, too, when the throne is likely to become vacant, — that is, when the king is old, or is attacked with any serious illness, — what secret canvassing and disturbance of men's minds will take place! The king himself will most likely wish that his son, or some other near relative or friend, should succeed him, and he will employ all his patronage with a view to such an election; appointing to public offices not the fittest men, but those whom he can reckon on as voters. And others will be exerting themselves to form a party against him; so that the country will be hardly ever tranquil, and very seldom well-governed.

"If, indeed, men were very different from what they are, there might be superior advantages in an elective royalty; but in the actual state of things, the disadvantages will in general greatly outweigh the benefits.

"Accordingly most nations have seen the advantage of hereditary royalty, notwithstanding the defects of such a constitution."

We heartily wish that all parents would remember and act upon the Archbishop's views, as expressed in the following passage. We believe the caution is extensively needed. We believe that many injudicious parents (with the best intention) trench upon the incommunicable prerogative of the All-wise and Almighty, by needlessly causing griefs and disappointments to their children, under the idea that all this forms a wholesome discipline. They forget that the nature and effect of every event partaking of the character of *pain* is determined by the source it comes from. When the heaviest sorrow comes by God's appointment, we bow in submission; and this not merely because we cannot help it, because it is vain to repine, because God *will* take his own way whether we like it or not, but because we have perfect confidence in the rightness of whatever God may do, and because we feel assured that there must be good reason for all He does, although we may not be able to discern that reason. As regards *man*, we have no such confidence. And parents may be assured that their foolish conduct towards their children in many cases *is* a training, but an extremely bad one; it trains the children to a spirit of fruitless and therefore bitter resistance, and of dogged resentment. The philanthropist Howard, by taking the course the Archbishop reprobates, drove his son into a lunatic asylum. *He* followed that course rigorously and universally, and so the worst degree of mental disease ensued upon it. Most parents follow it only in part; and the lesser evil follows, of alienated affection, loss of confidence, jaundiced views, and a soured heart. Yet if any parent, on a cold morning, insists on his children remaining in that part of the room most distant from the fire, when their warming their little blue hands *there* could do no harm to any human being; or systematically refuses to permit them to go to "children's parties," not because they are asked to too many, but merely because it is good for them to be disappointed; or, generally, seeks to repress the exhibition of gaiety and light-heartedness, because " we must through much tribulation enter the kingdom of God," — then let that parent be assured, that surely as the field sown with tares yielded a harvest of tares, so surely will this petty tyranny bring forth its natural result, of resentment and aversion.

" Most carefully should we avoid the error of which some parents, not (otherwise) deficient in good sense, commit, of imposing gratuitous restrictions and privations, and purposely inflicting needless disappointments, for the purpose of inuring children to the pains and troubles they will meet with in after-life. Yes, be assured they *will* meet with quite *enough*, in every portion of life, including childhood, without your strewing their path with thorns of your own providing. And often enough will you have to limit their amusements for the sake of needful study, to restrain their appetites for the sake of health, to chastise them for faults, and in various ways to inflict pain or privations for the sake of avoiding some greater evils. Let this always be explained to them whenever it is possible to do so; and endeavor in all cases to make them look on the parent as never the *voluntary* giver of anything but good. To any hardships which they are convinced you inflict reluctantly, and to those which occur through the dispensation of the All-wise, they will more easily be trained to submit with a good grace than to any gratuitous sufferings devised for them by fallible men. To raise hopes on purpose to produce disappointment, to give provocation merely to exercise the temper, and, in short, to inflict pain of any kind merely as a training for patience and fortitude, — this is a kind of discipline which man should not presume to attempt. If such trials prove a discipline, not so much of cheerful fortitude as of resentful aversion and suspicious distrust of the parent as a capricious tyrant, you will have only yourself to thank for this result." — (pp. 58, 59.)

Archbishop Whately is of opinion that the fear of punishment in a future life is a motive of more permanent force than that of temporal judgments. We quote his words : —

" It is true that some men, who are nearly strangers to such a habit, may be for a time more alarmed by the denunciation of immediate temporal judgments for their sins, than by any considerations relative to ' the things which are not seen and which are eternal.' But the effect thus produced is much less likely to be lasting, or while it lasts to be salutary, because temporal alarm does not tend to make men spiritually-minded, and any reformation of manners it may have produced will not have been founded on Christian principles." — (pp. 61, 62.)

Upon this we remark that there can be no question that, were future punishments realized as substantially as temporal evils, they ought to have, and would have, a much greater effect in deterring from sinful conduct. But the great difficulty with which men have to contend is the essential impossibility of realizing spiritual and unseen things in their true bulk and importance ; of feeling that a thing in the Bible, or in a sermon, is as *real* a thing as something in the daylight, material world. In no case is this difficulty more felt than in regard to future punishments in another life. We may be far mistaken ; but the result of considerable experience of the ways and feelings of a rustic population, is something of doubt whether in practice the fear of future punishment produces any effect in deterring from evil courses. A mountain far away may be concealed by a shilling held close to the eye ; and future woe seems to cross minds so distant and so misty, that a very small immediate gratification quite hides it from view.

We remember, as illustrative of this, a circumstance related by a neighboring clergyman. His parishioners were sadly addicted to drinking to excess. Men and women were alike given to this degrading vice. He did, of course, all he could to repress it, but all in vain. For many years, he said, he warned the drunkards in the most solemn manner of the doom they might expect in another world; but, so far as he knew, not a pot of ale or glass of spirits the less was drunk in the parish in consequence of his denunciations. Future woe melted into mist in the presence of a replenished jug on a market-day. A happy thought struck the clergyman. In the neighboring town there was a clever medical man, a vehement teetotaler. Him he summoned to his aid. The doctor came, and delivered a lecture on the *physical* consequences of drunkenness, illustrating his lecture with large diagrams which gave shocking representations of the stomach, lungs, heart, and other vital organs, as affected by alchohol. These things came home to the drunkards, who had not cared a rush for final perdition. The effect produced was tremendous. Almost all the men and women of the parish took the total-abstinence pledge; and since that day, drunkenness has nearly ceased in that parish. Nor was the improvement evanescent; it has lasted for two or three years.

The Archbishop, in the Annotations upon "Simulation and Dissimulation," discusses the question whether an author is justified in disowning the authorship of his anonymous productions. It is, indeed, a considerable annoyance when meddling and impertinent persons, in spite of every indication that the subject is a disagreeable one, persist in trying by *fishing questions* to discover whether we know who wrote such an article in *Fraser's Magazine* or the *Edinburgh Review;* and though no man of good sense or taste will do this, no author is safe in the existing abundance of men who are devoid of both these qualities. We have known instances in which the subject was recurred to time after time by impertinent questioners, and in which, by sudden inquiries put in the presence of many listeners, and by interrogating the relatives and intimate friends of the supposed writer, attempts were made to elicit the fact.

It is curious to remark the various opinions which have been put on record as to the casuistry of such cases. There is but one opinion as to the extreme impertinence of the questioners; and so far as *they* are concerned, the curtest refusal to answer their inquiries would be the fittest way of meeting them. But, unhappily, a refusal to reply will in many cases be regarded as an answer in the affirmative; and if the only alternatives were a *correct answer* and *no answer*, any meddling fool might reveal a literary secret of the highest importance. Dr. Johnson took up the ground that an author is justified in directly denying that he wrote his anonymous writings. Sir Walter Scott expressly declared that he was not the author of the Waverley Novels. Mr. Samuel Warren, when a lad at school, with characteristic presumption, wrote to Sir Walter as such, and Sir Walter's answer, published in Mr. Warren's *Miscellanies*, expressly repudiates the authorship. Mr. Samuel Rogers drew a nice distinction. Some forward individual, in his presence, taxed Scott with the authorship of *Waverley;* Sir Walter replied, " Upon my honor, I am not"; and Rogers thought that Scott might fairly have replied in the negative, but that he ought not to have said "Upon my honor." Swift's reply to Serjeant Bettesworth approached a shade nearer the fact:—.

"Mr. Bettesworth, I was in my youth acquainted with great lawyers, who, knowing my disposition to satire, advised me that if any scoundrel or blockhead whom I had lampooned should ask, 'Are you the author of this paper?' I should tell him that I was not the author: and THEREFORE I tell you, Mr. Bettesworth, that I am not the author of these lines."

A writer in a recent *Quarterly Review* * appears to be for exact truth at all risks; saying that the question really is, whether impertinence in one person will justify falsehood in another; and maintaining that, if the least departure from veracity is admitted in any instance, there is no saying where the thing will end.

Archbishop Whately is reluctant to advise a departure from the truth in any case, but advises a method of meeting prying questioners which we trust reviewers will make use of on occasion. We quote the passage in which his advice occurs; it is admirable for point and pungency:—

"A well-known author once received a letter from a peer with whom he was slightly acquainted, asking him whether he was the author of a certain article in the *Edinburgh Review*. He replied that he never made communications of that kind, except to intimate friends, selected by himself for the purpose, when he saw fit. His refusal to answer, however, pointed him out — which, as it happened, he did not care for — as the author. But a case might occur in which the revelation of the authorship might involve a friend in

<hr>

* Quarterly Review, Vol. XCIX. p. 302.

some serious difficulties. In any such case, he might have answered something in this style : ' I have received a letter purporting to be from your lordship, but the matter of it induces me to suspect that it is a forgery by some mischievous trickster. The writer asks whether I am the author of a certain article. It is a sort of question which no one has a right to ask ; and I think, therefore, that every one is bound to discourage such inquiries by answering them — whether one is or is not the author — with a rebuke for asking impertinent questions about private matters. I say ' private,' because, if an article be libellous or seditious, the law is open, and any one may proceed against the publisher, and compel him either to give up the author or to bear the penalty. If, again, it contains false statements, these, coming from an anonymous pen, may be simply contradicted. And if the arguments be unsound, the obvious course is to refute them. But *who* wrote it is a question of idle or of mischievous curiosity, as it relates to the private concerns of an individual.

" ' If I were to ask your lordship, ' Do you spend your income ? or lay by ? or outrun ? Do you and your lady ever have an altercation ? Was she your first love ? or were you attached to some one else before ? ' If I were to ask such questions, your lordship's answer would probably be, to desire the footman to show me out. Now, the present inquiry I regard as no less unjustifiable, and relating to private concerns, and therefore I think every one bound, when so questioned, always, whether he is the author or not, to meet the inquiry with a rebuke.

" ' Hoping that my conjecture is right, of the letter's being a forgery, I remain,' &c.

" In any case, however, in which a refusal to answer does not convey any information, the best way, perhaps, of meeting impertinent inquiries, is by saying, ' Can you keep a secret ? ' and when the other answers that he can, you may reply, ' Well, so can I.' " — (pp. 68, 69.)

There are some admirable remarks under the head of the Essay on " Parents and Children," upon the pro-priety of considering in what direction a boy's talents lie, in making choice of a profession for him. Too frequently, when we speak of a boy's mind having a bent to some particular course, it is understood that what is meant is, that he has an extraordinary genius for it; but it is to be remembered that —

" numbers of men who would never attain any extraordinary eminence in anything, are yet so constituted as to make a very respectable figure in the department that is suited for them, and to fall below mediocrity in a different one." — (pp. 72, 73.)

Mr. Thackeray would be delighted with the short Annotations on the Essay " Of Nobility." It is in the nature of the Anglo-Saxon race to worship rank; and when (as in the United States) rank is altogether ignored, the very violence of the reaction from the way in which things are done on this side of the Atlantic, indicates how resolute is the bent of the species in the contrary direction. It is the man who has a strong disposition to fall down at the feet of a duke that is most likely to deny a duke, because he is one, the courtesy due to a man. We think that Archbishop Whately holds the balance very fairly between the two extremes: —

" In reference to nobility in individuals, nothing was ever better said than by Bishop Warburton — as is reported — in the House of Lords, on the occasion of some angry dispute which had arisen between a peer of noble family and one of a new creation. He said that, ' High birth was a thing which he never knew any one disparage, except those who had it not; and he never knew any one make a boast of it who had anything else to be proud of.'

"It was a remark by a celebrated man, himself a gentleman born, but with nothing of nobility, that the difference between a man with a long line of noble ancestors and an upstart is, that 'the one knows for certain what the other only conjectures as highly probable, that several of his forefathers deserved hanging.'" — (pp. 121, 122.)

In the Annotations on the Essay "Of Friendship," the Archbishop puts down, by irresistible force of argument, one of the most silly, mischievous, purposeless, and groundless errors which have ever been taught: we mean the doctrine that in a future life, happy souls will be no longer capable of special individual friendship. We have often been filled with burning indignation at finding in the book of some empty-headed divine who never learned logic, or in the sermon of some popular preacher thoroughly devoid of sense, taste, scholarship, modesty, and the reasoning faculty, lengthy tirades about the perfection of another world consisting much in an entire elevation above such earthly things as specific attachments. We have seen and heard it stated that in a future life blessed spirits will never remember or recognize those who were dearest to them in this; and perhaps, indeed, will not remember or recognize their own identity. It is satisfactory to know that this doctrine is as groundless as it is revolting; and most truly does Archbishop Whately say, that —

" this is one of the many points in which views of the eternal state of the heirs of salvation are rendered more uninteresting to our feelings, and consequently more uninviting, than there is any need to make them."

There is much social wisdom in the remarks upon the Essay "Of Expense." And here the Archbishop, in a graver tone, propounds a like philosophy to that which Mr. Thackeray has in several of his writings enforced so well.   It would be hard to reckon up the misery and anxiety which are produced in this country by absurd and foolish straining to "keep up appearances"; that is, with five hundred a year to entertain precisely like a man with five thousand, and generally to present a false face to the world, and seem other than what one is. When will this curse of our civilized life cease?   Surely, if people knew how transparent are all the pretences by which they think to pass for wealthy folk, — how readily neighbors see through them, — how incomparably more respectable and more respected is sterling yet unaffected honesty in this matter, — this foolish display would cease, and the analogous forms of deception would cease with it.   No one is taken in by them.   Any one who knows the world knows thoroughly how, by an accompanying process of mental arithmetic, to make the deductions from the big talk or the pretentious show of some people, which are needed to bring the appearance down to the reality.   The green-grocer got in for the day is never mistaken for the family butler.   The fly jobbed by the hour is easily distinguished from the brougham which it personates.   And when Mr. Smith or Mrs. Jones talks largely of his or her aristocratic acquaintances, mentioning no name without "a handle to it," no one is for a moment misled into the belief that of such is the circle of society in which Mrs. Jones or Mr. Smith moves.

In the Annotations on the "Regimen of Health," there are some useful remarks upon early and late hours, and upon times of study, which we commend to the notice of hard-working college-men. And these remarks close with the following suggestive paragraph :—

" Of persons who have led a temperate life, those will have the best chance of longevity who have done hardly anything but live ; what may be called the *neuter verbs*, — not active or passive, but only *being ;* who have had little to do, little to suffer; but have led a life of quiet retirement, without exertion of body or mind, avoiding all troublesome enterprise, and seeking only a comfortable obscurity. Such men, if of a pretty strong constitution, and if they escape any remarkable calamities, are likely to live long. But much affliction, or much exertion, and, still more, both combined, will be sure to *tell* upon the constitution, if not at once, yet at least as years advance. One who is of the character of an active or passive verb, or, still more, both combined, though he may be said to have lived long in everything but years, will rarely reach the age of the neuters." — (p. 305.)

" It is better," said Bishop Cumberland, " to wear out than to rust out "; yet there can be no question that when the energies of body and mind are husbanded, they will go further and last longer. Never to light the candle is the way to make it last forever. Yet it may suffice the man who has crowded much living into a short life, to think that he has " lived long in everything but years."

> " We live in deeds, not years ; in thoughts, not breaths ;
> . In feelings, not in figures on a dial.
>   We should count time by heart-throbs. He most lives,
>   Who thinks most, feels the noblest, acts the best." *

In remarking on the Essay " Of Suspicion," the Archbishop writes as follows :—

* Bailey's *Festus.*

"Multitudes are haunted by the spectres, as it were, of vague surmises and indefinite suspicions, which continue thus to haunt them, just because they are vague and indefinite, because the mind has never ventured to look them boldly in the face, and put them into a shape in which reason can examine them." — (p. 317.)

A valuable practical lesson is to be drawn from the principle here laid down. Only experience can convince a man how wonderfully the mind's burden is lightened, by merely getting a clear view of what it has to do or bear or encounter. Some persons go through life in a ceaseless worry, oppressed and confused by an undefined feeling that they have a vast number and variety of things to do, and never feeling at rest or easy in their minds. If any man would just take a piece of paper and note down upon it what work he has to do, he will be surprised to find how much less formidable it will look; not that it will necessarily look little, but that the killing thing, the vague sense of undefined magnitude, will be gone. So it is with troubles, so with doubts. If any one who is possessed with the general impression that he is an extremely ill-used and unhappy man, would write down the special items of his troubles, even though the list should be of considerable length, he will find that matters are not so bad after all. There is nothing, we believe, that so aggravates all evil to the minds of most men, as when the sense of the vague, indeterminate, and innumerable, is added to it; and we are strong believers in the power of *the pen* to give most people clear and well-defined thoughts.

We may particularize as especially worthy of attention, Archbishop Whately's observations on the different periods of life at which different men attain their mental maturity (pp. 403, 404) ; on the license of counsel in pleading a client's cause (pp. 509 – 512) ; on the necessity of the forms and ceremonies of etiquette, even among the closest friends (p. 479) ; and upon the causes of sudden popularity (pp. 500 – 502).   Students will find some valuable advice at pp. 460, 461 ; and young preachers, at pp. 323, 324.   Dissenting ministers, and other persons who pretend an entire contempt for worldly wealth, either because the grapes hang beyond their reach, or from envy of people who are more fortunate, may turn with advantage to pp. 350, 351. Those amiable individuals who are wont to express their satisfaction that such an acquaintance has met with some disappointment, *because it will do him good,* are referred to the Archbishop's keen and just remark upon such as bestow posthumous praise upon a man whom they reviled and calumniated during his life, and may profitably consider whether the real motive from which they speak is not highly analogous : —

" It may fairly be suspected that the one circumstance respecting him which they se cretly dwell on with the most satisfaction, though they do not mention it, is that he is *dead ;* and that they delight in bestowing their posthumous honors on him, chiefly because they are *posthumous ;* according to the concluding couplet in the *Verses on the Death of Dean Swift :* —

> " And since you dread *no further lashes,*
> Methinks you may forgive his ashes."

— (p. 19.)

We must draw our remarks to a close.   We feel how imperfect an idea we have given of Archbishop Whately's Annotations, — of their range, their cogency, their wisdom, their experience, their practical instruction, their wit, their eloquence. The extracts we have quoted are like a sheaf of wheat brought from a field of a hundred acres; but we trust our readers may be induced to study the book for themselves.

CHAPTER XVI.

SOME FURTHER TALK ABOUT SCOTCH AFFAIRS.

A Letter to the Editor of "*Fraser's Magazine.*"

[In a former volume of Essays,* I filled a few pages with a letter written to. the editor of *Fraser's Magazine* by my neighbor and friend, Mr. Macdonald of Craig-Houlakim. That letter, when published in the Magazine, excited so much interest, that Mr. Macdonald was easily persuaded to follow it with another similar one; and, though not going all my friend's length, I have to confess the substantial truth of his statements. A little space in the present volume will not unfitly be spared for his epistle.]

GENERAL ASSEMBLY HALL, CASTLE-HILL,
EDINBURGH, May 29, 1857.

MY DEAR EDITOR:—A happy thought has just occurred to me. I am sitting here on one of the back benches of the General Assembly of the Kirk of Scotland, to which venerable Court the Presbytery of Whistle-binkie, with much appreciation of real merit, has sent me as one of its lay representatives. In company with some four or five hundred more, clergymen and laymen, I am legislating for the ecclesiastical good of the people of Scotland. I have been engaged in this work for a week past, and shall be for several days longer. I am look-

* Leisure Hours in Town, Chapter XIV.

ing out at this moment on a sea of anxious faces, inter-
spersed with many bald heads. The atmosphere is hot
and feverish. As I write, an outsider, name unknown,
is making a speech to which nobody is listening   A
booming sound of *Oarrdurr* occasionally proceeds from
the chair when the hum of conversation grows into a
roar; for my good friend Professor Robertson has been
elevated to the dignity of moderator, and has taken his
Aberdeenshire accent along with him. For the last
week I have been kept here to all hours of the night,
and I am uncommonly sleepy; and so it has occurred
to me that in the intervals when the business of the
House becomes devoid of interest, I might beguile
the time by writing a letter to you, and indulging in a
little further dissertation on the affairs of my adopted
country.

When I last wrote to you, it was on a gloomy day in
the end of November, — just that season- when you
London folk, who do not know anything better, delude
yourselves into the belief that a town life is preferable
to a country one. Since then we have seen once more,
what I trust I never shall see without leaping-up of the
heart, the gradual revival of the spring. Snowdrops
and crocuses came and went; the birch grew fragrant,
and the pine was tipped with delicate green ; the primroses sprang in the woods; and although the dire east
winds held all vegetation back for weeks beyond the
usual period, yet when I left home to come to the Assembly, I thought, with a grudge, that for many a day
I must forego the blossoming lilacs and hawthorns, the
fruit-trees bending with their weight of bloom, the soft
green of the beeches, and the floral glory of the horse-

chestnuts, around my Highland 'home. There is no place like the country, after all. But upon that subject you and I shall not agree, so I had better say no more about it.

Sitting in this atmosphere, my thoughts naturally take an ecclesiastical direction; and while I look at this great company of men, almost all well-educated, and many of them possessing high ability, who from Sunday to Sunday and from day to day are devoting their energies to the religious instruction of the Scotch people, the first reflection which rises to my mind is, the total severance which exists in many parts of Scotland between a sound creed and a righteous practice. Few things surprise me more than the utter lack of practical force in Scotch orthodoxy. I have no doubt that the same thing must be lamented in all countries, by all who are anxious for the moral elevation of mankind; but I believe that Scotland is the country which exhibits the evil in its most striking form. You can hardly find a church in this country in which sound doctrine is not regularly preached; you can hardly find in country places a child that has not been carefully instructed in the *Shorter Catechism*, or a grown-up man or woman who does not make some profession of religion, by attending church and receiving the Sacrament; but you would be regarded as an arrant simpleton if you fancied that nine farmers out of ten whom you saw most exemplary at their devotions on Sunday would not cheat you on Monday, if doing so would put five shillings in their pocket. Of course, you have plenty of grocers in England who mix sand with their sugar, and sugar with their tea; and abundance of farmers who will sell you a

lame horse as a sound one if they have an opportunity;
but if such a man among you English folk were scrupulous in maintaining morning and evening prayer in
his family, and given to shedding tears in church at the
practical pieces of the sermon, you would certainly conclude that he was adding hypocrisy to his other sins.
Not so here.   You would judge quite too severely were
you to conclude that a Scotch farmer was a hypocrite,
because you found him shaking his head sympathetically at the minister's warnings on Sunday, and then on
the following market-day at Whistle-binkie declaring
solemnly that he had paid fifty pounds for a broken-
winded nag which he had really bought for five.   The
true state of the case is that our friend Mr. Pawkie
does not feel that his religious belief has any connection
whatever with his daily life.   These are quite separate
things in his mind.   It is one thing for a doctrine to be
perfectly right in a sermon, and quite another for it to
be an axiom safe to act upon in the grain-market or at
the Falkirk Tryst.

Last Sunday, instead of remaining in Edinburgh, and
getting several ribs broken in an attempt to get into the
High Kirk to hear the " Sermon before the Commis-
sioner," I preferred going quietly into the country with
a friend who has a sweet place a few miles off, and attending church with him.   As we walked through the
quiet morning to the ivy-covered little kirk, surrounded
by a host of mouldering gravestones, on which a hand-
ful of simple-looking country folk were seated, awaiting
the hour of prayer, I should certainly have fancied that
the people were as Arcadian in innocence as the scene
was in peacefulness, had I not lived in Scotland for

some ten years past. While service was going on, I
was especially struck by the devout and sympathetic
attention of a venerable old fogy, apparently a respectable farmer, with long white hair and a most benevolent
expression. The sermon, which was an excellent one,
was upon the duty of mutual forbearance and kindliness;
its text was, " Forgive us our debts as we forgive our
debtors." The good old man's face was lighted up, and
he shook his head, and gently waved his hand in sympathy with the sentiments expressed by the preacher.
You would have said that he was recognizing the pa-
thetic delineation of the principles on which he was
himself acting in his daily life of charity and good will.
At length the sermon was finished, and the minister, as
is usual here, read the parting hymn. An expression
of high and holy joy beamed upon the patriarch's coun-
tenance as he listened to it; he laid his head back,
closed his eyes, and lifted his hand as though engaged in
silent prayer, as the clergyman read the lines:—

> " Let such as feel oppression's load
> Thy tender pity share;
> And let the helpless, homeless poor,
> Be thy peculiar care.

> " Go, bid the hungry orphan be
> With thy abundance blest;
> Invite the wanderer to thy door,
> And spread the couch of rest."

In walking home from church, I made inquiry of my
friend as to the benevolent and pious old gentleman
whose bearing had so charmed me. He *was* a farmer,
as I had surmised; a man paying some eight hundred
a year of rent, and enjoying a good income. I learned

in addition to this, that he was a thorough-going old scoundrel; a notorious cheat, swearer, drunkard, and worse. He had palmed off more lame horses than any man in the county, and told more lies in his time than would sink a man-of-war. The last of his doings, which he accomplished two days before I saw him, was seizing the bed from under a poor widow whose husband had died a few months previously, and who had been wearing her fingers to the bone to support her little children, but had failed to pay the old rascal a most exorbitant rent for a miserable hovel upon his ground. Yet this man was the most exemplary in the parish in his attention to the ordinances of religion: he never was absent from a sacrament; and on the Sunday after seizing the widow's poor sticks of furniture, I beheld him, radiant with holy joy, wagging his head and waving his hand in the church of C———. How I wished I were the Emperor of Russia, and the old gentleman one of my subjects. Should not I have given him a taste of the knout! shouldn't I have made him howl!

As I write these words, Professor Pirie of Aberdeen rises to make a speech. He begins, " Aw doant see thawt, Moaderahturr," as he raises his fist in the air. Had it been Mr. Phin, or Dr. Tulloch, or Mr. McLeod, I should have prepared to listen with all attention; but as it is quite certain that Mr. Pirie's speech will not be worth listening to, and equally certain that it will be a long one, I shall occupy its duration in telling you something about a very interesting Scotch institution, — that of our parish schools.

During the month of March, in that part of the country in which I reside, two days in each week are devoted to the examination of the schools by committees of the Presbytery; and as I feel a good deal of interest in the great education question, and am anxious to know the true condition of Scotland in regard to the training of the young, I accompanied my friend, the parish clergyman, this year to the examination of seven or eight of the neighboring schools. You must understand that every parish in Scotland has its parish school, as certainly as its parish church; and in these schools generally a sound, fair education may be obtained, quite adequate to the circumstances of the Scottish peasantry. Reading, writing, arithmetic, and religion as set out in the Catechism of the Scotch Church, are taught to all comers, without distinction of sect. The result of the existence of these schools is, that except in the large cities, in which the population has outgrown their reach, *all* Scotch men and women are able to read and write. Hardly ever is a bride or bridegroom under the necessity of affixing a cross to the registration paper, from want of capacity to sign the name. These parish schools are to all intents a part of the National Church. They are endowed from its revenues, their teachers must be churchmen, and they are under the supervision of the Presbytery of the district. A committee, consisting of three or four clerical members of the Presbytery, yearly examines each school; and I can testify from personal experience that the examination is no sham. Those at which I was this year present lasted from five to nine hours each.

The salaries of the schoolmasters are shamefully inadequate. They average some twenty-five pounds

13 *

a year in most cases, with a dwelling-house. The school-houses are often wretchedly bad. The buildings are maintained, and the salaries are paid, by the *heritors;* and you will be able to judge, from what I told you in my last letter, how much is in many cases to be expected from *their* liberality. Where the parish is large, — and parishes of twelve and fourteen miles in length are common, even in the Lowlands, — there are sometimes three or four schools; and in such cases this princely endowment is *divided* among their teachers. Besides the endowment, the teachers in all cases receive the school fees paid by the children. These fees vary from eighteen-pence to four or five shillings a quarter, according to the number of branches taught. The number of children attending a parish school may average from fifty to a hundred. I have known cases in which the numbers amounted to two and even three hundred; but these instances are rare, and *then* we find the teacher claiming for his school the more ambitious designation of *academy.* Many parochial teachers derive an increase of income from the Privy Council grants; but with that curious jealousy of state interference in religious matters which is ingrained into the Scotch character, many eminent clergymen refuse to receive the grant on the accompanying condition that the government inspector shall annually examine the school. This, it is maintained by some, with a feeling which appears to me Quixotic in the extreme, implies a doubt of the sufficiency of the examination by the Presbytery.

The Scotch parish schoolmaster toils away from nine o'clock in the morning till three or four in the afternoon,

with a single hour's intermission for dinner. He teaches
the alphabet, four or five reading classes, geography,
history, arithmetic, writing, Latin, Greek, French, ge-
ometry, and algebra. I have seen all these things
taught, and well taught, by a man who had not forty
pounds a year. In remote country districts, the ele-
mentary branches only are taught; but there are very
few schools in which there is not a Latin class. I venture to assert that the parish schools are for the most
part extremely well, and in many instances admirably,
taught; and any one who says otherwise must be altogether ignorant of the facts. The teachers are, with
rare exceptions, quite exemplary in conduct, and almost
always very intelligent men; many exhibit an energy
and spirit in conducting their classes which are extraordinary. They teach all the year round, except six
weeks in autumn. The holidays are at that season,
in order that the children may work in the harvest field,
reaping or attending upon the reapers. Indeed, it is a
matter of general complaint in country districts that the
children are frequently taken away from school to eke
out their parent's earnings by field-work. A child of
seven or eight years old can earn eightpence a day in
weeding turnips in the season. But when he returns to
school after some weeks' absence, the teacher finds that
he has forgotten all he had learned before.

I have seen school-rooms of all different degrees.
Sometimes they are spacious and airy, the walls well
furnished with maps and pictures, and presenting a
general aspect of cheerfulness and comfort. Much
more frequently I have found them wretched, ill-ven-
tilated, over-crowded apartments, with bare walls green

with damp, a moist earthen floor worn into deep hollows, and a ceiling from which the plaster had fallen in large patches. The forms and desks were rickety and creaking, cut almost in pieces by the knives of successive generations of school-boys; and the entire impression left by the place was stupefying and disheartening to the last degree. Shabby heritors find a pretext for allowing this state of things to continue, in the prospect of such a legislative act as shall put the entire educational system of Scotland upon a new footing. I heartily hope, my dear friend, that the day may not be far distant that shall give our hard-working parish teachers something like decent salaries, — fifty pounds a year is the highest salary contemplated, — and that shall rid us of those miserable school-buildings in which a boy is driven stupid by the din and the stifling atmosphere; but I cannot see why this should not be done without taking the parish schools from under the superintendence of the Church. Whatever may have been the case in past days, when both the churches of Britain were comatose enough, I can assure you that now the superintendence of the Presbytery is most effective and vigilant; and I can assure you, likewise, that the people of Scotland, as a whole, have perfect confidence in the schools as at present constituted. All sects of dissenters send their children most willingly to the parish school. The Lord Advocate, who has brought into Parliament repeated bills for separating the schools from the Church, is a mere tool in the hands of the leaders of the "Free Kirk." That "body" has built schools of its own in many parishes; and finding that it cannot support them, would like to get them taken off its hands.

This the Lord Advocate's bill would do. I do not expect, my dear editor, that you will entirely sympathize with me in what you may possibly regard my old-fashioned and illiberal notions upon this point ; but they are the result of a good deal of observation and no little reflection, and I hold them firmly.

A great day in the parish is that of the school examination. The children are all assembled betimes, with clean faces, and in their Sunday clothes. It is a time of solemn expectation ; and the teacher, as he walks up and down, giving his final directions, is a little nervous. The three or four clergymen who constitute the examining committee at length appear. The school-room is crowded with parents, who have come to enjoy the proficiency of their children ; and a heritor or two may be seen, who have sought a reflected happiness in spending two or three pounds in prize-books, which will make many little hearts light and proud for longer than that one day. It is whispered in the school that the master has got a new coat, which appears to-day for the first time. The proceedings are opened with a prayer, offered by one of the presiding ministers ; then the classes are successively called, beginning with the youngest. Who could be otherwise than interested and sympathizing, when two or three fluttered little things come up trembling, and say their A B C, making a host of mistakes, which they never would have made but for the awful presence of the Presbytery! Who but must feel for the poor cottager's wife on the back form, as she hears her little boy going all wrong in what he said to her perfectly right an hour before? Pat the little fellow on the head, and tell him he is a clever boy and has done capitally; it will tide him over one sad disappointment of his life, and the innocent fiction will never rise up against you elsewhere. Then come the reading classes; and here you may by degrees examine more sharply. Almost all read well — of course with the broadest Scotch accent; almost all spell admirably, and most understand completely what they read. The reading-books in general use are a series edited by Dr. M'Culloch, of Greenock; an excellent series, filled with pieces so attractive that children will read them for their interest, and almost forget that they are tasks. I must confess that when I have been at school examinations, I have sometimes found myself reading Dr. M'Culloch on my own account, instead of attending to the lesson that was going forward. The children generally exhibit a thorough acquaintance with Scripture history; and the *Shorter Catechism*, an admirable compend of sound theology, and quite in keeping with the Thirty-nine Articles, is at the finger-ends of all. Grammar is generally well taught; geography, sometimes extraordinarily well. Specimens of the writing of the pupils, each on a large sheet of paper, are hung up round the room. The Latin and Greek classes come last; and the exhibition is wound up by recitations, delivered by a few of the most distinguished scholars. Sometimes the effect of these is irresistibly ludicrous. A very favorite piece is Campbell's *Hohenlinden*. A boy stands up, amid awful silence, and elevating his right hand in the air, with a face utterly blank of expression, proceeds to repeat the poem, accentuating very strongly every alternate syllable, and completely ignoring the points : —

> " On Lunden whan the sahn was law
> Ul bloodless lah thuntroaden snaw
> Und dark uz wuntur wuz the flaw
> Avizar roallin rawpidlah."

Some clergymen pride themselves on their power of drawing out the intelligence of children by their mode of putting questions to them. And occasionally I have seen this well done; more frequently, very absurdly. The following is a specimen of a style of examination which I have myself more than once witnessed : —

" Wahl, deer cheldrun, what was it that swallowed Jonah? Was it a sh-sh-sh-sh-shark?" — " Yahs!" roar a host of voices. " Noa, deer cheldrun, it was not a shark. Then was it an al-al-al-allig-allig-alligator?" " Yahs!" exclaim the voices again. " Noa, deer cheldrun, it was not an alligator. Then was it a wh-wh-wh-whaaale?" " Noa," roar the voices, determined to be right this time. " Yahs, deer cheldrun, it was a whale."

The prizes are distributed; and then each clergyman in turn makes a speech, expressive of his opinion of the appearance which the scholars have made, and also of the skill and industry of the teacher. This opinion is always complimentary; and in cases where teacher and scholars are in an unsatisfactory state, it is amusing to witness the struggles of the speaker to say something which shall have a general tone of compliment, and yet mean nothing. Finally, one of the examiners gives an address to the children, inculcating the general doctrine that they ought to be good boys and mind their lessons. A prayer closes the proceedings; and then the ministers are off to the manse to dinner.

A great many parochial teachers add a little to their income by holding certain small parish offices; such as those of precentor, session-clerk, inspector of poor, postmaster, and the like. I have known all these offices accumulated upon one individual. Many teachers are very eccentric men. Indeed, one would say that no one but a rather singular being would continue for thirty or forty years in a post entailing so much toil and offering such poor remuneration. A short time since, at a school examination, I found a large piece of pasteboard, bearing in a very legible hand the following inscription, written by the teacher, and evidently intended to be exhibited to the children : —

"To Mr. Smith.

"*From a Correspondent.*

"Mr. Smith, thou art good and mild,
Beloved by every little child,
Thou wast formed for usefulness,
Boys to comfort and girls to bless."

You will hardly believe me when I tell you that the author of this remarkable poem was really a very efficient and successful teacher of young children; and possibly he was quite correct in judging that to exhibit such an effusion as something which he had received from an unknown admirer would tend to make his pupils hold him in greater veneration. My observation of many parochial schoolmasters has led me to the belief, not only that a total want of common sense in the affairs of ordinary life is quite compatible with a man's being an excellent teacher, but even that such a want of common sense is directly conducive to his success as a teacher. I have a theory by which I think I can both prove and explain this somewhat paradoxical opinion; but I need not bother you with it here.

The very best teachers I have ever known have been men of no great extent of information, and of no claims to scholarship, but who have possessed a wonderful power of communicating whatever knowledge they had got. I have known one or two men, rather stupid and indiscreet in daily life, but who seemed to become inspired when placed in the presence of a class of boys or girls (for both boys and girls are educated at our parish schools), and who displayed a positive genius for putting all they had to tell their pupils in the most attractive and striking shape. And once or twice I have come across quaint, respectable old characters, who have kept school for fifty or sixty years, content in their humble and useful vocation; much given to quoting Latin, especially in speaking to persons who did not understand it; treasuring up a little store of old classical authors *in usum Delphini*, one of which you might find them reading in their garden on a summer day; fond of talking about their old days at college, threescore years since; and recounting with pride how they had beaten, in the Latin class at St. Andrews, men who had become the dignitaries of the kirk, the bar, and the bench; or how they had lived for a term in the same lodgings with Smith, who became physician to the Court of St. Petersburg; with Brown, who rose to be Prime Minister to the King of Ashantee; or with Reid, who arrived at the dignity of an Austrian marshal. And philosophic men like you and me may perhaps bethink us, that to a Scotchman, with his yearning to the land of the mountain and the flood, it may have proved a less happy lot to rise to wordly honor far away, than to cuff the ears and win the hearts of many generations of school-boys, and to be the oracle of the neighborhood, the first man in his native village.

I have already said that the close of the school examination-day is a dinner at the manse, to which the schoolmasters are always asked, in addition to the clergymen who acted as examiners. I particularly enjoy dining with my parish clergymen on the days of the school examinations. I meet several of the neighboring clergy who would please you greatly; and I listen with a fresh interest to their conversation about church and college affairs. It opens a new field to me. I hear a great deal of men who, like the winner of the Derby, are great in their own sphere, but quite unknown to the world beyond it. I remember your telling me that you had never heard of our great preacher Caird till his sermon was published some months ago by the Queen's command. And I could mention the names of a score of Scotch preachers and professors, all great men in their way, but as unknown to you as is the name of the cook of the King of the Cannibal Islands. Now I like to hear about these men. I like to get an insight into a new set of interests and a new mode of life. I like to get a view of the Scotch character from a stand-point different from my own.

On such an occasion lately, I listened to much lamentation over the *pawkiness* and want of straightforwardness which are found in many country districts. *Apropos* of this, a minister who was present related how a country clergyman who died within the last twenty years,

one Sunday astonished his congregation in the following
manner. He announced his text with much solemnity.
It ran thus:—

I said in my haste, All men are liars.

Having read this verse twice with great emphasis, he
proceeded with his sermon in an abstracted and medita-
tive tone. "Ay, David," he exclaimed, "you said that
in your haste, did you? Gif you had leeved in this
parish, you would have said it at your leisure!"

"To show you," said another clergyman, "how little
feeling many persons, even of respectable standing, have,
that there is anything immoral in a falsehood told in the
way of business, I will tell you what occurred to myself
when I came to my parish. Like every minister with
an extensive parish, I wanted a horse. I mentioned my
need to a highly respectable farmer, who told me that
by great good luck he knew where I could be suited at
once. At a farm a few miles off there was for sale just
such an animal as I wanted. I said that I should lose
no time in going over to see the horse in question. 'Na,
na, sir,' said my friend, with a look of remarkable
shrewdness; 'na, na, *that* will never do. If you were
to gang over and say you wanted the beast, the farmer
would put an extra ten or fifteen pounds on his price.
But I'll tell you what we'll do. To-morrow forenoon
I'll drive you over to the farm, and I'll say to the farmer, 'This is Mr. Green, our new minister; I was jist
gieing him a bit drive to see the country. And as we
gaed by your house jist by chance, I telled him that you
had a bit beast to sell; and although I didna think it
wad suit him ava', yet it might do no harm to look at it
at ony rate. He wasna' for comin' in, the minister, for

he hadna time; but we have jist come in for ae minute, and if the beast's at hame, ye can let us see 't; but if no, it doesna matter a grain.' Noo, if I say *that* to him, he 'll think we dinna heed aboot the beast, and he 'll no raise the price o't.' I was quite surprised that a man of good character should propose to a clergyman to become his accomplice in a plan of trickery and falsehood; but when I recovered breath, I told my man exactly what I thought of his proposal, and said I should want a horse for ever rather than get one by telling a score of lies. But my friend was quite unabashed by my rebuke, and evidently thought I was a young man of Quixotic notions of honor, of which a little longer experience of life would happily rid me."

I was amused by a story I heard at the same time, of a simple-minded country parson, whose parish lay upon the Frith of Clyde, and so became gradually overspread with fashionable villas, to which families from Edinburgh and Glasgow resorted in summer and autumn. This worthy man persisted in exercising the same spiritual jurisdiction over these new-comers which he had been wont to exercise over his rustic parishioners before their arrival. And in particular, in his pastoral visitations, he insisted on examining the lady and gentleman of the house in *The Shorter Catechism*, in the presence of their children and servants. It happened, one autumn, that the late Lord Jeffrey, after the rising of the Court of Session, came to spend the long vacation in the parish of L——. Soon after his arrival, the minister intimated from the pulpit that upon a certain day he would "hold a diet of catechising" in the district which included the dwelling of the eminent judge. True to his time, he appeared at Lord Jeffrey's house, and requested that the entire establishment might be collected. This was readily done; for almost all Scotch clergymen, though the catechising process has become obsolete, still visit each house in the parish once a year, and collect the family to listen to a fireside lecture. But what was Lord Jeffrey's consternation when, the entire household being assembled in the drawing-room, the worthy minister said in a solemn voice, "My Lord, I always begin my examination with the head of the family. Will you tell me, then, 'What is Effectual Calling?'" Never was an Edinburgh Reviewer more thoroughly nonplussed. After a pause, during which the servants looked on in horror at the thought that a judge should not know his *Catechism*, his lordship recovered speech, and answered the question in terms which completely dumbfounded the minister, "Why, Mr. Smith, a man may be said to discharge the duties of his calling effectually when he performs them with ability and success." *

As I was writing these last words, the word *Episcopacy* caught my ear; and looking up, I observed a clergyman, unknown to me, addressing the House. The matter at the moment under discussion was some bill which it is proposed to introduce into Parliament to re-

* To explain Mr. Smith's consternation to an English reader, it may be well to give the question and answer in the form in which they are familiar to young Scotland.

Question. — What is Effectual Calling?

Answer. — Effectual Calling is the work of God's Spirit, whereby, convincing us of our sin and misery, enlightening our minds in the knowledge of Christ, and renewing our wills, he doth persuade and enable us to embrace Jesus Christ, freely offered to us in the Gospel.

move the disabilities of Scotch Episcopal ministers. The speaker, who spoke in the main smartly and cleverly, was evidently one of the last who cling to what may be called Presbyterian Puseyism. His speech manifested an enmity to prelatic government just such as many men in England bear towards Presbyterian. "The bishops of the Scotch Episcopal Church," said he, "illegally take to themselves territorial titles, and call themselves the Bishops of Glasgow, of Aberdeen, and so forth. Well, who cares? They have precisely the same right to these designations as the pickpockets who are taken before the London police-magistrates have to the *aliases* which they assume. And if a Scotch *soi-disant* bishop chooses to wear an apron, what have we to do with that? He is just as much entitled to wear a bit of silk as any other old woman. But if he goes to the pulpit with a cap, then indeed we have some reason to complain; for all things considered, it is unjustifiable that the cap should not be provided with bells." The intemperate speech of this gentleman was succeeded by a very judicious and excellent one from Mr. Sheriff Tait, the brother of the Bishop of London; and the Assembly came to some decision which I remember appeared to me a sensible one, but I have not the faintest recollection what it was.

But the little incident gave a new direction to my thoughts, and set me thinking upon the singular phase of feeling which has prevailed for some years in the Scotch Church. The horror of Episcopal government and ritual which prevailed in the minds of the founders of the Kirk was indescribably great. Not far from my door is the burying-place of two men who were hanged

in the persecuting days ; and the inscription on the stone
(which was often touched up by Old Mortality) states
that they died to bear witness "against Tyranny, Per-
jury, *and Prelacy.*" And in the mind of most Scotchmen then, and in the mind of the lower orders yet,
Prelacy is held in precisely the estimation which you
may infer from the connection in which it stands there.
A liturgy and a bishop were regarded as emanations
from the Devil. Yet now, singular to say, the Scotch
Church contains a body of clergymen, considerable in
point of numbers and pre-eminent in point of talent,
which you would say at once had a strong Episcopal
bias.

It would be invidious to mention names, but I venture to say that if you go to hear five out of six of our
most distinguished preachers, you will find their prayers
taken almost entirely from the Anglican liturgy, or from
the writings of the men who drew up the Anglican liturgy. If you should happen to converse with the ablest
and most cultivated of the Scotch clergy, you will find
that the wish for a liturgy is deeply felt, and almost
universal. I was informed within the last week that
one of the most conspicuous of the parish clergymen of
Edinburgh has compiled a liturgy for use in his own
church, which he intends to print and place in the hands
of the congregation. There is a strong and growing sense
among the educated people of Scotland that the Reformation in this country went a great deal too far, that the
ritual has been made repulsively bare and bald, and that
many things were tabooed for their association with
Popery, which formed no part of its essence, and are
founded upon feelings and principles which are integral

parts of man's higher nature.   There is a strong sense in this country that it was extremely absurd and wrong to refuse any recognition to the festivals of the Christian year.   There is a very general wish for some prescribed form of the marriage and baptism service.   There is an urgent demand for the introduction of a burial service; and indeed to any one who has often listened to the beautiful words of hope and consolation which in your country are breathed over a Christian grave, there is something inexpressibly revolting in the Scotch fashion of laying our friends down in their last resting-place without one Christian word, — without a syllable to tell in what belief we lay them there, or a prayer that we, when our day comes, " through the grave, and gate of death, may pass to our joyful resurrection."   And there is a strong movement, which is rigidly opposed by the ignorant and prejudiced, towards true ecclesiastical architecture.   Stained glass, which would have been smashed half a century ago, is common in large towns; and the use of the organ is evidently approaching.   One hears it often wished that the congregation, who now sit silent through the entire service (except joining in the Psalms), should at least respond so far as to utter *Amen* at the end of the prayers; and very many of the clergy take pains to have the whole worship of God conducted with an order and decency which the generation before last would assuredly have thought carnal and legal abomination.   The late Sir Henry Moncrief, who was minister of the West Church of Edinburgh, used to walk up to his pulpit every Sunday with his hat on his head, to testify to the grand Knoxite doctrine that no reverence is due to stone and lime; but any such proceeding now would excite just as much disgust for the pigheadedness of the individual that did it, in Scotland, as it would among you.

One hears occasionally of amusing instances of the pursuit of order under difficulties by the younger clergy. I heard of such a case the other day. The Scotch marriage service, you must know, is a very brief one. It is always performed by a single clergyman, who very rarely appears in canonicals. Two young clergymen, curates of a town in the west of Scotland, both (for I know them well) accomplished and able men, resolved to be the first to introduce a more imposing method. Accordingly, one of them having been asked to celebrate a marriage in town, both went to the place, arrayed in gown and band. One of them gave the very short address upon matrimonial duties which forms part of the service, and the other offered the prayers and received the declarations of the wedded couple. The parties, I believe, regard themselves as the only couple in Drumsleekie who ever were effectually and sufficiently married; but dire was the wrath of the true-blue Presbyterians of the place.

Now what is the meaning of all this? You must not fancy, my dear editor, that the Kirk of Scotland is growing ripe for amalgamation with the Church of England. Some members of what you might call the Episcopising party in the Scotch Church are really anxious for union with the Anglican Church; but by far the greater number of its adherents repudiate any such aim, and hold stoutly by Presbyterian Church-government. They say that they are striving for greater propriety and order in the worship of God; they maintain that although

Presbytery has generally been associated with an un-liturgical worship and a bald ritual, there is no necessary connexion between them; and they hold that, without going the length of Episcopal government, they may borrow from the Anglican Church its architecture, its prayers, its baptismal and burial services. They will take, they say, whatever they think good in itself, without thinking it has been contaminated by the touch of Prelacy. The Puritan reformers, on the contrary, never thought of considering any right or usage on its own merits. The simple question was, Has this been observed in the Episcopal Church? And if it had been observed there, *that* was quite sufficient. Right or wrong, it was sent packing. It would amuse you to see how exactly many of the most evangelical of the Scotch clergy, who never fail to denounce Puseyism as something dreadful, have copied the every-day dress which we are accustomed to consider the mark of Puseyism. I look up now, and glance round the Assembly Hall. A few years ago, the regular Scotch clerical attire was a dress-coat and a waistcoat revealing abundance of linen. But now I see nothing but those silk waistcoats, buttoning to the throat, which I am told tailors designate as the M. B., or Mark of the Beast; long frock-coats, many of them devoid of collars; plain white bands round the neck, devoid of tie of any kind; and cheeks from which the whiskers have been reaped. And did not that good old gentleman, Professor Robertson, when summoned in to take the chair of this Assembly, enter in full canonicals (which all moderators do), but wearing lavender kid gloves (which no moderator ever did before)? Some of the quaint old ministers from the Highlands shook their heads at the sight, and hoped we might not all be Prelatists soon !

As to the advantage, and indeed the necessity, of a liturgy, I think there cannot be two opinions among unprejudiced men. If you had attended a Scotch church, as I have done, for ten years, you would know what a horrid thing it is to see a stupid, vulgar fellow entering the pulpit, and to think that *that* man is to interpret and express your deepest wants for that day's worship. It is, indeed, a very hard task for even an able, a pious, and a judicious man to make new prayers each Sunday, suited to convey the confessions, thanksgivings, and supplications of a congregation of his fellow-men ; yet I have known this so well and beautifully done, that for one day I did not miss the liturgy, dear to me as it is. But you cannot count for certain upon each one of twelve or fourteen hundred men being possessed of common sense ; and when you think of the painful and revolting consequences of allowing a blockhead to conduct public prayer at his own discretion, you will feel what a blessing it would .be if some standard were put in the hands of the clergy that would assure us of decency. It is only just to say that the prayers one generally hears in Scotch churches are wonderfully respectable. They are sometimes, indeed, rather sermons or lectures than prayers ; and are spoken *at* the congregation rather than *to* the Almighty. And the truth is, that even in Scotland, where every minister prepares his own prayers, and where the prayers are very frequently *bonâ fide* extemporaneous, there is a sort of traditional liturgy ; a floating mass of stock phrases of prayer ; and each young man who goes into the Church takes up the kind of strain which he has been accustomed to hear all his life, and carries it on. If you hear a decent, commonplace, rather stupid Scotch minister pray, every separate sentence of the prayer would fall quite familiarly on your ear, if you were a Scotchman. It is the regular old thing, only the component parts a little shuffled. Where the preacher is a senseless and tasteless boor, of course his prayers are in keeping. I have sometimes had an intense wish to throw something at the head of some vulgar blockhead who was pouring forth a tide of unintelligible balderdash, in the name of a congregation of plain country folk, who could not understand, and still less join in, one syllable of the effusion. To show you that I am not saying this without reason, I quote a passage from a review of a work, entitled *Eutaxia, or the Presbyterian Liturgies*, which appeared in a Scotch Church periodical edited by one of the most eminent of Scotch ministers :—

" What a contrast between these prayers of Calvin and the ungrammatical, unprayerful exhibitions which are sometimes heard in the pulpit! It would be a shame to many ministers to rush into the presence of their earthly superiors as they rush into the presence of their God. The prayers of many betray an utter want of preparation, and even of active thought at the time of their utterance, as is evident from the almost absurd phrases which have become stereotyped forms, and which are poured forth every Sabbath in our pulpits. We give one instance which we have no doubt all will recognize: "We come before Thee, with our hands on our mouths, and our mouths in the dust, crying out," &c., while if one's hand is either on his mouth, or his mouth in the dust, crying out is out of the question, and much more so if both happen at once. We recollect a worthy who was in the habit of devoutly praying "that the time might soon come when Satan should be sent far hence, even unto the Gentiles"; and this is a type of too many of the stock phrases which are repeated in the sanctuary." *

There is no respect in which Scotch prayers generally are so bad as in that most important article, the confession of sin. One would say that in such a case the simplest and most direct way of acknowledging unworthiness would be the fittest; we do not know anything better than the familiar "We have left undone those things which we ought to have done, and we have done those things which we ought not to have done." But some preachers appear to think that confession should be set forth with sacred imagery, and accordingly express this part of prayer in terms which I believe convey no clear idea to plain people. I have often heard such sentences as the following: —

"We were planted as trees of righteousness, but we have yielded the grapes of Sodom, and the clusters of Gomorrah."

A still greater favorite is the following: —

"We have turned away from the fountain of living waters; and we have hewn out to ourselves cisterns, broken cisterns, that can hold no water."

My final instance to show what prayer may come to, when intrusted, without any directory, to each individual of a great number of men, shall be the beginning of a prayer which, I was told by a thoroughly credible friend, he himself heard delivered from a Scotch pulpit: —

"O God, Thou hast made the sun. O God, Thou

* *Edinburgh Christian Magazine*, p. 146, August, 1856.

hast made the moon. Thou hast made the stars. Thou hast also made the koamits, whech, in their eccentric oarbits in the immensity of space, occasionally approtch so necr the sun, that they are in imminent danger of being veetrifoyd. "

I heartily wish, my dear editor, that you could send down to the Scotch Kirk a number of those clever, accomplished young Oxford and Cambridge men who wish to devote themselves to clercial labor, and who, from want of interest, will never get more than eighty pounds a year in the English Church. We can hold out pretty fair inducements to such; and we need them sorely. The Scotch Church furnishes a remarkable proof of the soundness of Sydney Smith's views, that if you cannot make all the livings of the Church prizes, it is better to have a proportion of prizes and many blanks, than to reduce all benefices to a decent mediocrity. True, Sydney's plan may not tend to secure the happiness of the working clergy, but it assuredly tends to lead a superior class of men to enter the Church, each man hoping that he may be so fortunate as to draw a prize. I have heard wretched trash talked, to the effect that the right course to get a disinterested and unworldly clergy is to offer no temporal inducements to choose the clerical profession; and when heritors resist a minister's getting an increase of his stipend (each minister is entitled to apply for what is called an *augmentation* every twenty years), they are accustomed to quote with high approval the dictum of some old noodle of a judge in past days, that "a *puir* (poor) church is a *pure* church." Nothing can be more absurd. Cut down the livings of any church to what you choose, and you will have just as many men entering its service from mercenary motives as ever. All you will have secured will be that your recruits will be men of a lower class, to. whom a smaller provision is an inducement. Fix all the livings of the Church of England at thirty pounds a year each, and you will have no lack of men eager to get them; but they will be thirty pounds a year men.

Now, it is a fact which cannot be denied, that although there are very many exceptions to the statement, the majority of the Scotch clergy are drawn from the lower ranks of society, and many of them testify, by their appearance and their entire lack of that undefinable but keenly-felt quality which marks the *gentleman,* that they have not in any degree acquired that polish which the humblest origin is no bar against a man's attaining. As I look round this General Assembly, although the effect on the whole is good, and the principal places, with one or two exceptions, are filled by men fitted to adorn any circle of society, I yet am grieved to see here and there great loutish boors bursting out occasionally into horse-laughter, or apparently desirous of putting their hands and feet in their pockets, who never ought to have been in the Church, who cannot be supposed capable of maintaining the respect of even their humblest parishioners, and whom the squire of the parish would only make unhappy by asking to his table when he had anything but a second-chop party and entertainment.

Now, I say it most sincerely, God forbid that I should think less of a man of talent and piety, though of ever so humble origin. I must add, however, that so

far as my own experience has gone, the talent and piety
and practical usefulness of the Church are found almost
exclusively among its gentlemen. And you and I know
well how much a man's manners affect the estimation in
which the world holds him. You don't like to be told
of your sins by a man whom nature made for blacking
your boots; for I don't hesitate to assert that almost all
these recruits from the lowest orders are as deficient in
talent as they are in social standing. I do not like to
think that the spiritual interests of the country are to be
committed to an inferior class of men; and we know that
Holy Writ speaks with no approval of ancient kings
who "made priests of the lowest of the people." To
show you that I am not singular in this feeling, I quote
another passage from the article already referred to:—

"What can be more disgusting than to go into a church
where the pews are filled with people of refinement, who are
accustomed everywhere else to order and decency, and to see
in the pulpit, the centre of attraction, the cynosure of eyes,
the minister of God, a coarse vulgarian who ought to have
remained in the sphere in which he was converted? Piety
and earnestness make up for great defects; still, a clergyman, whether his parishioners be coalheavers, or the *élite* of
a cultivated city, should always be a gentleman and a man
of taste." *

And now you will be surprised to be told that the
livings of the Scotch Church average somewhat more
than those of the Church of England. Ay, cast in
your archbishoprics, bishoprics, deaneries, and rich rec-
tories, then strike an average, apportioning an equal

---

* *Edinburgh Christian Magazine*, p. 177, September, 1856. This
magazine is (avowedly) edited by the Rev. Norman MacLeod, of
Glasgow.

share to each cure of souls in England, and yet Scotland, with very few livings approaching a thousand a year, will yield a larger annual share to each of her charges. The average of the Kirk is, I am told, about two hundred and sixty pounds a year, with residence. And interest with patrons has little to do with a man's advance here. A young fellow, with a talent for popular preaching, may very reasonably expect, by the time he is seven or eight and twenty, to be settled in a snug manse, with an income of three or four hundred a year. Why is it that this does not tempt into clerical service those younger sons of gentlemen who are content to pinch themselves for years as briefless barristers, or ensigns and lieutenants tossed about the world with the chance of being shot, or clerks in government offices with an annual eighty pounds? The answer must be, that the Church can hold out nothing further. A man cannot get higher. The briefless barrister may be chief justice of England; the ensign may become a peer; the counting-house clerk, a millionnaire. Not one in ten thousand will, but one in twenty thousand *must;* and each hopes that he himself is to be the lucky man. Now this, I take it, is one great advantage of Episcopacy. It provides aims for honorable ambition. It holds out prizes which induce men of first-class social position to enter the Church. A man of the highest talent may enter an episcopal church without feeling that he is practising the unworldly self-denial of a Martyn. Between ourselves, my dear friend, notwithstanding all we used to talk long ago at Oxford, I am quite satisfied that a church may be a church though it have no bishops; and notwithstanding my Anglican up-bring-

<table><tr><td>14 *</td><td>U</td></tr></table>

ing, I think it my duty, living in Scotland, to maintain (so far as I can) the church of the country; and in the Church of Scotland I shall be content to die. I am not sure, if I were a clergyman, that I should much like to be ordered about by some cross-grained, crotchety old gentleman, neither wiser, better, nor more learned than myself, even if he were my bishop. And yet I see great good in Episcopacy; and I see it all the more for having resided these years in Scotland. First, a church with gradations of rank provides prizes which draw in men of social standing; and so long as this is a world of snobs, even a church will be thought the more of for numbering in its ranks the sons of peers. And secondly, Episcopacy provides clergymen who rank on terms of equality with the highest classes in the country. I regard this last as a most important matter. If a lord asks a parish clergyman, however eminent he may be, — say that it were Chalmers himself, — to his house, why, the latent feeling on both sides is, that the peer is rather patronizing the parson; while if a duke entertains an archbishop, the nobleman receives an honor rather than confers one. And as the clergy will always be, to the vulgar mind, the embodiment or at least the representatives of the Church, that which improves or depresses *their* social standing affects the credit in which the Church will be commonly held, in a proportionate degree.

Now, as I have said, very many Scotch parsons are of the humblest possible extraction; and most of these individuals have had no opportunity of getting a little polished up. They have not the chance that a man has who is going into the Church of England. If a man

lives at Oxford for four or five years, and has his wits
about him, he cannot but pick up some refinement from
the class with whom he in some degree associates, and
from the very air of the place. But if a man goes to
Glasgow or St. Andrews a clodhopper, a clodhopper he
remains to the end of his college course. While at the
University he lives in a garret on oatmeal; he never
mixes in decent society; he never sets foot in a drawing-room; he is completely shied by the small propor-
.tion of young men of·the better ranks who are his
class-fellows; he comes out into life a coarse, ungainly
cub, with perhaps a certain vulgar talent which gets
him a living at last. Then he goes out and drinks tea
and whisky-toddy with the neighboring drovers .and
small farmers; he deals in coarse jests which make one
long to kick him; he has an accurate knowledge of the
points of an ox or pig; and is much gratified when a
drunken grazier declares that " there's no a man goes
to Whistle-binkie market that kens aboot a· stot sae
weel as Mr. Horrid-beast." He gains, for a time, a certain popularity with the lowest class; but he drives off
the gentry of the parish to the nearest Episcopal chapel.
I am sure you will agree with me, my friend, when I
say that I regard it as self-evident that the parish priest
ought to possess the bearing, manners, and feelings of a
gentleman. He will be the better fitted for doing his
duty well, even among the poorest. He will be the
more respected; and if a clergyman is not respected,
he is useless. The poorest bodies know thoroughly
well when the minister is jack-fellow-alike, a man who
may be presumed upon, and when *that* will not do.
Nor does this imply a grain of affected stiffness, or the

very slightest lack of cordial kindness and sympathy
upon the part of the real gentleman.   On the contrary,
it is the vulgar boor who will walk into a decent labor-
er's cottage with his hat on; who will keep its mistress
standing while he sits; who will rudely say that the
preparations for dinner which he sees are far too good
for a family in such a position; who will abuse the poor
toiling creature because her little girl had some cheap
ribbons in her bonnet last Sunday at church; and say,
with a coarseness beyond the pigsty, that working people, who may soon need aid from the parish, have no
business with ornament, but should be thankful when
they can find food to eat.*   I know, indeed, that among
the heritors, — and every heritor with a fair rental is by
courtesy a county gentleman, — some miserable creatures may be found who don't want to see the clergyman a gentleman; who feel that in *that* case, superior
to themselves in education, ability, information, and
probably in birth, he becomes the subject of a comparison in which they come off second-best.   I have heard
a retired tradesman, who had bought a property in the
county, and been admitted to its society because his
misplaced aspirates made him an amusing laughing-
stock, lay down the principle that a clergyman would
not work if he were made too well off.   I have heard
vulgar-minded, purse-proud upstarts, taken from the
counter, and the oil-and-color way, say, with reference
to a neighboring parson, that the Apostle Paul did not
keep livery-servants or drive thorough-bred horses.   I
should never argue with any one who talked in this
fashion.   Leave such vulgarity to itself, and cut the

---

* All these particulars are taken from life.

creature dead. But the unhappy thing is, that the social standing of the entire clerical order is injured by the underbred vulgarians who are found in the Church here and there; men who cringe to the Pawtron, truckle to the laird, and sneak at the Heritors' meeting. I remember being struck by a passage in a speech made by the late Dr. Chalmers in this Assembly, in which he illustrates admirably the effect of the worldly standing of the clergy upon the moral estimation in which they will generally be held. He says:—

"It is quite ridiculous to say that the worth of the clergy will suffice to keep them up·in the estimation of society This worth must be combined with importance. Give both worth and importance to the same individual, and what are the terms employed in describing him? 'A distinguished member of society, the ornament of a most respectable profession, the virtuous companion of the great, and a generous consolation to all the sickness and poverty around him.' These, Moderator, appear to me to be the terms peculiarly descriptive of the appropriate character of a clergyman, and they serve to mark the place which he ought to occupy; but take away the importance, and leave only the worth, and what do you make of him? what is the descriptive term applied to him now? Precisely the term which I often find applied to many of my brethren, and which galls me to the very bone every moment I hear it, '*a fine body*'; a being whom you may like, but whom I defy you to esteem; a mere object of endearment; a being whom the great may at times honor with the condescension of a dinner, but whom they will never admit as a respectable addition to their society. Now all that I demand of the Court of Tiends is, to be raised, and that as speedily as possible, above the imputation of being '*a fine body*'; that they would add importance to my worth, and give splendor and efficacy to those exertions which have for their object the most exalted interests of the species."

Capital sound sense, and accurate knowledge of the world there!

Such, my dear Editor, are certain meditations, reasonings, facts, statements, and opinions, which have beguiled me from weariness (though they may have had quite a contrary effect on you) during the less interesting business of several Assembly days. It was good in me to think of you (and perhaps of the intellectual circle for which you monthly cater), and to combine my attendance upon my duties here with doing something that may amuse or inform an absent but not forgotten friend. But now the Assembly is drawing to its close: it is past eleven o'clock on the evening of the 1st of June, and I must put my note-book in my pocket, and attend to the closing proceedings. Then to-morrow morning I shall be off homewards; and O, how pleasant the rush from glaring pavements, a stifling atmosphere, and tedious·speeches, to the bright green fields and the thick leaves which I know await me. My home has seemed shadowy and far away during these days of occupation here; but now it is growing into reality again, as I think how a few hours are to take me back to it. I wonder how the horses are? I hope the dogs are all well. As for the children, I hear of their welfare daily; and I am taking with me a sufficient number of squeaking dogs, musical wagons, trumpets, and drums, to distract the nerves of a literary man for weeks to come. When shall we see you again? It cannot be too soon now.

Always your sincere friend,

C. A. MACDONALD.

CHAPTER XVII.

FROM SATURDAY TO MONDAY.

THERE are great people who have seen so much, that they are not surprised by anything. There are silly people who have not seen very much, but who think it a fine thing to pretend that they are not surprised by anything. As for the present writer, he has seen so little that he feels it very strange to find himself here; and he has not the least desire to pretend that he does not feel it so.

This morning the writer awoke in a bare little chamber, curtainless and carpetless, in that great hotel at Lucerne in Switzerland, which is called the *Schweizer Hof.* And having had breakfast in a very large and showy dining-room, along with two travelling companions, he is now standing at a window of that apartment, and looking out. Just in front, there spreads the green lake of Lucerne. Away to the left, is the Rigi; and to the right, beyond the lake, the lofty Pilatus, in a tarn on whose summit tradition says the banished governor of Judea drowned himself, stricken by conscience for his unjust condemnation of Christ. The town stands at this end of the lake; divided into two parts by the river Reuss, which here flows out of the lake in a swift green stream, running with almost the speed of a torrent. There is a glare of light and heat · everywhere in the town, most of all on the broad level piece of ground which at this point spreads between the lake and several hotels. On a rising ground, a few hundred yards off, rising steeply from the lake, stands the Roman Catholic cathedral, a somewhat shabby building, with two lofty slender spires at its west end. There are cloisters round it; and from several openings in the wall, on the side towards the lake, you have delightful peeps of the green water below, and of snow-capped hills beyond. If you enter that cathedral at almost any time, you will find its plain interior filled by a large congregation; and you will hear part of the service boisterously roared out by priests of unprepossessing aspect. Why do the Roman priests so furiously bellow?

This is a Saturday morning in August, — a beautiful bright morning.

There is no part of the week that is so well remembered by many people as the period from Saturday to Monday, including both the former and the latter days. That season of time has a character of its own; and many pleasant visits and expeditions have been comprised within it. Every one can sympathize with the poet Prior, and can understand the picture he calls up, when he describes himself as "in a little Dutch chaise on a Saturday night; on his left hand his Horace, and a friend on his right," going out to the country to stay till Monday with the friend so situated. I fear, indeed, that Prior would not go to church on the Sunday, which I can only regret. But I am going to spend this time in a way as different as may be from that in which I am accustomed to spend it, or in which I ever spent it before.

When the writer arises on common Saturdays, the thing he has in prospect is several quiet hours spent in going over the sermons he has to preach on the following day. I suppose that most clergymen who do their work as well as they can, do on Saturday morning after breakfast walk into their study, and sit down in that still retreat to work. And if, on other days, you are thinking all the while you are at work there of ten sick people you have to see, and of a host of other matters that must be attended to out of doors, you will much enjoy the affluent sense of abundant time for thinking, which you will have if you make it a rule that on Saturdays you shall do no pastoral nor other parochial work. Then you ought to take a long walk in the afternoon, and give the evening to entire rest, refreshing your mind by some light, cheerful reading.

This advice, however, need not be prolonged; as it is addressed to a limited order of men, and to men who are not likely to take it. And to-day, instead of sitting down to work, there is something quite different to be done.

For it is time to cease looking out of the window at the Schweizer Hof, and to walk the short distance to the spot where a little steamer is preparing to start. The baggage of the three travellers is contained in three black leather bags of modest size. The steamer departs, and leaves the town behind; but to-day, instead of sailing the length of the lake, to where it ends amid the wilds of Uri, we turn to the right hand into a retired bay, which gradually shallows, till the depth of water becomes very small. Pilatus is on the right, and the place where in former days there used to be the *Slide of Alpnach*. The sides of Pilatus are covered with great forests, the timber of which would be of great use if it could be readily got hold of. And the Slide was made for the purpose of bringing down great trees from spots from which any ordinary conveyance would be impossible. So a trough of wood was formed, eight miles in length, beginning high up the mountain, and ending at the lake. It was six feet wide, and four feet deep: a stream of water was made to flow through it, to lessen friction. It wound about to suit the ground, and was carried, bridge-like, over three deep ravines. The trees intended to be sent down by it were stripped of bark and branches, and then launched away. The biggest tree did the eight miles in six minutes, tearing down with a noise like thunder, an avalanche of wood. Sometimes a tree leapt out of the slide, in mid career, and was instantly smashed to atoms.

The steamer stops at a rude little wharf, near which a great lumbering diligence is waiting, very clumsy, but comfortable. Six horses draw it, whose harness, made mainly of rope, is covered with bells, that keep up a ceaseless tinkle as we go. In Britain, we wish a carriage to run as quietly as possible; in Switzerland, they like a good deal of noise. We go slowly on, into the Canton of Unterwalden, by the little town of Sarnen, along a valley richly wooded. For a while, the road is level, then we begin to climb. And now, as is usual with British travellers, we get out and walk on, leaving

the diligence to follow. We are entering the Brunig
Pass. In·former days, it could be traversed only on
foot or on mules; now a carriage road has been made,
a marvel of skilful engineering. We walk up a long
steep ascent. On the left hand, far below, are little green
lakes, and scattered châlets; on the right, rude hills.
Every here and there a little stream from the hills
crosses the road. It is now a mere trickling thread of
water; but acres on either side of it, covered with huge
stones, testify what a raging torrent it must be in winter.
So we go on, till we reach a spot where we are to witness a piece of ingenuity combined with bad taste. Turn
out of the highway by a little path to the right, and you
come in two hundred yards to a sawmill, driven by an
impetuous little stream. Where does the stream come
from? It seems to issue out of the rocky wall, which a
quarter of a mile above the sawmill here crosses the little upland valley. You follow the stream towards its
source. You reach the rocky wall. And. there, sure
enough, violently rushing out through a low-browed dark
tunnel, which it quite fills, you see the origin of the
stream. What is on the other side of the rocky wall?

Why, there is a considerable lake, which was once a
great deal bigger. The Lake of. Lungern was once a
beautiful sheet of water, with fine wood coming down to
its margin. But the people of the valley thought that,
by partially draining the lake, they might get some hundreds of acres of valuable land, and all consideration of
the picturesque had to give way. The tunnel we have
seen lowered the water in the lake by a hundred and
twenty feet, and diminished its size to half. With great
labor, the work of nineteen thousand days given by the

peasants, the tunnel was made, beginning at its lower end, through the rocky ridge, to within six feet of the water at the end of the lake. These six feet of friable rock were blown up with gunpowder, fired by three daring men who instantly fled; and in a few minutes a black stream of mud and water appeared at the lower end of the tunnel. The traveller, returning by the sawmill to the road, goes on till he reaches the village, whence you may see a bare, ugly tract of five hundred acres, dotted with wooden châlets, gained by spoiling the lake.

Passing through the village, you climb on and on; the diligence makes no sign of overtaking you. You reach the summit at last, 3,600 feet above the sea; whence you have a grand view of the vale of Hasli. Those tremendous snowy peaks beyond are the peaks of the Wetterhorn, one of the grandest of the Alps. All this way the road has been very lonely, but always richly wooded. Now you begin to go down. The road winds along the side of the mountain, cut out of the rock. In some places it is a mere notch, with great masses of rock hanging over far beyond its outer edge. And so, broken by a pause for some bread and wine at a little wayside inn, the day goes on towards evening.

All this while, one is trying to feel that it is Saturday, the familiar day one knows at home; for somehow it seems quite different. And in this strange country, where you are a foreigner, you feel yourself quite a different person from what you used to be at home. No doubt, by having two travelling companions from Britain, you keep a little of the British atmosphere about you. If you were walking down now into Hasli all alone, you would be much more keenly aware of

the genius of the place. All your life and your interests
at home would grow quite shadowy and unreal. But
this is one thing that makes a holiday season in a foreign country deliver you so thoroughly from your home
burden of care and labor. How very lightly the charge
of one's parish rests upon one when the parish is a
thousand miles away! The thing which at home is
always pressing on you so heavily, grows light, at that
distance, as one of those colored air-balls of India-
rubber.

And now, as the light is fading somewhat, the great
diligence, running swiftly down the hill, and zigzagging
round perilous corners, with little exertion of the six
plump horses, but with a tremendous jingling of their
bells, overtakes us, and for a mile or two you may enjoy a pleasant rest after the long walk. We stop at
a place where a roofed wooden bridge crosses the river,
turning sharp off to the left. Here we leave the big
diligence, and climb to the top of a lesser one which is
waiting, a vast height. And now, in the growing darkness, we proceed slowly up the valley, following the
course of the river Aar. On the right hand, huge precipices close in the valley, from which every now and
then a streak of white foam, hundreds of feet in height,
shows you a waterfall. It is perfectly silent, though
these seem so near; they are much farther off than you
are aware. On and on, up the river, till you can see
lights ahead, and you jolt along a very roughly-paved
street, where in the darkness you see picturesque wooden
houses on either hand. This is Meyringen, one of the
most thorough and beautiful Swiss villages to be found
in Switzerland. What an odd Saturday evening this

seems! Our old ways of thinking and feeling are quite dislocated. We stop at the door of a large hotel, built of wood. Everything in it seems of wood, except the stone staircase. It is eight o'clock in the evening, — quite dark; they have not our long beautiful twilights there. And now we have dinner. Then we inspect a room filled with carved work in wood which is for sale, and select some little things which will pleasantly remind us of this place and time when both are far away. Finally, before ten o'clock, we climb the long stair, each to his little bare chamber, with many thoughts of those at home, and trying unsuccessfully to feel that this is Saturday night.

But the glory and beauty of Meyringen appeared the next morning, — one of the sunniest, calmest, and brightest Sundays that ever shone since the creation. You go forth from the hotel, and walk down the street, with the most picturesque wooden houses on either hand, with their projecting galleries and great overhanging eaves. Above, there is the brightest blue sky, and all round, snowy peaks, dazzling white, rising into the deep blue. Walk on till you are clear of the village, and fields of coarse grass spread round you; for you will not find there the soft green turf of Britain, but a rough, harsh grass, alive with crickets and grasshoppers. We have some compensation for our uncertain climate and abundant rain. Yet, amid that scenery so sublime, still, and bright, you do not miss anything that could be desired. And now, on the silent Sunday morning, I have no doubt that, of several men whom I saw, who though arrayed in mountain dress each wore a white neckcloth, each one was thinking of his own church many hundreds of miles off, and hoping and asking that all might go well there that day.

All round Meyringen there stand those snowy Alps. Let the small critic understand that we all know that an alp does not strictly mean a mountain, but a pasture high in the mountains. But in Britain, Alps mean mountains, and nothing else. And all round are those white peaks, save in the narrow opening where the Aar comes down from above, and where it rolls away below. From great precipices on the left hand as you look up the valley, streams descend in foamy falls; and one among these has sometimes brought down in its flood such masses of mud and gravel as served to overspread half the valley. Turn up this little street, at whose end you can see the church, which is a Protestant one. Eighteen feet from the pavement there is a line drawn on the inside walls, showing the height to which the church was once filled with mud by an overflow of that torrent. Service is going on. We quietly enter and steal to a seat by the door. A clergyman, in very ugly robes, is standing in the pulpit, which looks diagonally across the plain interior. He is reading his sermon in a rather sleepy way. His robe is of blue, and a great white collar, turned over, is round his neck. Here is the best place to see a whole congregation, men and women, in their national dress. The men sit on one side of the church and the women on the other. Swiss women are for the most part far from pretty. They wear here a black bodice, with white sleeves starched till they seem as stiff as boards, a yellow petticoat, and a little black hat. The church was well filled, and the people seemed to listen very attentively to their pastor's words.

But, for one thing, I do not understand them, for they are expressed in German; and for another thing, I am going to worship elsewhere, so I slip quietly away. Just at the gate through which you pass into the churchyard, there is a shabby little building which I took for a school. No, it is the *Little Church;* and here, during the summer and autumn, you may join in the service of the Church of England. A succession of clergymen come for a few weeks each. A little before the hour of worship we enter the building. It is just like a very shabby Scotch parish school. Forms without backs occupy the floor; at one corner there is an odd little enclosure which serves as a reading-desk and a pulpit; and a little way off there is placed a very small table, which is to-day covered with white, and bears the elements of the Communion. As the congregation assembles, five-and-twenty persons, the clergyman puts on his surplice, and entering the little desk begins the service. I cannot but admire the determination this young minister shows, even in that shabby place, to make the worship of God as decorous as may be. Although there was no organ, there was quite a musical service; even the Psalms being chanted remarkably well. Five or six young English-women acted as a choir. The lessons were read by an old gentleman standing by the little communion table; but a second surplice was not forthcoming, and he was devoid of any robe. The sermon was a very decent one; not eloquent nor striking, but plain and earnest. I should have liked it better if the clergyman had prayed, before beginning it, in the words of one of the usual collects. But he simply prefaced his discourse by the words, " In the name of the Father and of the Son and of the Holy Ghost;" and by that exceedingly silly shibboleth, conveyed to me his adherence to a decaying party, which assuredly does not consist of the wisest or ablest of the Anglican clergy. There are, of course, two or three grand exceptions; but there is something fatuous in the parade of going as near Rome as may be, which some empty-headed youths exhibit. Let me add, that in the evening I went to service again. And now the sermon was so terribly bad, so weak and silly, that I found it hard to understand how any man who had brains to write the former discourse could possibly have produced it. Yet the text was one of the noblest in Holy Scripture.

After the forenoon service, we walk along a great wall, built to defend the valley from floods, towards the heights on the left hand, looking up the valley; and in the hot afternoon toil slowly up and up, till Meyringen is left far below. What is that distant sound? Well, it is that of rifle-shooting; for the men of Hasli think Sunday afternoon the best time for practice. Let me confess that the perpetual reports broke in very sadly on the silence of the Holy Day. Yet there never was a nobler temple than that on which you looked, sitting down on a rock and gazing at the valley far below, and the snowy Alps beyond. You could not but think of the words, chanted in that morning service, "The strength of the hills is His also"! And sitting here, can one forget that at this hour the text is being read out in the church far away; can one help shutting out the Alps for a little, and asking that the Blessed Spirit may carry the words that are to be spoken to many hearts, for warning, counsel, and comfort? It is quite true, that

when at a distance of hundreds of miles, your home
interests grow misty and unsubstantial; but it is likewise
true that at such an hour as this they press themselves
on one with a wonderful clearness and force. My friend
Smith told me that in two hours' lonely walking under
Mont Blanc, on a bright, clear autumn day, he felt more
worried by some little perplexity which soon . cleared
itself up, than at any other time in his life. And sitting
down on the edge of a glacier, whence a stream broke
away in thunder, with the Monarch of Mountains looking down, all he could think of was that wretched little
vexation.

The Sunday dinner hour at the *Sauvage* at Meyringen
is four; so let us slowly descend from this height. A
large party dines, chiefly English. The main characteristic of dinner was the fish called *lotte*, which is caught
in the river near. There was a certain quietness becoming the day; and it was pleasant to remark that the
greater number of our countrymen seemed to make
Sunday a day of rest. And indeed it is inexpressibly
pleasant, after the fatigue and hurry which attend
travelling rapidly on through grand scenery, to have an
occasional day on which to repose. And going to
church, with a little congregation of one's countrymen
and countrywomen, to join in the familiar service in a
 trange land, one felt something of that glow which
came into St. Paul's heart, when after his voyage he
was cheered by the sight of Christian friends, and
which made him " thank God and take courage."

Then to the evening service, when the congregation
was less, and the sermon so extremely bad. The setting
sun was casting a rosy color upon the snowy peaks, as

we returned to the only home one had there. And indeed Sunday is the worst day at an inn. There is a strongly felt inconsistency between the associations of the day, especially if you live in Scotland, and the whole look of the place. And sitting in a verandah behind the *Sauvage*, with the fragrance of the trees in the twilight coming up from the garden below, and looking across to the Falls of the Reichenbach on the other side of the valley, it was worrying to think of the weak sermon we had just heard, where one had hoped for that which might cheer and comfort and direct. On another day, in a church in a grander scene than even this, I sat beside a certain great preacher while a poor sermon was being preached with much attempt at oratorical effect, and thought how different it would have been had that man occupied the pulpit. Perhaps he thought so too, though he did not say so. But indeed, arrayed in garments of gray, and with a wideawake hat lying beside him, that eminent clergyman was like a locomotive engine when the steam is not up. He could not have preached then ; at least, not without two hours of previous thought. Before the best railway engine can dash away with its burden, you must fill its boiler with water, and kindle its fire. And when you may see that clergyman ascend his pulpit in decorous canonicals on a Sunday, charged with his subject, with every nerve tense, and with the most earnest purpose on his rather frightened face, to deliver his message to many hundreds of immortal beings ; if you had previously seen the easy figure in the light-gray suit sitting in a pew at Chamouni, you would discern a like difference to that between the engine standing cold and powerless in the shed, and the engine coming slowly up to the platform, with the compressed strength of a thousand horses fretting for escape or employment, to take away the express train.

To-morrow morning we have to be up at half-past four; so let us go to bed. First, let us have a look at the quiet street, indistinct in the twilight, and at the outline of encircling hills.

There are places in Switzerland where you do not sleep so well as might be desired. A host of wretched little enemies scarify your skin, and drive sleep from your eyes. The *Sauvage* at Meyringen is not one of these places. It is a thoroughly clean and respectable house. Yet for the guidance of tourists who may know even less than the writer (which is barely conceivable), let it be said that there is an effectual means of keeping such hostile troops away. Procure a quantity of camphor. Wear some of it in a bag about you, — a very little bag, — and even though you sit next a disgusting, infragrant, unwashed person in a diligence, nothing will assail you. And at night rub a little of that material into powder between your palms, and sprinkle it over your bed, having turned back the bed-clothes. Do that, and you are safe. If you rub yourself over with camphor besides, you are secure as though wrapped in triple brass. You have made yourself an offensive object to the æsthetic sensibilities of fleas, and they will reject you with contempt. They will do this, even though, uncamphored, you might be (in the South Sea Island sense) *a remarkably good man.* You remember how an Englishman once spoke to a chief of a tribe out there. He spoke of a certain zealous missionary. " Ah, he was a very good man, a very good man," said the Englishman, truly and heartily. " Yes," said the chief, not so warmly; "him was a good man, but him was very tough!" The chief spoke with the air of one who says critically, " The venison at Smith's was not so good as usual last night." And the Englishman forbore to enquire as to the *data* on which the chief pronounced his judgment. No doubt he had experimental knowledge on that subject.

It is a great deal easier to get up in the dark at half past four in the morning in Switzerland than it is anywhere in Britain. There is something so bracing and exhilarating in the mountain air, that you are easily equal to exertion which would knock you up elsewhere. Men who at home could not walk five or six miles without fatigue, walk their thirty miles over a Pass without difficulty; come in to dinner with a good appetite; and after dinner, without the least of that feeling of stiffness which commonly follows any unusual exertion, are out of doors again, sauntering in the twilight, or visiting some sight that is within easy reach. Yesterday was a resting day with us, so to-day we had breakfast a little after five; and then, the three black leather bags being disposed on a black horse, that scrambled like a cat over ground that would have ruined an English steed's knees in the first quarter of a mile, we set off at six o'clock to cross the Pass of the Great Scheideck to Grindelwald.

First, along the road up the valley for a mile or so; then turn to the right, and begin to climb the mountain which on that side walls the valley in. The ascent is very steep, and the path consists of smooth and slippery pieces of rock. You soon come to understand the wisdom of your guide, who requires you to walk at a very slow pace. *That* is your only chance, if you are to climb such ways for several successive hours. The inexperienced traveller pushes on at a rapid pace, and speedily is quite exhausted After a little climbing, you may turn to the right, where you will see the torrent of the Reichenbach go down nearly two thousand feet in a succession of rapids and falls, hurrying to the Aar in the valley below. On, higher and higher, till you see the huge snowy mass of the Wetterhorn far before you on the left, and you enter a little plain of bright green grass, dotted with many picturesque wooden châlets. On, higher and higher, till you stop to rest and have something to eat at the baths of Rosenlaui, a pretty inn near a rock where the Reichenbach comes roaring out of a cleft. In a large room here, you will be tempted to buy specimens of wood-carving, very beautifully done. Having rested, you determine to make a little deviation from your way. Twenty minutes' stiff pulling up the steep hillside, over a very rough path to the left, and you cross a bridge that spans a fissure in the rock two hundred feet deep, where a little stream foams along. Now you stand beside the glacier of Rosenlaui, not large, but beautifully pure. A cave has been cut out for many yards into the beautiful blue ice, and into it you go. It is a singular place in which to find yourself, that cave, or rather tunnel, in the solid ice. The air is cold, the floor is somewhat wet; a soft light comes through the ice from without. But there is no time to linger unduly, and we return down the rough slope to the spot, near the inn, where the guide and packhorse are waiting. Now, upwards again, by a very muddy path through a long wood of pines. But gradually the pines cease, and the ground grows bare, till you enter on a tract where the snow lies some inches deep. Parched as are your hands and your tongue, there is a great temptation to refresh both with handfuls of that snow, which in a little while will leave you more parched than ever. But after no long climbing on the snow, you reach the summit of the Pass, six thousand five hundred feet above the sea. Here you will find a little inn, the *Steinbock*, where a simple but abundant repast awaits the travellers. Thirty or forty, almost all English, sit down to copious supplies of stewed chamois, washed down with prodigious draughts of thin claret. Here you rest an hour. And going out, you look at the Wetterhorn, which rises in a perpendicular wall of limestone rock many thousand feet in height, beginning to rise apparently a hundred yards off. But your eye deceives you in this clear air and amid these tremendous magnitudes. The base of the precipice is more than a mile away. And when you begin to descend towards Grindelwald, the awful wall of rock seems to hang over you, though nowhere you approach within a mile of it. It is not safe to go nearer, for every now and then you hear a tremendous roar, and looking towards the Wetterhorn you see a mass of what looks like powdery snow sliding swiftly down the rock. You are astonished that so small a thing should make such a noise. But that is an avalanche; and if you were nearer, you would know that what seemed powdery snow was indeed hundreds of tons of ice, in huge blocks and masses. And if a village

of châlets had stood in the way, that slide of powdery
snow would have swept it to destruction.

It is a fact well known to students of physical philosophy, that it is incomparably easier to go down a steep
hill than to ascend one. This is a result of the great
and beneficial law of gravitation, according to which all
material bodies tend towards the centre of the earth.
And the consequence of this law is, that when we set off
to descend from this height, we do it very easily and
rapidly. A horse, indeed, looks a poor and awkward
figure scrambling down these paths; but if you have
in your hands that long, light, tough staff of ash shod
with iron which is called an Alpen-stock, you will
bound over the masses of rock at a great pace, doing
things which in a less exhilarating air you would shrink
from. All the way down on the left, apparently close
by, there is that awful wall of the Wetterhorn, and you
may see other peaks, of which the most noticeable or at
least the most memorable is the Schreckhorn. By and
by, by the path, you may discern a man standing beside a great square wooden box, like a small tub fixed
on a stake of wood four or five feet high. And when
the travellers approach, the man will fit to that box a
wooden pipe eight feet long, and sticking his tongue into
the lesser end of the pipe, will vehemently blow into it.
That rude apparatus is the Alpine horn, of which you
have heard folk talk and sing. There is nothing specially attractive to the ear, in the few notes brayed
forth; but what grand echoes, doubled and redoubled,
are awakened up in the breast of that huge wall, and
die away in the upper air and mountain! Produce
from your purse a liberal tip, and ask the mountaineer

to let you try his horn. You blow with all your might, like my friend Mac Puff sounding his own trumpet, but there is dead silence, as when to such as know him well Mac Puff does so sound; a feeble hissing of air from the great tub is all that rewards your labor. And one always respects a person who can do what one cannot do. Down along the slope, till, turning a little way to the left, you approach the Upper Glacier of Grindelwald, filling up the great gulf between the Wetterhorn and the Schreckhorn. Into this glacier you enter by an artificial tunnel; but the ice is dirty, and streams of water pour from it on your head. Thus you speedily retreat. Great belts of fir-trees fringe the glacier, which, like other glaciers, comes far below the snow-line. For as the ice which forms the glacier gradually melts away at the lower extremity next the valley, the ice from above presses on and fills its place. The glacier is in fact a slowly advancing stream of ice. And all the glaciers are gradually retreating into the mountains, as increasing cultivation and population make the lower extremity melt away somewhat faster than the waste can be supplied. Starting from far in the icy bosom of the Alps, in the region of perpetual snow, the Grindelwald glaciers come down to within a few yards of as green and rich grass as (if you were a cow) you would desire to eat.

Now we walk for an hour through meadows in the valley, pausing at a châlet to have some Alpine strawberries, small and flavorless; and so at five o'clock on Monday afternoon enter Grindelwald. The inns are filled with travellers; but we are lucky in finding space at the *Adler,* whose windows look full on the Lower

15 *

Glacier, at the distance of a mile. From a great black-looking cave at the end of the glacier, a river breaks away, of the dirty whity-brown water that comes from glaciers. It is a curious thing to see a river starting, full grown from the first. Look to the left of the lower end of the glacier, the ground meets the ice. Look to the right, and there a pretty big river, that looks as if it had burst out from the earth, is flowing away as if it had run a score of miles.

Let the traveller refresh himself by much-needed ablution; they give you pretty large basins here. And then descending, sit down to dinner at the *table-d'hôte.* A large party, almost all Germans. So are the waiters. Thus, if you express to a neighbor your conviction that something presented to you as chamois is in truth a portion of a very tough and aged goat, no offence is given.

Shall it be recorded how, after dinner, we sat in the twilight on a terrace hard by, looking at the glacier and the Alps; how, as it darkened down, we entered the dining-room again, and there beheld, seated at tea, a certain great Anglican prelate? Shall it be recorded how, if one had never seen nor heard of him before, you might have learned something of his eloquence, geniality, and tact, transcending those of ordinary men, even from that hour and a half before he retired to rest? Shall it be recorded how, having begun to tell a story to his own party, he gradually and easily, as he discerned others listening with interest, addressed himself to them, till he ended his story in the audience of all in that large chamber? And shall it be recorded how two pretty young English girls sat and gazed with·rapt and silent admiration on the great man's face? Two or three young fellows who had sought during that day to commend themselves to these fair beings felt themselves (you could see) hopelessly eclipsed and cut out, and regarded the unconscious bishop with looks of fury. Happily he did not know, so it did him no harm.

My friend Mac Spoon recently dilated, in my hearing, on the advantages of Pocket Diaries; which (as wise men know) are not records of passing and past events, but memoranda of engagements. " You note down in these," said he, " all you have to do; while yet if your book should be lost, and so fall into the hands of a stranger, he could not for his life understand the meaning of your inscriptions. Thus," he went on, " you see how under the head of Thursday, April 32d, 1864, I have marked *Jericho Train at* 10.30. Now if *that* were to fall into a stranger's possession, he could make nothing of it, he would not know what it meant at all. But as for me, the moment I look at it, I know that it means that on Thursday, April 32d, 1864, I am to go to Jericho by the 10.30 train." Such were the individual's words. And now, for the sake of those readers who could not understand that mysterious inscription, I think it expedient distinctly to aeclare, that the reason why this history is called *From Saturday to Monday* is, that it gives an account of historical events, beginning with Saturday and ending on Monday. And thus, having reached Monday evening (for soon after the bishop's story everybody went to bed), my task is done. It can never transpire, what happened on the Tuesday. Perhaps something happened of great public interest. But if I were to record it here, then it would appear as if what occurred on Tuesday occured between Saturday and Monday, which is absurd.

The remembrance of foreign travel is pleasanter than the travel itself. For in remembrance there are none of the hosts that are dispelled by copious camphor; no wear of the muscles, nor of the lungs and heart; no eyes hot and blinded with the sunshine on the snow; no parched throat and leathery tongue; no old goat's flesh disguished as chamois venison. The little drawbacks are forgot; but the absence of care and labor, the blue sky and the bright sun, glacier and cataract, and the snowy Alps, remain.

CONCLUSION.

IT is the way of Providence, in most cases, gradually to wean us from the things which we must learn to resign; and it has been so with this holiday-time, now all but ended. It is not now what it was when we came here. The leaves wore their summer green when we came, now they have faded into autumn russet and gold. The paths are strewn deep with those that have fallen; and even in the quiet sunshiny afternoon, some bare trees look wintry against the sky. Like the leaves, the holiday-time has faded, — it is outgrown. The appetite for work has revived, and all of us now look forward with as fresh interest to going back to the city to work as we once did to coming away from the city to rest and play.

We have been weaned by slow degrees. Nature is hedging us in. The days are shortening fast; the breeze strikes chill in the afternoons as they darken. The sea sometimes feels bitter, even though you enter it head foremost. Nor have there lacked days of ceaseless rain and of keen north wind. Two lighthouses, one casting fitful flashes across the water and one burning with a steady light, become great features of the scene

by seven o'clock in the evening. A little later, there is
a line of lights that stretches for miles at the base of
the dark hills along the opposite shore; indoor occupations have supplanted evening walks; yet a day or two,
and those lights will no more be seen. The inhabitants
of the dwellings they make visible will have returned to
the great city, and very many of the pretty cottages and
houses will remain untenanted through the long winter-
time.

As these last days are passing, one feels the vague remorse which is felt when most things draw to an end.
One feels as if we might have made more of this time
of quiet amid these beautiful hills. Surely we ought to
have enjoyed the place and the time more! Thus we
are disposed to blame ourselves, but to blame ourselves
unjustly. You would be aware of the like tendency,
parting from almost anything, no matter how much you
had made of it. You will know the vague remorse
when dear friends die, thinking you ought to have been
kinder to them; you will know it, though you did for
them all that could be done by mortal. And when you
come to die, my friend, looking back on the best-spent
life, you will think how differently you would spend it
were it to be spent again. You will feel as if your talent had been very poorly occupied, and doubtless with
good reason, here.

Last night, there was a magnificent sunset. You
saw the great red ball above the mountains, visibly
going down. It was curious to watch the space between the sun and the dark ridge beneath it lessening
moment by moment, till the sun slowly sunk from sight.

Of course, he had been approaching his setting just as fast all day as in those last minutes above the horizon; but there was something infinitely more striking about the very end. At broad noonday, it is not so easy to fully take in the great truth which Dr. Johnson had engraved on the dial of his watch, that he might be often reminded of it, — the solemn Νὺξ γὰρ ἔρχεται. It is in the last minutes that we are made to think that we ought to have valued the sun more when we had him, and valued more the day he measured out.

Day by day this volume has grown up through this holiday-time. In its earlier portion, the author diligently revised the chapters you have read. And by and by, the leisurely postman brought the daily pages of pleasing type, in which things look so different from what they look in the cramped magazine printing. Great is the enjoyment which antique ornaments and large initial letters afford to a simple mind.

And now it is the forenoon of our last day here; we go early to-morrow morning. Play-time is past, and work-time is to begin. I hear voices outside, and the pattering of little feet; there are the sea and the hills; and all the place is pervaded by the sound of the waves. On no day through our time here did the place look as it does now; it wears the peculiar aspect which comes over places from which you are parting. How fast the holidays have slipped away! And what a beautiful scene this is! What a pretty little Gothic church it is, in which for these Sundays that are gone the writer has taken part of the duty; how green the ivy on the cliffs, and the paths through the woods; what perpetual life in that ceaseless fluctuation of which you seldom lose sight for long! But we must all set our faces to the months of work once more, thankful to feel fit for them; not without some anxiety in the prospect of them; looking for the guidance and help of that kindest Hand which has led through the like before.

Cambridge: Stereotyped and Printed by Welch, Bigelow, & Co.